The

With her tradem⋯⋯ ⋯lling, Julia London br⋯⋯ ⋯treet, three dashing, aristocratic gentlemen whose scandalous exploits are the talk of the *ton*. Adrian Spence, Earl of Albright, has earned his notoriety on the dueling field, and in the finest drawing rooms—and boudoirs—of England. This is his story. . . .

THE DANGEROUS GENTLEMAN

It was strictly business as Adrian Spence claimed the woman his brother desired. A hasty wedding, and Lilliana Dashell was his—sweet revenge on the father who disinherited him and the brother who let it happen. Their wedding night is a revelation as passionate, innocent Lilliana ignites fires Adrian tries desperately to deny. By day he is a stranger. By night he is the lover of her dreams, and she a shameless wanton in his arms. But Adrian is determined that no woman will ever possess him. And Lilliana knows that her only hope of taming this very dangerous gentleman is to unlock his deepest mysteries and open his shuttered heart to love. . . .

THE ROGUES OF REGENT STREET

The Dangerous Gentleman

JULIA LONDON

A DELL BOOK

Published by
Dell Publishing
a division of
Random House, Inc.
1540 Broadway
New York, New York 10036

Cover Design by John Ennis
Hand Lettering by David Gatti

ISBN: 0-440-23561-8

Printed in the United States of America

Published simultaneously in Canada

April 2000

10 9 8 7 6

OPM

For this relief much thanks; 'tis bitter cold out
And I am sick at heart

HAMLET, ACT I, SCENE I

One

PHILLIP ROTHEMBOW WAS dead.

None of the mourners gathered around the grave had expected his demise to occur precisely this way, although there were certainly those who had wagered he would not live to see his thirty-third year. They never dreamed he would die by forcing the hand of his very own cousin. And they all agreed—rather adamantly in front of the justice of the peace—that Adrian Spence, the Earl of Albright, did not have a choice—it was either kill or be killed.

Still, some of the mourners privately argued (at the public house, before the services commenced) that Albright might have avoided the confrontation had he not asked Rothembow to stop cheating. Not that anyone could dispute that Rothembow's cheating was legion, or that Albright had been a virtual saint of patience through the years. But he might have thought twice before accusing his cousin before a roomful of people.

That sentiment was met with the equally insistent

one that as Rothembow had been cheating so very blatantly, he had obviously been asking to be called on it. A few tried to put forth that Rothembow had been simply too drunk to know what he was doing, particularly evidenced by his calling Albright a coward. Of all men, the Earl of Albright was the last one any of them would have called a coward, and furthermore, they argued, what could Albright have done? A man could hardly have his character challenged in the face of so many peers and not avenge his honor. Not one of the mourners could fault Albright for accepting Rothembow's drunken challenge.

Not one of them could believe that either man had actually gone through with it.

So it was the collective opinion of the mourners that no matter how Rothembow and Albright came to be standing in that yellow field, Albright had had no choice. And he *had* done the honorable thing by deloping. Rothembow, who was still staggering drunk that morning, had responded by firing on him (a sin so great that the men shuddered each time they recalled it) and missing badly. Yet that paled in comparison to what Rothembow did next, and the mourners were divided on the subject of Lord Fitzhugh's culpability.

Having recently obtained a fine double-barreled German pistol inlaid with mother-of-pearl, Lord Fitzhugh had felt compelled to wear it in his new leather holster for the entire weekend in the event the party was set upon by thieves or an otherwise marauding band of ne'er-do-wells. So confident was he in his new pistol that he was in the habit of draping his coat in a manner that clearly displayed the firearm. Which was exactly how he was wearing it when Rothembow grabbed it from its holster. He had lunged for that pistol—primed for any event, naturally—and had fired a second time at Albright, clearly intending to kill him. Albright *had* to defend himself, and most agreed it was a bloody miracle that he was able to retrieve his own pistol and fire before his cousin gunned him down with a third shot. Fitz-

hugh had been the fool and Rothembow the coward—
although one mourner noted that the wild look in Rothembow's eyes suggested he was perhaps more deranged than cowardly.

That, naturally, had prompted another round of debate as to whether Rothembow had actually *meant* Albright to kill him. It was hardly a secret among their set
that Rothembow was drowning in debt, having squandered his funds and his life on excessive drink and
Madam Farantino's women, and was seemingly bent on
self-destruction. That notwithstanding, it was inconceivable to them that a man might want to end his own life
so desperately he would go to such extraordinary mea-
sures. Inconceivable, but apparently possible.

Now, at the gravesite, all of the mourners who had
come to witness the fantastic end to their hunting trip in
the country covertly watched Albright and his friends
beneath the brims of their hats as the vicar droned on.

"Know ye in this death the light of our Lord . . ."

The Rogues of Regent Street—Adrian Spence, Phillip
Rothembow, Arthur Christian, and Julian Dane—were
the idols of every man of the Quality. In fact, the final
argument that had risen over the din of the public house
was just how, exactly, the four childhood friends had
come by that moniker. None could really recall, but they
agreed the name had been earned honestly enough. The
four had met at Eton, earning themselves reputations as
young reprobates even then. But it was when their
names started to appear with alarming frequency in the
Times a few years ago that the name had stuck. The
Rogues exhibited a penchant for breaking the hearts of
proper young debutantes who strolled amid the Regent
Street shops during the day. Capable of charming the
young ladies and their mamas to the tips of their toes,
they also were ruthless in winning their dowries from
their fathers in the gaming clubs at night.

"Know ye the quality of love . . ."

That habit hardly endeared the four men to the Regent Street set, and for the more conservative members,

their habit of openly frequenting the notorious Regent
Street boudoirs in the early hours of the morning was the
most egregious of their many sins.

"And the quality of life . . ."

Nonetheless, the Rogues were an enviable group who
lived by their own code and amassed great sums of
wealth in their various business ventures. They lived on
the edge, never fearing danger, never fearing the law,
and flaunting their disdain of society's expectations for
titled young men in the *ton*'s collective face—exactly
what every mourner privately wished *he* had the courage to do. Until today.

"And know ye the quality of mercy . . ."

Until the solemn pain on the faces of the surviving
Rogues suggested they had tasted their own mortality.

And the mourners had tasted their own.

"Amen."

Having seen what they had come to see, the mourners at last began to drift away from the gravesite in
search of shelter from the threatening skies. Only five
remained. Two were gravediggers, working to fill the
hole before the rains came. The three surviving Rogues
stood slightly apart, seemingly oblivious to the light rain
as they stared blankly into the yawning grave.

Adrian could not tear his eyes away from his cousin's
pine box as the words of the vicar rattled about his head,
taunting him. *Know ye the quality of mercy,* indeed, he
thought bitterly. He certainly would never know mercy
again. He would never know *peace* again. He had killed
his cousin, one of his dearest friends, and had destroyed
the quality of his own life in the process. There would be
no mercy for him, not in this lifetime.

He glanced at Arthur, who stood grimly rigid as the
gravediggers pushed the earth onto the casket. Arthur,
who in a moment of grief last evening had confessed that
Phillip was the only one who had ever really looked up
to him. In the unenviable position of being the third son
of a duke, Lord Arthur Christian had, as long as Adrian
had known him, felt inconsequential. Only Phillip, he

said, had thought him capable of moving mountains. Only Phillip wanted to go where he led. But, Arthur lamented, he had never led him anywhere because he had nowhere to lead him to. And then he had harshly censured himself for not seeing the downward spiral sooner.

Hell, Adrian hadn't seen it, either. He never really understood it until Phillip was dead.

But Julian had seen it. For two days now, the Earl of Kettering had barely spoken, except to admit last evening—having been moved by Arthur's confession—that he had seen Phillip's fall from grace and hadn't done enough to stop it. Julian, who stood now with his greatcoat gathered tightly around him, a frown etched deeply into his face, had been Phillip's constant companion the last five years or so. There had always been a special bond between the two of them, and Phillip's demise was particularly difficult for Julian to bear—he feared he hadn't taken his friend's desperation seriously enough. That was perhaps because Julian was having a hard time himself. The sole guardian of four younger sisters for many years, Julian had been struggling since losing one of them a few years ago. Understandably restless since Valerie's death, Julian had taken to following Phillip on increasingly aimless escapades, looking for something to fascinate him.

Julian had seen Phillip's downfall, he said, but had been too mindful of his pride, too trusting of his strength, too confident that Phillip's esteem of Lady Claudia Whitney would bring him out of it to do anything about it. He had allowed it to happen, and no argument Adrian or Arthur put forth would convince him otherwise.

But for all of Arthur and Julian's pain, they had not killed him. Adrian had. As their unofficial leader for more than twenty years, he had let them all down by doing the unthinkable. The infamous control for which he was known had snapped like a twig under the pressure of a little fear and a stunning disbelief at what was happening. The events of the weekend played a thousand times over in his mind's eye as he searched for a reason, anything that would help make sense of this horrible tragedy.

It had started so innocently! Sick to death of Phillip's cheating, Adrian had asked him to stop, plain and simple, and like a fool, had smirked when a drunken Phillip demanded satisfaction. He should have walked away. But his pride wouldn't allow it, and he had convinced himself that when Phillip sobered they would end their foolish argument peacefully. But Phillip never sobered, and when he had actually *fired* on him, Adrian had turned away with sickening disgust. Lord God, everything happened so *fast*—Arthur's cry of warning, the shot fired above his head, the frantic lunge for the small stand where his pistol lay, and the blurred moment in which he whirled around and shot Phillip through the heart.

Somewhere in the distance the death knell rang. The gravediggers finished covering the grave and quickly departed with a wary look at the three remaining gentlemen. A fine rain was falling now, but Adrian could not make his feet move from the gravesite.

"Come on, then. It's over," Arthur said quietly. Unable to make his legs move, Adrian ignored him. "Albright? The rain—"

"I was a goddamned fool for letting him unnerve me," he suddenly muttered to no one in particular, his eyes locked on the mound of earth.

Arthur exhaled slowly as he glanced at the grave. "You may have pulled the trigger, but he wanted you to do it. Don't torture yourself—he wanted it."

A sharp pain stabbed directly behind Adrian's eyes, and squeezing them tightly shut, he blurted, "Good God, no one wants to *die*!"

"*He* did," Julian muttered angrily. "Come on, then," he said, and put a hand on Adrian's forearm.

No mercy! Adrian's mind screamed, and he angrily jerked away, unworthy of the compassion. "I didn't see what was happening. That is . . . I knew he was in trouble, but I didn't know he was *drowning*," he muttered helplessly.

"Neither did I, God help me," Arthur sighed. "I should have seen it." He glanced warily at Adrian and Julian. "Look here, we don't see each other as often as we ought. We should make more of an effort."

The sentiment of a man who had attended a funeral, Adrian thought blandly. He could hardly fault Arthur. If he had thought this was the last time he would see Phillip—

"Our lives have taken us on different paths, Arthur," Julian muttered. "It's not the same as it once was."

"I'm not asking that it be the same. I just believe . . . come now, a vow. A vow among us, today, on Phillip's grave, that we will never allow another of us to slip away. Nothing will go unsaid between us. I vow that at least once a year, on the anniversary of Phillip's death, I will assure myself that all is well with the two of you, that not another of us will fall," he said, almost desperately.

"Arthur, you are overwrought," Julian insisted, and glanced helplessly at Adrian.

"Bloody hell, Kettering, what harm is there in it?" Arthur snapped.

Julian frowned and looked at Phillip's grave. But Adrian merely shrugged—there was no harm in it, and if it eased Arthur's anguish any, what difference did it make? Their lives *had* taken different paths, and no graveside vow was going to change that. "I vow," he muttered. Arthur looked anxiously to Julian.

Julian groaned. "What sentimental folly, Christian," he complained, and rolled his eyes at the pointed look Arthur and Adrian gave him. With a snort of exasperation, he nodded his head. "All right, I vow, I *vow*! Are you satisfied?"

Arthur's gaze slid to Phillip's grave again. "Hardly," he mumbled.

Adrian winced, too, as he looked at the earthen

mound. He should have paid more heed, but it was too damned late now. Phillip was dead. Suddenly sick, he pivoted sharply and walked away from the gravesite, his cloak snapping furiously about his boots. With a final look, Arthur and Julian fell in behind him.

Two

KEALING PARK, NORTHAMPTON, ENGLAND

ADRIAN LEFT JULIAN and Arthur at the road to London and headed north, racing fast and hard from Dunwoody and the unspeakable thing he had done. But there was no place he could run to, no refuge from his guilt. London was out of the question—he had no desire to face the *ton* after what he had done, or his father, whom he knew to be there. Kealing Park was the last place he *should* seek refuge. But it was the family's home, the one place on earth where he was capable of finding a measure of peace. Not that he had any hope of that.

He rode mindlessly, feeling as if his entire being had been scattered in a thousand different directions like the leaves his stallion, Thunder, kicked up. He relived every moment from the time they had arrived at Dunwoody until the fatal morning, searching for an explanation that would enable him to put the pieces back together again. He saw every turn of card in his mind's eye, and now questioned if Phillip had been cheating at all—perhaps he had just been losing badly. Perhaps, for once in his life, Phillip had not been cheating.

In the village of St. Albans he was forced to a halt by market traffic, and as he waited, he happened to see two gentlemen. One was golden-haired, just like Phillip. And he walked with that same easy gait, twirling his hat absently on one finger as Phillip used to do. A cold shiver ran through Adrian, and he had shouted after that man, only to have his heart plummet. Of course it wasn't Phillip. Phillip was dead.

He rode quickly from the village before anyone could see the madness he was so certain had overcome him, his heart pounding against his chest. Was he losing his mind? Could he be so ridiculously sentimental? *Phillip was dead!*

Phillip, who had arrived at Dunwoody with a flask of whiskey under one arm and a particularly notorious woman on the other, signaling the start of a weekend of debauchery so typical of their gatherings. Phillip, who was so drunk that night that Adrian could recall marveling at his ability to remain standing. "Then why did you sit for cards?" he asked himself aloud. The bastard always cheated, the severity determined by the amount of liquor he had consumed. *Why hadn't he just walked away?*

He would never know why, but he hadn't, and the next thing he knew, the accusation had tumbled out of his mouth. Then Phillip was unsteadily on his feet, a dark, strangely victorious look on his face. Or had Adrian just imagined that was so? "You insult me, Albright. I demand satisfaction!"

That had stunned him completely—it was the last thing he had ever thought to hear from Phillip's mouth. He had not meant Phillip to take offense. God, no, he had never meant that. And when he had tried to laugh it off, to make light of Phillip's intoxicated state, his cousin had looked him squarely in the eye and demanded, "Are you a coward?"

Adrian moaned and shook his head. Thunder was

beginning to labor, he noticed, and he pulled up on the reins, slowing their pace. As the horse slowed to a trot he recalled the whirlwind of unfamiliar emotions that had unbalanced him that night: a desire to hit Phillip in his fool mouth; absolute horror at what his friend was apparently doing; gross confusion as to *why*. "Wh-what?" he had stammered stupidly.

"By God, I think you *are* afraid! You are a bloody coward, Albright!" Phillip had shouted, and by so saying, pushed Adrian and his foolish pride into a corner.

But even then he had no intention of dueling him. "All right, Rothembow. Pistols at dawn," he had shot back, and heard Arthur's gasp as Julian jerked around and stared at him as if he were insane, which he certainly must have been.

As he certainly must be now. Adrian pressed a gloved hand to his forehead, seeing in his mind's eye only that strange, dark smile on Phillip's lips. "Marvelous," his cousin had drawled, and grabbing Tina's wrist, pulled her along with him as he quit the room, presumably to wait for dawn.

Would that it had ended there, Adrian thought miserably. But no. Dawn had come all too quickly, and incredibly, Phillip had not changed his mind. Nor had he sobered any.

Standing in that field, Adrian had felt like he was the lead actor in some sort of bad dream. Everyone in their party had come out, along with their valets. Their cheerful laughter indicated that they, too, thought the so-called duel was far more entertaining than it was dangerous. But disbelief and fear had muted Adrian, and only Arthur and Julian had seemed as fearful as he was as they desperately tried to reason with Phillip. But the man was unrelenting, his determination bordering on macabre. So Adrian had gritted his teeth, swallowed his pride, and had selected a dueling pistol, frowning darkly at Fitzhugh when he had laughingly offered his new pistol before carefully stuffing it into his holster. He then had taken the requisite twenty paces, silently cursing

Phillip and vowing to beat his cousin within an inch of his sorry life for putting him through this. Then, when the mark had been called, he had fired into the air, deloping.

Would that it had ended *there*. But Phillip, damn him, had chuckled nastily, and weaving unsteadily, raised his pistol and fired.

Something died in Adrian at that moment. Phillip had actually *fired* upon him, and he had turned away in disgust, striding toward the tree stump where he had left his gun, his only thought to be gone from Dunwoody and Phillip.

Arthur's fierce cry had raised the hackles on his neck. Adrian jerked around to see Fitzhugh on his rump and Phillip pointing that fancy pistol at him. At his *back*. He had no time to think; he dove for his gun as a bullet whizzed over his head. It was blind instinct, the sort of mindless reaction one draws upon when attacked. Somehow his hand had landed on the pistol. Somehow he had cocked it as he rolled onto his back, and somehow he had fired it with deadly aim before Phillip could fire again.

Adrian yanked Thunder to a dead stop and pressed his knuckles against the burn in his eyes. The vision of Phillip, knocked from his feet by the force of the bullet, would haunt him all his days. But . . . but had Phillip actually *fired* on him? Or had he purposely shot over his head? Had Phillip actually cocked the pistol to fire again, or had he just convinced himself of it? Adrian tried to remind himself that he had had no choice—Phillip would have killed him. He kept telling himself that, desperate to believe it, but he could not erase the image of Phillip's eyes. Jesus, his *eyes*.

He suddenly spurred Thunder again, pushing him into a gallop in a vain attempt to escape the burning in his soul. His heart, dear God, his heart was positively bursting with the ache of having lost one so dear to him. He had not felt so empty since his mother died almost twenty years ago. No, that was not quite accurate. He had not *felt* since his mother's death. Archie had seen to that.

Archie, as he disparagingly thought of his father, was Archibald Spence, the Marquis of Kealing—tyrant, misogynist, and coward. To the country set and the *ton* he was a shining example of what a peer of the realm should aspire to be. No one outside their little family, save a few longtime servants, knew of the vile contempt he had heaped on Adrian's mother, Lady Evelyn Kealing, and on him, his oldest son and heir, day after miserable day.

Adrian's earliest childhood memory was of him and his younger brother, Benedict, cowering in the nursery as words like *whore* and *slut* filtered up to them through the chimney shared with the green drawing room below. The verbal abuse was a constant barrage it seemed, and was sometimes backed with Archie's fist. On those occasions, the young fool that he had been, Adrian had tried to fight for her, only to be beaten and called every invective that came to his father's demented mind. Those were the days he had begun to teach himself not to feel. *Feel nothing, feel nothing, feel nothing.*

There was never a reason for the abuse, no particular incident or misdeed that Adrian could recall. Archie simply despised him, had despised him from the moment of his birth, apparently, and Adrian had sought his refuge in the quiet solitude of the hills and streams and valleys of Kealing Park.

But his mother was trapped and she died a broken woman when Adrian was only twelve. Archie turned the full brunt of his abuse on him then, but as Adrian grew older Archie could not affect him with his words and fists as he once had been able to do. So he had taken to banishing him from the Park for one infraction or another. The first time had been for fighting on Phillip's behalf. On that particular occasion he had not allowed Adrian to come home during the Christmas season, and the boy had spent the holidays at Eton with the dormitory housekeeper. He had been all of thirteen years old.

The last time had been five years ago when Adrian had refused to invest in his father's newly acquired coal mine. He abhorred the conditions in the mines, particularly when owners like Archie enjoyed obscene profits at the expense of the children who labored there. But Archie complained that his profits were not as great as those of other mines of similar size and demanded that Adrian supply him with an infusion of cash. When Adrian refused, Archie had angrily banished him from the Park.

And Adrian, of course, had responded as he always did—by enlarging his holdings again. It was the one thing he could do that Archie couldn't. Since he had come of age he had invested wisely by joining ventures he knew to be sound. He bought a majority holding in a Boston shipyard, and as a result he now enjoyed a reputation for building the fastest and sturdiest clippers that skimmed the Atlantic between England and America. His partnership with Arthur in the manufacture of iron was earning beyond his wildest expectations. Everything he owned was of far greater value and earned much higher profits than anything Archie did—because Adrian spent almost every waking hour making sure of it.

But for all that, it was Kealing Park he really wanted.

Gathering his cloak around him, Adrian stared blindly at the road in front of him. For reasons that he did not fully understand, Kealing Park had become precious to him. It was the last thing he had, the last thread to distant feelings of love and comfort he had experienced in his mother's arms, or the freedom he had known as a lad roaming the backwoods and valleys. When his grandfather had died five years ago with no surviving heirs save his two grandsons, Adrian had inherited the title Earl of Albright and the earl's seat, the estate of Longbridge. Yet it did nothing to appease his desire for the Park. Adrian had been to Longbridge only a handful of times—it held no sentimental value for him and, being a few hours east of the Park, was not on any of the thoroughfares he typically used to travel about the country. No, it was Kealing Park he wanted, and one day he would have it, in spite of Archie's complete disdain.

As Thunder loped easily along the road, Adrian sighed thoughtfully. Though his father had never been very clear in his reasons for his contempt, he had heard enough through the years to deduce the truth. Actually, it was so bloody obvious—the horrible things Archie had said to his mother, the disgust he showed his heir at every turn, the absolute adoration of Benedict, Adrian's weak-willed younger brother. Adrian had never asked another living soul, but he knew he was an illegitimate child. It was a secret that would die with him, because to tell it would be to free Archie to give everything that was rightfully his to Benedict.

Legally, Archie could leave his many personal holdings to Benedict if he so desired, and Lord knew he threatened it enough. Kealing Park, the coal mines, the house in London and château in France—none of it was part of the Marquis of Kealing's original entail. There was nothing left to Archie's title but an old, crumbling manor on the southern edge of the Park—everything else, Archie and his father had acquired. Nonetheless, there was no law in the land that would prevent the title of marquis and its entail from passing to Adrian, and that was killing Archie.

Adrian was more than happy to let it. Unless Archie was prepared to announce to the world that his wife had cuckolded him and his firstborn was a bastard he had been forced to raise as his own, his only recourse was to find fault with Adrian and disown him. There was no other way to give Benedict everything as Archie was so obviously desperate to do, but the scoundrel had no valid grounds to do it short of scandal. As Archie was loath to sully his own name, it meant one day Kealing Park would pass to Adrian.

And it would be his great pleasure to allow his father to go to his grave unable to complete the one thing in life he truly wanted—Adrian's demise and Ben's ascendancy to the Spence throne.

Unfortunately, although Kealing Park was blissfully free of Archie, Adrian found no comfort for his ravaged heart or refuge from the guilt that was eating him alive. Even worse, Benedict was not in London with Archie as Adrian had thought, but at the Park, hovering about. Every place Adrian sought solace, Benedict appeared, anxious and fretful and trying far too hard to befriend him. Three days at the Park quickly turned into three days of agony.

"Ah! There you are!"

Speak of the devil. Adrian glanced from the corner of his eye as Benedict strode into the library. "I've been looking everywhere for you!"

"Have you?" Adrian asked indifferently, and pushed aside the letter to Phillip's family that he had been trying to write for two hours. Actually, he had been trying to write it since Dunwoody.

Benedict paused halfway across the room and nervously clasped his hands in front of him. "Father has finally returned from London. He requests an audience in the study."

An audience with Archie. Bloody hell, that was the last thing Adrian needed today. There was nothing he detested more than interviews with his father, and this one had to do with Phillip, that much he was certain. The news had reached London the day after Phillip's death almost ten days ago. Well, he would be on his way to London as soon as they could ready his chaise. "He's returned, has he? What does he want?" he muttered impassively.

"Why, I can't say that I know, really!" his brother said, a little too quickly. "No doubt he means to see if you are well."

Adrian gave him a lazy, knowing smile. Benedict was

good at some things, but lying was not one of them. "When did he arrive?"

Benedict's eyes darted to the sideboard. "Um, an hour or two ago. What, did Brian forget to bring round some whiskey? I told him to fill the decanters."

"Oh, but he has," Adrian drawled as he lazily shoved to his feet. "I've been draining it as quickly as he fills it." Ignoring Benedict's startled look, he began walking toward the door.

"Adrian!" Benedict suddenly blurted. "I . . . I suppose you'll be leaving soon?"

Adrian paused to slice a disinterested glance across his tight-lipped younger brother. "I don't know, Ben . . . am I going somewhere? Perhaps I've been banished again?"

Benedict flushed. "I wouldn't know. I just . . . I just assumed you would be going. You always do."

He would be going all right, and the sooner the better. He turned away.

"Are you to London? Pardon, but would it be a terrible imposition if I should come too?" Benedict asked quickly.

Sometimes Ben sounded like a child. Frowning, Adrian glanced impatiently at him. "Your father owns a very expensive house in London. Why don't you just go if you like?"

"I didn't mean to imply . . . I rather thought . . . I've some business there, and as we never seem to encounter one another, I thought it would be easier to travel together."

A distant memory of a little boy running after him flitted across Adrian's mind. Then, his brother's near idolatry of him had amused him. He might have even cared for the lad. But Benedict had shown no particular affection for many years now—with the promise of Kealing Park dangling in front of him, he had succumbed to his father's machinations. And Adrian long ago had lost whatever feeling he might once have had for his brother.

Benedict apparently sensed his hesitation, because he

quickly crossed the room to Adrian. "There was a time when you welcomed my tagging along. I thought it might be entertaining, that's all."

Hardly. But as it was with most things, Adrian could not have cared less if Benedict accompanied him to London or not. "Whatever suits you," he remarked unemotionally, and walked out the door before Benedict could say more.

Fortunately, Archie was not a coy fellow. The moment Adrian entered the study, he shot out of his seat, holding a crumpled paper in one hand. "*Murderer!* I should have known it would come to this! Gambling and whoring were never enough for you, were they?" he bellowed.

Well, they were off to a fine start, as usual. "Please, Father, you mustn't fawn over me," Adrian said dryly as Benedict timidly slipped past him and hurried to the window.

"God's blood, Albright, don't belittle me! You are a *murderer!*"

Years of practiced indifference had made Adrian a master at masking all emotion, and he leaned casually against the door with his hands shoved deep in his pockets, coolly observing his father. "As usual, you have your facts a bit backward. I did not murder him; he tried to murder *me*. If you have cause to question that fact, you might speak with the justice in Pemberheath."

Archie scowled deeply. "That's just like you, to make light of something so reprehensible! God knows how you could possibly disparage the death of my cousin's son! Have you no conscience?"

God, did *he*? He had not seen his cousin in fifteen years—as was so bloody typical of him, Archie hated Phillip's father because of some vague falling out over money.

"You are no son of mine, do you hear me? I will not have a murderer in my house!" Archie shouted angrily. "I have done it this time, you worthless—"

"Father!" Benedict cried. "Please!"

"Ah, Ben, he was just getting started," Adrian said, smiling. "Go on, Father . . . you were saying?"

Archie's flaccid face turned red. He growled and raised the crumpled paper he held. "Do you see this? I have done it, you worthless cur! You don't deserve the title of earl, much less marquis! I may not be able to keep you from my title, but by God, I can keep you from my fortune! *This*," he shouted, waving the paper, "says it all! I have done what I should have done long ago and disinherited you at last! It belongs to Benedict now, *all* of it! Kealing Park, the house in London, the château in France! It is all *his* now!"

Behind him, Benedict shamefully bowed his head. Adrian chuckled derisively—the little rat had known it all along. "Well, Ben, I suppose you will want to visit your own house in London now," he drawled, and smiled at the twitch in Benedict's shoulders.

"Everything is a jest to you, isn't it?" Archie hissed. "You have mocked me for the last time, do you understand? You disgust me! A bad seed from the start, you were! That shameless mother of yours—"

A cold chill shot down Adrian's back and he pushed away from the door. "Leave her out of it, Father."

"Why should I? That whore had this coming!"

Adrian lunged across the room before Archie could react and grabbed his father's neckcloth, twisting it as he glared down at him. "Not another word against her, or I shall give you true cause to call me murderer," he breathed.

His father's eyes bulged with fear, and disgusted, Adrian shoved him away. Gaping fearfully, Archie quickly grabbed his neck. "My God, are you *insane*?" Oh yes, he was. With a nonchalant shrug, Adrian started for the door. "You have dishonored me from the moment you were born! I have been exceedingly generous to you, and for what? So that you could drag my good name through the mud? So that you could kill my cousin's son? You are a blight on this house, Albright!" Archie roared as Adrian walked to the door. "I am ashamed to call you son, you reckless heathen! May God have mercy upon your soul!''

Too late for that, Adrian thought wryly and paused to glance over his shoulder. Benedict had not lifted his head. Not a word of protest or indignation passed his quivering lips as he cowered behind Archie and the piece of paper that gave him everything that was rightfully Adrian's. His expression bland, Adrian slid a cool, unaffected gaze to his father. Archie's jowls were purple with rage, and for one bizarre moment, Adrian was reminded of a turkey. ''Be careful, Father,'' he said, smiling. ''You have finally achieved what you have sought for thirty-two years. You wouldn't want to spoil it with a heart seizure,'' he said flippantly, and casually strolled out the door.

Three

MR. PEARLE PRIDED himself on being a solicitor with a heart. Having served Kealing and the neighboring villages for nigh on twenty-five years, he could count among his clientele such noteworthy personages as Lords Kealing and Carmichael and Baron Huffington— exactly three more nobles on his rolls than his chief competitor, Mr. Farnsworth of Newhall, could claim. His success was due, he thought proudly as he marched down Kealing's main thoroughfare, to his penchant for learning things about his clients that made them unique. For *caring* about them.

Pausing in front of the apothecary's shop, Mr. Pearle checked the alignment of his neckcloth in the reflection of the front windows. He spotted Mrs. Rasworthy inside, rapped lightly on the window, and waved. She was one of his best clients, he thought as she frowned back at him, because he had taken the time to learn about her. He knew, for example, that she was a rather avid fan of the country horse races held twice yearly at Barstone. So avid a fan, in fact, that she had lost much of what her father had settled on her. This *he* knew about Mrs. Rasworthy, but Mr. Rasworthy did not.

With a cheerful smile, he continued his march down the street, musing that Mrs. Rasworthy was one of many who appreciated his skills—which *far* surpassed those of Mr. Farnsworth—as well as his impeccable discretion. The effort he put into learning about his clients enabled him to help them if the need arose. Such as the fact that Mr. Tinsley had an ailment that prevented him from fathering children. Or that Lord Huffington was descended from mental imbalance on his mother's side. There were so many small details, that he had, several years ago, taken to chronicling them in a series of leatherbound journals he kept safely hidden in his offices. Appropriately titled *Pearles of Wisdom,* his journal contained twenty-five years of interesting tidbits about practically everyone in Kealing, Newhall, and Fairlington.

He paused at the corner of the thoroughfare and Grayson's Alley to look carefully in both directions before continuing across to the bakery he owned, above which he received his clients in a tidy little office. Even *that* was discreet—one never knew if a person entered his establishment for bread or for legal services. As he neared the door he fumbled in his pocket for a key and promptly dropped it at his feet. Bracing his legs far apart, he cautiously leaned forward to retrieve it. When he lifted his head, he saw the expensive traveling chaise coasting down the thoroughfare, its distinctive crest identifying it as belonging to the Earl of Albright. Now *there* was an interesting family, he thought as he pocketed the key again, and mentally flipped through the journal pages cataloguing the Spence family tribulations. Pity that Lord Kealing had disowned the earl in favor of his youngest son, Benedict. Mr. Pearle knew this because just this morning he had reviewed the details of the revised will to make sure nothing was left unclear—or to Lord Albright—and had promptly entered the latest information into his journal over luncheon.

As he watched, the traveling chaise drew to a halt just outside Randolph's Sundries; a man sitting with the driver leapt to the ground and strode inside. Mr. Pearle unconsciously adjusted his neckcloth. He had an obligation to make sure Lord Albright understood all interpretations of the disownment, really, and without hesitation strolled to the traveling chaise.

Fortunately the chaise curtains were open, so Mr. Pearle could see Lord Albright was alone inside, reading a newspaper. Clearing his throat, he tapped lightly on the window. "Good afternoon, my lord!" he called cheerfully. Lord Albright glanced at him and nodded— at least it *seemed* like a nod—then turned back to his paper. A bit of heat crept under Mr. Pearle's collar, and he cleared his throat again. "I trust you have come from Kealing Park?" he asked loudly. "Rather unfortunate turn of events, I must say."

Lord Albright turned his head slowly and considered him with a cool nonchalance that reminded Mr. Pearle just how chilly the day was turning. After a moment of casual perusal, the earl reached for the door and flicked it open. "Good afternoon, Mr. Pearle. Would you care to join me inside while I wait?" he asked smoothly.

Indeed he would! Mr. Pearle eagerly clambered inside, rocking the coach with his clumsy entry. Settling himself against the velvet squabs, he nervously straightened his neckcloth. "I had heard you were at Kealing Park, of course. And as your lord father was by early this morning, I rather imagine you have learned the regretful news by now." Instantly, he recognized how forward that sounded, and in an attempt to explain blurted out, "Naturally, Lord Kealing entrusted me to review the documents."

"Naturally," Lord Albright drawled.

Heat seeped into Mr. Pearle's face. "Terrible pity that you weren't able to resolve your differences. But I suppose if something like this *had* to happen, it is fortunate that you are quite able to fend for yourself, what with your title and the Longbridge estate. And, of course, the entail that will one day come with your father's title. I suppose if one was to look on the positive side, one could hardly ignore the fact that young Benedict's finances will be secure. It is not very often the younger son has such security, you may trust me.''

Lord Albright nodded and settled further into the squabs with such an unconcerned expression that Mr. Pearle had to wonder if he did indeed know what his father had done. ''Well,'' he said in a nervous croak, ''behind every cloud there lies a silver lining! It is important for a young man to have security if he intends to marry well, and Lord Benedict is quite enamored of Miss Dashell—Lilliana, that is, not Caroline, as one might expect.'' At that, Lord Albright cocked his head to one side; his hazel eyes pierced Mr. Pearle's until he felt the heat spread to the top of his scalp. He swallowed. ''What I mean to say is that since *you* do not stand to suffer, not *really,* then one might be pleased that Lord Benedict's offer will seem, ah, more palatable to Baron Dashell. That would be your silver lining, you see.''

''An offer? I am afraid I have not heard of this . . . *fortunate* . . . turn of events, sir,'' Lord Albright admitted casually.

Mr. Pearle squirmed uncomfortably. ''Haven't you? I should think Lord Benedict might have mentioned it.''

''Ah. But as he did not, perhaps you would be so kind as to enlighten me?''

''Yes, well, I know of it only because Lord Kealing called upon me in an effort to gain some . . . ah, information . . . about Lord Dashell,'' Mr. Pearle said cautiously. ''He hasn't exactly been careful with his funds, you see.''

Lord Albright glanced at his paper and asked, ''Gambling debts?''

''Oh no!'' Mr. Pearle said, shaking his head vigorously. ''Well, not *entirely.* Lord Dashell had a particularly bad crop three years past, and it was hardly improved the following year. And what with the taxes . . . well, I rather think he meant to make it up at the gaming table, but he was not very successful. And now there is the matter of keeping Blackfield Grange afloat.''

"I see. And I gather Benedict proposes to help him, so that Dashell will look favorably upon his suit," the earl remarked as he casually studied a cuticle.

Mr. Pearle relaxed a bit, warming to the topic about which he was so well informed. "In a manner of speaking, yes. Miss Dashell does not have a dowry to speak of, so Lord Kealing thought to offer a betrothal gift of her father's debts in exchange for her hand."

Lord Albright looked up, smiling thinly. "It seems a bit extreme for my father to pay Dashell's debts, doesn't it? I should think a waiver of the dowry would be sufficient to earn the young lady's favor."

Recalling almost every word he had recorded in his journal about it, Mr. Pearle was quite proud of knowing the answer. "One would think so, yes. But Lord Dashell's creditors have grown quite insistent, I'm afraid. Lord Kealing intends to pay his debts in exchange for the gel's hand *and* a controlling interest in Blackfield Grange. Very clever, your father," he said with a nod.

Odd, but Lord Albright's smile seemed almost a sneer. "Yes, isn't he? But I wonder why he should want a controlling interest in an estate that is not producing," he mused, and arched an inquisitive brow.

"Oh! That's quite simple! Blackfield Grange sits on some of the richest soil in the parish. But Lord Dashell could not manage to withdraw his kerchief from his pocket efficiently, if you take my meaning. He does not have a head for things agricultural in nature."

"I see." Lord Albright nodded thoughtfully. "Then I must agree with your assessment, sir. It appears my brother has gained himself the silver lining."

Mr. Pearle beamed with pleasure that the earl had recognized his keen powers of deductive reasoning. He was still beaming when the door opened and the earl's man stuck his head inside. "Beggin' your pardon, milord, we are ready now," he announced.

Lord Albright graciously inclined his head to Mr.

Pearle. "Thank you for the visit, sir. It has been my pleasure."

Mr. Pearle saw that his time was up, and inched his way to the door. "Thank *you*, my lord. I am glad I had the opportunity to say good-bye and to give you perhaps a more cheerful interpretation of events. I suppose you will go to Longbridge now? Or perhaps London?" he asked as he carefully extended his legs through the small doorway.

"Good day, Mr. Pearle," the earl said.

The solicitor made his way onto terra firma and glanced back; Lord Albright had resumed reading his paper. He tipped his hat at the earl's man and, straightening his neckcloth, turned around and marched to the bakery.

So, Benedict was to marry, Adrian thought bitterly as he watched Pearle waddle away. And Archie was going to hold a man's estate as ransom for the privilege. As if the man needed Blackfield Grange—but with Archie, the conquest was just as enticing as the spoils.

As the chaise started forward, Adrian clamped his jaw tightly shut against an indignation that was beginning to soar in him. He could hardly bring himself to admit it, but the loss of Kealing Park had wounded him deeply. Somehow he had foolishly convinced himself he could hold Archie at bay until his death. He'd been stupid enough to think so even after he had killed Phillip.

A familiar stab of pain jabbed at him, and Adrian closed his eyes. He should have known Benedict would have the Park in the end. Benedict, who had never lifted a finger in all his life to earn a blasted thing, would benefit from Adrian's misfortune just as he always did. Benedict the Coward would have everything that rightfully belonged to *him*, the heir.

A budding anger took firm root and began to feed on years of suppressed emotion. Suddenly, Adrian could not allow Archie and Benedict to have their way in this. He had lost his father's esteem long ago, and now, his rightful inheritance. He would never have them back—at the moment, he didn't *want* them back—but neither did he want Benedict to have them. He suddenly lunged toward the ceiling vent and jerked it open. "Arlo!" he bellowed. "Stop the coach!" As the conveyance shuddered to a halt, Adrian slowly leaned against the squabs, turning a nugget of an idea over and over in his mind, looking for holes, for pitfalls, anything that might persuade him to continue on to Longbridge as he fully intended, having lost the will to return to London just yet.

The groom's face appeared in the narrow doorway. "Have Wyatt turn the coach around and drive to the village inn," Adrian said curtly. Arlo's eyes widened, but he nodded directly and closed the door. As the coach began to move again, Adrian glanced out the window, his mind churning. He could find no obvious flaws in his thinking. His idea, much to his great surprise, suddenly made a great deal of sense to him.

Archie had chosen well. Reined to a stop on top of a hill, Adrian surveyed the valley below him where Blackfield Grange sat. A little ragged around the edges, it was nonetheless a fine estate of Georgian design, with two modern wings sweeping out from either side of the main hall. The fields beyond the house were dotted with haystacks, feed supply left for the winter. A spread of gardens graced the east wing, a bowling lawn was off the west terrace, and two riders raced headlong into a wooded area that bordered the west side of the estate.

Adrian only vaguely remembered the owners, Lord and Lady Dashell, and had racked his brain for a memory of the children, but to no avail. He seemed to recall that Lady Dashell had visited his mother with her brood in tow on occasion, but his lack of any other memory had forced him to call on the odious Mr. Pearle to find out exactly how many children, and of what age and gender. Pearle had eagerly ticked off Master Tom Dashell, the heir, his younger sister, Lilliana, and the youngest of them all, Caroline, the family beauty. Both girls were of marrying age and, as Pearle so delicately put it, Lilliana was even a smidgen past a suitable age at two and twenty.

The fat little solicitor had also added that the girls were healthy feminine specimens, and in his words, "built to produce an abundance of heirs." Adrian had certainly not inquired as to that, but was glad that Pearle had volunteered it all the same. The debate warring inside him argued that he was doing this, in part, because he needed an heir. Phillip's death had rudely awakened him to the reality of his own mortality, and he would not allow one foot of Longbridge or any of his other holdings to pass to Benedict.

He needed an heir.

It was the rationalization he clung to, but he was not so obtuse that he didn't recognize that this was also revenge, plain and simple. He simply could not allow Benedict and Archie to have Blackfield Grange in addition to everything else they had taken. Apparently he was in luck—another interesting piece of news Pearle had passed along was that a final agreement between the Spence and Dashell families had not been reached. And to Pearle's knowledge, Miss Dashell was not aware of the particulars of the offer.

Adrian adjusted the brim of his hat with a wry smile. Miss Dashell would be aware of *his* offer, just as soon as he had his audience with Lord Dashell. It would no doubt seem like a godsend to Dashell. It was so simple, really. He would pay the man's debts, just as Archie had offered to do. But instead of taking a controlling interest of Blackfield Grange, Adrian would offer to give the baron twenty-five thousand pounds over and above the twenty-five thousand he needed to settle his affairs. In exchange for that extraordinary sum of money, Adrian would request only that the marriage occur as quickly as possible—and he had taken the liberty of obtaining a special license to ensure that it did. As for the matter of never having met Miss Dashell, well, he would finesse that when the time came. He was banking on the fact that Dashell would realize there would never be a chance like this again in his lifetime.

The smile slowly faded from his lips as he asked himself again why he should care if Benedict married the Dashell girl or if Archie got a piece of Blackfield Grange. He didn't really know the answer, and he certainly didn't care to analyze it. The only thing he knew was that he wanted revenge. Revenge for a lifetime of Archie's abuse, for the many times he had tried to please his father. Revenge for his mother and the loss of Kealing Park. He wanted revenge, and the longer he sat here, the longer he would have to wait for it.

He spurred his horse forward.

Jason, a groom at Blackfield Grange, could see Lilliana crashing through the trees just ahead, starting to put distance between them. He gave his horse his head and crashed after her, but she was an expert rider. When he caught up with her, she veered sharply to the right. Jason managed to keep pace parallel to her, catching glimpses of her blue riding habit through the copse of trees through which they recklessly rode. As they neared a meadow stretching beyond the woods, they broke through the trees at the same time, both bent over the necks of their mounts. Jason saw the mound of brush and rocks looming directly in front of Lilliana and caught a nervous breath in his throat. But she led her horse to leap agilely over the brush, never losing speed.

They tore down the length of the west meadow and around the lone oak at the far end, neck and neck. As they raced down the return stretch, Jason gained a nose on her. Lilliana suddenly pulled up short, her cry fading swiftly as Jason shot past. Panic assaulted him— immediately he yanked on the reins and jerked the roan around, just as Lilliana flew past.

"Damnation!" he shouted, and yanked the roan around again. But it was too late and too well done on

Lilliana's part. He saw her disappear into the woods ahead of him, and when he emerged on the other side a few minutes later, Lilliana was at the finish line. Laughing.

"You *cheated*!" he cried angrily.

"I certainly did!" she readily agreed, and laughed gleefully.

Jason couldn't help himself—he smiled broadly. "That was hardly sporting, Miss Lilliana! I wonder what your lady mother would say to your racing *and* cheating!"

"She would flay me alive, I assure you," Lilliana responded cheerfully.

Jason's gaze flicked to her gown, spattered with mud and bunched around the tops of her boots. She rode astride—terribly improper, but effective. "She may flay you alive yet. Your gown is ruined," he remarked, and motioned to her hem.

Lilliana's smile faded as she leaned to one side to have a look. "Oh, *no*," she moaned, then sighed wearily. "Well. There you have it. I am to be flayed alive." She glanced up, a devilish grin on her face. "Therefore, I should take full advantage of the opportunity. Come on then, I am simply *dying* to see Mrs. Oakley's baby boy!"

Jason instantly shook his head. "Lady Dashell said you weren't to go there."

Lilliana smiled brightly. "I'm not to race, either, and you did not protest too strongly. Oh, *do* come with me!" she urged him, and started Susie in the direction of the tenant cottages, blithely ignoring Jason's calls to turn back before her mother discovered where she had gone.

When they returned to the Grange two hours later, Lilliana was a bit more frantic than she let on. She really had not intended to be gone so long and had little doubt her mother was already scouring the countryside in search of her. This would earn her a grand tongue-lashing at a minimum, which she prayed would be all. Heaven help her, she just could not please her mother.

Inside the stables, Lilliana donned a drab brown cloak she kept there just for emergencies such as this, and was frantically trying to stuff errant strands of blond hair into something resembling a coif when she heard her mother calling. Wincing, she redoubled her efforts to repair her hair.

"Hurry, Miss Lilliana!" At sixteen, Jason had just been promoted to the position of groom, of which he was exceedingly proud. Which was why the prospect of facing Lady Alice Dashell at the moment scared him more than it did Lilliana. Not two days ago Lady Dashell had threatened to hang him if she discovered him racing Lilliana again. He peered nervously out the stable door. "She is coming this way!" he hissed.

"Hurry and get yourself up in the loft!" Lilliana whispered frantically, and yanked her cloak tightly around her. Jason did not argue; he pivoted and bolted for the back of the stables, disappearing into the loft just as Alice Dashell swung the door open.

"*Lilliana!* God in heaven, where have you been?" her mother snapped.

Bloody hell, judging by the tone of her voice, this could be worse than she thought. Lilliana forced a cheerful smile to her lips. "I was just saying hello to the horses, Mama. I'm very sorry, I did not hear you."

The frown that creased Lady Dashell's face would have made a warrior cringe. "I find it rather hard to believe that you did not hear me just moments ago, miss," she said as she stalked toward the stall.

"Oh! Did you call?" Lilliana asked sweetly, her smile widening as her mother closed in on her. Dear God, *please* don't let her see the mud on my gown, she pleaded silently, and to be safe, moved to the horse's side as her mother marched to a halt in front of her.

"What on earth are you doing?" Lady Dashell demanded.

"Why, nothing, Mother! Oh, you mean *now*? I am, ah, brushing Susie, because she—"

"Not in one of your good gowns, I should hope!"

"Oh no, mum. I put on this old cloak so as not to spoil my gown."

Alice Dashell punched her fists to her hips and glared at the horse. "And just where have you been?" When Lilliana hesitated in a frantic effort to think of an answer, her mother angrily shook her head. "Never mind! Come now, and leave the task to that worthless groom. There is a gentleman caller for you," she said, and impossibly, her stern frown deepened.

"Lord Benedict?" Lilliana asked, and suppressed the strange urge to yawn. Benedict had, of course, hinted at his intentions, and Lilliana supposed she was prepared to accept him. He was a nice sort of fellow, although a little weak in the knees. She had discovered that one morning when they were strolling the grounds and a poor little bird fell from its nest. Benedict had gone positively green, but she had thought to save it and had become rather disgusted with Benedict's squeamishness. But she supposed it hardly mattered that he did not share her enthusiasm for life—he was as good a match as she could ever hope to find in the middle of absolutely nowhere as she was.

How painfully aware she was of *that,* just as she was painfully aware of her advanced age. At two and twenty, she should have been married by now, maybe have a babe or two. And to make matters worse, her sister Caroline was absolutely desperate to marry Mr. Horace Feather. Unfortunately, she could not until Lilliana had married, because, as their mother pointed out to Caroline on an almost daily basis, that was the way things were done in the country. So her sister spent every day absolutely frantic that Lilliana stood in her way of everlasting happiness. Benedict would solve all that, Caroline reasoned, and Lilliana could not *dream* of doing better.

"I wasn't expecting Lord Benedict today," she added, and sighed unconsciously.

"No, not Lord Benedict," Lady Dashell replied impatiently.

Lilliana glanced curiously over her shoulder as she smoothed Susie's mane. "Then who? Please don't tell me it is that mean Mr. Willard again! I did *not* harm his silly old clock! That old thing was broken *long* before I tried to wind it—"

"Not Mr. Willard!" Lady Dashell fairly shouted. "It is Lord Benedict's brother."

It took several seconds for that to register. Stunned, Lilliana jerked her head to her mother. *Adrian* Spence had come to call on her? The Earl of Albright? The most fantastically masculine man in all of England? "Wh-what? What did you say?" she gasped.

"Oh dear, what have you done to your hair?" her mother moaned.

Lilliana suddenly lunged at her mother and grabbed her shoulders, causing the woman to shriek in surprise. "Mother, is it *Adrian* Spence? Lord Albright? Do you mean to tell me he is *here*? Oh my God, oh my *God*!"

"Lilliana, get ahold of yourself!" Alice Dashell demanded, and grabbed her wrists, forcing her arms to her sides. "Turn around so that I might do something with your hair!" she snapped, and shoved her around to begin jabbing her hair into place.

"But what is he doing *here*?" Lilliana cried. Her mother did not answer immediately, and pushed Lilliana's head around when she tried to look over her shoulder. *"Mother!"*

"He wants to speak with you!" Lady Dashell snapped, as if it was perfectly obvious. "Now listen to me, Lilliana. You will remember that Lord Benedict has been very persistent in his courtship, and you have given him every reason to believe his attentions are welcome. I should not be surprised if things may have been said between the two of you, but you must be cognizant that there are other suitors—"

"Lord Albright wants to *court* me?" she gasped in disbelief.

"There are other suitors," her mother continued
evenly, "and your duty is to choose the one who can give
you the most comfortable and prosperous existence . . .
without making too great a demand on your family. Do
you understand? You know we have been through a
rough patch recently, and while I know you are fond of
Lord Benedict, you must be aware—"

Lilliana wrenched free of her mother and whirled
around, gaping at her in astonishment. She was going to
swoon. Jesus, Mary, and Joseph, she was going to drop
dead where she stood! Adrian Spence wanted to court
her? It was not to be believed! This was some sort of
waking dream, and to prove it, she quickly pinched her
arm. That hurt—oh God, she was not dreaming!

"Lilliana." Her mother sighed heavily. "Do not look
so overjoyed. It makes you appear simple."

"But . . . but there must be some *mistake*! Are you
quite certain he did not ask for Caroline? Surely he
asked for Caroline! A man such as Lord Albright would
call on *Caroline,* not *me*!"

"I am quite certain he asked for you, dear. Please
stop twisting the buttons on your cloak before they
break off."

"But . . . but *why*? Mother, do you realize that
Lord Albright could court whomever he wants—and believe me, the rumors are that he *has*—"

"Lilliana!"

"But not someone like me! I don't understand why
he would call on *me*!"

Lady Dashell frowned as she reached to straighten
the collar of Lilliana's cloak. "You won't understand
until you see him, will you? Now come with me—and do
not gush like a simpleton, and do *not* show him such
blatant favor right away! It is quite unseemly for a
young woman to pounce on the first compliment she re-
ceives!"

Lilliana barely heard her mother—her head was reeling. There was some mistake. Or someone was playing a

cruel joke on her, a very cruel joke. From almost the time she could walk, she had dreamed about Adrian Spence. When she was a child, her mother would take her and her siblings along when she visited Lady Kealing. She remembered Adrian as tall and handsome and *terribly* dashing. He would tweak her nose and give her sweets and entice her to sing little ditties. She had worshiped Adrian Spence even then, had followed every word ever said about him— and God knew there was no lack of gossip. Everyone in Kealing, Newhall, and Fairlington knew he was a rogue, a scoundrel, and a daring adventurer. *A dangerous gentleman,* they said, who fought with his father—about what, she had no earthly idea—and anyone else who crossed him. He had traveled extensively and made himself an *enormous* fortune, one so great that everyone in the parish felt compelled to whisper when they spoke of it. He was reputedly a high-stakes gambler, had questionable taste in feminine companions, and had participated in at least two duels, one even in *France.*

The Earl of Albright was a man who knew how to live life to its fullest, to experience all there was. He did exactly what she craved—to live! Except that she was not allowed to live, not here, not socked away at Blackfield Grange like some country bumpkin. Good Lord, given half a chance, she would *soar,* just as Adrian Spence did every day of his life! The fact that he, of all people, had come to call on her was enough to make her think she had finally died and gone to heaven.

"Stop staring off like that! Oh my Lord, he will think you are completely addled!" her mother said with a twinge of desperation.

Lilliana smiled broadly. "I can't believe it! He has come to call . . . on *me!*" she cried, and impulsively threw her arms wide and twirled around in the stable.

"Stop that!" Lady Dashell insisted, and grabbed Lilliana's wrist. "Come along, the man has been waiting long enough as it is! Jason! Bring yourself down here and rub this horse down! And if I catch you racing again, I shall hang you from the oak on the bowling lawn, do you hear me?'' she shouted.

"Yes, mum!'' came the muffled reply, but Lady Dashell was already pushing Lilliana out of the stable.

Four

LADY DASHELL PUSHED her daughter toward
the formal drawing room with the whispered admonish-
ment that she should *never* keep an earl waiting so long,
as if Lilliana had done it on purpose. When they reached
the closed oaken doors, Lady Dashell jerked the cloak
from her shoulders, reached for the brass handle, and
flung them open. Lilliana barely registered the presence
of her father and brother inside with Lord Albright before her mother pushed her across the threshold.

"Lord Albright, may I introduce my daughter, Lilliana?" her father said, coming to his feet. Her mother
nudged her none too gently with her foot, and Lilliana
immediately sank into a curtsy . . . at which point she
remembered the mud on her gown, and artfully stepped
behind a high-backed settee. She smiled at the earl—or
rather, she *hoped* she was smiling. With her hair all
mussed and her exuberance spilling from every pore, she
suspected she looked something like a goose. If Lord Albright thought so, he was very careful not to show it.

"Miss Dashell, it is my extreme pleasure to make
your acquaintance again," he said smoothly as he

crossed the room to take the hand she clumsily thrust at him. Smiling at her, he lifted it to his lips.

Oh hell, how very *dashing*, she thought dreamily as he lowered her hand, as dashing as she remembered him, and Lord knew she remembered every single thing about him. Except how very handsome he was. Good God, he was handsome—hair neither brown nor blond, but a rich mixture of both, hazel eyes flecked with gold, and his lips, heaven help her, his lips were full and soft and the very deep color of raspberries.

"Lilliana?" her mother squeaked.

"I, um, the pleasure is mine, my lord," she said hoarsely. Wonderful. She was making a cake of herself and had barely opened her mouth.

"You are too kind," he murmured, and smiled so warmly that the corners of his eyes crinkled.

Lilliana's knees buckled.

"Well!" her father exclaimed, and coughed loudly. "Shall we sit?" He took Lady Dashell's arm and led her to a couch. Lord Albright politely extended his arm to Lilliana, and she very gingerly laid her hand on it, taking care not to touch him *too* much. Clutching the front of her skirt so that he would not see the mud, she allowed him to seat her on the settee. Tom remained standing at the pianoforte, his eyes narrowed on Lord Albright as he seated himself in a chair nearby.

Her father cleared his throat. "Pleasant weather for the time of year," he said, and began speaking of the weather—it was unusually warm. The southern breezes were particularly delightful in the early evening hours, but it would be a mild winter. Lord Albright agreed, and mentioned an unusually warm winter spent in Rome. *Rome*—how terribly romantic! But why on earth Tom should roll his eyes at that was beyond Lilliana. Honestly, Tom was acting as if he was miffed. Actually, everyone was acting odd, she noticed with a quick glance at her parents. Her very prim and proper mother did not so much as open her mouth, but sat stiffly beside her husband, staring blankly at the vase of fresh-cut flowers on a little table near the hearth. Even her father looked very uncomfortable, which was very unlike his amicable self.

As for *her,* well, she had to concentrate to keep from gaping, and speaking was out of the question. It was impossible to comprehend how he had come to be in her drawing room, and to think he was actually *calling* on her completely unfathomable. And worse yet, it was absolutely breathtaking to behold him. From his long, tapered fingers drumming absently on one astoundingly muscular thigh, to the perfectly tied silk neckcloth that just brushed his square jaw, to the wavy hair that extended well past his collar—he was, in a word, magnificent. So magnificent that Lilliana was awestruck.

Not that anyone noticed, fortunately. Only her father chatted with the earl, and wonder of wonders, the Spence Family Scoundrel responded with effortless grace on the most boring topics in the world. *Farming?* Her father spoke of farming! Lilliana suppressed a groan of mortification, but Lord Albright managed to converse rather cheerfully on the subject. Just when she had convinced herself that she had to be dreaming—for surely a man like him would not be remotely interested in *farming*—her father abruptly stood.

"Alice, I could use your help in the library. Tom, weren't you off to the stables to have a look at that new colt?" he asked, then glanced uneasily at the earl. "You will please excuse us, my lord?"

Excuse them? Oh no, what was *this*? They were going to *leave* her here with him? Lilliana jerked a frantic glance at her mother, but she stood and took her husband's arm as if it were the most natural thing in the world to leave her daughter unchaperoned. That was absurd, as absurd as the notion that Tom, who was skulking to the door, would bother with a new colt—especially one that didn't exist! "Mama?" Lilliana asked, her voice quavering slightly. "Wouldn't you like to sit with us?"

Lady Dashell's eyes flicked to Lord Albright, then

back to Lilliana. "No. Ah, no dear—your father needs help with the . . . ah . . . accounts." Lilliana's eyes widened at that ridiculous lie, and she panicked. They *were* contriving to leave her alone with him! What would she say? How on earth would she converse with a man like *him*? "You might offer some tea," her mother added with a frown, and before Lilliana could speak, her father was moving toward the door, pulling her mother with him and forcing Tom out in front of him.

She gripped the arm of the settee as her family trooped out the door. What in blazes was happening here? Had some strange star struck the Grange and caused them all to take leave of their senses? She was completely unprepared—no, *inept*—to amuse a man of his position and experience! He was used to the finest the world had to offer, women far more sophisticated than she was!

"Your parents are graciously allowing me a moment to speak with you alone," he said.

A strange little flurry of nerves shot through the pit of Lilliana's stomach at that remark, and she dragged an astonished gaze to him. She knew what *speaking alone* meant in the country, but the idea was so unbelievable, so ridiculously preposterous, that she almost laughed. He arched a quizzical brow, and she thought it might be necessary to remind him that he was a man of the world, a scoundrel of the highest order, the exceedingly wealthy Earl of Albright. He was mistaken—he did *not* want to speak alone with her, not to Lilliana Dashell of Blackfield Grange. That idea was so ludicrous that she choked on a hysterical giggle.

Lord Albright smiled fully then, and the flurry in her belly turned into a full-blown churning. "You look positively horrified. Am I as odious as all that, Lilliana?"

Oh God, but her name sounded like heaven on his lips, especially since it was not supposed to be there. A gentleman would not be so familiar—well, at least not a *country* gentleman, but who knew what the fast set of London did?

He was staring at her. She swallowed. "Forgive me, I did not mean to look . . . horrified," she muttered uncertainly. "Shall I . . . shall I ring for some tea?" she asked, her tongue moving despite her frozen brain.

"Perhaps a little later," he said, and smiled charmingly. Lilliana frantically racked her brain for something to say as those lovely hazel eyes thoughtfully roamed her face and then her . . . oh *my* . . . a deep blush flamed Lilliana's cheeks, and she quickly lowered her gaze— only to see the hideous splatter of mud on her lap. Hastily, she snatched a handful of her skirt and folded it over the stain.

"Please don't look so frightened," he said with a low, silky chuckle. "I am perilously close to having my tender feelings crushed."

Tender feelings? "Oh! Do I look frightened? I assure you I am not," she said uneasily. "Not in the least. I am just . . . I am just—"

"Surprised?" he offered helpfully.

"Surprised!" she agreed, nodding furiously to emphasize just *how* surprised.

"I regret that I have not called sooner. Unfortunately, I am often in London—"

"Yes of course, London is a very large town—"

"And I do not get to the country as often as I would like. Kealing Park is a good half-day's ride from London."

"It is a good half-day's ride from *Hades*," she hastily agreed.

He smiled again, sending another quiver through her belly. "Nevertheless, I pray you will forgive my deplorable lack of manners."

What on earth was he talking about? She hadn't expected him to call at all, much less before now! Her mind flicked through all sorts of useless information she had dragged out of Benedict about him. Had Benedict mentioned his brother was coming? Was there some rule of etiquette that required him to call on her before Benedict offered?

"But I am a man of action, Lilliana, and when I have determined my course, I waste little time."

Whatever he should mean by that, she could certainly believe it. A man of action and sophistication and excitement and—

"I have recently determined that I have certain responsibilities to be fulfilled now that I have reached my thirty-second year, and it is that which brings me to you. I apologize for arriving unannounced, but in my haste to get here, I am afraid it was unavoidable."

Responsibility. All right, all right, she was beginning to understand, she thought, and took a deep breath. He was speaking of something to do with Benedict, and almost sighed with relief.

He rose so suddenly that her perfect posture slipped for a moment; in two steps he was sitting beside her on the settee. Astounded, Lilliana's eyes widened with surprise. Acutely aware that she was gaping at him like a fool, she gasped when he pried her hand from its grip on her gown. In stunned amazement, she watched as he carefully placed it between his two, strong hands, jolting every nerve in her. What responsibility did he have that required such delicate touch? God, did she bloody well care? *Don't you dare swoon!*

"You are aware, I am sure, that among the *ton*, two people of suitable lineage and fortune enter into matrimony for the purpose of extending the family name and increasing their holdings." Yes, yes, she knew all that, and nodded dumbly as her mind raced ahead, offering up and rejecting different suppositions for his wildly absurd call. "I am certain you are equally aware that a man in my position must make a match with a woman who has been trained to manage a large household, is dutiful in her role as a countess and can provide an heir. Above all, a woman who is a good companion," he continued.

Lilliana nodded unconsciously. This had to do with Benedict, that much was clear, what with the reference to matrimony and the rattling off of society's expectations. Did he think she and Benedict did not suit? Was *that* what this was all about? She should hardly be surprised—she was the daughter of a downtrodden baron, had left Blackfield Grange exactly twice in her twenty-two years, and had no real connections to the Quality other than some distant cousin on her mother's side. Benedict, on the other hand, was the son of a wealthy marquis and could certainly do better than her. Honestly, she had often wondered why he did not seem to realize that.

The earl's hazel eyes flicked to his hands and long dark lashes swept his high cheekbones, momentarily hiding his gaze from her. The mad notion that he was here to tell her that Benedict could not marry her popped into her numbed brain. Funny, but she felt nothing in particular about that—except a sense of irritation that Benedict had not come to do the deed himself. All right, then, she was unsuitable. And when had the Spence family reached this astounding conclusion? Certainly since Monday, because Benedict had almost cried with despair when she had begged a reprieve from his call, citing a very bad headache. Well, good God, she had not expected him that day, and she had promised to race Jason. It wasn't as if she hadn't responded every other—

"Of course, companionship is not the best of reasons to make a match, but it is very pleasing to have it all the same. I have thought long and hard about this, and I have determined that you are the woman," Lord Albright said, and looked up, his eyes suddenly piercing hers.

Lilliana blinked. She must have been swooning when he was speaking, because she had no earthly idea what he was talking about. "*What* woman?" she asked, confused.

"The woman I would have as my wife," he responded casually.

With a shriek, Lilliana jerked her hand from his.

He quickly lifted his hands. "I know this must come as something of a surprise—"

"A *surprise*? I beg your pardon, my lord, but is this some sort of *joke*?" she cried.

"Not in the least, madam!"

"Because if it is, I shall beg you *not* to jest about something so . . . so . . ."

"I am quite serious, Lilliana."

Stunned, she shot off the settee and stumbled blindly to the pianoforte. This was inconceivable! The man she had admired from almost the beginning of time would suddenly stroll into Blackfield Grange and offer her *marriage*? For heaven's sake, what strange dream was this? Something was wrong. Perhaps he had been hit on the head—it happened to Mr. Perry and the poor man didn't know who he was for a full three days—

"Lilliana," the earl said in a terribly rich, terribly soothing voice as he slowly rose to his feet, "please do not rush to judgment. At least hear me out." Oh, but he was in luck on that score. She was too overwhelmed to think or move! "I am an extraordinarily busy man. I do not have the luxury of time to call on a lady as a gentleman should, particularly one who resides so far from my affairs. It would have been impossible to have courted you properly."

"D-did you remember me as a child?" she asked, desperately searching for a reason, something that made sense of his astonishing announcement. "Is it possible you could have remembered me after all these years? Did you care for me then?" she blurted frantically, and whirled around to face him.

He looked almost chagrined. "I will not lie to you. I do not remember you as a child."

Certainly *that* did not reassure her. But honestly, how could she even think he would remember her? She had not seen him in fifteen years, and could hardly expect a man of his stature to recall some little girl from the country. "Then . . . then is it my father? Do you know my father?" she asked breathlessly. "You must," she said, nodding, trying to convince herself. "You remember Papa fondly, don't you!"

Lord Albright sighed and slowly shook his head. "I remember him only vaguely."

He did not know her family? What in God's name was *happening* here? "Then . . . then *why*? What possible reason could you have to come here and ask . . . Are you ridiculing me?" she cried.

"Of course not!" he said sternly, and strode across the room to quickly take her hands in his. "I came because I want you as my wife, Lilliana. We would make an excellent match, you and I. I can give you a life of luxury, anything your heart desires." He spoke softly and earnestly, his eyes peering deeply into her own, and Lilliana wondered if he could see her heart fluttering madly. "I had every intention of calling on you before now, but I began to wonder what possible difference would a few hours of chaperoned courtship make in your decision? Why should we waste that time when we could reach the conclusion, and therefore our marriage, much sooner?"

"But . . . but you can't just come in here and offer *marriage*! We might not suit! Did . . . did you think of that?" she sputtered hysterically.

"Of course we suit! A few hours sitting on your settee with your parents in this room would not tell me more than I already know. You are of gentle birth, you have been properly schooled, and you have a reputation for a warm and generous spirit and lively character. You are a good match for a man in my position, an excellent companion. What more should I hope to know? No, I am quite determined in this. But perhaps there is something about me that gives you pause?"

Lord God, there was *nothing* about him that would give her pause! He was right—six minutes, six days, or six years would not alter her opinion of him—she had adored him far too long. But she was not so silly that she could not see how sudden, how incredible this was! *He did not know her!*

"Lilliana? Have you a concern about my character?

Undoubtedly you have heard the rumors that circulate—
is that what upsets you?'' he asked softly.

If only he knew how she relished the rumors that
circulated about him, the tales of adventure, of daring
exploration, of defying society's edicts! She slowly shook
her head. He smiled. ''Then perhaps you are loath to be
a countess?'' She practically snorted at that—she was
unconventional, but she was not stupid. ''Then do you
agree that a few hours of courting would not change
your conclusion?''

Her heart was hammering wildly now, and she
forced herself to take a deep breath before she became
apoplectic. She would walk to the ends of the earth to
marry a man like him, but that did not make his offer
any less insane. *Insane!* ''Yes,'' she said meekly, and
inwardly winced at her traitorous tongue.

His charming smile deepened, warming her to the
tips of her toes. Giving herself a sharp reminder to
breathe, Lilliana jerked her hand from his. ''I beg your
pardon, my lord, but this makes no sense! You could
marry any woman! A woman with connections, and
. . . there must be women far more agreeable to you—''

''There are none,'' he said resolutely.

''Or beautiful! I am not beautiful, and I know you
enjoy the company of—''

''A woman's beauty is in her character—''

''Ladies who frequent the finest salons of London—''

''They bore me.''

She gulped. His smile seemed to widen, and she realized how very close he was. So close, she could smell the
spicy scent of his cologne. Now her heart was beating so
wildly that she was quite certain it would break through
her chest at any moment. ''But . . . but there is Benedict! He . . . he, ah, he plans to offer, too, you see,'' she
stammered.

Impossible, but the man moved as close as he could
without crawling into her gown with her. ''But he has
not, has he?'' Before she could answer, he smiled that
devastating smile of his again and promptly made her

mute. "As I told your father, we are not the first brothers to have settled on the same woman. No matter what you may decide, Benedict and I will sort it out. The choice is yours, Lilliana. A life of luxury as a countess—or, if you prefer, the familiar comfort of Kealing Park, near your family and your home."

Why did it suddenly sound like a choice between heaven and hell? Lilliana had accepted what she thought was an inevitable match with Benedict, but she had not thought it so terribly ordinary until this very moment. She abruptly turned away and collided with the pianoforte she had forgotten was behind her. A candlestick toppled over onto the wood flooring. "Please forgive me, but I can't think! This is all so very fantastic! No! So insane! Oh, Lord, it's insane all right, so sudden, so unexpected—"

"Lilliana," he murmured, his voice falling over her like a silken drape. "It is sudden because I am quite eager in my desire." In his *what*? She could not help herself; she glanced suspiciously at him from the corner of her eye. He leaned forward, his lips almost brushing her cheek. "*Quite* eager," he said softly, and his warm breath fanned her skin. "Please forgive me for having startled you, but try to understand. You know it is a good match, and I give you my word I shall make you happy."

He leaned closer, and through no will of her own Lilliana turned slightly toward him. His lips brushed hers, singeing her. She did not move, stood as rigid as a statue, her gaze riveted on his cheek. Slowly he lowered his head again, teasing her lips with the whisper of his before carefully shaping her mouth to fit his.

Liquid fire spread rapidly, heating every inch of her body, then suddenly swelled to a full-blown panic. She had never been kissed before, not like this, not so sweetly and tenderly and *earnestly* that she turned molten. It was a strange, enticing sensation—she felt almost weightless, quivering when his hand ran a fiery path down her arm.

And then he suddenly lifted his head. Lilliana grabbed the edge of the pianoforte, her eyes locked on his lips. Those lips had touched hers. Adrian Spence had *kissed* her! It was unimaginable, incredible—"It is unfathomable, my lord!" she suddenly blurted out. "Please, I must . . . I need to think!"

"Of course," he murmured soothingly. "May I call again tomorrow? Perhaps that will give you time to digest my offer and we might discuss it further."

She rather doubted she would be able to digest a single thing for the rest of the day, but she nodded dumbly. The charming smile he flashed her was full of white teeth as he lifted her hand to his lips. When he turned her hand over and kissed the soft inside of her wrist, another startling spark ignited deep inside her and sent a chain of tingles up her spine. "I will make you a good husband, Lilliana," he murmured, and a suggestive grin curled his lips. "In every conceivable way."

A deep heat instantly flooded her cheeks; he chuckled and dropped her hand, then turned and strode to the door, where he paused to glance over his shoulder. "Until tomorrow?"

"I, ah, I . . . tomorrow," she stammered. And then he was gone, leaving her to absorb the most incredible, most unbelievable thing that had ever happened in all her twenty-two years. Lilliana closed her eyes. It was absurd; the whole thing was patently absurd.

Almost as absurd as her giddy feeling of *complete* elation.

She suddenly pushed away from the pianoforte and rushed to an oval mirror to peer at her reflection. Nothing had changed—it was *her* looking back, the same, simple Lilliana Dashell. Slowly she brought her hands to her cheeks as she stared at her wide-eyed reflection. Heaven help her, but if she could have knocked on the pearly gates and asked God for just one favor, it would have been Adrian Spence. If she were married to a man like him, she might soar where others feared to, far away from Blackfield Grange and her mother's rigid rules and the expectations of a gently reared miss! Mother of God, she might actually *experience* life! She could travel to the ends of the earth, see things that most people could not even imagine, and best of all, she could gaze at his handsome face every day! It was more than she had ever dared to dream, but here it was, presented to her on a silver platter.

The bothersome image of Benedict appeared in her mind's eye, and she felt no small amount of guilt for what she was thinking. Yet she knew as she turned and blindly made her way to the door that she would accept Lord Albright's offer. As patently ridiculous as it was, she knew that as well as she knew the sun would come up in the morning.

Adrian accepted the reins from a groom who glared at him as if he had stolen the crown jewels, and sent Thunder trotting toward Newhall, the little village just five miles east of Kealing and the closest accommodations to Blackfield Grange. At least, he thought as he glanced at the fields around him, she seemed to take it well. He had expected some indignation, but Lilliana Dashell had taken his unorthodox offer rather well once she was capable of speaking instead of staring at him as if he were some sort of apparition.

He was not displeased with his progress.

And he was not entirely displeased with her. For all of Pearle's praise of the younger sister, he had feared she would be homely. She was not homely, but neither was she pretty. Just . . . average. Average height and build, average looks—exactly what one might expect in a parish princess. Her blond hair was pretty, he thought idly, or rather, *could* be pretty—it looked a bit like a bird's nest today. And the mud on her gown might be cause for wonder, but he shrugged to himself, unaffected by it. She was, in a word, unremarkable, and he couldn't help wondering briefly what Benedict saw in her. He didn't really care—he only cared that her father seemed to be a wise man.

Not that Dashell wasn't astounded, and that son of his rather indignant. But the baron had quickly understood the enormity of his offer, and had quickly agreed that while it was Lilliana's decision, he would not be disinclined to a match. What else could the man say? He was offering Dashell a solution to his many problems, and giving his daughter a match far above what she could hope for otherwise. Adrian had no doubt his offer would be accepted.

Lilliana descended the stairs very slowly, careful to step in such a way that the wood did not creak. If there was one thing that infuriated her mother even more than her racing, it was her habit of taking moonlit walks.

Yes, well, she was a bit restless, thank you, and her mother would just have to bear it.

How could she blame her? There was too much to think about! With a bewildered shake of her head, Lilliana paused in the corridor to fetch a heavy cloak. The sound of raised voices coming from the drawing room startled her, and she froze, straining to hear. It was quite extraordinary, really, as she could not recall ever having heard her parents argue. No one had to tell her that they argued about Lord Albright's offer. She quietly moved closer, listening carefully to the muffled voices, then catching her breath when she overheard her mother demand that the earl's offer be denied. "Oh, Walter, the entire parish will think Lilliana has jilted Lord Benedict! Everyone knows he intends to offer for her—can you not see how it will look when she marries his *brother*? Not to mention that there will be talk of *why*, exactly, they were married in such a rush!"

"My dear," her father answered patiently, "if she accepts the earl, they will be gone from the parish in a fortnight. What little talk there is will soon vanish, and we can ill afford to let a little scandal cloud our judgment.''

That remark astounded Lilliana, seeing as how her mother lived in *constant* fear of scandal, and very deliberately, she crept to the door. The scrape of a chair on the wood floor was followed by the sound of her father's footfall. ''Don't look so ill, love. He offers us a freedom I could never give you, you know that. Fifty thousand pounds, Alice! Kealing offers us little more than servitude—he may pay our debts, but he takes the Grange in return. Think of our Tom! Think of what he will inherit if we are forced to accept Kealing's offer—a mere forty percent!''

''I *do* think of Tom, but I also think of Lilliana!'' her mother moaned. ''She does not know this man! He has a horrid reputation—''

''Granted, he is known as a rogue, but he also has a very fine reputation of being fair and reputable in his business dealings. And you can hardly ignore the fact that he can give her a rich life. We could never hope for a better offer, my love.''

''He can give her a rich life, but he can also break her heart. I'm sorry, Walter, but it is all very suspect that he should come now. He does not know her, and—''

''He does not need to know her, Alice. He needs the requisite connections and good breeding stock, nothing more,'' her father said flatly.

A curious silence had followed that remark, and then her mother sighed sadly. ''Oh Lord, the rift this is bound to cause in that family is not to be borne! We should refuse *both* sons and take our chances!''

''It *can* be borne if it means keeping us from debtor's prison and giving Tom his due. Alice, you know that we must accept one of the offers, or we are ruined. You *must* think of Tom! And I daresay, Lilliana's chances for a good match grow smaller with each passing day!''

Lilliana stood perfectly still, her head swimming with confusion. Debtor's prison? She knew that they had experienced what her mother called a rough patch . . .

but debtor's prison? A band of fear tightened around her
chest as she imagined the authorities dragging her father
away. And exactly when had Lord Kealing made an offer? Her father had told her only that the marquis had
mentioned his son's interest in her!

She heard the scrape of the chair again. "Ah, Alice. It
is Lilliana's decision, not ours. If she chooses the earl,
well then, I am quite confident she will bear it well. She
is a spirited girl."

Her mother snorted her opinion of that, and Lilliana
could not bear to hear more. She didn't *need* to hear
more—everything was suddenly very clear now, and she
turned and walked quietly away.

Outside, she ran to the edge of bowling lawn, her
breath frosting in the night air. The icy cold felt good in
her lungs and cleared her mind. In truth, the conversation she had overheard had shaken her badly, but not for
the obvious reasons. Oh, she thought Lord Kealing's
terms were as odious as Lord Albright's were suspect.
But instead of being shocked and outraged, she felt an
enormous sense of relief. Her parents did not think her
particularly marriageable. That was not new—although
they had never said it to her, it was something she just
knew. It logically followed, then, that they did not believe a man like Lord Albright could want her. Well, she
could not believe it either. But all that aside, if what they
said was true, then Lord Albright had given her the reason to do what she knew she would do this very afternoon, what she *longed* to do. He had given her a sane
reason to accept his offer—to save her family's home.

She paused at the edge of the lawn and looked up at
the crystal night and stars twinkling like so many gems
above her. A distant memory came to her, when she had
been a small child, looking out the window of the drawing room at a night sky just like this one. *I want to be a
star when I grow up, Mama,* she had said. *Don't be ridiculous, Lilliana! Now look at what you've done! You've
missed another stitch!* But Lilliana had not cared about
stitches; she had wanted to be up there, flying high

above the earth seeing what God saw. She still did. But at Blackfield Grange she was earthbound, stifled by boredom and a desire to know more. There was nothing in this parish to hold her except the overbearing sense of duty and propriety that had been drilled into her from the crib.

She could not let this one chance at heaven slip by. If she did, she would die, extinguished by a life so mundane as to stifle the breath from her. It didn't matter what others said of Lord Albright—he was the man of her dreams, had always been, and she was not going to let him slip through her fingers because of some outdated fear of scandal. And her father was right—if she did not accept one of the two offers, Lord only knew what would become of her. She was two and twenty and lived in the middle of nowhere where less than a handful of eligible men knew of her existence. And without a suitable dowry her choices were extremely limited. So were Caroline's, and she was blocking her sister's chance at happiness with that ridiculously foppish Horace Feather—assuming, of course, her father ever agreed to accept "Mr. Featherbrain."

Nonetheless, she felt terribly guilty and foolish and appalled by her reckless determination. But heaven help her, all she could think of was how perfect her life would be married to the most exciting man in all of Great Britain. God was smiling on her for once, offering her the one person who could make her truly happy—Adrian Spence.

At long last, she might soar.

Five

A SMILING LORD DASHELL greeted Adrian the next day when a footman showed him to the solarium, and Adrian took that to be a good sign.

Crossing the threshold of the brightly lit room, he noticed the sister before anything else. He bowed over her hand as Dashell introduced her, taking in the heavily lashed green eyes and hair the rich color of honey. In spite of Miss Caroline Dashell's uncontrollable giggling, Adrian could see why Pearle had described her as the family beauty.

Dashell pointed him toward his other daughter. Lilliana was seated at an easel, but she came quickly to her feet as he crossed the room to greet her. "Lilliana," he murmured, and bowed over her hand, allowing his lips to linger a moment longer than etiquette allowed. The rustic parish princess flushed furiously. "You look lovely," he said, and her flush turned to a delightful smile, ending in a lone dimple in one cheek.

Behind him, Lord Dashell cleared his throat. "If you will excuse me, my lord. I have some business that cannot wait," he said, and receiving a nod from Adrian, cast a pointed look at Lilliana before quitting the room.

That left them with Caroline, who was still grinning like a simpleton.

Adrian turned his attention to Lilliana. "What are you painting?" he asked, and casually walked around to see her canvas. It was a painting of a vase stuffed with showy pink and white flowers, and it was actually quite good.

"Just some flowers," she mumbled, and clasping her hands demurely, smiled shyly. "They grew in our garden last spring." Across the room, Caroline giggled again, but was abruptly silenced by a sharp look from Lilliana.

"You are quite talented," he said, and meant it; she obviously had an artist's eye.

"Oh!" She blushed again, and looked at her feet. "Thank you, my lord, but I am not really very talented." Obviously embarrassed, she turned and walked hastily to the cluster of chairs in the middle of the room, where she sat daintily on the edge of one, and looked at Caroline again. Her sister dutifully dropped into a chair next to her. Adrian smiled to himself—how long had it been since he had courted a woman in her drawing room? Never, actually, save that one unfortunate incident when he was eighteen years old. He preferred the uncomplicated liaisons at Madam Farantino's.

"The, ah, weather is much warmer today," Lilliana stammered as Adrian selected a chair directly across from her. Caroline giggled. "It is a mild winter," she added, "but I suppose we could use some rain." Adrian nodded again. She bit her lower lip and stole a glance at Caroline. "It is particularly dry," she said, and locked her gaze on his mouth.

Well, one thing was certain—the Princess of the Grange was not very good at small talk. As for Caroline, that young simpleton could hardly contain herself. The two of them lacked the sophistication Adrian was accustomed to. They would never survive a London Season, not with such a blatant lack of feminine finesse. Fortunately, he didn't need a society belle for a wife.

"I prefer mild weather, because the house gets so

drafty when it is very cold," Lilliana muttered, and dropped her gaze to her hands.

Adrian suppressed the urge to chuckle at her helplessness. As he was feeling a bit charitable, he decided to end her agony. He suddenly leaned forward, and propping his forearms on his thighs, let his hands dangle between his legs. "Lilliana? Have you thought about my offer?" he asked softly, and arched a brow at the girls' collective gasps. Caroline gaped at him. Lilliana blinked. Several times. A bolt of lightning could have struck that solarium and not moved them. "Have you?" he asked, inserting a hint of anxiousness in his voice.

Lilliana and Caroline exchanged sidelong glances. "Umm, yes. Yes. Yes I have," she said slowly, and bravely lifted her chin.

"Might you share your decision with me? Or shall I be forced to endure the agony of waiting for your reply?"

Caroline turned at least three shades of red and, giggling hysterically, jerked around to gape at her sister. In stark contrast, Lilliana had gone deathly pale. She gulped. "Caroline, I do believe Mother could use some help with the sewing."

That caused Caroline to pierce Adrian with a sharp look. "But she said—"

"She said she needed help with the sewing. In the sitting room," Lilliana replied with a bit more confidence.

Her sister squirmed a bit, looked at her hands, then reluctantly came to her feet. "Yes, the sewing," she said unconvincingly. "If you need me, I shall be *in the sitting room*." She said it so distinctly that Adrian had to suppress another smile of amusement. Caroline looked once more at him, then practically sprinted for the door. She peered carefully into the corridor before slipping through, and closed the door softly behind her.

Thankful to be free of the giggler, Adrian smiled warmly at Lilliana. "You must assure your sister that I am not accustomed to offending women in their father's study."

The tension seemed to have left her, and she flicked a dismissive hand toward the door. "Oh, that is my mother's doing. Caroline lives in mortal fear that I shall receive another tongue-lashing," she said absently.

"I beg your pardon?"

Lilliana jerked a wide-eyed gaze to him. "I mean . . . I mean . . . Mother worries that I will be un-chaperoned. Quite a lot," she added with a quick, impatient roll of her eyes.

"Indeed? And are you in need of a chaperone?"

Her indelicate snort surprised him. "Hardly! What on earth could happen at Blackfield Grange?"

And so did her naiveté. "If one were so inclined, I rather imagine anything."

She frowned thoughtfully at him. "Indeed? Such as?"

Adrian chuckled. "Lilliana, my offer?" he prompted her. She did not immediately answer, but gave him a soft shrug of her shoulders. All right, she was going to make him work for it. "Would you torture me with your silence? If your answer is no, then please, do me the favor of ending this uncertainty."

That made her wince ever so slightly. "I . . . I think it very kind of you, my lord, but I should . . . It's just that . . . it's just that I should very much like to know some things," she said uneasily.

"Anything."

She glanced up, assessing him. "Well . . . I should like to know why you offered my father such a large sum of money."

God, had Dashell told her the terms? Rather indelicate, but then Lord knew what customs ruled in the country. "Quite simple. I wanted to make sure he understood how determined I am. I hold you in great esteem, Lilliana, and I did not want to dicker over the terms of the betrothal if you would have me."

For a fleeting second she looked confused, then

startled him by laughing gaily. "Oh my, you are not very practiced, are you?"

Oddly, that remark made him want to squirm. "I beg your pardon?"

"At least I may surmise that you have not offered for many others, as you would know that my father would have accepted *far* less than what you proposed. Without dickering." She laughed again, flashing the lone dimple.

"You have me there. I am quite new to this," he agreed, feeling a sense of relief. "Is there more you would know?"

She sobered immediately and glanced at the carpet again. "What of Benedict? Do you really think the two of you shall, ah, come to an understanding? He is rather tenderhearted, and I do believe he will be quite . . . well, perturbed."

She peeked up at him with such genuine concern that Adrian bit his tongue on the point that Benedict would fare well enough and always did. "We have suffered through worse and remain brothers." It was not a lie. Lilliana said nothing, but drew her bottom lip between her teeth again. Adrian shifted forward in his chair. "What else would you like to know?"

A soft frown creased her brow. "Where shall we live?"

That should not have caught him by surprise, but he did not know the answer she wanted to hear. "Longbridge, for now," he said carefully, "but if you prefer—"

"Is it very far away?" she asked earnestly.

Adrian nodded, thinking it best to leave the exact distance unsaid. "Not so far to prevent you from visiting your parents whenever you desire, but far enough one might think twice before arriving unannounced," he said. To his considerable relief, she smiled fully and glanced at the window, a faraway look in her eye. "Is there more?" he asked cautiously.

She nodded and squared her shoulders, unconsciously, he thought, before meeting his gaze again. "I gather I have the requisite connections and breeding to be considered a suitable match—"

"Of course," Adrian interjected.

"And I agree that either we suit or we don't, but that there is no point in some protracted courtship in my father's house." Sensing victory, Adrian almost smiled. "I am not certain that we *do* suit," she continued, deflating him a little, "but I hardly think one knows that sort of thing until one has . . . ah . . . resided in, ah . . . *matrimony*." Coloring slightly, she gave him a tremulous smile.

"I agree," he offered helpfully. "But?"

She drew a deep breath. "But . . . you implied we should be companions. Is that true?"

Companions? Had he actually said that? "Yes," he said carefully.

Nodding thoughtfully, she leaned back.

"Is that not to your liking?"

"Oh no!" she said hastily. "I *want* to be a good companion to you. But I must have some assurance that I may . . ." Her voice trailed off; her fingers nervously plucked at the embroidery in the arm of the chair.

"What, Lilliana? What is it you want? I have the means to give you anything, you know that, don't you?" he asked earnestly.

"I want . . . I want to . . . *live*," she muttered, and jerked her gaze to him. "I want assurances I will be allowed to live. Experience life, that sort of thing. I want to live *freely*," she added nervously.

Of all the things she could have asked him, that had to be the last one he expected. She wanted to live *freely*? What in the hell did that mean? "I beg your pardon?"

Lilliana suddenly shifted to the edge of her chair and eagerly leaned forward. "I want to *live*! I want to know true adventure! I want to *see* things, to travel to new places and hear strange foreign tongues and eat exotic foods!" she exclaimed, her hands gesturing wildly. "I want to meet people who would *never* come to Blackfield Grange! People who think the sky is red, not blue, and the earth *flat* not round!'' she breathed excitedly.

Adrian was speechless—he had never heard such fantasy from a woman's mouth! His jaw clenched tightly shut as he considered this unsophisticated Grange Princess. A whirlwind of thoughts tore through his brain, not the least of which was that he might have made a terrible mistake. Not ten minutes ago she had been a demure country girl with absolutely no idea of what to say to a man. At the moment, she sounded like a budding lunatic with her talk of red skies and a flat earth.

Her expression crumpled into bewilderment, and she sagged against her chair. ''I have offended you, haven't I? Proper ladies would never profess to wanting more than what your good name and title could give them, would they?'' Good God, certainly not, he thought, and unthinkingly shook his head. ''I was afraid of this,'' she muttered sadly. ''I am very sorry, my lord, but I cannot accept your offer.''

What? What in the bloody hell was this? *He* was the one who should have the opportunity to cry off at this moment, *not* her! And because he had not, apparently, responded to her absurdity in the earnest manner she seemed to think was necessary, she would *refuse* him? Irrationally disgruntled, he almost came out of his seat. ''I, too, am sorry, but I cannot accept your refusal,'' he said curtly.

''Pardon?'' she squeaked.

''You may live however you please, madam. If you want to wear grass skirts or speak in foreign tongues or howl at the moon, I will not stop you. If you want to believe the sky is red, I will be the last person to contradict you.''

Lilliana's mouth dropped open. ''You . . . you will honor my wish to experience life?''

He didn't give a damn what she did with her life, but she would *not* refuse him. ''Of course I shall,'' he said bluntly. ''Insofar as you do it without slandering my name,'' he added, a little more roughly than he intended.

"Of *course* not!" she gasped. "How very wonderful that we may travel, and meet new people, and explore the world!" she exclaimed happily.

Explore the world with this bumpkin? Lord God, he could hardly imagine her beyond her own sitting room, much less in some of the finest salons of Europe. What nonsense . . . but what difference? He might take her to Europe once, let her *experience* life. Surely that would take care of her naive desire to meet savages in the far corners of the earth. The lass beamed at him as if he had just handed her a fistful of diamonds. "Lord Albright! I should very happily accept your offer!" she exclaimed. "I can hardly wait to tell Caroline! To think that I might actually see the Levant! I've read all about it, you see," she eagerly explained, and launched into a monologue of some book she had read.

Adrian smiled as she spoke, but his victory over Archie did not taste nearly as sweet as he had anticipated.

The wedding took place exactly five days later. As Adrian was not welcome at Kealing Park, the traditional wedding breakfast was held in the village assembly rooms following the ceremony. It was the one thing Adrian had insisted upon, despite the Dashell pleas to host the affair at Blackfield Grange. On that point he was unyielding—the ceremony had to be in Kealing. He wanted everyone to see his victory.

And everyone seemed to be in attendance. If he had had to guess, Adrian suspected no fewer than five houses had been put to the task of preparing the wedding breakfast. He had no inkling of the details; his sole task had been to provide an endless stream of funds.

And inform Lord Kealing and his son of the happy occasion.

He would have liked to do that in person, but his requests for an audience were returned unopened. So he had resorted to informing them in writing. His note had been short and sweet: *To the Right Honorable Marquis*

*of Kealing, Archibald Spence, and Lord Benedict, it is
with great happiness that I inform you I am to be wed on
Saturday next to Miss Lilliana Dashell of Blackfield
Grange. Please do me the great honor of joining us on
this, the happiest of occasions.*

Lilliana had also sent a note to Benedict with his, one
she labored over for a good hour. It had been the one
unhappy moment Adrian had seen in her all week.

Beyond that, the Princess of Blackfield Grange had
been completely ecstatic. He dutifully called every afternoon, more to occupy his time than to prove his sincer-
ity, because he was making himself mad idly waiting for
a response to his letter to Lord Rothembow. Every afternoon he was greeted with a flurry of anxious activity.
Lord and Lady Dashell were frazzled by the daunting
prospect of launching a wedding suitable for a baron's
daughter in less than a week, and had, in Adrian's opinion, unwisely added to the melee by deciding to take the
waters at Bath after the wedding. Apparently Baron
Dashell, feeling a new sense of freedom with Adrian's
generous settlement, had determined that spending the
winter months in Bath would be just the thing for Lady
Dashell's humor and to convince Caroline to set her
sights on someone other than Horace Featherbrain.
Young Tom remained quite sullen, rarely leaving his
rooms when Adrian came. Caroline bounced about like
an india rubber ball, chattering endlessly about gowns
and trousseaus and little family secrets.

Adrian did feel honor-bound to explain his circumstance to his fiancée. He told her he was estranged from
his father, but did not offer the details of why. The very
thought of Phillip still made him ill—mentioning his
name aloud was impossible. To her credit, Lilliana had
listened attentively, then flashed a smile with that tantalizing little dimple and insisted that while she was sorry
about his estrangement from his father, it did not concern her in the least. She did not ask any questions, and
for that he was extremely grateful. And the next moment
she was up and flitting about the drawing room, peering

closely at her paintings—of which there were *many*—and asking his opinion of which would do at Long-bridge. Lilliana, apparently, beamed from sunup to sundown.

Because Lilliana had never been so terribly happy in all her life. She helped her mother convert an old ball gown into her wedding dress, laughed at her father's complaints about the size of the wedding breakfast, and despite her mother's disapproval, made an increasingly long list of keepsakes she must have for her trousseau.

When she wasn't caught up in the activity of planning the wedding, she was making a concerted effort to see all the tenants and bid them good-bye. She rode recklessly across the fields, feeling very much like the hawk that circled lazily above—in a matter of days she would be free, and her ebullient anticipation spilled out with everything she did. The servants and residents of the Grange congratulated one another on the wonderful match Miss Dashell had made, as if it were *their* daughter who had landed such a fortune.

And what a handsome lord for their miss, they said. The Earl of Albright was as darkly handsome as he was mysterious. They caught glimpses of him quietly reading when Miss Lilliana worked on the invitations, or standing to one side as Miss Dashell and her father packaged her paintings for the journey. The earl would be a good husband, they said, not anything like the rumors about him might suggest.

Lilliana had to agree—her future husband was as marvelous as he was in her dreams. He smiled whenever she spoke, assured her that whatever she wanted to take was welcome in his home, and didn't even seem to mind when she and Caroline practiced the wedding ceremony, collapsing into a fit of giggles on the settee.

None of the harried preparations or the sense of excitement building at the Grange seemed to fluster him in the least, not even Tom's sullen behavior or her mother's obvious disapproval of the whole thing. Every day that passed convinced Lilliana that she had made the right

decision, and she could hardly wait for the day of liberation to finally come.

On the day of liberation, Adrian sat alone in the
crowded assembly room, watching his laughing wife
flutter from table to table. He had to admit she looked
particularly radiant today. At the ceremony he had been
mildly surprised by how lovely his undistinguished fiancée looked in her wedding gown. But then again, he had
never seen an unappealing bride. At the conclusion of
that mercifully short ceremony, he had cupped her face
with one hand and had kissed her fully on the lips. It
was a short, perfunctory little kiss, but when he had
lifted his head, her eyes were shimmering. He had noticed then, for the first time, really, that they were pale,
almost smoky green. For a single, odd moment he had
been briefly fascinated with them.

A very brief moment, which he now shrugged off as
he reached for his pocket watch. They needed to be under way if they were to reach Longbridge before nightfall. He stuffed his pocket watch away and scanned the
crowd, wondering absently if Arlo had finished seeing to
her portmanteaus. He had dispatched a hired carriage to
Longbridge just yesterday, filled to the brim with her
many trunks and paintings. It was nothing short of
amazing to him that one could assemble such a large
trousseau in less than a week—and of what? He was
mulling that over when he caught sight of Benedict.

Adrian started badly. When had he come in? It was
unnerving to see his brother now, standing in the corner
as he was. His eyes were fixed on Lilliana, and there was
no mistaking the look of abject misery on his face.
Adrian's eyes narrowed speculatively . . . his brother
was smitten!

Benedict was honestly smitten with her.

Adrian flicked his gaze to Lilliana, who had yet to
notice his brother. He glanced at Benedict again; with
his hands shoved deep in his pockets, he leaned against

the wall as if he needed it to hold him up. Adrian swallowed hard; he had waited for this moment, had dreamed of the moment he would wrest something from that weakling, something that would avenge the loss of Kealing Park. Jesus, he *wanted* to strike back at Archie and hurt Benedict in the process! But he could take no pleasure in the expression of complete bewilderment on his brother's face. He felt no sense of victory, no satisfaction. Just an odd feeling of disgust for himself.

And as Adrian was trying to understand it, Ben found his nerve and approached Lilliana. She looked as stricken at seeing Benedict as Adrian felt, nervously pulling at the trim of a dainty little lace handkerchief she had carried all morning. Just bloody grand, he thought miserably, and tossing aside his linen napkin, moved to rescue his wife.

This day had been absolutely glorious, far better than she had dreamed—until now. Lilliana kept her eyes fixed on the path as Benedict led her around to a small lawn behind the assembly rooms. He had not uttered a word since he had given her his congratulations and then had asked if he might have a word. She could hardly refuse under the circumstances—he was, after all, her brother now.

He stopped in the middle of the lawn and glanced around them, unseeing, before he finally turned to look at her. He eyed her face and her gown before finally settling on her hands, which she held tightly together at her waist. "You look beautiful, Lilliana," he murmured.

Heat flooded her cheeks at the sound of misery in his voice. "Thank you," she choked.

"Why?" he whispered, and slowly lifted his lashes to look her directly in the eye. "Why did you do it?"

"It is as I wrote you," she whispered faintly.

"You honestly expect me to believe you have harbored some . . . *childish* adoration for him all these years?" he snapped. "You have not seen him in fifte years or more, Lilliana. It is inconceivable to me that you would have an affection for him after all that time!''

That was fair, because Benedict could never hope to conceive how she adored Lord Albright, or why. How could she possibly make him understand that Adrian was the key to her living, the very sort of free spirit she longed to be? Or that he was the exact opposite of that ideal? Yes, for Benedict it must be inconceivable. ''I have held him in great esteem for a long time,'' she forced herself to respond. ''I am truly sorry if I have hurt you, Benedict, but it was against my very nature to refuse him. And . . . and his offer was . . . very generous.''

Benedict's brown eyes hardened. ''His offer? What was it? Did he convince you with expensive jewels?'' he snarled sarcastically.

Lilliana quietly lifted her chin at the insult. ''He offered to save my father from debtor's prison and ensure that my family would never want again. And he did not require Blackfield Grange in exchange for his generosity,'' she said calmly.

Benedict's eyes widened, and he suddenly looked away. ''I see,'' he muttered coldly. ''Then I suppose there is nothing left for me to do but wish you happiness, is there?''

''That would be very kind of you,'' she murmured.

Benedict frowned and forced himself to look at her again. His gaze locked with hers for a long moment, until he winced and looked at her hands again. ''God forgive me. Lilliana . . . I am sorry. I am so very sorry. I had honestly hoped that you and I—''

''Benedict, please don't,'' she softly warned him.

He drew a deep breath and made a halfhearted attempt to straighten his shoulders. ''I wish you well, Lilliana, and I pray you will not be terribly disappointed by what you've done.''

Oh, she would not be disappointed. This was the miracle of all miracles, and it had happened to her. She glanced at the simple gold band on her finger, unable to suppress her smile. She would *never* be disappointed.

"What a wonderful surprise. You honor us with your presence, Ben."

Lilliana jerked toward the sound of his voice. Adrian was standing at the edge of the lawn, his hands clasped behind his back. "Lilliana, it is time we began our good-byes," he said casually, and held out his hand to her. Lilliana did not hesitate; she went to her husband and slipped her hand into his. Adrian brought it to his lips before gracing her with an exceedingly charming smile. "Go on ahead. I should like a word with my brother."

She glanced over her shoulder at Ben—he was watching her closely, watching her smile at Adrian. "You . . . you will come to say good-bye, won't you?"

"Naturally," he said tightly.

Adrian squeezed her hand, drawing her attention back to him. "I'll be along shortly," he said, smiling. A delirious sense of happiness washed over her with the warmth of his smile, and Lilliana beamed at her husband before walking inside, her thoughts already on their departure.

Six

LONGBRIDGE

LADY DASHELL ALLOWED her rigid spine to bend long enough to sob hysterically when the couple's departure was announced. Lord Dashell tried to comfort his wife with a pat or two on the shoulder, but the man was overwhelmed himself. And it was not particularly helpful that Caroline hung on to her sister—sobbing alternately for Lilliana or Mr. Feather—until Adrian was forced to pry them apart. It took a good half hour of tearful good-byes and promises to write from Bath along with Adrian's cajoling—and, finally, demanding—before he was able to pull Lilliana from the bosom of her family and put her into the coach that would take them to Longbridge.

Good God.

Worse yet, that scene was immediately followed by the uncomfortable discovery that the new Lady Albright chattered like a magpie.

Lilliana had begun the moment the post chaise rolled down Kealing's main thoroughfare, reviewing every single detail of the ceremony and the breakfast, seemingly oblivious to the fact that she was the only one participating in the conversation. She had then segued effortlessly into a discourse on the things she had forgotten, although Adrian would have sworn she had packed every inch of the Grange into one of the dozen or more trunks already at Longbridge. Tiring of that, she had begun to chatter about all the things she would do at Longbridge, beginning, apparently, with a thorough cleaning. Why she thought the place was in such disarray, he had no idea, and as she had rattled off all the rooms she supposed Longbridge had, including a ballroom, which it did not, Adrian had stared at her, quite simply fascinated.

It was the first time he had been alone with her, *really* alone with her. Hell, he thought as he watched her lips move, it was the first time he had been alone with a woman for any appreciable length of time that did not include a bottle of good wine and a bed.

This was new to him, completely foreign, and the woman's incessant chatter was starting to frighten him. Was this what he was to expect? Did *all* gently bred women eventually show themselves unable to let a moment of silence pass? Moreover, was he expected to actually *know* what the hell she was talking about? He certainly hoped not, because he had lost track of the conversation somewhere between Newhall and the turn onto the eastbound road. But she kept looking at him as if she expected some sort of response, and feeling a little desperate, Adrian pulled a book from his bag and opened it, hoping that would silence her.

It did not.

Much to his morbid fascination, Lilliana spent the first half of the drive glued to the window and calling his attention to such engaging scenes as oh, *flocks of sheep*. Lord help him, he did not think he would be able to bear it if she talked so much on a regular basis. No matter how many ways he tried to dissect it, the drive was bringing home to him the fact that he had married an unremarkable country bumpkin who was enthralled with dairies, among other things. The Grange Princess was, he was slowly beginning to understand, as alien to him as one of those strange countries she had talked about all through luncheon. This marriage had been a monumental, irreparable gaffe, thank you, and the biggest mistake of his life—no small feat, that—and one with terrifying consequence. But he would find a way to deal with it, Adrian thought, and resolutely clamped his jaw shut. He'd be damned if he was to spend the rest of his life looking at trees and birds and, dear God, *cattle*.

After a while, fortunately, she apparently tired of her own chatter, and was at the moment sitting peacefully, gazing out the window.

Would that he could be so peaceful, he thought miserably, but he could not, not after having discovered his folly. And certainly not after seeing Benedict.

With a slight wince Adrian shifted his gaze to the book he held, pretending to read. He had expected a confrontation with his brother, but Benedict had surprised him by congratulating him. Nevertheless, he could not mask his expression, and Adrian knew by his eyes that he was distraught. And instead of triumph, Adrian had felt nauseatingly contrite. The distasteful realization that he had snatched someone's happiness, even if it was his oh so deserving brother's, disturbed him far more than he would have imagined. Guilt, the one emotion that was becoming extremely familiar to him of late, had taken hold. Again.

Well, it was too bloody late to turn back now, he thought as he surreptitiously glanced at Lilliana. He had earned his victory over Archie and had wounded Benedict in the process, just as he had set out to do. These sudden feelings of contrition were annoying, as annoying as the prospect of having a wife he did not know or really cared to know. What an idiot he was! Recklessness was part of his life, but it had never manifested itself with such a permanent consequence as this!

He glanced at the pages of his book again, only to see Benedict and that pained look in his eyes.

He was a goddamned fool.

Adrian's lungs were burning; he was being chased through the trees, along the stream where he had fished for trout as a boy. Phillip was close behind, firing that German gun above his head. Frantic, Adrian ducked behind a tree, and peered back. But it was Benedict he saw now, and terrified, he whirled away from the tree and struggled to run—but he could not move his limbs.

Suddenly his eyes flew open. After a brief, clouded moment of terror, he realized he had fallen asleep, propped awkwardly against the squabs. God, he was bathed in sweat again. He extracted a handkerchief from his breast pocket, and as he wiped his brow he realized the post chaise was slowing. Lilliana, he noticed, was pasted to the window, and he struggled to see over her shoulder.

Longbridge.

Nestled on the banks of a river, the eighteenth-century mansion was exactly as Adrian remembered—an ornate estate to which he had no real connection, no sense of belonging. As the chaise coasted around the long circular drive, Lilliana turned a beguiling grin to him, her pale green eyes sparkling with enthusiasm. "It's *beautiful!*" He nodded and shifted his gaze to the house, feeling a bad humor that had no basis in anything.

Mr. Brent Maximilian, Adrian's longtime butler, was the first to greet Lord and Lady Albright, bowing respectfully as Adrian helped Lilliana from the chaise. "A pleasure to have you home, my lord," he intoned.

"Thank you, Max. I trust your journey from London was uneventful?"

"Quite, my lord. I believe you will find everything in order."

"Madam, allow me to introduce Maximilian, otherwise known as Max," he said to Lilliana.

The poor girl was so excited, she actually curtsied to his butler. "It is a pleasure to meet you, Mr. Maximilian," she said, and smiled brightly.

The usually fussy Max looked a little surprised—no doubt he had expected a woman of a more sophisticated countenance. "The pleasure is undoubtedly mine, my lady. I hope you shall find all at Longbridge to your satisfaction."

"Oh! I am quite certain I shall! It's so very lovely, don't you think?" she chirped. Max inclined his head as he stole a fretful glance at Adrian from the corner of his eye. Hardly in a mood to entertain curious looks from his butler, Adrian grasped Lilliana's elbow before she could speak further, and swiftly led her to the row of servants who had filed out to meet them in the early twilight. Much to his surprise and annoyance, Lilliana stopped to speak to every one of the twenty-two staff gathered, beaming as if she was being presented at court.

By the time he had managed to pull her inside, she was positively glowing with exuberance. As she pulled off her bonnet in the foyer, she gasped at the opulent surroundings. "Oooo, this is positively *wonderful*!" she exclaimed, and did a slow pirouette beneath the dome above the entry, painted with some scene from the Greek tragedies. Indifferent to all of it, Adrian removed his gloves and tossed them to a footman standing nearby in the black and gold livery of Albright. "This is *just* as I imagined it, you know! Caroline and I knew you would be surrounded by splendor!"

He had no earthly idea what she meant by that, and simply smiled as he glanced over his shoulder at Max. "Have a bath drawn for her ladyship and a light supper brought to her rooms."

"Yes, my lord," Max drawled. "My lady? If you will follow me?" he asked, and gestured toward a huge curving staircase spiraling upward beneath old portraits and coats of armor and one massive crystal chandelier. "This way, if you please." As they trailed up the stairs with a footman carrying her bags close behind, Adrian heard his wife ask *Mr. Maximilian* if his name was Greek, if he had any family, and if he had been at Longbridge for very long. Remarkably, Max answered her questions with a lilt in his voice Adrian was quite certain he had never heard from the fastidious man. If the Princess of the Grange had that effect on his butler, then he could only surmise Max had been without the company of a woman for far too long.

Lilliana's cheeks were beginning to hurt from the smile she forced to her lips so that Mr. Maximilian would not see how very mortified she was. Dear Lord, what had she *done*? She had been so ecstatically happy when they had left Kealing, so anxious to begin her life of adventure with the most magnificent man alive, she had feared she might very well float away. Naturally, she had assumed he would be happy.

If he was, he had a peculiar way of showing it.

From the moment they had begun the trip to Longbridge, she had tried to engage him in conversation. She could not say that he did not oblige her, because he did, and was exceedingly polite about it. But he didn't really *respond* to her. His answers were short, or he responded with questions of his own, forcing her to talk of herself. He revealed nothing of what he really thought about anything.

As the drive to Longbridge was the first time they had been alone for more than a few minutes since he had appeared at the Grange, that botched attempt at conversation had made her extremely self-conscious. She tried to take solace in the passing scenery, pointing out interesting things as they rushed by. Adrian looked up every time she asked, nodded politely without really seeing anything, then returned to his reading. Of a *French* book. That made her just as self-conscious, and unfortunately, the more nervous she became, the more she talked.

Things hardly improved over a late luncheon. He

made her eat a meat pie at a quaint little inn, and even ordered her a pint of ale to wash it down. Lilliana had never tasted ale in her life, but after a few sips the bitter drink was going down rather smoothly—so smoothly that she hesitantly requested a second one. "Whatever you would like, Lilliana, you need only ask," Adrian had said, and she was left with the strange feeling that she could have whatever she liked as long as she stopped talking.

As Mr. Maximilian directed the footman to stoke the fire in the large hearth, she told herself that she was experiencing wedding nerves, nothing more. But the nervousness had grown to terrifying proportions the more miles they covered. Her husband was not even remotely interested in the things she found fascinating; she could not find a topic that interested him, and she could not read French.

Well, what in God's name had she expected? He was a man of the world and it was little wonder he found her conversation boring. She had *nothing* to compare to his vast experience, nothing to capture his superior attention. And here she was, acting as if she was somehow *surprised* that she hardly knew the man she had married. She angrily reminded herself that it would take some time to grow comfortable in each other's company. Nonetheless, for the first time in a week a faint hint of doubt crept into her conscience, unwelcome and unsettling.

"I shall have some bread and cheese sent up, if that pleases you, my lady," she heard the diminutive butler say. "And some wine."

Wine. Yes, she would very much like some wine. A barrel of it. "Yes, please," she said.

"I shall leave you now. Lucy will attend you tonight. I have taken the liberty of engaging a lady's maid for you, Mrs. Polly Dismuke. She shall attend you first thing in the morning," he said, and with an efficient bow, left her with a tiny young chambermaid who was already laying out her nightclothes.

"They've brought the water for your bath, Lady Albright," Lucy said, and motioned toward a door near the far wall.

That name registered somewhere in her brain, and Lilliana felt dangerously close to fainting. It had sounded so terribly important when she and Caroline had laughingly practiced it, but now it sounded almost ominous. Lord help her, she was his *wife*! She could almost hear her mother's anxious voice as she had delicately explained what to expect tonight. It would happen *here*, in this room. But she hardly knew him! The thought of his powerful body coupled with hers made her knees shake, and she stumbled toward the door Lucy had indicated. The girl looked curiously at her; Lilliana hastily tilted her chin up, determined she would not see what a coward she was, but oh God, she *was* a coward!

The hot bath did nothing to soothe her. How in heaven's name would she lie with him? Would he at last speak to her, or would he approach it with the same damned patience he had shown her all day long? She changed into the silk night rail and dressing gown her mother had bought from Mrs. Peavey, who had brought it all the way from London. She was hardly aware of Lucy braiding her hair; she hardly remembered getting *married*, she thought, a little hysterically, and when Lucy announced she was done, she only barely managed to drag herself into the main suite again.

Some food and wine had been brought up. Lucy poured a glass for her, and with a final, curious glance at her, she took her leave. The moment the door shut, Lilliana began to pace anxiously. No matter how wonderful she thought him, the vision of the impending invasion unnerved her so badly that Lilliana suddenly lunged for the wineglass, quickly downing half the contents. Blast it all, but it did nothing to ease her tension—if anything, it made it soar. Squeezing her eyes tightly shut, she commanded herself to stop being so childish. She was a grown woman, for heaven's sake! She would endure this!

More wine.

"Ah, the wine has come."

She hadn't heard him enter, and started so violently that she spilled a bit of wine onto the table. Quickly, she put the glass down and swiped at the spilled wine before turning to face him. He strolled into the room wearing a black velvet dressing gown that swept the carpet. He looked quite imposing, and she thought for a moment that he looked even taller in bare feet, perhaps as much as two or three inches above six feet. And terribly virile. Lord God, *terribly* virile. He perused her, too, from the top of her head to the tips of her toes, then lifted his gaze to hers as he shoved a hand through his hair. "Well. It seems you've been hiding beautiful hair beneath your bonnets," he remarked.

She blushed furiously. "Thank you," she said, and unconsciously smoothed an errant strand from her temple.

He advanced farther into the room, now looking at anything but her. "Max has outdone himself, hasn't he? The last time I saw this room, it was quite bare."

At that, insane questions popped into her head. When had he been in this room? And with *whom*? They said he was a scoundrel, and it was a well-known fact around the parish that Adrian Spence did not keep company with reputable women.

With a convulsive shiver, she swallowed again.

He paused in his perusal of the room and slanted a look at her. "Naturally, you may do as you wish to it," he offered.

"No, my lord," she managed to choke, and felt herself color, impossibly, even more. "I, uh, I think it is quite lovely."

The Adonis moved slowly toward her. "As we are quite married now, I think it time you called me Adrian."

Hadn't she? That she had not actually voiced her husband's Christian name aloud astounded her, and she frantically attempted to recall everything she had said over the last few days.

"Please don't feel any need on my account. You may call me whatever you like—assuming it is acceptable to Polite Society."

He was teasing her now. And gaining ground. Lilliana forced her breath as he came to stand in front of her. His hazel eyes swept her face, her neck, and lingered on her bosom. She might as well have been standing naked in front of him, so pointed was his gaze. And it didn't help that the room was suddenly *stifling*. When he lifted his hand and placed it gently against her cheek, everything in Lilliana froze with fear. Focusing on the lapels of his robe, she took what seemed like giant gulps of air to steady herself.

"Why don't you eat something? You will feel better," he suggested. But no, thank you, nothing was going to make her feel better. Adrian grasped her hand. "You are making me feel a bit like an ogre, madam, looking as horrified as all that." Before she could respond, he pulled her around the little table and helped her into a chair. "Relax," he whispered into her ear, and patted her arm before placing some bread and cheese on a small wooden platter. "Eat," he said, motioning to the food, and sat himself across from her.

Yes, she should eat something. But she reached for the wine instead, taking another good, long sip that warmed her from the top of her head to the tips of her toes. Adrian watched her beneath long, thick lashes as he munched on a thick slice of bread. When she finished the glass, he wordlessly refilled it.

"I didn't know you cared for wine," he remarked as she reached for the glass.

"Neither did I," she mumbled hoarsely.

The briefest hint of a smile grazed his lips. "Perhaps it is that particular vintage. If I know Max, it has fermented for all of two weeks now."

Lilliana smiled in spite of herself and risked a look at him. His robe was open at the neck, and she glimpsed a bit of the crisp hair that covered his chest. His sandy brown hair was all curl, his jaw impossibly square. She took another generous sip of wine as she watched his broad hands tear the bread. Such strong hands, she thought, and suddenly imagined them engaged in a variety of activities. Like dueling. Or gambling. Or on a woman. That thought caused her traitorous cheeks to flame. Just how many women had his hands touched? And more importantly, exactly *how* had his hands touched them?

Again he lifted a single, quizzical brow. Lilliana hastily took another sip of wine. "You have hardly touched your food," he remarked.

"I am really not very hungry," she admitted.

"I see," he said, and unfortunately, she rather imagined he did. The burn in her cheeks spread to her neck; she quickly dropped her gaze to her platter. "Perhaps we should retire."

Oh God, it was *time*! She had imagined this moment would be a bit more tender, perhaps a bit of wooing on his part. Exactly where she had come up with that idea escaped her—certainly it was nothing her mother had said. Well, there was nothing to be done for it. As her mother had drilled into her several times the last week, a woman submitted to her husband without complaint. Nonetheless, she felt every fiber tense as he stood and walked around the table to stand behind her. She swallowed a gasp when he put his hands on her shoulders and lightly massaged them. What was *this*?

"You are trembling, Lilliana," he murmured and, with his fingers, lightly rubbed her neck. Oh, she was trembling all right. And if she didn't get this over and done with soon, she might very well faint. He leaned down. "Don't be frightened," he whispered, his breath tickling her skin. But when his lips touched her neck, she jumped like a scared rabbit, and the top of her head collided with his chin. "Oh! I'm sorry," she hastily muttered.

He gave her a strange look as he rubbed the offended

chin. "It's quite all right." Even though he did not sound so very reassuring, he resumed his caress, his hands sliding slowly over her shoulders and down her arms. She tried not to squirm. "Relax, Lilliana, or we'll never get through this," he murmured, and touched his lips to her neck again. He was right, they would never get through this, she thought as he nuzzled her neck and caressed her arms.

But then something started to happen. Her whole body seemed to pulsate with each gentle touch of his fingers. She felt his hands grip her arms, felt herself rising to her feet. Slipping his arms around her waist, he pulled her into his chest. The silk dressing gown she wore was so thin, she could feel the hard wall of his chest against her back. His lips were on her cheek now, so soft and warm on her skin, and he smelled so . . . well, *masculine*.

He pulled her away from the table, forced her to turn in his arms, then gave her a half-smile as he artfully released her hair from its braid. "Beautiful hair," he muttered as his lips descended to her mouth.

Lilliana's breath froze in her lungs as his lips slowly slid across hers. The sensation was paralyzing; she stood rigid as he carefully and artfully moved his lips on hers, shaping them to match his own. The sweetness of the kiss began to flow through her like molten rock. His hold tightened around her, coaxing her closer to him by caressing her spine. It was not supposed to be like this! She had the sensation of drifting as he continued his gentle assault with his mouth and hands—

He lifted his head and looked down at her, frowning slightly. He grasped her hands, which she realized were fisted tautly at her sides, and draped them loosely around his waist. "That's better," he murmured. Yes, it *was* better. At least she would not crumple to the floor. She could actually feel his breath in his chest as he slipped a finger under her chin and tilted it upward. "Now," he murmured as his head slowly descended to hers, "open your mouth."

"Pardon?" she whispered into the fog, and his tongue slid between her lips.

The room suddenly pitched as he stroked her with his tongue. His sweet breath mingled with hers, filling her with awe and a longing that was indescribable. Her body began to tingle in a most unusual way, starting somewhere in her belly and unfurling throughout her limbs. Through no will of her own she felt herself leaning into him. Oh, Lord, his body was lean; his waist slender, and his hips rock hard. Vaguely aware that her hands had begun a journey of their own, she was conscious of the feel of his spine, the muscles in his back, the ripple of flesh in his shoulders. At the same time, he caressed her shoulders, her arms, and the curve of her waist into her hips. Just when she thought she might possibly be in heaven after all, his hand swept up and cupped her breast.

Lilliana unwittingly gasped against his mouth, and he plunged farther into her recesses. He filled the palm of his hand with her breast, and instantly feeling faint, she unthinkingly clutched at his arms as his hand moved the silk of her gown across the rigid peak of her breast. He hardly touched her at all, yet a furious desire was pooling deep in her belly.

Adrian dragged his mouth to her ear as his hand continued its seductive dance on her breast. "Put your arms around my neck," he whispered, and caught her earlobe between his teeth. Shaking like a leaf, Lilliana tentatively ran her hands up his chest and around his neck. He dropped his hand from her breast then, and wrapped his arms tightly around her, pressing her against the hardness of his frame, his thighs . . . and oh *God*. The unmistakable hardness between them, the full length pressed against her abdomen was *him*. Her inexperience burned her neck and face.

And then he began to move. Heaven help her, she was going to die of shame or longing or both! He moved almost imperceptibly at first, a slow, grinding movement against her as he toyed with her lobe. She tensed, uncertain what to make of it, uncertain what to do in response, and all the while feeling the unimaginable heat building in her. Suddenly his hands came between them, searching for the tie to her wrapper. Fear shook her to consciousness, and she grabbed his hand.

He let go of the knot and lifted one hand to her temple, tenderly brushing the hair from her brow. "There is nothing to be afraid of. I would never willingly hurt you." Those seductive words ignited a burn in her all over again. He kissed her, and this time she did not try to stop him as he effortlessly untied the very secure knot she had made earlier. The silk wrapper slid from her shoulders; with a soft sigh, he put his hands on her bare skin and bent to kiss the curve of her neck into her shoulders. His hands slipped down and under her breasts, carefully lifting them in his palms. They swelled in his hands, Lilliana numbly realized, and her head fell backward as he traced a warm path from her shoulder to the hollow of her throat. His lips were intoxicating, his touch making her completely mindless. When her knees started to buckle, he swept her into his arms and carried her to the bed, never breaking the kiss.

When her feet touched the carpet, her knees did give way, and Adrian caught her with a firm arm around her waist as he bent to douse the candle at her bedside. In the pale light of the hearth he turned to face her, allowing his gaze to peruse her before reaching to push the thin straps of her silk sleeping gown from her shoulders. A rush of shameful alarm filled her as the thin fabric slipped down her arms and breasts. She clutched his arm, her fingers spanning muscle that rippled beneath her touch. He did not seem to notice her death grip; his hazel eyes were focused on her breasts. Completely exposed to him, they stood swollen, the tips protruding from what he had done to her. Lilliana frantically caught the thin silk before it fell to the floor and held it tightly at her waist, mesmerized by the strange dark light in his eyes.

"My God," he murmured, and with his knuckles

traced lightly across the top of her breasts and the valley between them.

Lilliana shivered, with fear or great anticipation, she did not know. She felt exposed and raw, as if she would shatter into a thousand pieces at the slightest touch. Adrian did not notice; he was suddenly kissing her senseless again, and the next thing she knew she was lying on the bed, his body stretched beside her. He grabbed a fistful of her hair and inhaled it, then lowered his head to hers again, feathering her face and neck with light kisses, moving lower until his breath fanned her breasts.

She sucked in a sharp breath at the stark sensuality, but she almost came up off the bed when his tongue flicked across her nipple. Adrian very smoothly anchored her with one hand on her abdomen, then began a painstaking exploration of her breasts with his lips and tongue, tugging, sucking, and nipping lightly until she thought she would go mad. The desire awakening deep inside frightened her—it was building to a sinful pitch, turning hot and moist between her legs. When he pushed the silk gown from her waist and over her hips, she could hardly catch her breath. Oh, God, she was going to suffocate!

When Adrian paused momentarily to shrug out of his dressing gown, Lilliana felt the incredible length of his manhood slide against her bare thigh and pulse against her flesh. And she was gulping desperately for air. Adrian grasped her hand and bent to kiss her. *"Touch me,"* he murmured against her lips.

And he guided her to feel his passion.

Lilliana recoiled in horror at the feel of his engorged member. He chuckled low and deep as his hand flitted across the level plane of her belly. "It will be all right," he muttered, but that was a lie—it was bloody *impossible,* she thought, and was once again struggling for air as his fingers traced a line down one thigh.

"You must trust me, Lillie," he murmured, and nipped the rigid peak of her breast between his teeth as his knuckles brushed the blond curls at the apex of her thighs. The endearing use of her childhood nickname and the shock of being touched in the most forbidden place of all suddenly vanquished all thoughts from her head. Her body seized with panic as he fingered the curls there, his knuckles brushing the silken mound dangerously low. When his fingers slipped between her legs and touched the very core of her, Lilliana strangled on her breath and pushed deep into the feather mattress, alarmed by the erotic sensation and exquisite feeling of lightness. But Adrian shamelessly stroked her, urging her thighs open with little effort. He buried his face in her breasts, suckling them while his shaft brushed her abdomen and thigh, its heat burning her skin. She clutched frantically at the bedcovers as he slowly slipped one finger inside her, then two, and gently forced her body to open. But when he moved over her, pushing her legs apart with his knee and leaning over her until his manhood brushed against the swell of her own sex, her body seized again, and she unthinkingly tried to close her legs.

"Relax," he muttered, and guided the velvet tip to brush her sheath. She wrenched her body beneath him, instinctively looking for an escape from the invasion. With his hands, he pushed her thighs farther apart. *"Relax,"* he whispered again, and slowly, gently, he entered her, pushing a little farther, and then a little farther again, before settling down around her to begin a delicate movement inside her. He kissed her tenderly, catching her bottom lip between his teeth, swirling his tongue inside her mouth as he continued his exquisite assault. Her body opened to receive him so naturally, so instinctively, that she was astounded both physically and emotionally by nature's joining of a man and woman. He lowered himself to her completely and buried his face in her neck as he carefully slid deeper into her.

And then he paused, his own breathing as ragged as hers. His hand stretched out to where hers clutched the bedcovers, and covered it. With a soft groan, he lifted his hips and suddenly thrust forward.

The sharpness of the pain caught her by surprise, and she unconsciously cried out as her whole body tensed in anticipation of more pain. She heard Adrian's hiss of breath, felt his grip on her shoulder tighten as he stilled inside her. "God, I'm sorry, Lillie. I'm so sorry," he murmured, and with the back of his hand, caressed her cheek. "Rest easy, don't move, all right?"

Lilliana barely heard him; she had no idea what to expect. Even though the initial pain was slowly subsiding, she feared what he might do next. "Please don't hurt me," she muttered unthinkingly.

Adrian groaned. "No, never again. I promise you," he said, then gently kissed her eyes and mouth. "We'll stop at any time you want. You just tell me, and we'll stop." His fingers traced a gentle path from her temple to her chin, and Lilliana felt the tingle beneath her skin. "Don't be afraid, Lillie . . . the worst is over."

She shifted beneath him, felt the mound of her sex brush against the hair that covered his groin. His lips brushed across hers; his tongue slipped into her mouth and began to tangle with hers. Carefully, he withdrew then stroked into her depths again, until Lilliana was arching beneath him as the unbearably sweet pressure began to mount again. She whimpered, and his hand tightened around her wrist in response. "Easy, easy," he breathed into her neck, and repeated the torturous movement, pushing her toward an anticipation of ecstasy she was certain would destroy her.

But what *magnificent* destruction! It felt as if she were lifting, floating almost above them as he continued his even course of stroking her with his body, lengthening inside her. She began to squirm beneath him, seeking the release her body suddenly craved. When his hand slipped between their joined bodies and began to stroke her, Lilliana choked on a cry of pleasure. Every fiber tingled with great anticipation, every muscle strained to surround him. His strokes took on a new urgency, at once leaving her and filling her so violently that the heavy sacs of his life's blood met her body with a fierceness that was, incredibly, not fierce enough.

"Hold me," he whispered roughly. With her hands, she eagerly sought the corded muscles in his shoulders and back as he held himself above her. Her legs, too, came up of their own accord and circled his hips, urging him deeper into her.

Then suddenly, it happened. Without warning, she was all at once soaring high above herself as overlapping waves of pleasure spilled over her. Yet the erotic assault continued, building to another frightening climax, and when she thought she could bear no more, her body released itself again. Dizzy with the unearthly sensation, she only vaguely heard his low grown as he thrust into her the last time.

They lay in each other's arms, each fighting for breath, his heart beating rapidly against her breast. *That* had been the most beautiful thing she had ever experienced, she thought dreamily. It was nothing as her mother had described, but almost preternatural, a release of her soul into the night. It was the intimate act of freedom, and she reveled in its glow.

After several moments Adrian lifted his head. "Are you all right? Do you still hurt?"

All right? She was *ecstatic*. She had dreaded this thing, never knowing that it could be so liberating. "I am deliriously happy," she said with a broad smile.

He looked at her for a long moment as his breathing returned to normal, his eyes quietly roaming her face, seemingly memorizing her features. But then he kissed her lightly and rolled onto his back, propping one arm behind his head. One hand tangled with hers, stroking her palm and twining with her fingers. He said nothing, but looked toward the fire. Lilliana rolled into his side, nuzzling her face in his neck, but after what seemed like only a few moments he gripped her hand. "You should try and get some rest now." He shoved up and kissed her shoulder before swinging his legs over the side of the bed and standing.

Startled, Lilliana sat up and hastily gathered the bedcovers around her. "Are you going?"

"It is rather late," he said, and strolled across the room to stir the embers in the fire, completely oblivious of his nakedness. She watched him, shamelessly fascinated by his male physique as he stood and casually strolled back to the bed, astounding her with his openness as he donned his dressing gown. He leaned over and kissed her. "Sleep well," he murmured.

It could not be over so soon! She caught his hand, a little desperately, she knew, but impulsively brought it to her mouth and kissed his knuckles. "Adrian," she whispered, testing his name on her lips. "Must you go now?"

Adrian smiled so that his eyes crinkled at the corners, and he sat on the edge of the bed. "You must be exhausted. You've had quite a full day and I don't want to overtire you. Get some sleep," he said, and with a final kiss to the top of her head, stood and disappeared through the door that adjoined their rooms. Ashamed by her own brazenness and strangely disheartened, she stared at the door. His lovemaking had been the most glorious thing that had ever happened to her, perhaps the most defining moment of her life. But it had also left her with a peculiar sort of emptiness. Shivering, she pulled the bedcovers around her shoulders before falling against the goose down pillows.

On the other side of the door, Adrian walked to the drink cart Max kept stocked for him, poured himself a whiskey, downed that, and poured another one. What in the hell was the matter with him? Disgusted, he turned and walked to the hearth. Propping one elbow on the mantel, he stared unseeing into the dying flames.

She had affected him. Not affected, exactly, but it was just . . . hell, he didn't know what it was. It wasn't as if she had any sense about lovemaking. She had been stiff as a post, clutching the bedcovers in fear until . . . until she *had* started to respond. With great abandon. With complete exhilaration. Her response, while hardly practiced, was as primal as his in claiming her virginity.

Adrian took a long sip of whiskey as he contemplated that. He had never broken a woman's maidenhead before tonight. There was something terribly earthy about it, something that spoke to the very essence of life in that act. It had captured him, had conjured extraordinary feelings of possession and masculinity. It was a profound act, one that had created an infallible bond between them. Such experiences were foreign to him, and it suddenly made him shudder.

Whatever it was, it had compelled him to claim her fully, invading her untouched body with a strength he had not known in years. And that simple, innocent country girl had opened to him like a flower, returning his passion as well as she knew how, with the same strength he had shown her. He was growing hard again just *thinking* about it.

Dammit, he did not want to feel anything about her—there was nothing but trouble in that. Regardless of how primal that experience had been, she was still the same innocent, the same unremarkable country girl he had so foolishly married.

A Princess of the Grange with a tantalizing dimple in one cheek.

Surely, *surely,* this strange reaction was no more than the release of days of frustration and weariness after his duel with Phillip. Yes, it was that and nothing more, he convinced himself, and poured the last bit of whiskey down his throat.

Exhausted, his nerves raw, he tossed aside his dressing gown and fell naked onto his massive bed. Completely spent, he closed his eyes and prayed that just once, Phillip would not appear in his dreams. *"Just once,"* he muttered, and slung an arm over his eyes, knowing it was too much to ask for.

Seven

Mrs. Polly Dismuke announced her arrival the next morning by flinging open the drapes. As Lilliana blinked against the bright sunlight that flooded the room, Mrs. Dismuke began a discourse on the ill effects of sleeping so late. Alarmed, Lilliana sat up. She never slept so late. But neither had she ever slept so badly, tossing and turning all night in the unfamiliar surroundings, tortured by an increasing number of doubts.

Fine time for doubts!

Mrs. Dismuke—or Polly, as the boisterous woman loudly proclaimed—shoved a cup of hot chocolate at her and insisted she drink it before she dressed. Lilliana obediently gulped it down, sensing that the woman had an overpowering opinion of the proper order of things. Then she insisted on helping Lilliana dress. Built sturdy and square, Polly looked as if her corset was pulled so tight that she was exploding out of both ends. Broad, masculine hands yanked and pulled at Lilliana's hair, her night rail, and her arms and legs as Polly chattered brightly of how her mother had served Lord Albright's grandmother, and she her daughters.

Lilliana hardly listened at all—her nerves were too

frayed, and Polly's presence seemed yet another sign that things were not quite right. Her father always woke her mother. Every morning, without fail, his was the first face she saw. It was already noon, and Adrian had not come to see about her. Yesterday, he had hardly even looked at her, much less given her any sign—of *anything*.

Except last night.

With the single exception of the incredible things he did to her, he had shown her no emotion at all. Even worse, his lovemaking had made her feel larger than life, almost beyond herself. She was dangerously enamored of a man who had obviously discovered he loathed her. Good God, how could she have possibly gotten off to such a bad start? As if she had to ask herself that, she thought disgustedly. She had been too busy planning her life of freedom, too caught up in the fantasy to notice the warning signs. Foolish, *foolish* girl!

All right, she thought as Polly roughly fastened her gown, she was obviously doing something terribly wrong, and for once she wished her mother were there. She had never put much store into what her mother said about how young ladies should comport themselves; her lessons had seemed positively archaic and demeaning. How many times had she heard the lectures? Never mind that—*think*! All right, well, she *did* talk too much. Mother had said men do not care for ladies who talk too much. And she was not demure, not at all. If she had had one bit of sense in her feeble head, she would have sat quietly reading throughout the drive, *not* leaning out the window and *not* calling attention to every piece of scenery. Worse yet, she was not beautiful to make up for her gaffes, not like Caroline. Caroline had the luxury of being an absolute pill when she wanted to be, but Mr. Feather doted on her nonetheless because she was beautiful.

Exactly how did one make up for the lack of beauty and ladylike demeanor?

"Fine head of hair, milady. I shall look forward to dressing it for you. Now, if you will follow me, I shall take you to Max. He is in an absolute dither to show you about,'' Mrs. Dismuke said with a roll of her eyes. She marched to the door of the suite, threw it wide open with brute force, and proceeded to march into the corridor.

Afraid to disobey her, Lilliana rose from the vanity and reluctantly followed.

And Polly was right—Max, as the butler insisted she call him, was as diminutive as Polly was large, and truly was in something of a dither. He seemed to flit from one side of the drawing room to the other, straightening figurines and portraits and wiping imaginary specks of dust from mahogany tabletops. Just when Lilliana thought he might actually work himself into a frenzy and whirl right through the roof, the tour of Longbridge began.

In the course of it, when she wasn't sprinting to keep up with Max, Lilliana learned that Adrian had spent very little time at Longbridge, and that most of the enormous house remained as the late Lord Albright had left it. Which was one reason Max exclaimed over the many paintings she had brought from the Grange, declaring they would be the perfect pick-me-up to some of the drab decoration. When she confessed that she had painted them, Max clasped his hands to his chest and excitedly confided that he, *too*, was a budding artist. Which naturally gave rise to his idea that she might paint in the orangery, a building that had not been used in many years, and he instantly ushered her down to the rectangular brick building for a proper artist's inspection.

Lilliana managed to keep a cheerful facade throughout the tour by sheer force of will. In truth, she walked about in something of a daze, nodding politely with feigned interest in the things Max showed her, or appearing to listen attentively to Polly's rather long-winded history of the Albright house. And, naturally, nodding politely to both points of view during Max and Polly's frequent arguments about who, exactly, had done what to Longbridge and in what year. More than once she opened her mouth to ask about her husband. More than once she shut it before she foolishly did so. *Don't ask. Don't let them know.*

Apparently, miracles could happen, she told herself as she took her tea alone. Because for the first time in her twenty-two years, it looked as if her mother might possibly be right. Lady Dashell had always stressed the importance of being a lady. How many times had she rebuked her for unladylike behavior? How many times had she warned her that no gentleman would want a ruffian as a wife? Lord, how many times had she thrown up her hands, complaining it was all quite hopeless?

Lilliana had ignored her mother, assuming she was as old-fashioned as she was unyielding in her beliefs. And she was too desperate to soar to worry about what others might think of her. She had never cared a whit about being a proper lady, and despite her mother's pleas she preferred racing at reckless speeds on horseback to needlework. Romping with children or exploring the caves by the river suited her interests far more than drills in deportment and elocution. Lady Dashell positively wailed when Lilliana chose novels of daring adventure and travel above the required poetry and biblical text. But it was the only way Lilliana knew how to exist in the oppressive confines of Blackfield Grange; her only solace was the dream of escape.

Silly girl, she had thought she had found her escape in Adrian. How very ridiculous to think he would be pleased with•a ruffian, or to ignore how odd she would seem to a man of his stature and sophistication. Unfortunately, he had offered based on her reputation—a reputation that her mother had fought to maintain for her. He could not have possibly known she was as unladylike as he should ever hope to find or that she longed for adventure and travel and worldly amusements.

But he suspected now, did he not, that she was not the gently bred woman so well suited to him? Her only option—now that her mother was in Bath with the rest of the family—was to recall every fragment of memory of her mother's hundreds of lessons and become the demure woman a gentleman would want at his side. It seemed the only way, and definitely her only hope.

Adrian plunged his arms into the coat his valet, Roger, held out for him, a deep frown on his face and a blinding headache to boot. Roger's attention to his neckcloth was grating on him; he was far too exhausted to care about his appearance. As was happening with alarming frequency, he had spent another sleepless night with visions of Phillip, and sometimes Benedict, plaguing him.

"Thank you, Roger," he muttered, impatiently slapped the man's hand away, and started for the door. He was famished; he had not eaten since sunup. A good supper and several glasses of port seemed in order, and then, God help him, perhaps sleep would come.

"I'm to tell you that her ladyship is in the south drawing room, my lord," Roger said behind him.

Adrian paused at the door and glanced at his valet in a moment of confusion. *Lilliana*. He had almost forgotten. "Thank you," he said curtly, and strode from the master suite. He had forgotten his new wife sometime early this morning when he had come upon the first tenant's cottage in great need of repair. The next cottage had been no better, nor the next. The tenants were clearly suffering, and as he had ridden into the fields he had seen why. The harvested stalks were spindly, and judging by the look of the soil, there wouldn't be much point in sowing the fields in the spring.

That was when the idea had come to him. Longbridge had once been a place of splendor—and it could be so again. As he had ridden about the estate he had begun to see how easily Longbridge might rival Kealing Park. It was brilliant—if Archie thought to deprive him, then Adrian would create his own Park. Only one much grander than Archie should ever hope to see at Kealing Park.

As Adrian strode along the corridor of the ground floor, he tried to recall when he had last seen a report on

Longbridge since inheriting the title and estate after his grandfather's death some five years ago. Reaching the drawing room, he opened the doors and walked inside, his mind quickly running through the places he might have left that report.

Lilliana sprang to her feet as he entered and stood nervously. She wore a gown of ivory brocade, and her thick blond hair was arranged in a pleasing style. Adrian was struck by the odd notion that she looked . . . *attractive* . . . in a country sort of way. "Good evening," he said, and strolled to where she was standing to place a perfunctory kiss on her temple.

"Good evening," she murmured, and smiled nervously. "Shall I fetch you a drink?"

Yes, and a stout one at that, he thought, and sank onto a damask-covered couch. "A whiskey."

Lilliana hurried to the sideboard and poured it herself before the footman attending them could reach it. She returned, holding the liquor out to him with a slight tremble in her hand. "How was your day?" she asked.

"Exhausting," he muttered, and took a healthy sip of the amber liquid. Lilliana perched herself carefully on the edge of a chair, primly arranged her skirts, and straightened her spine. She then looked at him expectantly.

Adrian belatedly remembered himself. "And how was your first day at Longbridge?"

She smiled prettily. "Quite informative. Max took me on a tour of the house. It is quite grand. The southern rooms get wonderful light."

"Yes," he said simply, and sipped his whiskey, his thoughts having returned to where he had seen the latest report on Longbridge. In London, that much he remembered. But what had he done with it?

From the corner of his eye he noticed Lilliana fidgeting with the seam of her gown. "I hope you don't mind, my lord, but I have set up a studio of sorts in the orangery. It does not appear to have been used in many years, and Max said—"

"Whatever you would like," he said, cutting her off. Had he actually opened the packet?

"Oh. Thank you," she muttered. "I . . . I, uh, also thought to make some changes in your study. The drapes are too heavy, I think, for the oak paneling. And the gold salon could use some new sofas."

"Whatever you would like to do, Lilliana, you have my leave," he repeated absently. He had seen the packet on the desk in his London study, clearly labeled. He had intended to read it . . . but then Julian and Phillip had come. Ah yes, he thought, and frowned lightly. Yes, yes, he had been working late that evening and had every intention of reviewing the packet when Max had announced Lords Rothembow and Kettering. The two rogues had come staggering into his study, already a bit in their cups, and had enticed him to join them at Madam Farantino's. It had been easy enough—they had claimed a great beauty had joined the madam's ranks, which had piqued his interest greatly. Indeed, the lass *was* a great beauty, and extremely skilled in pleasuring a man.

"Are you feeling well?"

Lilliana's voice jolted him back to the present. "I beg your pardon?"

"Are you feeling well?" she asked again, and nervously cleared her throat. He couldn't help noticing that her hands were now clutching her gown on either side.

"Of course! I'm rather famished, that's all. Where do you suppose Max is?"

"I shall go fetch him," she said, and came quickly to her feet. He thought to tell her that the footman would do it, but his stomach was protesting the lack of food, and she was already at the door. By the time she returned and mumbled something about supper being served, he had finished his drink and was pacing in front of a bank of pane-glass windows, feeling faint from hunger.

In the dining room, he ate as if he had not tasted food in days. "I don't know where he found the cook, but I shall have to thank Max for his efforts. This soup is extraordinarily good," he remarked.

"Mr. Deavers comes to us from Keswick," Lilliana replied. "Max happened upon him quite by accident."

Adrian shot her a curious look as he fit another spoonful of soup into his mouth. "Indeed? I take it then you have had the opportunity to review the staff?"

She looked puzzled. "Review them? I went to the kitchens for a cup of tea, if that is what you mean."

Country lass. Adrian smiled indulgently as he reached for his wine. "You need not serve yourself tea, Lilliana. There are more than enough servants here to do that for you. Just call when you want something," he said, and motioned apathetically at the bellpull.

Lilliana blinked her large green eyes, and Adrian experienced a fleeting image of them half closed, the golden lashes fluttering in the throes of passion. "I am not helpless," she said, and laughed tautly. "I should be able to fetch a cup of tea."

"Not helpless, but a countess. You should feel free to act the part." The Grange Princess looked positively perplexed by that, and he grinned at how uncomfortable she was in assuming her rightful role. Extremely uncomfortable, judging by the way she now bowed her head and looked at her hands. Ah well, Adrian thought, and returned his attention to his soup. She would grow accustomed to it—*all* women grew accustomed to leisure. Now, Albright, he silently reminded himself. What exactly did you do with that packet after a night of whoring with Julian and Phillip?

Occupied with his thoughts, he hardly noticed when Lilliana launched into a little monologue having something to do with her many trunks and paintings. He nodded at what seemed appropriate moments as he devoured the leek soup. When he had at last cleaned the bowl, he looked expectantly at one of two footmen who were serving them.

"I rather suspect they have more in common than they would ever admit," Lilliana said.

"What?" he asked absently, and glanced impatiently at her before turning a menacing gaze to the footman.

"Polly and Max. I think they have quite a lot in common."

Adrian looked fully at her then—what on earth was she talking about? "Max and who?" he heard himself ask, and looked at her soup bowl. She had barely touched it. "Aren't you hungry?" he asked, casting another frown at the footman. He was ravenous, but the damned footman would not remove his plate until Lilliana had finished. Blasted rules of etiquette!

"Oh! I . . . not really, but it is delicious! I should very much like to send my mother the recipe. Papa is wild about leek soup."

"Are you quite finished, then?" he asked sharply. She nodded uncertainly. He threw a quick glance at the footman that the man could not possibly misinterpret. And Bertram did not—he moved very quickly to remove the soup bowls. As he waited for the main course to be served, Adrian drummed his fingers restlessly on the table.

"Max had all my things unpacked and put away. I thought that was very grand of him, because I had no notion what to do with it all. Except the paintings, of course. He has placed them in a sitting room upstairs, which he said he believed would be the mistress's sitting room—assuming, of course, you agree."

"That's nice," Adrian mumbled.

She sighed softly and began to turn her fork over, onto its back, then to its front, then back again. "And he said the orangery could be converted into a little studio. But he thinks it might be rather drafty in the winter, and said there is a seldom-used drawing room on the ground floor where I might be allowed to paint if the orangery is not to my liking," she continued.

"Mmm." At the moment, Adrian was far more intent on the trout Bertram placed in front of him than where she might paint.

"Would that meet with your approval?"

"I beg your pardon?" Adrian asked, momentarily distracted from the fine piece of fish in front of him.

"Painting," she said hesitantly. "In the orangery. Or the little drawing room."

Now what was she talking about? Something to do with her painting, as if she hadn't done enough of that already. As if he cared a whit where she painted—she could paint in the foyer for all he cared. She could *paint* the foyer for that matter. Was he to expect that she would ask his permission for every little thing? "Lilliana," he said impatiently, "whatever you would like, you may have. You may do as you please at Longbridge, and you need not bother yourself with seeking my permission," he said flatly, and flashed her a brief smile just before he attacked the trout.

"Thank you," she muttered. She did not speak after that, which was just fine with him. He could hardly be counted on to think of where she might do her sewing, or her correspondence, or any of the other little things women did with their time. When the meal was finished—which he could not help noticing Lilliana hardly even tasted—he relaxed with a glass of his favorite port.

Ah, but Max had done an excellent job of stocking the larder and sideboard. And he would have to compliment the old chap on his choice of cooks—that was some of the finest trout he had ever tasted. He glanced at his pocket watch; it was just ten o'clock. It would serve him well to get an early start the next morning, he thought absently. There was much to plan—a few statues around the place, perhaps some fountains in the gardens. And new gutters. He would replace them all, and the spot on the roof that appeared to be damaged. But first he would repair the cottages and bring in the latest farming technology. Yes, reconstructing Longbridge would provide him the diversion from his life that he so desperately needed at the moment, the perfect thing to occupy his thoughts and his days. He sipped his port, quite satisfied with his little stroke of brilliance.

The clink of china snapped him from his ruminations, and he slid his gaze to Lilliana. She was sitting quietly, gazing demurely at her hands in her lap. The candlelight caught the darker gold sprinkled in her blond hair, and the memory of that hair in his mouth, on her skin, came flooding back to him. Funny how a little port and a fine meal had made him much more disposed to do his duty. In fact, the idea did not give him the least bit of pause.

He placed his port on the table. "Lilliana, perhaps you would like to go and prepare for bed." She started, blinking those wide green eyes. He smiled. "Why don't you go on up? I shall be along directly." Her gaze flicked to the footman, then back to him. "To . . . to my, ah, *room*?" she asked hesitantly. Conscious of the footman, he merely nodded. Her cheeks flamed. "Yes. Well. I suppose it is rather, ah . . . late. Very late," she muttered, and came unsteadily to her feet. Glancing uneasily at the footman, she looked as if she might speak, but chose instead to make a hasty departure from the dining room. Adrian shrugged to himself as he motioned for more port to be poured. If the Princess kept looking at him like that, he really was going to start feeling like a bit of an ogre.

But after another glass of port Adrian was suddenly feeling the weight of exhaustion. At last, he thought desperately, at last he could sleep, and went directly to bed, only to be awakened a scant two hours later, perspiring and breathless. It was the same dream he had had several times now, the one in which he realized that Phillip had fired over his head and never even cocked the second barrel. Phillip had not intended to kill him. He had purposely missed, had no intention of firing a second time, and Adrian had shot him through the heart.

He rose from the bed, pacing restlessly as the blinding headache of his doubts came crashing down on his skull. Phillip had never intended to harm him. He had reacted in fear and had shot down his cousin for no reason. He was, as Archie had so succinctly put it, a murderer.

Exhausted and desolate, Adrian's mood was hardly improved the next morning when a messenger delivered the reply to the letter he had written Phillip's father. His first instinct was to leave it unopened, but guilt pushed him. With his thumb, he broke the wax seal and unfolded the heavy vellum. Scanning the page, words leapt out at him: *reckless, dangerous, shameful*. Lord Rothembow had taken his son's death as any man but Archie would do—hard and personally. Adrian blinked as he read the last thing Lord Rothembow had written: *May God have mercy on your soul*. He folded the vellum and placed it in his pocket, then practically bit a footman's head off when he lingered a shade too long in the foyer after being told to have Thunder saddled. He stalked to the breakfast room from there and was greeted by the Princess of the Grange. "Good morning," he forced himself to say.

"Good morning," she squeaked.

He landed heavily in a chair, scowling at the footman who placed a cup of coffee in front of him.

"Shall I prepare a plate for you?" Lilliana asked softly.

He sliced an impatient glance across her. Dressed in brown, she looked drab and ordinary. "Have the footman do it," he said curtly.

"I should be happy to do it," she insisted. He watched her spring to her feet and walk quickly to the sideboard. Her hair was fixed in an unappealing bun at her nape—good God, she looked like a country spinster dressed like that. He turned his attention back to his coffee, barely acknowledging the plate of steaming eggs and ham she placed in front of him.

"W-what have you planned for today?" she asked nervously when she resumed her seat across from him.

"Work," he informed her through a mouthful of eggs.

"Is there something I could do for you? Perhaps I could help."

The last thing he needed was a plain little country

mouse following him about. "No," he said hastily. "I intend to be in the fields most of the day. You had best occupy your time here." Her shoulders sagged slightly, and he realized he sounded harsh. He put his fork down. "There is much work to be done around the mansion, Lilliana. Wouldn't you like to rearrange a room or two to your liking?"

Funny, but he would have sworn her eyes narrowed. It must have been his imagination, because when she blinked, they were as wide and innocent as ever. "Perhaps I shall paint," she muttered.

"A splendid idea," he responded, and quickly finished his breakfast.

She painted all right, alone in the orangery for days that turned into weeks. At least there, amid her canvases, she felt some measure of comfort. Honestly, Longbridge felt more of a prison than Blackfield Grange ever had, she thought grimly as she dabbed a bit of paint on her brush. At Longbridge she felt hemmed in, so terribly out of place, without purpose. At least at the Grange she had been surrounded by her family. What she wouldn't give to be in Bath with them now! *Terrible pity, that, Lady Albright. You created this folly.*

And it was sheer folly. She could hardly complain that Adrian was cruel to her, because nothing could be further from the truth. He gave her leave to do what she wanted, to *have* anything she wanted. He never spoke a harsh word to her, and was politely civil at all times.

That was precisely the problem.

He never said much of anything except *how was your day,* the answer to which he never heard, and *whatever you would like.* Her attempts to converse with him left her feeling simple. Everything she said was met with a polite nod or a look of decided indifference. It created a crushing insecurity in her—she felt herself becoming increasingly inhibited and terribly ill at ease. She worried constantly that her conversation bored him, and if something was on *his* mind, well, she likely would never know. The man was exceedingly civil to her, but he never allowed her to know what he was feeling.

Except at night, in bed.

Lilliana inadvertently dropped her brush as a peculiar warmth filled her. When he came to her at night, he would whisper *Lillie* in her ear and take her to new heights of physical liberation each and every time. His lovemaking was magical; when he was deep inside her, she felt desirable and vibrantly alive.

Which was why his leaving her each night made it so much harder to bear. She longed for him to hold her for just a little while, but he never lingered. He would kiss her good night, wish her sweet dreams, and disappear through the door that adjoined their rooms. Oh, Lord, how she yearned to be held by him, to feel the power of him surround and protect her!

"What a foolish dream," she mumbled to herself. Adrian Spence had no use for such intimacy. At least not with her. He apparently did not even want the companionship he had claimed when he had offered for her. Adrian spent his days out on the estate somewhere. From Max she had learned that he planned to renovate the estate with the latest agricultural technology and to embellish the mansion to rival any other. Naturally *he* had not said a word to her of such plans—when she tried to ask what he did during the day, he was politely evasive. "A number of business dealings, Lilliana," he would say with a charming smile. "You would not be interested." Naturally she never disputed him—the nagging voice of her mother reminded her it was terribly unladylike to be disagreeable. But damn it all, she would very *much* like to have listened to his plans for Longbridge!

Even if she did summon the courage to ask, she rarely saw him long enough to discuss something so important. He worked from sunup to sundown and was often in his study until the early hours of the morning. She knew this from Max, too, who proudly told her how hard he was working, how impressed the tenants were with his willingness to toil alongside them in resurrecting what had once been such a grand estate. And the little man almost suffered a bout of worshipful apoplexy when he told her that her husband's generosity was unparalleled. He had set up a school for their children, demanded that abundant food stores be purchased, and even went so far as to help several of them erect a new barn. With his *bare hands*.

Would that she could work alongside him, Lilliana thought miserably, and dabbed paint on her brush. At least make herself useful! As it was, she spent her days wandering aimlessly about the house and spending far too much time chatting with Max. There was nothing much for her to do; the staff was efficient and everywhere. She would have given everything she owned to have escaped her chores at the Grange, but now she would give anything to have a *single* chore. The idleness was *suffocating* her.

So there it was. Three weeks at Longbridge and she was the useless mistress of a household that did not need her and an inept wife to a husband who did not notice her. And to think she had thought she would soar here. Honestly, what pathetic folly! What shameful naiveté! With no thought to reality or consequence, she had married a man she hardly knew, all because of some silly, romantic, and terribly childish notion of life!

And as if to make things bloody impossible for her, she recognized that she was falling in love with him.

Oh yes, she certainly was, and she actually snorted out loud at the very idea. Only silly Lilliana Dashell would love a man who did not seem to notice she existed. But she had loved the image of him for as long as she could remember, and the stories Max filled her head with excited her on a level she could hardly fathom. He was an adventurer, a man who was not afraid of hard work, and generous to a fault. And he was a scoundrel, too. The things he did to her in bed were absolutely wicked. But he was also a gentleman. Unerringly polite, he never raised his voice, yet commanded respect among all those around him, including herself. If only she could command the same respect from him. If only she could be the sort of wife he deserved. A man like Adrian Spence deserved far better, a woman of great connection and sophistication and bearing, not a dormouse like her! She should be thankful he spoke to her at all. Perhaps she should be thankful he *didn't* notice her—or else he might very well see how bloody insignificant she was.

Eight

Lilliana put the finishing touches on her latest creation, a still-life portrait of a basket stuffed with red apples. She stepped back from the canvas, and cocking her head to one side, eyed it critically. Apples. How perfectly boring.

Frowning, she tossed her brush aside and wiped her hands on the apron tied beneath her bosom. Having painted every conceivable object at Longbridge, she was now reduced to apples. Lilliana glanced irritably about the orangery—the walls were covered with her paintings, as were those of the house, the quarters above the stables, and the guest house. Paintings of trees and horses and houses and servants. What she had not brought from Blackfield Grange, she was quickly creating. For weeks now she had done nothing but paint, welcoming the task that filled the endless hours of her lonely existence. But the weight of emptiness was pressing down on her harder and harder, and painting, which had once given her such solace, no longer filled the void.

Apples, for heaven's sake!

Dear God, she had to do *something!* She suddenly jerked the strings of her apron free, tossed the garment aside, and marched through the door of the orangery into the bright sunlight. She would find something new to occupy her time and her thoughts, propriety be damned! She marched across the meticulously manicured lawn, her pale blue and white skirt rustling against the yellowed grass. Perhaps she would go and find Adrian and *demand* he allow her to help him!

On most days she felt completely inadequate and cowed by her title and by being the wife of a man like him. But *this* was one of the days she despised him and cursed him for marrying her. This was one of those days she felt her heartache keenly and blamed him for everything wrong with her life, including the blasted apples!

She noticed Max rushing toward her across the lawn and paused to allow him to catch up. "Good afternoon, milady! Have you finished your painting so soon?" he asked breathlessly.

She had finished, all right. Forever. "Apples, Max. I have painted apples."

"Ooh, a *lovely* subject."

"A boring subject, sir. It seems I have quite exhausted my imagination."

Max shook his head fiercely, as he was wont to do. "Your paintings are quite lovely, and I am quite certain your apples are painted to *perfection*."

Lilliana snorted impatiently. "It is not terribly difficult to paint apples to perfection, is it, Max? One simply paints a circle, then colors it red."

"If it were so easy, we should all paint apples," Max informed her with a sniff, and paused to brush an imaginary piece of lint from his sleeve. "You are fortunate to have such unique talent—why, if it were not for your lovely paintings, Longbridge would be quite plain."

Lilliana laughed at that. There was nothing about Longbridge that could be even remotely described as plain. "Nonetheless, I've decided to retire for a time."

"I suppose it's just as well, milady. You have callers."

An immediate sense of foreboding descended on Lilliana. "Callers?"

"Yes, milady," Max responded, looking terribly pleased. "Lady Paddington and Mrs. Clark from *London*!"

Callers from London! This was a catastrophe! "Does . . . does my husband—"

"Oh yes, madam. He is with them now and bade me fetch you."

She forced herself to smile at Max, who was obviously quite pleased she had actual guests. "Very well then," she said with an airy flick of her wrist, and proceeded to walk toward the house, Max anxiously on her heels. *Callers!* Oh *Lord!* These women, whoever they were, would see that the Earl of Albright did not care for his new wife.

As they walked into the house through the terrace sitting room, Lilliana paused to look at her hair in the mirror. Max, beaming his approval, assured her she looked quite fetching, and nervously hopped from one foot to another until she was satisfied there was nothing she could do. When they reached the gold salon, Max proudly swept the doors open.

Two elderly women jumped to their feet as Lilliana entered, both talking excitedly as Adrian strode forward. He smiled absently at her and beckoned her into the room. "Lady Paddington, Mrs. Clark, may I present Lady Lilliana Albright," he said smoothly. Lilliana curtsied, intended to extend a proper greeting, but the women immediately began chattering before she could open her mouth.

"Lady *Albright*! My, what a wonderful ring the name has to it, don't you think, Mrs. Clark?"

"It is positively divine, particularly since we were never expecting there to *be* a Lady Albright!"

"Oh my, never!" Lady Paddington echoed.

Uncertain how to respond, Lilliana stammered, "I, uh, thank you."

"Lady Paddington is the great-aunt of my close

friend, Lord Arthur Christian,'' Adrian informed her. "And Mrs. Clark is her companion. They have stopped on their way to Cambridge, to visit with Mrs. Clark's sister.''

"Cambridge is such a quaint little town,'' Lady Paddington said with a sigh. "It reminds one of—''

"London!'' Mrs. Clark chirped.

"London!'' Lady Paddington echoed, and folded her chubby hands over her middle. "Have you been to Cambridge, Lady Albright?''

Good Lord, she had hardly been to Newhall! "I'm afraid I've not had the pleasure,'' she said, and the recently familiar sensation of awkwardness began to creep into her bones. She gestured helplessly toward some chairs. "Please, do sit.''

The ladies did so eagerly, and launched into a disjointed discussion of their travel plans. Not a single detail was left out as far as Lilliana could tell, including the ladies' shared relief that Mrs. Clark's sister lived in Cambridge and *not* in London. Why they were undertaking a journey to see her would, apparently, remain a mystery.

They talked incessantly; when one finished, the other began. And they did most of their talking at Adrian. Lilliana tried to converse, but their chatter was daunting and she had absolutely nothing to add. If she did manage to say something, it seemed the women barely heard her. Oh, they smiled and nodded their heads at her pleasantly enough, but their attentions were most decidedly on Adrian.

And *he*, of course, gave no sign that he heard anything she said, but conversed with the ladies easily enough, just as Lilliana had seen him converse with her father.

When the ladies had completed their dissertation on Cambridge, they began to prattle about events in London, talking of people and places Lilliana did not know. Not once did they attempt to explain to her who the Devil of Darfield really was, or why Bavaria was men-

tioned so often in the same breath as the Duchess of
Sutherland. Nor did they attempt to explain the signifi-
cance of Harrison Green, who apparently hosted several
bawdy gatherings in his home, which all of them had, at
one time or another, attended. They had had a grand
time of it, too, judging by the uproarious laughter as
several incidents were recalled.

Abandoning her feeble attempts to join in the conversation in which she was so obviously an outsider, Lilliana sank against the plush armchair, convinced she
was indistinguishable from the floral print. When Lady
Paddington stood and started wandering about the
room, she thought to stroll with her, but Adrian was
quickly to his feet, walking beside her and nodding
thoughtfully at one of Lilliana's paintings the woman
admired.

And then her misery gave way to a rising anger.
When Lady Paddington asked after the artist, Adrian
merely shook his head. "Probably a local," he said dis-
missively, and pointed her toward an expensive oriental
vase that had recently arrived. That bloody husband of
hers did not know it was her painting! After weeks of
feeling like a country bumpkin, an indignant anger ignited and flamed through Lilliana at a frightening pace.
He did not really speak to her, he did not acknowledge
her in any way, and he did not know she painted! *Damn*
him! He said he wanted a companion! He said they
suited! He was a liar if nothing else, a bloody *liar*!

When Max announced tea, the ladies eagerly accepted Adrian's invitation, swearing in the same breath
that they simply had to be on their way. Adrian extended an arm to each of them, smiling politely at their
simultaneous chatter. Lilliana remained seated, glaring
at the lot of them as they sauntered toward the salon
door. When they reached it, Lady Paddington paused
and glanced so quickly over her shoulder that her sau-
sage curls danced wildly. "Lady Albright, aren't you
joining us?" she asked sweetly.

Adrian jerked around. "Lilliana! I'm terribly sorry,

I'm afraid I forgot you," he said with a disarming little chuckle, and smiled charmingly at the ladies.

He had forgotten her—but wasn't *that* fine! And why should she be surprised? He hardly knew she existed, so she should hardly take offense that he had *forgotten* her! But offense she did take, and hard. Slowly she pushed herself from her chair and walked to where they were standing, glaring at Adrian the whole way. He quirked a lazy brow, then smiled down at his companions. "You are in for a treat, ladies. We have had the good fortune of engaging a particularly good cook. I think you will find his pastries quite delightful."

"Ooh, I simply *adore* pastries!" Mrs. Clark chirped, and out the three of them walked, strolling abreast down the corridor, leaving Lilliana to walk behind.

The chatter continued, unabated, during tea. After insisting she would introduce Lilliana around when Adrian brought her to London for the Season— something Lady Paddington seemed terribly certain would actually happen—she began telling some outrageous tale about a game of loo in which she had lost against one Lady Thistlecourt. "I vow, I so desperately wished I was a man so I could avenge my honor properly," she huffed, and stuffed a whole strawberry into her mouth. "Do you play, dear?" she asked Lilliana, carefully spitting the strawberry crown into her napkin.

"No, I'm afraid I don't know the rules," she answered truthfully, and wanted to smash Lady Paddington's scone when she exchanged a brief but undeniable look of pity with Mrs. Clark.

"I once came dangerously close to having to defend my honor with Lady Thistlecourt," Adrian said, chuckling softly. "She can hardly abide my presence since the Wilmingtons' closing ball last Season."

"Ooh, you are a *dangerous* gentleman, my lord!" Lady Paddington cried, and playfully slapped Adrian on the arm as Mrs. Clark howled with laughter.

Defeated, Lilliana sagged into her chair and began separating her raisins from her scone, piling them mind-

lessly on one side of her plate. Somewhere in the middle
of a detailed description of all Lady Thistlecourt's faults,
she caught Adrian looking at her plate. She responded
with a heated glare, but he did not so much as blink, and
instead responded politely to Mrs. Clark's inquiry as to
his last trip to London. And then Lady Paddington casually mentioned seeing the "unfortunate" Lord Rothembow. A sudden chill seemed to descend upon the room;
Lilliana quickly looked up from her pile of raisins.

"*Clara!*" Mrs. Clark hissed.

"I am *terribly* sorry, my lord!" Lady Paddington
gasped. "I don't know what I was thinking! You must
forgive me!"

"There is nothing to forgive, my lady," Adrian said
coolly. Lilliana looked from Adrian to the ladies and
back again. His expression remained inscrutable. "Who
is Lord Rothembow?" she asked. Three pairs of eyes
suddenly locked on her face.

"An acquaintance, dear. No one you know," Mrs.
Clark mumbled.

Yes, just like everyone else they had discussed! Lilliana put her fork down. "Only an acquaintance? Then
why are you so terribly sorry, Lady Paddington?" she
asked sweetly, and could almost feel Adrian's displeasure emanate from across the little table.

"He is my father's cousin, Lilliana. His son is
recently deceased," he said tightly. Lady Paddington
suddenly took a great interest in her scone; Mrs. Clark
pretended to closely examine the flowers on the table.

"I am very sorry," Lilliana said, but she wasn't
sorry, not in the least. How could she possibly know he
had a relative who had recently died? It wasn't as if he
had deigned to tell her a bloody thing about himself! If
he was uncomfortable, it was his own fault, and she
blithely continued rearranging the raisins on her plate.

A man would have to be blind and deaf not to see that
his wife was miffed. Lilliana had acted like a petulant

child during their tea with the ladies, digging her raisins out of her scone and making a little mountain of them. Fortunately, the ladies had been so engrossed with the cataloguing of Lady Thistlecourt's many faults they had not seemed to notice. And when the ladies were finally on their way, Lilliana had gone to her rooms, where she had remained for the rest of the day, refusing even to join him for supper. As she was typically such an unobtrusive sort of girl, taking her meals with him in companionable silence, he could not help wondering what had come over her. He thought to send for her, but then thought better of it. At the mention of Lord Rothembow, he had acquired another one of the miserable, blinding headaches that often came with a reminder of Phillip or Benedict.

Seated in front of the fire in his master suite of rooms, Adrian pinched the bridge of his nose between his finger and thumb. He had not had a headache in several days now—in the process of pouring his heart and energy into the resurrection of Longbridge, he had managed to push his conscience into some remote and dusty corner of his soul.

For weeks now, he had worked hard in the fields, shored up the tenant homes, pored over the accounts, and planned several extensive enhancements to the mansion. The sweat, the exertion, the mind-numbing review of years of mangled accounting had gradually freed him from the intense guilt that had been eating away at him, little by little. He was by no means completely free of it; God help him, he would *never* be completely free of it. But his bouts of melancholy and blinding headaches were becoming less frequent, and his ability to block the horrible events beginning in Dunwoody and ending in Kealing was growing stronger.

But then Lady Paddington and Mrs. Clark, two old bats who frequented the best salons of London in search of gossip and a card game, had unexpectedly appeared. After an absence from the same salons of more than six weeks, Adrian had been rather delighted to see them and

anxious for news of London. He had been amused by
their little tales, eager to hear of friends and acquain-
tances. The talk of London had left him thinking how
much he missed it, and he had been mulling over the
idea of leaving Longbridge in the care of his steward,
Mr. Lewis, when they had mentioned Lord Rothembow.
The reminder of Phillip's death and his father's grief—
Adrian hadn't looked at that letter in days now—had
sent him spiraling backward into the pit of guilt and
desolation from which he had been working so hard to
claw his way out.

Speaking of guilt, hadn't the Princess of the Grange
been in fine form this afternoon! How he regretted his
hasty decision to marry her! As a result of his rash anger,
he had gotten himself a little country wife who no more
suited him than he suited her. She would have been
much happier in her home parish with Benedict—now
there was a pair that suited. Unfortunately, he had
ruined any hope of that, and despite having realized the
gravity of his mistake several times over, it was too
damn late. He had no choice but to keep her, and for the
most part he had managed to put her out of his mind
along with everything else.

Until today.

Until he had seen those gray-green eyes, and the
pangs of his old, familiar friend Guilt had crept into his
bones.

He sighed and pushed himself from the leather wing
chair and strode to the windows of his master suite.
Shoving the heavy velvet drapes aside, he stared blindly
into the night, wondering how to make life bearable for
them both. He should give her an expensive bauble to
cheer her; he had never known a woman whose disposi-
tion did not improve with an expensive piece of jewelry.
He would dispatch a letter to his solicitor first thing in
the morning, recognizing that it was a pathetic gesture
for having ruined her life but hoping it might at least
make her smile. He remembered that smile—broad and

bright and ending in a lone dimple in one cheek. He had not seen her smile for days now.

Except when she lay beneath him.

That sudden thought brought a rush of warmth to his loins. The one thing about her that had surprised him enormously was how unconventional she was between the sheets. Since the first night he had bedded her, she had astounded him with her passion. She was a little hellion, he thought with a wry smile, unafraid to try anything and searing him with her demanding, untutored responses. Hell, he could hardly call her untutored—she was a quick learner and seemed almost desperate to please him. The memory of her mounting him with such exhilaration just last night was making him quite hard. He suddenly pushed away from the window and turned toward the door connecting their rooms.

He entered quietly, but in the faint glow of the dying embers in her hearth he saw her quickly flip to her side, her back to him. Still miffed, he thought as he removed his dressing gown. The Princess did not so much as move when he lifted the bed linens and slid in next to her.

Neither of them spoke. His fingers grazed her shoulder then slid slowly down her arm, to her waist, and over the silk night rail covering her belly. "I had a rather lonely supper," he murmured against her shoulder. "Max said you were not feeling well."

"I was feeling perfectly fine," she muttered irritably.

Interesting. Definitely not her typically demure reply. He continued his gentle caress, his fingers trailing languidly across the curve of her waist into her hip, then her leg. "Then perhaps you are not quite as enamored of our cook as I am?" he asked pleasantly, inhaling the subtle scent of rosewater in her luxurious hair. She shrugged. His fingers trailed up her leg, over her hip, and up her arm until they reached her shoulder, where he brushed the hair from her neck. "Perhaps, then, it was the prospect of my company," he said, and feathered her neck with light kisses. She squirmed, moving away from him.

With a quiet smile Adrian slid his hand down her arm until he reached her hand. Grasping it tightly, he pushed it against her belly, forcing her against his body and anchoring her to his chest. He leaned over and kissed her cheek. The salty taste of her tears surprised him as she helplessly jerked her hand from his and pressed her fingers to her eyelids.

He had no idea what had upset her so, but if there was one thing he could not abide, it was a woman's tears. Not that he had ever really seen them, except on Eloise, the French whore who had fallen in love with him after a particularly memorable night. He hadn't liked it then, and he didn't like it now. Gently but firmly he rolled Lilliana onto her back and came over her, kissing one eye, then the other. "Don't cry, Lillie," he whispered. "Please don't cry." Her tears began to flow then, and he quietly kissed them away while his hands provocatively roamed her body, seducing her to his throbbing arousal. She took several sharp breaths as she fought her tears, and almost reluctantly, he thought, she put her hands on his shoulders, then swept them down his chest, fingering his hardened nipples. With his mouth he teased hers open, then plunged into her warmth, savoring the taste of mint on her breath. His hands roamed wildly now, his senses inflamed by the satin feel of her skin. Her hands, too, ran across his shoulders, his back, and down his torso. And then she reached between his legs, lifted him in her hand, feeling the weight of him.

And pushing him past the point of all reason.

He groaned her name as he entered her; her body tensed at the sudden invasion. "Lillie," he whispered, "hold me." She shook her head and tried to resist him. But his knowledge of the female body was the one thing he knew about women with all certainty, and within the space of a heartbeat she was panting and stroking the corded muscles of his back and buttocks, demanding with her hips that he fill her completely.

When they had both found their release in another explosive climax, Adrian rolled to his side, taking her with him. She made a ragged sound of distress, and confused by it, he held her close. "What has upset you?" he asked softly. He heard her breath catch in her throat, felt her stiffen in his arms. "Lilliana?"

"I . . . I want to be a good wife," she began in a whisper.

"You are a good wife," he said quickly, relieved that was all there was to this show of tears.

"No, I mean a wife you can be proud of."

Honestly, he didn't mean to hesitate. But it was enough for her to pull from his arms and roll away, and for him to feel like a cad. "You are," he said, choosing his words carefully, "a wife any man would be proud of." Her body shuddered as if he had jabbed her in the back. What a miserable liar he was! He racked his brain for something to say, but with no sense of what had caused this misery, his mind reverted to ingrained, reflexive habits learned in notorious boudoirs. Flattery.

He put his hand on her shoulder and leaned over her, nuzzling her ear. "There are many admirable qualities about you, don't you know? You are kind, and . . . thoughtful. And you have beautiful flaxen hair," he said, grabbing a fistful of her silken mane. It wasn't a lie—she *did* have beautiful hair. She stirred beside him, turning her face farther into the pillows. "I would imagine that others are quite envious of it."

"Thank you," she muttered.

Satisfied that he had at least gotten a response, he rolled away from her. Whatever was bothering her would seem much better by morning's light, he was certain. Lilliana did not seem the maudlin sort. But she kept her back to him as he got out of bed and slipped into his dressing gown. He leaned over and pulled the counterpane over her shoulder, then kissed her temple. "Sweet dreams, Lilliana," he murmured, brushed a strand of hair from her cheek, and left her room, his appetite sated and his conscience at least appeased.

When the door closed, Lilliana slowly pushed herself

up and glared at it, her brows knit into a deep vee. "He adores my hair," she muttered to herself. "My *hair*!"

Humiliated by her inability to resist him, fury rifled through her. Damn it, but *he* had come to *her* at Blackfield Grange and offered her a life as his companion! The memory of his blithe conviction that they would suit made her ill—that man had shown her nothing but polite indifference since the moment they had said their vows. His only concession was to stoke her passion under the veil of night, making her believe he desired her with his hands and his mouth but never putting a voice to his desires. Well, perhaps that was because the only thing he could find to admire about her was her bloody *hair*.

She hated him.

She threw the linens back and leapt from her bed. Marching to the hearth, she lit a candelabrum, turned on her heel, and marched to a scattering of chairs. Retrieving a sewing basket, she continued her march to her vanity and sat heavily on the little bench. She stared at her reflection a long moment before fishing a pair of shears from the basket. He adored her hair, did he? Well then, he could bloody well *have* it! Lilliana grabbed a handful of the heavy blond locks and snipped.

Her hand slowly came down, and horrified, she gaped at the tress in her hand. *Her hair!* Yes, and what difference did it make? Other than it was one of the few "admirable qualities" about her! With a gleam of fury in her eye, she grabbed another handful.

Polly Dismuke thought Lady Albright had lost her mind. She had arrived later than usual this morning, having quite a head on her after one too many pints at the Dog and Duck on her weekly holiday. And Lord, this time it was a whopper—she blinked several times as she entered her mistress's rooms, quite certain she was seeing things.

But there was no mistaking the clumps of blond hair

strewn about the little bench at the vanity—big, thick clumps of her lady's glorious hair. Polly cried out as she rushed into the room and picked up a handful of the shorn tresses, prompting Lady Albright to emerge from her dressing room. Without the weight of a lifetime in her locks, the shoulder-length tresses bounced into a riot of curl. The darker shades of gold, long since covered by the heavier flaxen tresses on top, peeked through, revealing several different shades of blond.

"What have you *done,* milady?"

"I have cut my hair," her ladyship responded matter-of-factly.

"But *why?*"

Lady Albright smiled cheerfully. "I thought it would be a nice change. I've had that hair all my life, you know."

Polly's jaw dropped. And then she noticed what her mistress was wearing and actually stumbled backward, quite certain she was apoplectic. *"Trousers?"* she gasped.

Lady Albright nodded. "They are perfect for riding."

"You intend to *wear* them?"

Another smiling nod. "I am quite determined to ride, actually. It's a glorious day and I haven't been on the back of a horse in over a month, I'd wager. Do you like to ride, Polly?"

No, she did not. And if she did, she most certainly would not like it in trousers! She shook her head, afraid to speak.

"Really? I adore it!" Lady Albright said in a sing-song voice, and disappeared into the dressing room again. When her ladyship came strolling out a few moments later, Polly felt the apoplexy coming on. Her mistress still wore the trousers that fit her too snugly, and had added a man's waistcoat over the lawn shirt she had gotten from God knew where. Polly, who had served the daughters of the late Lord Albright, was certain about one thing: It was the height of impropriety for her mistress to wear those clothes. She was also certain it was her duty to warn her ladyship of the error in her decision.

Squaring her broad shoulders, she planted her hands on her hips. "Lady Albright, I would be remiss in my service to you if I did not point out that it is not quite seemly for women to be seen running about in"—she could hardly spit out the word—"*trousers*."

Lady Albright blinked her big green eyes. "No?"

Polly fiercely shook her head.

"I see," her ladyship mused, tapping a finger against her cheek. "Well then, I suppose I shouldn't leave the estate," she said, and with a grin, walked to the corridor door.

Polly took several frantic steps after her. "B-but the estate is rather large, milady. What about the *tenants*!" she cried as Lady Albright walked out of the room.

Lady Albright paused in the corridor, pondering that. "You are absolutely right!" she said after a moment. Polly's shoulders sagged with relief. "I should have introduced myself to them long ago. Thank you for that kind reminder; I shall meet every last one of them today, you have my word," she said, and with a jaunty wave disappeared from view, leaving Polly gaping at the open door.

Polly wasn't the only one who thought the mistress had lost her mind. Max came flying across the marble foyer, stumbling to a halt next to Polly, who was peering out the front door and wringing her big hands. *"Disaster!"* he whispered frantically.

"I'll say," Polly muttered, her gaze riveted on something outside.

"I might very well lose my post!" Max whispered, and looked furtively over his shoulder as he grasped Polly's arm.

Polly snorted and shook him off. "What are you rattling about?" she muttered angrily.

"Early this morning her ladyship said she intended

to cut a pattern for a gown, and I thought nothing of it, but why should I? She *is* the mistress of this house, is she not? Oh Lord, oh Lord, I saw her enter the library, and I thought to say something, but I didn't! It's not my *place*, do you hear me? And . . . and I saw no harm in it, truly I did not! Yet I can scarcely believe it, even though I saw it with my own eyes!'' he continued madly.

With an impatient roll of her eyes, Polly huffed, ''I've no idea what you are going on about, but—''

''She moved his papers!''

Polly stopped and looked fully at the little man. ''Papers! *What* papers?'' she snapped.

''*All* of them!'' Max squeaked, sounding as if he might weep at any moment. ''He had the accounts all there on the table, spread out, arranged by date. They go back *years*, I tell you! And she . . . she *moved* them!''

''So she moved them!'' Polly said, and jerked her gaze outside once again.

''No, no, you don't understand. She not only moved them, she *rearranged* them! His lordship had . . . had sorted them and very carefully arranged them so that he might follow the income against expenditures!'' Max wailed, his hands waving furiously as he tried to depict just how carefully they had been arranged. ''God help us all, because she took papers out of their leather bindings, she stacked them willy-nilly on chairs and the floor! She even''—his voice dropped so that it was almost inaudible—''she even used the back of one page to *mark some figures*! Heaven help me, he will have my head, I am quite certain!''

''No,'' said Polly, solemnly shaking her head. She stepped aside so that Max could see what attracted her attention. ''He will have *her* head, and I am quite fearful for her!'' Max turned to see what Polly was watching. To his utter amazement, Lady Albright rode by. Astride. Wearing trousers.

Atop *Thunder*.

No one, not even the stable master was allowed to ride Thunder. That stallion was the earl's pride and joy, and there was not a person in his employ who did not know the horse was almost sacred.

Max groaned. "Oh dear. And I really thought so very highly of her," he said sadly, and he and Polly stood side by side, watching her until she had disappeared over a crest, shaking their heads in unison.

Nine

WHAT IN THE hell was the matter with everyone?

Adrian glanced irritably at a footman who was trying
very hard to blend into the wall as he passed him in the
expansive foyer. He wouldn't have thought much of it,
except that Mrs. Dismuke had quickly disappeared into
Lilliana's room when she had seen him in the corridor,
and Max had definitely changed course and ducked into
a seldom-used parlor when he had rounded the corner
on his way to the library.

The servants were acting as if he had suddenly
sprouted horns, and he'd be damned if he knew what
had brought that on. Never mind that now, he thought
testily as he walked to the library. He had work to do—
an idea had come to him this morning. Archie was exceedingly proud of the gazebo he had built at Kealing
Park, but it was rather small. He would build a larger
one, a monument to the beauty of Longbridge. And he
had a brilliant idea how to pay for it. Adrian walked
across the library threshold and glanced at the table
where the account books for the last ten years had been
carefully laid out.

He could not believe what he was seeing.

He shook his head, then stared at the table, trying to fathom it. The account books, so painstakingly arranged so that he could follow expenditures, investments, and revenues through the years, were strewn over two chairs, an ottoman, and the floor. They were stacked haphazardly, papers sticking out of the leather bindings every which way. His pulse began to beat at a clip and he walked to the bellpull, yanking so hard that he almost ripped it from its fastenings. Then he waited, glaring at the table, until Max appeared, looking quite pale.

"Max, do come inside," Adrian said evenly, and strolled toward the table where he had made extensive notes on the accounts. "Do you notice anything unusual in this room?" he asked in a deceptively calm voice.

"Ah. Well. Yes, my lord," Max mumbled.

Adrian turned halfway to look at him over his shoulder. "Really? And what would that be?"

Max's thin face took on an almost purple caste. "The . . . the account books, my lord. It would appear they have been . . . ah, moved."

"Yes, it would seem so," Adrian said amicably. "And why is that?"

"I . . . I don't know, my lord," Max squeaked.

"Don't you? As you are charged with the task of keeping my house in a reasonable semblance of order, might you offer *any* explanation?" Adrian asked, turning to face his suddenly meek butler.

"Umm . . . No," Max muttered, clearing his throat, and shifting his gaze to the hearth.

Adrian shoved an impatient hand through his hair. "Max, what in God's name would possess you—"

"Not *me,* my lord! I beg you do not force me to say more," he said, and clasped his hands together so tightly that it looked as if they might explode.

"Not you? Then who in the hell would you suggest? That timid little maid who is almost too frightened to touch anything?"

"I am begging you, my lord—"

"What in the hell is the matter with you?" Adrian angrily demanded.

"It was Lady Albright!" Max cried, and immediately winced, dropping his head in shame.

Thunderstruck, Adrian gaped at him. *"Who?"*

"On my honor, I have no idea why, except that she said they seemed like a lot of musty old books, and she needed the table to cut a pattern for a new gown—"

"A *gown?*" he all but bellowed.

Max nodded his head furiously and gulped a deep breath. "It was a pattern her mother sent all the way from Bath! And she, ah, she needed a *large* table, and, well, it *is* a large table. But I never thought she would *touch* them, no, no, I never thought that! And then, I thought *surely* she would ask if she couldn't find paper, but she is obviously the industrious sort, because she used . . . she used . . ." Max paused and stuck a finger under his collar and tugged anxiously.

"Go on," Adrian said flatly, his pulse now pounding soundly at his neck and temples.

"She . . . she used a page from the account books to write some figures. Year 1829, I believe," he muttered miserably.

Adrian glared at him for a long moment before turning and walking slowly to the window. He took several steadying breaths. *Deep* breaths. All right, all right, the Princess of the Grange obviously did not know what she was doing. It wasn't as if he had explained to her the work he was doing here. It was an honest mistake. He and Max would simply put them back together. How long could it possibly take? A few hours? A bloody *week*? Damnation! "Have Lady Albright sent in," he ground out.

"Um, I beg your pardon, my lord, but she has gone out."

Gone out. Well, then, he would wait until she returned. In the meantime he would leave things as they were and use her carelessness to make a point. "Leave things as they are," he said gruffly, and pivoting on his heel, quit the library, striding past his butler without looking at him.

A ride. A nice long ride to calm him down a bit, he decided, and walked swiftly to the foyer, gesturing to the footman for his coat and gloves. The footman eyed him warily as he timidly handed him his gloves. With an impatient roll of his eyes, Adrian stalked out of the house, bound for the stables.

As he stepped into the paddock, he noticed two young grooms suddenly scamper around the corner of the stable, disappearing from view. Dear God, what did they think, that he would beat her for moving some account books? What sort of man did they take him for? Irritated, he marched into the stable, spying Mr. Bottoms before the stable master saw him. The moment he caught sight of his employer, he nervously dropped the bucket he held.

"Saddle Thunder," Adrian barked, and began walking toward the largest stall at the very end of the row. Mr. Bottoms did not move, and seemed paralyzed. "Well? What are you waiting for?" Adrian snapped, his patience wearing very thin, and glanced at Thunder's stall.

His horse had been stolen!

A rush of panic gripped him, and he jerked around toward Bottoms, who was trembling so badly that the bucket he had just retrieved was about to shake loose from his hands again. "What has happened? Where is Thunder?" he exploded.

"Ah . . . Lady Albright, my lord," the stable master gasped.

Speechless. He was totally, utterly speechless. *"Lady Albright?"* he roared.

"She said you gave her leave!" he cried, and dropped the bucket. "I thought . . . I mean, I suggested she take the mare, but she was rather insistent, my lord. She promised me!" he frantically added, and quickly bent to retrieve the bucket.

"Promised you?" Adrian choked out. "Promised you *what*?"

"That you said she may have whatever she fancied," he said, and nervously swiped his arm across his forehead. "Including Thunder," he mumbled miserably.

Deep breaths, he reminded himself. She was on Thunder. Good God, that foolish little idiot could get herself killed! "Did it occur to you that she might not be able to handle Thunder?" he ground out.

Bottoms paled. "Aye, my lord. But she had begun to saddle him herself, and what was I to do? She . . . she seemed all right, on my honor she did," he said, his voice pleading.

Now what in the hell was he to do? "Saddle the mare," Adrian snapped, and whirled around, glaring out the door. That parish princess, that Thief-of-Stallions would be very, *very* sorry indeed that she had pulled such a childish, foolish stunt. For all he knew, she had already broken her silly neck. What was she thinking? Of course he had given her leave to do whatever she wanted, but he had thought she might at least use a bit of common sense! What was in a woman's mind? Hell, it hardly mattered, because—

A thought suddenly struck him, and slowly he folded his arms across his chest, quietly seething. Was it possible that the little featherbrain was still pouting about something? Was she *trying* to anger him? Well, the evil country bumpkin had succeeded admirably. Lord help her when he found her scrawny little hide!

He glared at Bottoms as he swept up onto the mare, demanded to know which direction she had taken, and sent the horse galloping after her.

His humor did not improve, given that he had quite a time finding the little wretch. Several of the tenants had seen her, beaming with idiotic grins as they pointed in the direction she had ridden. What a darling, some of them said. A darling all right, he thought, still seething. A darling of the devil!

He was on the verge of giving up and assembling a

search party—convinced the stallion had killed her by
now—when he saw Thunder grazing peacefully under a
tree. He jerked the mare hard right and galloped across
the field. As he neared his horse he could see the banks
of a small stream. A young man—a boy, really—was
lying on his woolen riding coat next to the stream, his
feet crossed at the ankles, his arms pillowing his head.

But there was no sign of Lilliana.

He reined the mare to a violent halt and swung
down.

Intent on an explanation, he started for the boy but
drew up short when the lad scrambled to his feet.
Squinting, he peered at him . . . *that* was no boy.

For the third time that day Adrian was badly startled. Startled? He had to remind himself to breathe, because *this* time, the Princess of the Grange had
succeeded in knocking the wind from him. What in
bloody hell had she done? Astounded, he stared at Lilliana—the only thing recognizable about her was that
smile and that single dimple in her cheek. He took an
unsteady step forward as his gaze landed on the top of
her head and the riot of blond curls, then slowly traveled
to the *waistcoat,* for chrissakes, and the boy's trousers
that fit her like a glove, and the pair of men's leather
boots that fit snug around her calves. That . . . that *boy*
was his wife!

And he was infuriatingly, positively captivated.

"Ah, my lord husband! How marvelous that you
should join me!" she called, and with a beguiling grin
tossed her coat over her shoulder and started walking
toward him. Adrian forced himself to tear his gaze away
from her hips as they swung softly in those buckskin
trousers, leaving *nothing* to his imagination. She stopped
in front of him and, still grinning, pushed a curl from her
forehead with the back of her hand. "Glorious day for
riding, isn't it?" she chirped. "Awfully warm for this
time of year." Adrian exhaled sharply—the lawn shirt
and waistcoat she wore clung to her round bosom.

"I have never seen the estate, you know, and today

seemed a grand time to do it," she added, and cocked her head to one side, peering up at him with those smoky green eyes.

Hell, there was something different about *them,* too, he thought madly. They were . . . sparkling. Ah yes, there was a definite glint to those pretty eyes—a demonic little glint! "It is indeed a lovely day," he said, and forced a polite smile to his lips.

She grinned fully then, and he noticed that flashing back at him in a rather gleeful smirk were teeth that were straight, white, and even. "Do you think so? I thought—judging from your expression, I should say— that you might not be terribly inclined to a long ride today." Still grinning, she clasped her hands behind her back and rocked up to the balls of her feet and down. Then up. Then down again.

"My expression? Why madam, I am merely relieved you are quite alive," he drawled, his eyes narrowing slightly.

Incredibly, she practically laughed at him! "Of *course* I am quite alive! Thunder and I had a wonderful time of it—we've taken quite a liking to one another," she said cheerfully.

It was all Adrian could do to keep from snatching her up and shaking some sense into her. But he was extremely practiced at maintaining his composure, and with a grin of his own, inclined his head toward Thunder. "Shall we see about him?" he asked pleasantly, and signaled for her to precede him. With a careless shrug of her shoulders, she walked to where the horses were grazing. Adrian gamely tried to look anywhere but at the round little derriere bouncing along in those tight buckskins. Where in the bloody hell had she gotten *those*? When they reached the horses, Lilliana tossed her cloak across Thunder's neck and began stroking his nose. And that traitorous horse of his actually dipped his head to nuzzle her.

"You've cut your hair," he observed bluntly.

She self-consciously ran a hand through the curls. "It

was getting a bit bothersome." A deep smile appeared on her lips again, dimpling on one side. "Do you like it?"

"It is quite nice," he begrudgingly admitted. He would not have believed it but there was something terribly erotic about that mass of curl, the shimmering intermingled shades of wheat and flax. The smile faded from his wife's lips and she blinked up at him, an unmistakable cloud of disappointment shadowing her eyes, confusing Adrian completely. "I'm a bit surprised, I will admit," he added. Surprised, hell—he was quickly coming to the conclusion that the Princess might very well be mad, because Lilliana grinned at that remark.

"Oh, you are surprised? How wonderful! And I thought you wouldn't notice."

All right, she *was* mad. How could he *not* notice her hair, her trousers—*enough*! She might be a mad fool, but he wasn't going to allow her to come to harm because of it.

"Lilliana," he began patiently, working hard to keep his voice even, "Mr. Bottoms tells me you did not care to ride the mare."

That wicked little smile appeared again. "That's very true. I prefer a faster horse, and Thunder is more to my liking." As if to prove it, she buried her face in the horse's neck and glanced at Adrian from the corner of her eye.

She was a demon. "He is indeed a fine horse. However, I am concerned for your safety. Thunder is a powerful horse, and I fear you will have difficulty controlling him."

Much to his great irritation, she laughed roundly, as if that had been a perfectly absurd thing to say. "Thunder is quite easy to handle! Really, I am *surprised* at how easily he handles! One would think he is quite powerful, but he is really docile. *Very* docile."

Adrian pressed his lips together and looked heavenward for a long moment until he could speak civilly. "I assure you, he is not docile. You may ride whichever horse you please, whenever you please, but I would ask that you leave Thunder to a more experienced hand.''

The Princess's eyes narrowed as her gaze boldly swept the length of him and her hands found her waist. ''A more experienced hand. I suppose you think that is *you*?''

Adrian blinked. ''Naturally! I am a horseman, and you are a—''

''What?'' she demanded heatedly.

''A novice,'' he calmly informed her.

Something hard flashed in those green eyes, and Lilliana suddenly flung herself at him, crushing her lips to his as she wrapped her arms tightly around his neck. Stunned, Adrian stumbled backward as he grabbed her waist to steady them both.

And then she bit his lip. Adrian started to protest, but her tongue was in his mouth, painting him with light little strokes. God Almighty, he was suddenly on fire! Pure male instinct kicked in, and he crushed her to him, deepening the kiss. One hand roamed the round curve of her bottom, the slender waist, the full breasts encased in men's clothing. It was horribly seductive, and he was madly wondering how to get the trousers off her when he realized anyone passing by might think he was kissing a boy. Instantly, he broke free and hastily set her away from him.

''But might you allow me to ride him when you are with me?'' she asked breathlessly, and swept the back of her hand across her lips.

What? His blood was still pumping furiously, his eyes riveted on her breasts. ''I suppose,'' he muttered unthinkingly. He had to get out of there, quickly, before he took her on the banks of the stream. ''If you will excuse me, I really must get back. I have quite a lot of work to do.'' He moved toward Thunder, intent on trading mounts with her, but Lilliana quickly stepped in his path.

''Then I shall ride back with you. On Thunder. I shall be with you, after all, and you *did* just agree.'' She did not wait for his answer; he clamped his jaw firmly shut as she eagerly gathered Thunder's reins. Lord *God*, she was exasperating! When he silently acquiesced and moved forward to help her, she startled him again by scrambling up unaided. Sitting high atop his very own stallion—astride, naturally—she smiled down at him with a look of decided superiority. "Come on, then," she chirped, and quickly shrugged into her coat.

The Princess had duped him with a searing kiss. Muttering the things he intended to do to her under his breath, Adrian fetched the mare. Absolutely boiling that she had maneuvered him into it in full view of God and Lord knew who else, he swung up into the saddle and frowned lightly at her.

Obviously delighted, she flashed a charming smile. "Do you think you will be able to keep up?" she asked, and with a throaty little laugh suddenly spurred Thunder forward, galloping across the field at full speed. Astounded, Adrian spurred the mare forward, slapping his crop mercilessly on the horse's hindquarters. But Lilliana was too far ahead, and Thunder was too much horse for the mare. After a few minutes the mare began to labor, and growling, Adrian watched his demon-wife disappear over a hill. He cursed the mare for several minutes before finally sighing with frustration and giving up.

She had bested him. Openly, purposely, and dammit, rather artfully. He really did not have the patience for capricious feminine games, but the demon in buckskins had started it, and by God, two could play! He did not understand why she was doing her damnedest to goad him—that would require an understanding of the female brain—but he would not be goaded, never again. He had been goaded once before to the point of distraction, and it had ended in the disastrous death of his cousin.

Well, the Princess of the Grange would be the last person on the face of this earth to rattle him. She was going to have to do a lot more than cut her hair or steal his horse.

When he at last reached the stables, Lilliana was sitting on the top railing of the paddock fence, watching Mr. Bottoms unsaddle Thunder. As he trotted through the gate on the despicable mare, she laughed. *Laughed.* "Oh my, she is not terribly fast, is she?" she unabashedly observed. Mr. Bottoms looked as if he would be ill at any moment, and turned his attention fully to Thunder. A groom tentatively came toward Adrian, his steps measured and cautious. Exasperated, Adrian tossed the reins in his direction. Lilliana bounced down from her perch, wearing a brilliant smile that suddenly seemed all dimples. "Thank you again, Mr. Bottoms! I shall see you again on the morrow," she called cheerfully.

Adrian cast a dark look at the stable master. "Mr. Bottoms, Lady Albright has agreed she will not ride Thunder without my accompaniment. Isn't that so, Lilliana?" he asked with a menacing frown.

She snorted her opinion. "It is true, Mr. Bottoms," she said grudgingly, and with a pert toss of her head she blithely started for the house. Adrian quickly caught her arm, forcing her to walk with him. She wanted to play games? All right, he would play.

"Lilliana, I understand you would like to use the library," he remarked casually.

She jerked her head up; her eyes widened slightly, but she quickly recovered with a smile. "Oh yes, the table there is *perfect* for dress patterns and such. I used it this morning—I hope you don't mind, but as no one was about, I rather thought it was all right. It's very quiet, you know. One can do a lot of important work there."

Ah, so she knew very well what she had done. In spite of himself Adrian somehow managed to smile graciously. "I often use the library to work," he agreed. "It is very conducive to long periods of intense concentration." Her grin began to fade, and he silently applauded himself. Obviously, the Princess had hoped for a little more from him. "It must suit you. For your dressmaking and such," he continued. "So I shall move my things to my private study. You may feel free to use the library whenever you would like." And he would bolt the door to his study, she could count on it.

"Oh. That is very generous of you, Adrian. Very kind," she muttered. A slight frown creased her brow, and she dropped her gaze to the gravel path in front of them as they strolled toward the house. "Is there . . . is there anything *else* you would say to me?" she asked hesitantly.

There was no *end* to the things he would say to her! But habit forced him to indifference. That, and the vague discomfort that he didn't know all the rules to this particular game. "Only that whatever you would like, you need only ask. Whatever you may wish to do, I don't care—except when it comes to your safety, naturally," he said, and released her elbow.

"Naturally," she muttered, the frown deepening.

"I shall leave you to your own devices, madam. Good afternoon," he said politely, and shoving his hands in his pocket, he jogged up the terrace steps, whistling.

He was *insufferably* unflappable, Lilliana thought as she lay watching the shadows of a tree play in the moonlight that came into her room. Completely devoid of normal human sentiment! She had cut her hair, ruined his papers, and ridden about his estate in full view of his tenants dressed like a man. On his prized stallion, for heaven's sake, and *none* of it had moved him! He acted as if everything she had done today was a jolly little stroll in the woods!

She rolled to her side and closed her eyes. After weeks of trying to be like her mother, to be the wife an earl should want, she had given up. Something had to move him—to anger, to disgust; she didn't care, just as long as it was *something*. But her best attempts to provoke a reaction had failed at every turn. Even when she had eaten like a glutton at supper, he had merely smiled and said he was glad to see she had an appetite. When she had asked if she might have his untouched pudding—after devouring hers—he had pushed it toward her and had casually sipped his port, as if it were perfectly natural for her to eat her weight in pudding. *That* attempt to move him had earned her nothing but a ferocious bellyache, and because of it, she was thankful he hadn't come to her tonight.

But God help her, she missed him.

Part of her needed to feel his strong arms about her body, his weight so carefully balanced above her as he lifted her to a higher plane. Yet part of her despised him, *loathed* him for making her want it, for making her desperate for his affection. And just when she had all but succeeded in convincing herself he was an ogre, the tenants had sung their praises of him. It was obvious what he had done for them as they proudly pointed to new roofs, barns, and fences. Their praise epitomized everything she loved about him. That a man of the world, a fearless scoundrel, would care for his tenants as he did touched her somewhere deep inside.

She could not deny the truth—it was *her*. There was something about her that he found repulsive. But how could he show her such incredible passion at night without feeling at least a *little* something? A tear slipped from the corner of her eye and made its lazy path down her cheek and Lilliana squeezed her eyes tighter still. He was destroying her with his lovemaking. When he touched her, when he filled her so completely, he gave her a glimmer of hope that he might one day return her love. And then he would ruin it by leaving her alone and empty when he was finished with her body. It was a searing emptiness. Without true affection, without intimacy, she was like a fruit dying on the vine.

Lilliana swiped angrily at the wet path on her cheek. All she had ever wanted was to soar, and he had given her leave to do that. The only thing he had asked is that she not ride Thunder. She could generally wreak havoc if she wanted, and he did not give a damn, did not so much as lift that imperious brow. How terribly ironic that she finally had leave to do as she wished, but did not want her freedom. He had taken the joy out of that, too.

She hated him.

Oh God, but she really *loved* him, and it was killing her!

Adrian glanced again at his steward and frowned. Mr. Lewis had sidled over to the window at least half a dozen times now to stand on tiptoe and peer around the corner of the house. "I beg your pardon, Lewis, but may I know what you find so terribly interesting out that window?" he asked blandly as he jotted a number in a column.

Lewis glanced sheepishly over his shoulder. "The match, my lord. I hoped to see a bit of it," he admitted weakly.

"Match? What match?"

"Why, between Bertram and that groom, Roderick. Surely you have heard of The Match?" Lewis asked cautiously. When Adrian replied he had not, Lewis hesitantly explained to him what was obviously occurring, at that very moment, in the old stables: a little boxing match to settle an old score going back many years between a footman and a groom. It had to do with a woman, naturally, and as they could hardly be civil to one another, Lewis explained it was Lady Albright who had suggested the boxing match as a way to settle the argument once and for all. When Lewis finally admitted he had a few pounds riding on the outcome, Adrian wryly suggested they go see about his wager.

Given Lewis's description, he expected a little mayhem, but the sight that greeted him was astonishing. Lilliana stood in the center of the ring with the two contestants, whose hands were wrapped in shorn wool. The old stables were packed to the rafters with servants and tenants, all anxiously waiting for the contest to begin. Even Polly Dismuke was on hand, perched on a barrel in the first row, loudly proclaiming her lad would be the easy winner. More surprising was that finicky Max glared at her from across the haphazardly fashioned ring and shouted back that *his* lad would be the easy victor. Then Lilliana beckoned Mr. Baines forward—who Adrian had thought was hard at work clearing a small field on the east side of the river, and said as much to Lewis.

He would have been, Lewis responded, had Lady Albright not pleaded with him to officiate. Lewis further confided that he believed her ladyship had meant this to be a private affair, but Max and Polly's bickering about it had garnered far too much interest.

"Ladies and gentlemen, if you please!" Lilliana called, and the din lessened considerably. "Mr. Bertram and Mr. Roderick have graciously agreed to settle their dispute in a gentlemanly manner. Mr. Baines?" That man stepped forward like a king, and Lilliana quickly scampered out of the way as he reviewed the rules with the opponents. With great flourish, he began the first round.

Bertram and Roderick started off slowly, cautiously circling each other, oblivious to the cheers and jeers from the small crowd. Mrs. Dismuke, who apparently was an avid fan of boxing, leaned forward on the barrel on which she was perched, her hands braced on her knees, and shouted, "I've got a month's wages riding on you, Bertram! Get those fists up!"

Bertram was the first to throw a punch, and the crowd heaved as one toward the little ring, exclaiming at his skill. Or lack of it—he barely clipped Roderick on the shoulder. The groom's face grew quite red, and pressing his lips firmly together, he swiped at Bertram, just grazing his ear. The two men, now sporting identical murderous glares, continued circling each other. Mr. Baines rushed from side to side, carefully watching for any sign of unsporting conduct.

Bertram suddenly threw a left jab, followed quickly by a right, winging Roderick hard on the chin and shoul-

der. It stunned the groom as much as it angered him,
and all at once he was battering away at Bertram.
Adrian suppressed a smile at Lilliana's look of horror as
the two men began to whale away at one another, landing blows in the belly, the chest, the chin and shoulders,
between strangled cries of pain. The little crowd grew
frantic, all shouting at their favorite. But then Roderick
punched Bertram in the eye with his right fist, and
quickly followed it with an uppercut to the chin that
knocked Bertram backward, and the crowd caught its
breath.

Lilliana's hands flew to her mouth as the taller man
teetered unsteadily on his feet, staring in shock at
Roderick. "Excellent punch, sir," he gasped, and
promptly fell over backward, landing with a thud on the
soft earth.

And then it was pandemonium. The crowd roared,
Mrs. Dismuke leapt off her barrel shrieking at Bertram
to get up, and Roderick gasped in horror, covering his
mouth with both padded hands. Lilliana rushed to Bertram's side and fell to her knees beside Mr. Baines.

"Oh God," Bertram moaned, and gingerly opened
one eye, then the other, which was beginning to swell.
Very slowly, he moved his jaw, then touched his eye. He
gasped in horror and suddenly cried, "I concede, I concede!" Mr. Baines shot up from his crouch and turned to
the crowd. Grasping Roderick's hand, he lifted it high in
the air. "Mr. Roderick is declared the winner!"

The little crowd went wild. Lilliana tried to help Bertram into a sitting position, Mrs. Dismuke and Max
loudly argued their wager, and Roderick was hysterically explaining to anyone who would listen that he had
not really meant to hurt Bertram. And as Lilliana
searched frantically for someone to help her, she caught
sight of Adrian standing in the doorway, his arms folded
across his chest, gazing impassively at the melee.

Beside him, Lewis said sheepishly, "I rather thought
it would be an interesting match." An interesting match
indeed, Adrian thought dryly. His gaze locked with Lil-

liana's horrified one, and he lifted one brow, silently questioning her. Wincing slightly, she glanced heavenward, then quickly turned her attention to Bertram.

''See to it that the bets are paid,'' he said to Lewis, and walked out of the stables. His country mouse of a wife was not only capricious, she was a lunatic. He had not married a demure little flower as he had thought, but a menace to every man, woman, and child who lived on the Longbridge estate.

And something about that notion made him smile.

Ten

LILLIANA DECLARED AN all-out war.

She tried everything, her actions growing more outra-geous every day. It was maddening—it seemed the more she tried, the more indifferent he became. Having long surpassed the desire to please him, Lilliana now sought only a reaction. *Any* reaction.

In her sitting room, she carefully cut the crown from his best hat, thinking about the evening that she had entered the dining room wearing a drape made from a selection of his silk neckcloths. That *had* to be the most enraging. Adrian had peered suspiciously at the garment as she took her seat complaining of a draft, and for a brief moment she had thought victory was in hand.

"A draft, madam?" he asked dryly, and settled back in his chair to study her. "I had not noticed. But I sup-pose your wrap will come in quite handy," he had said, and casually motioned for the footman to begin serving.

Her first thought was that he did not realize from what her wrap had been fashioned, and had offered, "I made it myself." He graced her with the sort of kind smile one reserves for the deranged, and reached for his wineglass. Not only was he bereft of emotions, he was apparently as blind as a bat. "It took me several days to sew it," she had added testily.

"Oh? And what did you use to achieve such a . . . colorful effect?"

Lilliana shrugged. "Just a few pieces of cloth."

He sipped his wine, regarding her over the rim. "Any particular *sort* of cloth?"

"Well . . . they might have been neckcloths," she said, and had looked him straight in the eye, daring him to react.

"I see. Might they have been *my* neckcloths?" he had asked amicably.

"Might have been," she said, and smiled broadly, waiting for the reprimand, the words of indignation she so richly deserved.

"They make for an unusual design," he said simply.

Oh, what an exasperating man! "That's all?" she had asked incredulously. "But they are your *neck-cloths*!" It was undoubtedly her imagination, but she could have sworn a smile was tugging at the corner of his mouth.

"I can see that."

That was all, nothing more. Furious, she had demanded, "Aren't you even the least bit angry?"

"Of course not. I want you to have whatever makes you happy, Lilliana. Ah, the beef looks particularly good this evening," he remarked as the footman place a plate in front of him.

Lilliana stopped her work on his hat and released a sigh of great aggravation. Did *nothing* move him? Apparently not. Having failed to provoke him with the destruction of his neckcloths, she had tried to alarm him. But he did not so much as blink when she spoke of her intention to climb the highest peaks in India. He had merely lifted that intolerable brow and had remarked, "You will need a pair of sturdy shoes." When she had suggested she would like to sail to the West Indies—on a merchant ship, no less—he had chuckled. "That should prove rather amusing for the crew."

Nothing moved him.

But, oh God, he moved her.

In the darkness, he moved her to touch the stars. *"Lillie,"* he would whisper in her ear, *"hold me tight."* And his strokes would lengthen, driving her to the brink of madness before releasing her into the heavens.

Lilliana paused in her work on his hat, lifting cool fingers to her face as she recalled how, just last night, he had lain there with her in his arms for a few moments afterward, his fingers drifting idly through the curls on her head, his breath steady on her cheek. The intimacy of the moment was more moving to her than the physical lovemaking, so when he had disentangled himself from her, she had frantically grasped his arm. "Adrian," she whispered, "please stay."

Gathering her in his arms, he had lightly kissed her temple. "What is it, Lillie?"

Lilliana picked up the shears and renewed her work with a vengeance. God help her, what an *idiot* she was! Of course she had had no idea how to answer—it was such a vague feeling of distress that plagued her, a hopelessness that had no basis in any one thing. Overcome by cowardice at the last moment, she had muttered miserably, "I . . . I'm cold."

"I'm cold," she mimicked now, and rolled her eyes in frustration as she yanked the crown of the hat from the brim. He had chuckled, leaned down to kiss her, his tongue dancing languidly with hers for a moment, and then lifted his head. "I'll stir the embers for you." And he had left her, fumbling in the dark for his dressing gown. When he was through with the fire, he came back to the bed. "Sweet dreams," he murmured, and kissed her forehead then pulled the counterpane over her shoulders as he always did before disappearing soundlessly through the door.

Lilliana tossed the brim aside and stared blindly at the crown of his hat. *Sweet dreams.* Impossible. This loneliness, the emptiness she felt when he left her was killing her, eating away at her very being. Physically, he gave himself completely to her, and although she enjoyed that—her cheeks burned just thinking about how *much* she enjoyed it—it was not enough. There was no affection, no indication that he cared for her one way or another. And it certainly didn't help matters that she was such a bloody coward, unable to summon the words she so desperately wanted to say because the fear of rejection stilled her tongue. She would rather not know his touch at all than this painful emptiness.

There was no ready answer for it, and Lilliana worked diligently to transform his obliterated hat into a sewing basket. Once that was done, she discarded the stupid thing in a place he was sure to see it, and made her way to the orangery to work on the portrait of Adrian she had started two weeks ago. Restless, she quickly tired of that, and had the little mare she had named Lightning saddled. As she trotted out of the paddock she thought that life at Longbridge was no different from what she had left at Blackfield Grange.

Why in God's name had he married her?

It was that she was thinking about when she rode by the Baineses' cottage on another aimless afternoon ride. Just past the cottage, Adrian and some men were working to repair a granary. She paused, unnoticed by them. Adrian had shed his coat and waistcoat, had rolled up the sleeves and bound his thick sandy hair with a leather tie at his nape. His forearms rippled as he hammered a row of nails into a railing; perspiration stained the back of his shirt. He was built strong and hard, and Lilliana swallowed a lump of strong desire.

As she sat there watching him she heard a whimpering coming from a hut that the sheepherders sometimes used. She looked around and squealed with delight when she saw the litter of puppies in the corner of the small yard. They were yellow puppies, with legs as thick as the wood beams in the ceiling at Blackfield Grange. There were eight altogether, and they swarmed around her when she climbed down from Lightning. Lilliana went down on her haunches and scooped two of them into her arms; their paws, she noticed, were the size of her palm. They were adorable, and she smiled broadly as she buried her face in the puppy fur.

She was still beaming when she entered the terrace sitting room a little later with one particularly fat puppy close on her heels. Max's face pinched with horror. "Oh my. Oh *my*," he gasped.

"Max!" Lilliana exclaimed, giggling. "Isn't he adorable?"

"Oh milady!" Max cried as the little fellow began to dig at the edge of the expensive Aubusson carpet. "Haven't you ever noticed there are no dogs at Longbridge?" he asked frantically.

It had never occurred to her, but oddly enough, Lilliana realized she had not seen a single dog anywhere near Longbridge. She looked at Max in confusion. "I . . . I don't understand."

Max groaned.

"Please don't tell me someone has an aversion to *dogs*," she said, and laughed at the absurdity of it. But Max's wince turned into a painful grimace. "Max? Why are there no dogs at Longbridge?"

"Dear me, it's not my place, mum . . . but Mrs. Dismuke told me."

"Told you what?"

"Everything," he muttered miserably. "One of the grooms . . . oh, no matter how it came up. Mrs. Dismuke, she said Lady Kealing corresponded with her once upon a time, and I suppose it goes that when his lordship was a lad, he was quite fond of the hounds Lord Kealing kept. Had a right large kennel, and there was one pup, the runt, which the earl took a shining to. His lady mother wrote Mrs. Dismuke that he coddled that pup."

Lilliana tried to imagine a young Adrian and his dog. "I should *hope* he would like dogs!" she said, and pressed her face into the side of the fat pup she had scooped into her arms.

Max sighed sadly and shook his head. "Terrible

story, really. Lord Kealing didn't like the earl playing with those pups. Those were hunting dogs, and he told the earl he was not to play at the kennel. But Lady Kealing wrote that the runt was too small to keep up with the rest of them—had a good nose, that was all. He wasn't suited for the hunt.''

"Then Adrian kept him as a pet?" Lilliana asked uncertainly.

Max shook his head. "Apparently Lord Kealing didn't allow it. But it seems his lordship continued to go to the kennels, and took to letting the little fellow out of his pen. The two of them would explore the grounds. The pup *must* have had a good nose," Max continued, his face going red, "because he sniffed out a trap and stuck his nose where it didn't belong. Trap came down on his leg, almost severing it clean. The poor little fellow had to be put down, naturally."

"How horrible," Lilliana muttered.

"It's worse than that, milady. Mrs. Dismuke said the boy was devastated, but his papa thought to teach him a proper lesson all the same. To punish him for disobeying, the marquis dragged his lordship out to the kennels and made him watch while he shot the dog dead."

Lilliana gasped in horror and quickly set the pup free of her arms as if he were a hot coal. What sort of monster would do that to a boy?

"To this day, Lord Albright *despises* dogs," Max whispered. "Best you take it back, milady."

Lilliana did not move, unable to fathom the horror Adrian must have felt. Yet it had been many years ago— *surely* he did not fault every dog for that terrible mishap. That her husband could despise dogs for that reason broke her heart. But it also intrigued her—he must have loved that hound to be so overly sensitive now, she mused. And if anything could provoke a feeling of genuine affection in a person, it was a dog. If any one thing could make that man *feel,* it just might be a dog. "That was a long time ago," she said softly, and lifted her gaze to Max. "It is high time he overcame that tragedy, don't you think?"

Max started, his eyes rounding in shock. "Lady Albright! You *wouldn't*!" he gasped, clutching his hands to his chest.

Lilliana smiled. "Wouldn't I?" she asked sweetly.

When Adrian strolled into the gold salon, Lilliana graced him with a beguiling smile from her perch on a china silk settee in the middle of the room. "Good evening."

The demon looked rather appealing in the gown of dark blue. "Good evening," he intoned with a quick smile, and walked toward the sideboard, nodding politely to the footman. "What have we got?" he asked amicably, and surveyed the various decanters and bottles. The sound of growling caused him to turn sharply toward the room. Lilliana was still sitting, still smiling . . . but that evil little spark had appeared in her eye, the same spark he was coming to recognize as trouble. And to prove it, she suddenly leaned over her knees just as Adrian heard the growling again. A rush of uneasiness swept over him, and he walked cautiously to the collection of furniture where she sat.

The sight of the fat pup ferociously shaking a small pillow clamped firmly in his jaw caused Adrian to hastily and involuntarily step back. "What in the hell is *that*?" he asked, stupefied.

"A dog," Lilliana responded cheerfully, and with her foot nudged the pillow the little fellow was chewing on.

Adrian flushed and took another, unconscious step backward. "I can *see* that. What is it doing in here?" he demanded.

Lilliana laughed. "Fighting a big, ugly pillow, aren't you, boy?" she purred, and leaned down to scratch him behind the ears.

"Where . . ." He hesitated as the dog suddenly dropped the pillow and bounded over to a chair to sniff the legs. "Where? Where did it come from?" he asked, his voice suddenly hoarse.

"I found him while I was riding today." She glanced up, openly assessing his reaction.

Bloody hell, she was at it again! He frowned down at the pup, his mind whirling with ancient emotions and long-buried, sickening turmoil. Good God, the little beast had paws the size of tea saucers. Suddenly the dog came bounding over to him, and Adrian stumbled backward, fighting the urge to flee the beast. The pup sniffed his shoes before attempting to take one in his mouth. Adrian hastily shook him off.

"He is a water dog and his name is Hugo," Lilliana announced with great amusement. Adrian hardly heard her as he tried to move away from the dog's ardent attentions, but the pup was quite determined to have his shoe. Lilliana put a hand over her mouth in a vain attempt to keep from laughing as she slipped to her knees on the floor.

"Are you aware that this dog will grow to be the size of a horse?" Adrian demanded, and shoved at the pup. That only served to excite the little fellow, and he pounced on Adrian's foot, chewing excitedly at the tip. "He is eating my shoe!" he exclaimed gruffly. "Call him off!"

Laughing gaily, Lilliana clapped her hands. "Come here, Hugo!" she called in a singsong voice, and waved the pillow. The puppy went loping toward her, his thick legs tangling with one another at each step.

Adrian rubbed the tension from the back of his neck as he watched her scoop the puppy up and nuzzle his fur. "Do you intend to keep him?" he asked cautiously, knowing full well how stupid *that* question was.

"Why yes, of course!" she said, her eyes sparkling. "Isn't he precious?"

"That is not the word that comes to mind," Adrian muttered. "I wasn't aware you were fond of dogs."

She stopped making those silly little cooing sounds to the enormous little monster and glanced up at him.

"Actually there are many things I am fond of that you don't know. You like him, don't you? Hugo, go and greet your papa," she said, and pushed the puppy forward.

"I am most decidedly *not* his papa," Adrian growled, but he might as well have waved a bone at the little beast. The pup eagerly waddled forward and began sniffing the leg of his trousers.

Lilliana came to her feet. "You do like him, don't you Adrian?"

Hell no, he didn't like him. He despised dogs, especially little ones that chewed on his foot. He glanced warily at her through the veil of his lashes. Was it possible this beast could end the onslaught of her bizarre behavior? "I don't mind," he forced out, and gave another mighty shove to the pup. "If a dog is what you want, then of course I don't *mind*," he said, and shoved the dog away again with such force the puppy yelped.

Lilliana's bright smile quickly faded. "Hugo!" The pup, apparently unnoticing of the shoving, took a roundabout way to Lilliana's side, stopping to smell every piece of furniture on his way. She picked him up and started quickly toward the door. "Thank you," she said as she passed Adrian. "Because I very much want a dog." She walked out of the room, her face buried in Hugo's hide, and Adrian turned and strode for the sideboard, gratefully accepting the glass of whiskey the footman held out to him.

Christ Jesus, a *dog*!

That evening, he considered having the dog evicted, but assumed that would earn him some form of bizarre punishment, and convinced himself that he could live with the horror of having a dog about. After all, it wasn't as if he saw her very often. It could not be that bad.

It could be that bad.

The next afternoon he stopped dead in his tracks and blinked to make sure he wasn't seeing double. In the corridor, on the expensive carpet he had brought in from

Belgium, *two* yellow pups rolled over each other, chewing on legs and tails and ears. Lilliana suddenly appeared from the door of the library, carrying a bolt of cloth. "Oh! I didn't know you were in," she cheerfully remarked.

"Has Hugo multiplied already?" he asked dryly.

"Oh, Adrian," she laughed. "That is Hugo's sister, Maude. I have decided I should like two dogs. You know, for companionship." She flashed him a devilish smile.

Lord help him, was there no end to his punishment? "Two," he forced out.

"At *least* two!" she said, and cocked her head prettily to one side.

"In the house."

"Of course in the house! They are my *companions*," she said, as if that had not been made sufficiently clear. "Oh, you must be worried about your new carpet—well you shouldn't, because Mr. Bottoms said it will only be a matter of a week or so before they . . . well, before they can control themselves."

"Control themselves?" he asked, madly hoping that meant they would stop chewing legs of expensive walnut consoles as they were, at this very moment, doing.

Lilliana wrinkled her nose. "Before they step outside when nature calls."

With an impatient roll of his eyes, Adrian continued to his study, desperately hoping he could cope with the invasion of the little mongrels.

He survived them well enough to brave a visit to her rooms later. It had been the first visit in several nights, as he had made himself stay away, alarmed at how much he was beginning to desire the Princess of the Grange. When he entered her room, Lilliana was sleeping, and when he slipped into bed next to her, she sleepily opened her arms to him. It was a simple but seductive gesture, and Adrian took her slowly, prolonging the experience of which he was so suddenly fearful. Their lovemaking was explosive; they reached a pinnacle together, then drifted slowly downward in a rain of tender kisses.

And when he left her, he paused on the other side of her dressing room door, listening to the faint sound of her crying as he had so many nights before. He fought the urge to go back to her and gather her in his embrace until the pitiful sound of her tears had vanished. But as always, he backed away from the door, turned away, and entered his own suite.

As much as he wanted to deny it, something was happening to him, changing him.

He did not like it. Not at all.

He walked to the drink cart and poured a brandy, then settled in front of the fire, staring thoughtfully at the flames. What was changing was Lilliana, he realized, and it was having a profound effect on him. He might have seen it coming, but against his will and breaking every rule he lived by, their lovemaking was stirring something deep inside him, something that had lain dormant for many years. When he buried himself inside her, when her hips moved with his and she parted her lips to breathe him in, he sometimes felt as if their souls touched. The Grange Princess fulfilled him in a way he had never thought possible.

It had been easy to ignore her in the beginning. Other than the hour or so he spent in her bedroom at night, he thought little of the demure lass he had married. There was nothing about her that captured his imagination, other than the passion she showed him in her bed. But that was slowly changing. Impossible though it seemed, Lilliana was becoming vibrantly alive.

Whatever he had done to anger her had turned her around so completely, so totally, that he had felt like he was living with a different woman than the one he had married, one with moments of great charm and a unique enthusiasm for life that was contagious. Adrian smiled absently at the memory of her in those wonderful trousers, her gorgeous hair now a mop of curl. He thought of that devilish little light that appeared in her eyes when she attempted to goad him with the neckcloths. She had pretty, expressive eyes, something he had not really noticed before, but Lord, how he noticed them now.

And there was more—such as how the tenants adored her. How many times in the course of a single week did someone ask him with breathless eagerness when Lady Albright might ride by again? Max hung on every word she said, the cook made her pudding every night, and even stiff Mrs. Dismuke gushed around her.

Adrian felt besieged in his own house. If there wasn't some stout puppy getting underfoot, there was something else to take him by surprise. And there was laughter—constant, light, and coming from all corners of his house. Before the Grange Princess had come into his life, his servants jumped out of his way, nervously tended to him, and never uttered a word unless spoken to. They certainly never *laughed,* not until she had come and illuminated the musty old place. It was almost as if some strange light shone all around her, and drawn to it, they all lived in a pleasant state of derangement.

Yet there were times at night when he was quite certain Lilliana would never laugh again. Why did she cry herself to sleep? What was it that caused her such heartache at night? He treated her well enough—certainly better than other husbands he had witnessed through the years. She had everything she wanted, and if she did not, she had only to ask. Her life was complete as far as he could see; yet *something* made her privately miserable, despite all the gaiety she created. Despite being able to stir the deepest of longings in him.

He squirmed at that thought—such sentiments were dangerous. He did not want to feel, had spent *years* learning not to feel. The few times he had allowed himself the privilege disaster had struck. His mother, God rest her soul. Benedict. Lord God, his cousin Phillip, whose death stood as a grotesque monument to the pain his feelings brought him. The moment he allowed himself to feel was the moment disaster struck. *That* was the quality of his mercy.

Yet he *was* feeling something, and it scared him to death.

Adrian suddenly drained the snifter. Disaster would not happen here. It was his duty to see to it that their lives were kept perfectly normal, that they lived without the entanglement of needless, hurtful emotions that were neither necessary nor welcome.

He closed his eyes against a headache that was threatening to erupt. Whatever Lilliana wanted of him, whatever made her cry at night, she would eventually learn to overcome. Her youth made her fragile, and he had a responsibility to make sure some misguided feelings for him did not destroy her. And to make sure that they did not, he would do her the enormous favor of keeping a respectable distance, both figuratively and physically.

He was doing just that when he heard the crash the next morning. Frowning, he glanced at the door, hearing the distinct sounds of giant paws and tiny yelps in the corridor. With a sigh, he walked to the door and pulled it open, scowling at the detestable little creatures who were apparently oblivious of the expensive vase they had knocked from a console in their play. "Idiot runts," he muttered, ignoring the excited wagging of their tails. "Go find your mistress," he said, walking back into his study and yanking on the bellpull. He paused then to check his pocket watch against the mantel clock, not bothering to look up when the door opened, intent on setting the time of his watch. "Have someone clean that mess," he uttered.

"Yes, my lord," Max said.

"Good day, Adrian."

Adrian's head jerked up; his heart suddenly began thumping with a surge of anxiety.

Benedict.

Eleven

His HEART WAS beating erratically, but Adrian calmly snapped his pocket watch shut and slipped it into his waistcoat. "What brings you to Longbridge? Did Archie send you?" he asked casually, and glanced up at his brother.

Benedict flushed. "No!"

Adrian's brow lifted with skepticism. "Then you came to see Lilliana—"

"No!" Benedict hastily responded, his flush turning crimson. "I came to see *you*, Adrian."

He didn't believe that for a moment, and chuckled derisively. "Perhaps I should assume you covet Longbridge too?"

With an uncharacteristically icy glare, Benedict snapped, "I do not covet anything of yours, and I never have! I can hardly abide what has happened, so much so that I have come to see if we can set things right between us!"

Set things right between them? And how in God's name did he propose to do *that*? Years stood between them, years of distrust, of turmoil . . . the sound of laughter suddenly drifted into Adrian's consciousness.

Lilliana was somewhere nearby, and he suddenly and irrationally did not want her to see his brother. "Rather ambitious undertaking," he said with a shrug, and strolled to the door, feeling a strange sense of bafflement.

He had assumed he would never see Benedict again, and that was exactly how he had wanted it. The sycophant was a traitor as far as Adrian was concerned, his cowardice keeping him squarely behind Archie until he had obtained Adrian's rightful inheritance. But as he soundlessly closed the door of his study, the only thing Adrian could see was Benedict's eyes the day of the wedding. The longing as he had watched Lilliana. The unambiguous look of grief.

A pain stabbed at his eyes. "Shall I fetch you a drink? A brandy perhaps?" Adrian offered.

"Whiskey," Benedict muttered.

Silently, Adrian moved to the sideboard and poured two very stout whiskeys. He handed one to Benedict, who took it uncertainly. "Adrian, please believe me. What Father did . . . I had no prior knowledge of it. It surprised me as much as it did you."

Adrian smiled thinly. "Do you honestly expect me to believe that?" he asked, and lifting his glass in a mock toast, gulped a mouthful of whiskey, hoping the burn would dull the pain in his head.

"It is so!" Benedict blustered impatiently. "How could I have known? Father was in London and I was at the Park. I did not know about Phillip—"

"Phillip's death," Adrian interjected impassionedly, "had little to do with it, Benedict. Archie has contrived for years to do what he did. You know that."

Benedict blinked and shifted his gaze to the whiskey he held, staring into the small glass for a long moment before swigging a mouthful. "Nonetheless, it was Phillip's death at your hand that drove him to it," he muttered hoarsely.

Phillip's death at his hand—how succinctly put, Adrian mused, and turned to the sideboard for more whiskey.

"Bloody hell, I had not meant to start this way, I swear it," Benedict groaned. "You must believe that I want only to make amends. I know there is much between you and Father—I don't know why, I have *never* known why! But . . . but I am not a party to it. I am helpless to affect the situation, and as you say, he was bound and determined. I cannot change what he did, but it doesn't alter my feelings for you!"

Adrian stood with his back to Benedict, pouring another whiskey and quietly absorbing each word like a knife in his back. "Your feelings for me?" he asked, and turned slowly, eyeing his brother with disdain. "Your *feelings* for me were decidedly absent that morning at the Park."

"I was as stunned as you were," Benedict said meekly.

Benedict was a liar. He had known before Adrian ever stepped foot in that library what Archie had done. Adrian strolled to his desk where he absently and blindly sifted through a stack of papers. Benedict had damn well known. But . . . what could he have done? What could one weak-willed man have done?

"I scarcely believed it," Benedict continued raggedly. "I *still* cannot believe it. So many times I have tried to understand, but I see no reason for his disdain. It is as it has always been . . . unwavering. And unfounded. I have no idea why—"

"Have you ever asked him?" Adrian asked quietly.

A palpable tension filled the room; silence stretched between them as Adrian nonchalantly flipped through the papers. "No," Benedict mumbled at last. "Have you?"

Adrian briefly considered telling his brother the truth, but to do so would denigrate his mother. Moreover, it would allow Benedict to know the true power he held over him. He shrugged carelessly and sipped his whiskey.

Benedict sighed. "Whatever his reasoning, it is not fair. And I tried, I swear to you I *tried* to make him understand that you are . . . I have tried to make him see you as I do,'' he said wearily, and Adrian heard him put the glass down and move toward him. ''I have admired you since I was a lad, Adrian, and the thought of a permanent estrangement between us is not to be borne.''

Staring blindly at the desk, Adrian did not for a moment believe the words he was hearing, yet he could see nothing but the pain on Benedict's face at the wedding. And then, as was inevitable, the pain on Phillip's face in death. Phillip had admired him too. And he had let both men down.

The pain in his head was excruciating. Adrian closed his eyes tightly shut against the images and downed the second glass of whiskey. Whatever Benedict was, he was not, in all fairness, Archie. Adrian's sole complaint against his brother was that he had taken his father's side in a monumental battle of wills. And for that, Adrian had struck back by marrying Lilliana. How contemptible it all seemed now. ''I am sorry about Lilliana,'' he said suddenly, surprised that the secret sentiment should somehow find its way to his tongue.

''Lilliana?'' Benedict said uncertainly.

Adrian turned to face him, expressionless. ''I am sorry if I caused you any hurt by marrying her,'' he said simply.

Benedict's face darkened, and he suddenly focused on the cuff of his shirt, straightening it to perfection. ''You didn't hurt me,'' he snorted. ''I never harbored any real affection for her. She just seemed the sort to make a good wife. She was nothing to me.''

Liar. Even now, fidgeting with his cuff as he was, Adrian could read much into the firm set of his brother's mouth—he had held her in great esteem.

And naturally, the object of his esteem should choose that inopportune time to poke her head in the library. ''Adrian?'' She gasped upon seeing Benedict, and suddenly sailed through, the two mongrels close behind. *''Benedict!''* she cried. For a moment Adrian thought she would fling herself into his brother's arms, and gritted his teeth. But she stopped just short, grabbing Benedict's hand and gracing him with a gorgeous dimpled smile.

Benedict caught her elbow as he kicked at one of the dogs that had sprung up on his hind legs and planted two soggy paws on his trouser leg. "Lilliana, how good to see you," he exclaimed, turning his attention to her fully when the pups spied Adrian and came loping forward. For once, Adrian hardly noticed the insufferable little creatures. "You look radiant," Benedict was saying, and smiled at her like a simpleton. *She was nothing, eh, Benedict?* Only a blind man could not see how he adored her.

Lilliana's eyes danced with laughter. "Did you come alone? Are you to stay on awhile? I must hear all the news! I had a letter from Caroline, and she fears—"

"You may tell your sister that Mr. Feather eagerly awaits her return! I daresay he will never give up!" Benedict said, smiling.

"Oh, how *charming*. I hope Papa relents. He calls him Mr. Featherbrain, you know," Lilliana said, pulling Benedict to a settee. "And have you heard from Tom? He has written only once since I left!"

"Tom is quite content in Bath. Now if only someone would explain that to Miss Mary Davis," Benedict laughingly responded.

"No!" Lilliana exclaimed. "Oh, you must tell me everything!"

And Benedict eagerly began to relate what had transpired at some country dance, puffing up like a rooster every time she smiled—which was often. Lilliana anxiously sat forward, hanging on every word he uttered as the pups collapsed at her feet to have their midday wash.

An extraordinary feeling of distress swept over Adrian as he watched them. He had kept them apart, two people who clearly deserved each other. He had not seen such joy on Lilliana's face since—

The surprising pang of jealousy roiled through his belly, and he clamped his jaw firmly shut. *Unbelievable!*

He had to be mad to feel any jealousy! Was this the quality of his mercy—the guilt, the jealousy, the lifetime of knowing he had caused another being unnecessary pain? His headache was beginning to blind him now, and he started for the door, glad to let the two of them ramble on about people he did not know or want to know, events he could not care less about.

"Adrian?" Lilliana's voice stopped him. "Please sit with us! Surely you want to hear all the news?" she asked anxiously.

Adrian glanced at Benedict. "I rather think he shall be here for a few days, won't you, Ben? Enjoy your chat. I will catch up with him later," he said, and walked out of the door before the pain in his head brought him to his knees.

A few days quickly turned into a week; Benedict showed no sign of leaving. As Adrian watched his brother escort his wife to the orangery one morning, he knew he had nothing to complain of, really. Benedict had been on his best behavior, and from all outward appearances, he genuinely seemed to desire reconciliation between them. He was exceedingly respectful of Lilliana—and she certainly seemed to enjoy his company.

Adrian could hardly look at the two of them without feeling the burden of his enormous guilt. Somehow, Benedict and Phillip had joined together in his mind, both painful reminders of his failures. And Lilliana—even years of studied practice at suppressing emotion could not keep him from the oppressive distress he felt about her any longer. If by some miracle she did not cry when he left her at night, he was made miserable by the knowledge that the man who might have made her happy was in his house. He found himself sullenly wondering if she might have shown Benedict the same stark passion, if she might have released *him* to the heavens with her lovemaking.

Adrian watched the two of them bundled up against

the late winter chill, walking side by side. Benedict walked with his face tilted toward her as if what she had to say was the most fascinating thing on earth. It was too late for them now. He had created this hell for all of them, and there was nothing that could be done for it.

But work.

Adrian was not the only one wondering how long Benedict would be at Longbridge. Lilliana surreptitiously watched her brother-in-law stroll about the orangery, admiring the many paintings she had hung there. His constant presence was beginning to grate on her; there seemed no place she could go to be away from him—or his quips about Adrian.

"Your talent is remarkable, Lilliana," he said.

Uncomplimentary little quips, she thought, and smiled sheepishly as she donned her apron. "You mustn't flatter me, Benedict."

"I do not flatter you! You really are very talented!" he insisted, and pivoted, looking at her curiously. "There is so much about you that is unique. I marvel at it."

Lilliana laughed and sheepishly turned to study the canvas in front of her.

"Ah, this is particularly lovely," Benedict said, and pointed to a painting of the river that ran through Longbridge. "Such talent, Lilliana. But surely Adrian tells you so all the time."

A queasiness in the pit of her belly rose up, the same queasiness she felt every time Benedict mentioned Adrian. It was as if she were playing a part in some strange little play, a role in which she must pretend all was well with her husband because she was desperate that Benedict not discover the truth. If he knew how unimportant she was in her own household, he would certainly tell Tom, if not her parents. How long would it be before the entire parish knew the Rogue could scarcely tolerate her? The sting of humiliation began to creep up her neck.

"Surely he has said as much!" he insisted.

Lilliana forced a cheerful laugh. "Adrian is rather busy with his work."

Benedict crossed the room to stand at her canvas. "He hasn't, has he?"

She shrugged and picked up her brush. How could he? He had never so much as stepped foot in the orangery, and Lord knew he paid no attention to the paintings she had hung in his study. "He's really not very interested in art," she said, dipping her brush onto her pallet.

"Yes, he is. He has one of the finest collections in London," Benedict said abruptly.

The queasiness roiled up into her chest. "Well," she said lightly, "I paint only for the pleasure of it."

"Oh, God," Benedict groaned. "I was afraid of this!" He suddenly came down on one knee beside her, grasping her wrist. "He's made you unhappy, hasn't he? Don't deny it—it's painfully obvious."

"Benedict!" she said, and forcing a smile, tried to wrench her wrist free of his grip. "You have no idea what you are saying!"

Benedict held fast. "Oh, but I do. I've seen the two of you, and I know what sort of man he is! If he truly held you in the highest regard, he would not . . . you *know* what I am saying, don't you?"

She had absolutely no idea what he was saying! "Know what? He is rather occupied with his work, that's all."

Benedict frowned down at her hand for a moment. "He is rather distant, even *I* can see it. I shouldn't be the one to tell you, but I feel . . . oh hell! Lilliana, *think*! Has he been away from you for any length of time? At night? Has he made any trips or received any correspondence he did not want you—"

"I beg your pardon?" she asked, her forced smile

fading with her confusion. "Adrian is working very hard to make repairs to Longbridge."

"Of course," Benedict said, with such a piteous smile that she wanted to strike it from his face. "It is Longbridge he devotes his attention to during those evenings he cannot even take the time to dine with you."

Lilliana suddenly understood his implication and it jolted her. She surged upward from the little bench and jerked free of Benedict. "I don't know what you are attempting to imply, my lord, but it is none of your concern! Everything is quite *fine*!"

Benedict rose slowly. "Do you honestly want me to believe that?" he asked softly.

Mortified, Lilliana yanked at the ties of her smock. "I don't know what you believe, but I would thank you to keep your thoughts to yourself! They are unwelcome!" she snapped as she discarded the smock. With a heated glare, she moved quickly to retrieve her cloak.

"I only want your happiness, Lilliana, it's all I have ever wanted!" Benedict insisted earnestly. "Don't you know I will help you with everything in my power? If he cannot bring himself to care for you, if he must turn his attentions elsewhere—"

"Stop it!" she cried. "How *dare* you insinuate yourself into my marriage? For God's sake, Benedict, if you are still angry with me for marrying him, then say so! But please do not be cruel!"

Benedict immediately came forward, grabbing her cloak even though she tried to slap his hand away, and held it up so she could slip into it. "I could never be cruel to you. I am so sorry, so *very* sorry for you, don't you see that? You cannot hide from me, Lilliana, I know you too well. I know you both too well, and I can plainly see what you will not admit. I cannot bear to see how he is hurting you with his indiscretion!"

Lilliana lurched away from him and jerked the door open without looking back, flying across the lawn to the house, frantic to be away from him and his lies. Stumbling up a narrow servants' staircase, she made her way to her rooms, bolted the door behind her, and fell onto her bed.

He *knew*! God help her, it was so bloody obvious— Benedict had already surmised that Adrian despised her! The tiny thread of hope she had so stubbornly clung to in the last weeks, the hope that Adrian would grow to accept her, had vanished in the orangery when Benedict suggested there was another.

Her heart constricted painfully, and she gasped for air. There was no *other*! How could there be? He had not left Longbridge! *But he is gone every day, all day*. "Longbridge is *huge*!" she sobbed. And there were many cottages and houses occupied by dozens of tenants, and little villages nearby, and public houses and inns— plenty of opportunity for a man who was a celebrated womanizer.

Oh, Lord, how could she be so angry with Benedict when she had wondered the very same thing about him? Such doubts and fears were not new, but to hear them voiced aloud by another . . .

She suddenly pounded her fist into the bed. She would not accept it! She would *not* believe it!

She believed it.

Adrian was lost to her.

Honestly, as if he had ever been hers to lose! Lilliana gulped down a sob and hit the bed again and again, fighting to keep the awful truth from burying her.

She did not attend supper that evening, but sent a note to Adrian saying she had a sick headache. No one questioned her, no one came to see after her, except Polly, whom she managed to anger by refusing the soup she brought. Polly clucked her tongue disapprovingly and said sharply, "The Albright girls were just the same, you know. Would get some bee in their bonnet and not eat a bite."

Lilliana was too miserable to care what the Albright girls did or did not do. Her life looked terribly bleak— was she to be shut away at Longbridge for the rest of her life, longing for him while she endured his disdain? The attempt to accept her loveless fate was excruciatingly difficult—but not nearly as difficult as the thought that he would come to her tonight, make her love him all over again, then leave her so that the cold emptiness could creep into her soul until she was mad with it.

Well, she would rather be dead than know pleasure at his hand. She was nothing more than a vessel to him, a piece of flesh on which he might get a son. He was indifferent to all else, and by God, so should she be.

Adrian did not realize that he might actually miss the company of the Grange Princess until he was forced to dine with Benedict alone. The dining room seemed unusually large and quiet without her bubbling laughter or eager discussion of which pudding the cook was sure to have made. Benedict seemed to notice it, too, and the first course passed in awkward silence as the two brothers consumed their wine as if they had thirsted in a desert. By the time the third course was served, the wine had eased the tension between them somewhat.

"Honestly, I have never known you to stay in one place for so long," Benedict said amicably through a mouthful of fish.

Adrian shrugged. "There is a lot of work to be done at Longbridge."

"But don't you yearn even a bit for London? The Rogues and all that?"

Another painful reminder of Phillip, which Benedict innocently managed rather frequently. "Not at all," Adrian lied. "However, I am going in a day or so to see after a few things." An idea that had come to him just today, actually.

"Then I suppose you'll be introducing Lilliana around?" Benedict asked, almost hopefully. "High time London saw the sort of woman Albright would take as a wife."

Adrian glanced at him. Was it his imagination, or did Benedict's eyes take on a peculiar little glint? "I think not this time. I should be no more than a day or two. The trip would be too hard on her," he said carefully.

Benedict nodded as he reached for his wineglass. "Traveling with a woman is a bit like torture, isn't it? I shouldn't blame you."

"Indeed?" Adrian drawled, eyeing his brother curiously.

Benedict chuckled. "I have hardly lived the life of a monk, Adrian. Granted, my exploits are fewer in number and far less entertaining than yours, but I am a man after all."

How strange, Adrian thought absently, that he really did not know what sort of life Benedict lived. He really didn't know his brother at all. He had always assumed he was a pasty country squire, dabbling with his garden and dining with Archie at precisely nine o'clock each evening. A mollycoddle, more in need of creature comforts than he would ever imagine a woman needing.

"This is excellent news, by the by, for I, too, am to London. We could travel together," Benedict said, and turned to look at Adrian.

Fabulous. The only reason Adrian had offered his plans was in the hope that Benedict might at last leave Longbridge. "You've a coach here. I intend to travel on horseback—"

"Of course! I shall ride with you and return for my coach."

"It is a half day's hard ride from Kealing Park," Adrian reminded him.

Benedict snorted. "What of it? It is not so far out of the way, really. Come on, then, Adrian. It will be entertaining, just the two of us. Remember when we were packed off to Eton together?"

He remembered all right. But Benedict was not that impish little boy anymore, and had not been for a very long time.

Benedict suddenly laughed. "God, Adrian, do you despise me so much?" he asked, but his eyes definitely belied the light laughter.

"No, Ben, of course not," Adrian quickly answered. Truly, he didn't *despise* him—he could not even, in good conscience, hold him partly responsible for Archie's madness. It was just that he wished Benedict could have been more of a man. That was it, wasn't it, the true root of his discomfort with him? Benedict's smile faded, and Adrian quickly agreed. "We may travel together if you like, naturally." Benedict smiled again, and Adrian ignored the feeling of uneasiness it gave him.

He declined his brother's offer to play chess, citing his own headache. That was true enough; a dull, bothersome headache had been with him since Benedict had first appeared at Longbridge. But there was more, he grudgingly admitted to himself as he climbed the stairs.

He wanted to see Lilliana. He wanted to run his fingers through that mess of blond curl, to look into those gray-green eyes as he plunged into her warmth.

Fortunately, Lilliana had not gone to sleep. She was sitting at her vanity in the glow of a single candle, looking at some paper when he came into the room. She did not look up, as if she had not heard him.

"How are you feeling?" he asked as he strolled into the room.

"Fine, thank you," she muttered, and still she did not look up, did not grace him with that smile she seemed to flash at Benedict at every turn.

He walked to where she sat and put his hands on her shoulder, peering at her reflection in the mirror over the top of her head. "What are you reading?"

"A letter from Caroline."

He bent to nuzzle her neck. Lilliana squirmed as he flicked his tongue across her earlobe. "We missed you at supper," he murmured. He got no response to that. Wordlessly, she folded the paper and slipped it under her jewelry box, then folded her hands primly in her lap. Mildly surprised, Adrian lifted his head—she was usually eager for his caress. His hand drifted down from her shoulder to cup her breast, but Lilliana did not move.

Adrian frowned at her reflection. "Madam, do I detect a bit of unwillingness?" he asked bluntly.

"I am your wife. I would never be unwilling."

And what in the hell was *that* supposed to mean? Adrian abruptly stepped away and shoved a hand through his hair. "Not the most charming thing you have ever said," he muttered irritably.

She turned to look at him, her eyes oddly vacant. Slowly, she rose from the bench—in the soft candlelight the white silk wrapper she wore gave the illusion of a mist rising on the lake. Her eyes locked on his, never leaving him as she walked to the bed. Mildly confused, Adrian wondered if she was playing some sort of game with him. Hesitantly he followed her, drawing up short when she untied the wrapper and let it fall to the floor. She did not speak, just stood there looking at him with that oddly vacant expression.

Completely naked.

Lord God, but the woman had a sumptuous body. His gaze hungrily roamed the smooth slope of her shoulders, the ripe fullness of her breasts and the dark, rigid peaks, the slender waist flaring into softly rounded hips, the golden triangle of curls between her legs. She had never done this—she stood before him without artifice, allowing him to feast on her feminine curves at his leisure. It wouldn't be long; his arousal was swift and hard, jutting against his trousers.

A lazy smile spread across his lips. "Is this an invitation, madam? If so, it is one I cannot refuse," he drawled, and quickly shrugged out of his waistcoat and shirt. He gathered her in his arms, crushing her lithe body into his hard one, pressing his erection against the soft flesh of her belly as he caressed the curve of her spine. He devoured her neck, moving eagerly to her mouth as he eased her onto the bed. His lips moved roughly over hers, tasting them, feeling the softly plump flesh against his teeth. Desire spread uncontrollably, clouding his brain. It wasn't until he thrust his tongue in her mouth that he realized she was not responding.

He lifted his head. "Hold me, Lillie," he whispered urgently, then claimed her mouth again, forcing his tongue past her lips. He allowed himself the pleasure of languishing there as his hands roamed her body, skating the peaks and valleys, savoring the incredible softness of a woman's body that penetrated the most hardened of his senses.

Until he understood he was the only one enjoying this dance.

Hell, he was the only one *participating*! He came up on his elbows, peering down at her with a frown of great exasperation. Lilliana's eyes narrowed slightly as she returned his gaze.

It was so unlike her. All right, all right, he barely knew what she was like anymore, but that was out *there*, beyond these walls. In *here*, he knew her very well, and this . . . this was so unlike her that it sent a strange shiver down his spine. Slowly he pushed himself up and sat back on his heels, his eyes angrily demanding an explanation.

Lilliana responded, all right. Her gaze never wavered as she slowly snaked her arms out perpendicular to her body and then spread her legs wide.

Like a whore.

Adrian exploded. He slapped at one knee as he came off the bed. "What in the hell do you think you are doing?" he roared.

"It's what you want, isn't it?"

Insulted, he shoved her legs together. "It's disgusting! Stop it at once!"

"I offer my body for your pleasure, like any wife should."

Her words angered him beyond comprehension. He grabbed her wrist and jerked her upright. "You would that I feel like a monster? Because you have succeeded, madam," he breathed.

"I would that you *feel*," she responded softly, and all at once, her eyes were glistening with goddamned tears.

In a moment of panic, Adrian shoved her away.

"What is it you want, Lilliana? What in God's name do you want of me?" he demanded hoarsely.

One tear slid haphazardly down her cheek. "I want your attention!" she said on a ragged breath.

She had lost her bloody mind. "You *have* it! Completely and undivided!" he snapped. Lilliana blinked, and more tears rolled down her face as she gazed up at him. "Well? What do you want *now*, Lady Albright?" he demanded. Her silence sparked a fit of fury in him, and he suddenly launched himself at her, toppling her onto her back, then roughly parted her thighs with his hands. He shoved himself between them as he fumbled with his trousers. His erection was dangerously tantalized when the swollen tip sprang free against the moist lips of her sex. "Is this what you want? You want me to take you like a common whore? Is *that* the kind of attention you want?" he muttered, and thrust hard into her.

Lilliana struggled beneath him, trying to push him off, but he easily caught her arms and pinned them above her head with one hand. "You want my attention, Lillie, you have it," he breathed into her neck. His mouth found her breast, and he laved the hardened nipple, catching it in his teeth, rolling it between his lips. With his free hand, he stroked her where they were joined, swirling around and over the tiny core of her pleasure. He heard her moan from somewhere deep inside, and slowly, he began to move.

He plunged deep inside her, thrusting harder with each stroke. In a frenzied attempt to reach the very core of her, he lifted her by the waist while he devoured her breasts with his mouth. He rode her until she was writhing uncontrollably beneath him, her hips thrusting upward to meet every onslaught. He denied his fulfillment until he could bear it no more, fearing he might literally explode.

And when she convulsed around him, crying his name, he released himself into her with white-hot fury, pumping his seed somewhere deep inside. Twice. Three times.

The fury ebbed slowly, and Adrian buried his face in the valley between her breasts as he released her hands. And still she did not touch him. He could not have imagined that it would affect him so, but the absence of her touch crushed him. He waited for what seemed an eternity, but she lay limply beneath him, her arms once again spread wide on the bed. At last he rolled away in disgust, off the bed, and hitched his trousers up, feeling very much as if he had tumbled a tavern wench in some dark alley.

"Was that attention enough for you?" he asked bitterly as he retrieved his waistcoat, and glanced at her over his shoulder. She was curled into a ball, her head turned where he could not see her face. He almost hated her at that moment. Or himself. He really didn't know which of them he loathed more. "Jesus, what is wrong with you? Can't you answer me?" he demanded hopelessly.

She gave him no response; his heart lurched and the fury took hold again, refreshed by her silence. "Perhaps you need time to think about what it is you want so desperately that you would treat this union like some dockside assignation! So help me, Lilliana, if you ever treat our marriage bed like you did tonight, I cannot be responsible for my actions, you may depend on it."

The Princess did not so much as move. Adrian turned and strode out of her room, his heart leaden in his throat.

Twelve

Standing in the master suite of his London townhouse, Adrian stared out the window at the dreary, mist-filled night, reminding himself for the hundredth time it was just as well that he had left immediately for London. It was just as well because if he had seen her before he left, she might have provoked him to murder, and God knew he was capable. The more he dwelled on that extraordinary episode in her bed, the more unsettled he became.

Dammit, but guilt had returned in full force and was exacting its recompense.

He deserved it—he had taken her in a moment of anger, a sickening realization. It didn't matter that she had reached her fulfillment, crying out his name as he had rammed into her. It did not change the fact that he had taken his wife like a wench, spilling his anger deep in her womb in a shattering climax.

Sighing wearily, he turned from the window. The worst was that he had not been able to stop thinking about her. This quiet despondency was making him believe that he was at last slipping into madness. He had to be—only a madman would feel the extraordinary pangs of longing after an experience like that. This, he thought miserably, was the continuing evolution of the quality of his mercy—he was captivated by a lunatic.

God help him.

He picked up the note he had received this afternoon. Arthur had heard he was in town from one of his solicitors; he and Kettering were to the exclusive Tam O'Shanter for a round of cards, the note said. Did Adrian care to join them?

Did he? Adrian had not seen the Rogues since the terrible events at Dunwoody, and he was loath to renew that painful memory on top of everything else. But he was in dire need of an escape from Benedict, and the Tam O'Shanter was one of those exclusive clubs where men like his brother rarely ventured. A wry smile snaked across Adrian's lips. The Rogues had given the out-of-the-way Regent Street club its exclusivity, having discovered it was a haven from the mindless routs and balls, angry fathers and incensed lovers.

In a moment of decisiveness, he tossed the note aside, picked up his gloves, and headed for the Tam O'Shanter.

Arthur Christian knew Adrian was not himself the moment he appeared at the door of the Tam O'Shanter. Immediately surrounded by those who had not seen him since the infamous incident at Dunwoody, he greeted them with a lopsided smile and a faint shrug of the shoulders that suggested nothing affected him. Just like the old Albright might have done.

But having known Adrian for more than twenty years now, Arthur could see he was not the same old Albright. Something had definitely affected him—his eyes were hollow and dark, his bronzed skin oddly pale. *Phillip,* Arthur thought wearily.

"I told you." Arthur glanced at Julian, whose long legs stretched in front of their corner table, his eyes narrowed above his frown as he watched Adrian. "The fool will never forgive himself, will he?"

Wordlessly, Arthur shifted his gaze toward Adrian again just as Fitzhugh clapped him on the shoulder as if he was the prodigal son returning home. "You look well, Albright, indeed you do! Marriage agrees with you!" he boomed cheerfully, and unconsciously adjusted his coat around his goddammed prized pistol. The man was an idiot.

"It suits me as well as any, I should think. If you will excuse me, Fitzhugh, I've come to divest Kettering of all his money." With that, Adrian effortlessly broke away from the men gathered around him and sauntered toward the Rogues' corner table.

"Speaking of marriage," Julian drawled as Adrian approached, "you might have mentioned it to a body."

A faint smile appeared on Adrian's lips as he dropped into a leather chair. "It all happened rather quickly," he said casually, and signaled a footman.

"I suppose as those things go, it's better that it go quickly if it must go at all," Julian responded with a grin. "But next time you are thinking of doing something so terribly rash, do give a fellow an opportunity to talk some sense into you. Where is the lovely little countess, by the by?"

"Longbridge. I've only come to Town for a day or so."

"So," Arthur said, "you've gone and done it, have you? And where did you find our Lady Albright? Or did I somehow miss your tale of sweet love?"

Adrian snorted. "Quite the romantic, aren't you, Christian?" he muttered, and lifted the snifter the footman deposited on the table, actually beating Julian to it, which in itself was quite a feat. "Lilliana Dashell hails from Newhall, near the Park," he offered after swallowing a mouthful of brandy. "Her family has been known to mine for years."

Known to his family indeed! For a man who had never claimed a particular attachment to any woman, Adrian's sudden plunge into matrimony was nothing short of extraordinary. "Seemed rather sudden," Arthur remarked. "You never breathed a word of your intent."

Adrian merely shrugged. "My intent? Isn't it inevitably every man's intent?"

"Hell no," Julian responded flatly.

Adrian shot him a cool glance. "Personally, I saw no point in waiting. It wasn't as if she was going to make herself any better known to me in the course of some rustic courting ritual."

That caused Julian to snort with delight. "Good God, did you know her a*'tall?*"

Adrian did not answer immediately, but glanced about the room, nodding to an acquaintance who caught his eye. "I can't say that I did." He frowned lightly. "Can't say that it would have mattered, either."

Ah, so it wasn't Phillip who'd put that look in his eye, Arthur thought, and was oddly relieved. This woman, whoever she was, had done it. But what *woman* could affect Adrian Spence? He had always been so smooth with the ladies, preferring Madam Farantino's stable to a mistress or debutante. It was easier that way, he had said, no complications. But God, Arthur had never seen a man look quite so miserable, with the sole exception of his brother Alex. But he had been—

He suddenly leaned back and gaped at Adrian.

He *had* seen that look before, on Alex, when he had ended his long-standing engagement to Marlaine Reese. Because he loved Lauren Hill—desperately, completely, and to the point of throwing away everything he had ever been. Alex had worn that exact same look during those dark hours when he could not fathom the depth of his feelings for her. Mother, Mary and Joseph, was it possible that *Adrian* . . . ?

No. Absolutely not. Not Adrian Spence, of all men. Not *this* Rogue. Albright needed no one! But it *was* that look—God help him but Arthur knew that look.

Adrian scowled at Arthur's strange grin. He was beginning to feel a little like a circus oddity; old friends peered curiously at him, as if trying to see from what well the insanity had sprung the day he had killed Phillip. Lords Dwyer and Parker, both of whom had been in attendance that day, kept stealing glimpses of him from over the tops of their cards, and Arthur and Julian kept observing him as if they expected him to *do* something. Honestly, he was on the verge of assuring the entire room that he had not killed anyone recently.

Instead, he asked Julian how his sisters fared, then tried to look interested, ignoring the looks in his direction as Julian ranted about one very pregnant and very emotional sister between several snifters of brandy. He tried to ignore Arthur, who kept staring at him as if he was desperate to ask something. He tried not to think of Lilliana, or the discomfort of being here without Phillip, or the gnawing guilt at having avoided his brother so he would not be forced to invite him along. It took three snifters of brandy and an expensive cheroot provided by Julian before he finally began to relax a little.

But Julian grew increasingly restless the further he fell into his cups. In the middle of some convoluted story, he suddenly muttered, "What in God's name is everyone looking at?" Clearly irritated, he glanced over his shoulder at a group of men who had cast several furtive glances in their direction.

Arthur grinned around a cheroot clamped firmly between his teeth. "That is the fourth time you have asked, Kettering."

"It's rather irksome," Julian growled. "I don't care to be watched so closely."

"You've had too much to drink, my friend. There is no one watching you."

"Well they certainly aren't watching *you*," Julian countered, glaring at Arthur.

"They are looking for Phillip," Adrian said blandly. When his companions swung startled gazes to him, he shrugged. "It will never be the same for us, and they know it. Once there were four, now there are three, and one of us is responsible for the reduction in our number."

His words had the same, instant effect as a bucket of cold water. Julian snubbed his cheroot dead with a snort of disgust and leaned back. "You can't go on punishing yourself, you know," he said as he tried to fit a hand in the waist of his trousers. "Bloody well time you stopped dwelling on it if you ask me. It was a goddamned accident."

` "Is that so?" Adrian asked with more bitterness than he intended. "Thank you, Lord Kettering, but as it was *I* who killed one of our dearest friends, I find it rather impossible to stop thinking about it. Forgive me if that annoys you."

"It not only annoys me, it infuriates me," Julian snapped. "On my honor, if we've told you once, we've told you a thousand times. You didn't *kill* him precisely—"

"What precisely would you call it?" Adrian shot back, and shook his head. "I don't know why I am bothering . . . just look at you, soaked to the gills. You're just like him—"

With a start, Julian came forward, and so did Adrian. Arthur quickly inserted himself between them and held up his hands. "Please God, can we never put it behind us? Look here, Albright, Phillip wanted to die. He chose a vile way to do it, but he *wanted* to die. Yes, yes, I know you reject that theory," he said quickly as Adrian opened his mouth to deny it. "But no one else does. He was determined, and if you hadn't done it, one of us would have before he gunned you down in cold blood. He killed *himself*. You happened to be the unfortunate method he chose to do it."

Adrian looked from Arthur to Julian, both glaring at him, daring him to disagree. There was no point in dredging up the fact that Phillip would not have gunned him down, that he had shot well over his head and had not even *cocked* the second hammer. They would believe what they wanted, cope as best they knew how. But he knew. Lord God, he knew deep in his soul that Phillip would not have shot him.

His head was suddenly pounding.

"Yes, Arthur, Phillip killed himself before he ever arrived at Dunwoody," Adrian muttered as he rubbed his forehead. "And we can only blame ourselves for it. If even one of us had understood his course of self-destruction, it might never have ended like that. I didn't pay him heed, you know. I turned a blind eye."

"The same could be said for all of us," Arthur said wearily. "God knows how often I have lain awake at night, knowing that I might have prevented it—"

"Do you lay awake, Arthur?" Julian snidely interrupted, and gave them both an impatient look. "Well I *did* pay him heed. I saw everything, every bloody self-destructive act, and yet I didn't do enough to help him. Can you imagine how that feels? I *let* him fall," he snapped.

Yes, one of them had fallen hard, Adrian thought bitterly, and he'd be damned to eternal hell if he let another one fall. He glanced at Julian's empty glass; he had drained several more snifters than his companions had, and it made Adrian angry. It was so like Phillip! Looking for a solution to his grief in a bottle! Adrian lifted his gaze to Julian, who had turned his attention to the back of the room, in search of a footman. "You drink like a fish. Just like Phillip did," he snapped, nodding his head toward the empty glass.

With a groan, Julian threw up his hands. "Thank you, but I don't recall inviting any one of my sisters to join us. So I've had a few brandies!" he blustered angrily. "Don't worry about me, Albright. I am not in debt, I do not want to *die,* and I am quite capable of walking away from it!"

"Perhaps, but I would be vastly relieved if I thought you could pass a single day without drowning your guilt in whiskey," Arthur interjected, which earned him a look of indignation from Julian. "You, too, Adrian," he continued, undaunted. "Between the two of you, I'm not sure who is more worrisome."

"Me?" Adrian fairly shouted.

Arthur calmly nodded his head. "You cannot deny that something is eating away at you. You look like hell, man."

"How very kind of you." Adrian snorted with exasperation. "But at least I am not tearfully sentimental. You, on the other hand, rather *do* sound like one of Kettering's sisters!"

Resentment flashed in Arthur's eyes. "Well, forgive me for the unpardonable sin of caring about the two of you. But I look at Julian, who is well into his cups more often than not, and you, looking rather desolate, and I know that *I* have not had a decent night's sleep since Phillip died! I know if I had paid him more heed, if I hadn't shut my eyes to what was happening, he might bloody well be here tonight, begging us to accompany him to Madam Farantino's!" he exclaimed loudly.

A stunned hush fell over the table as several heads swiveled to see what the commotion was about. An awkward silence fell between them; Arthur shifted uncomfortably, and Julian twisted about in his chair, now apparently desperate for a footman. Adrian winced; the last thing he wanted to talk about was *this,* especially with his head pounding like a drum. But Arthur was right, and he bloody well knew it. They had lost Phillip, not so much because he had pulled the trigger, but because each of them had ignored what was happening, hoping it would go away, and pretending it was no cause for alarm. They had pushed it down with everything unpleasant, as they so often did.

"Bloody fools, the two of you," Arthur muttered.

"Oh God, this is really so unnecessary," Julian groaned. "Let's change the subject, shall we?"

"I just want to assure myself that not another of us will fall," Arthur stubbornly reiterated.

"Then perhaps we should prick our fingers and swear our fealty to one another," Julian sarcastically shot back, and finally catching the eye of a footman, anxiously motioned him over.

"We've a vow between us," Adrian carefully reminded them. "We swore at Dunwoody to meet for the purpose of assuring ourselves another would not fall."

"Oh *Lord*," Julian moaned. "All right, all right, we've a *vow*. Enough of this now, before the world discovers how impossibly sentimental the two of you are! Come on, then, I am bored with this place. Shall we call on Madam Farantino? I am quite certain she has missed our smiling faces."

"Now *that* would be a perfect antidote to this morbid conversation," Arthur drawled, and pushed his brandy aside.

Madame Farantino's. It had been a long time since Adrian had sampled the delectable flesh there. "Go ahead then, why don't you? I'll find my way home well enough," he said, surprising even himself.

"Oh *no*." His tone grave, Julian leaned forward and peered closely at Adrian. "Don't tell me that rustic wife of yours has made you soft!"

Adrian chuckled. "I beg your pardon, but I am married."

"Yes, and so are the majority of patrons at Madam Farantino's. Surely you will not deny yourself pleasure when she is safely tucked away?"

"Leave him be, Julian. He is smitten with her," Arthur interjected with a broad grin. "As smitten as Romeo was with his Juliet."

That was preposterous, and Adrian snorted. "I am not smitten with her," he grumbled. And he *wasn't* smitten with her. How could he be smitten with an obnoxious little—

"My God, I think you must be right! He *is* smitten with her!" Julian gleefully exclaimed.

"I am not *smitten* with her!" Adrian insisted more forcefully. "Believe me, she is the most exasperating, impudent, insane county bumpkin you could ever hope to meet!"

Much to his exasperation, Arthur and Julian exchanged a glance and laughed at that. Ignoring Adrian's dark frown, Arthur asked, "If she is so . . . exasperating, is that it? Why in God's name did you marry her?"

Good Lord. Adrian sighed and lifted his brandy, then set it aside again without drinking. "You wouldn't believe me if I told you."

"Try us," Julian said, chuckling.

"For revenge." There, he had said it, and glanced impassionately at the twin looks of shock.

"Wh-what?" Arthur stammered.

"Revenge, plain and simple," Adrian repeated. And with the inevitable momentum gained from having opened his mouth in the first place, he calmly began speaking of the events that had occurred after Dunwoody. He told them of the disownment, which they apparently already knew, judging by the sheepish looks on their faces. He told them of his discovery that Benedict planned to offer for the parish princess, of his rash decision to marry her, of being catapulted into a strange world of horse thieves and drapes made of neckcloths, and perfectly good hats turned into baskets. He shook his head when he told them of Hugo and Maude, and how those beasts were slowly and systematically destroying his home.

And for reasons he would never fully understand, he spoke of the emotional distance between him and his wife, overlooking Julian's dramatic groan when he covered his face with his hands at Adrian's obvious weakness. Amazingly, as Arthur gaped at him in rapt attention, muttering, *"I knew it,"* the distress came tumbling out of him. He was able to put into words his inability to understand the Princess of the Grange, or women for that matter, and his fear that she loved Benedict. When he at last finished, he pushed away his empty glass feeling completely drained. Never in his life had he spoken so openly about himself, and he was already regretting it. He felt exposed and raw.

The men were silent for a long moment, until at last Julian spoke. "Take a mistress," he said flatly. "Trust me, you will never be able to understand her, and if what you say is true, it won't matter. You come from different worlds, really, and if it is Benedict she desires, then . . . Take a mistress," he said gruffly.

"No," Arthur hastily interjected. "No. It is possible there is something you don't see. Perhaps she doesn't love Benedict. You should go and tell her what you have told us."

Julian laughed. "And when did you become such a fool? Confessing that he married her to avenge the loss of his inheritance might not endear him to her."

"I daresay it will be more appealing to her than a mistress," Arthur shot back. "He deserves to know how she feels. And she deserves to know how *he* feels."

Did he feel? Adrian wondered, and pressed his lips together, slowly shaking his head as Julian groaned his disgust again, muttering that feelings and a halfpenny would get him a pint. Was he even capable of feeling? After years of suppressing his feelings, it was exceedingly difficult to recognize them when they surfaced.

"Go home to her, Adrian," Arthur insisted.

"Get yourself a mistress and thank me another time," Julian said, and shoved away from the table. "I'm to Madam Farantino's. Who will join me?" When Adrian declined again, Julian blithely remarked to Arthur that was just as well since Adrian always helped himself to the prettiest, and slung his arm around Arthur's shoulder. With bright farewells until the morrow, the two Rogues sauntered from the Tam O'Shanter with all the confidence of a pair of roosters.

Adrian spent the next day behind closed doors with his solicitors. When he emerged in the early evening, he headed straight for the blue drawing room and the cup of coffee he had craved all afternoon. No thanks to Arthur, he had slept restlessly. The suggestion that he tell Lilliana how he felt had tumbled roughly about his brain like a rock all night, jabbing sharply at his dull headache. If it hadn't been for that wretched scene in her bedroom, had she not presented herself like a wench, he would not have paid Arthur any heed. But that strange event had him thinking perhaps Arthur was right—there was more than he knew, and he should return to Longbridge at once to speak with her. To the extent that he was capable, he should at least be honest with her.

And himself.

He grudgingly recognized that perhaps he had not been completely attentive to her, really, as he had thrown himself into the resurrection of Longbridge. A gift. Yes, he would bring her a proper gift, a peace offering. He would have his secretary check on the emerald bracelet and necklace he had commissioned several weeks ago. That would be a proper peace offering.

Unfortunately, he could not yet depart, as his solicitors had advised him there were some papers concerning his Boston shipyard that needed to be drawn up immediately. It would take a few days to have everything in order, but they needed his signature so they might be dispatched at once. Ah well. Another day or so would not make any difference, and in truth he could stand a trip to the exclusive shops on Jermyn Street to replace his two best hats and the silk neckcloths she had destroyed. No, he thought with a wry smile, another day or so would not make much difference.

Except that he needed to see her.

Thankfully, Benedict did not want to remain in London any longer. He made some vague excuse of having business elsewhere, but Adrian suspected he was anxious to return to Kealing Park before he angered Archie with his prolonged absence. He asked Benedict to explain to Lilliana why he had been detained, which his brother eagerly assured him he would. With a cheerful wave, Benedict departed for Longbridge to retrieve his coach.

Thirteen

IN THE ORANGERY at Longbridge, Lilliana
stared at the nearly finished portrait of Adrian and commended herself—she'd actually done a rather good job
with it. His handsome face stared back at her, impassive,
unfeeling. . . .

He had left her at Longbridge with nothing more
than a terse note informing her he had gone to London
for a few days. To *London*. She had been there once as a
child, remembered it as noisy and dirty and teeming
with all sorts of people. It was a vivid memory, and one
so grand she would give anything to see it again. But
after her little display she been abruptly left behind. Perhaps it was an indication of how things were to be with
them. He would see the world; she would remain at
Longbridge. Painting.

His abrupt departure had hurt her terribly and had
angered her to an extent she had never before experienced. In some respects she was glad he had not returned before now, because Lord only knew what she
might have said or done. But that was before the unmistakable feelings of contrition and shame began to creep
into her conscience. Her actions had been abominable—

an image of her mother's likely horror if she knew how Lilliana had acted kept playing in her mind's eye—screams, a plea to God to have mercy on her daughter, then certain heart failure. Like a silly, wanton child, so in need of attention, she had pushed the limits of decency.

What demon had possessed her? What monstrous illness had robbed her of all reason? She was deeply ashamed that she would so readily and completely believe Benedict's innuendoes. Again, like a child.

She paused in her painting and leaned back, cocking her head to one side as she assessed her work with a critical eye. It was a very good likeness of Adrian, but it did not quite capture the essence of him, the sheer magnetism that practically oozed from him. *Please come back,* her heart whispered. She missed him. She needed to apologize, to explain how foolish she had been, to finally speak of *why* she had done it. *Please come back.*

But a little voice in her head sounding suspiciously like Alice Dashell warned her that he might never come back to her. Not in spirit, anyway. "You wanted a reaction?" she muttered angrily. "Well, you got one!" She had succeeded, apparently, all too well.

The sound of her name from somewhere outside startled her, and she yanked her gaze to the window. Benedict! Her heart skipped several beats. They were home! Lilliana anxiously leapt to her feet and yanked at the ties of her apron. Discarding it, she quickly ran a hand through her hair, pinched her cheeks to hide the paleness, and hurried to the door. Flinging it open, she rushed outside, oblivious to the cold of the final gasp of winter. Beaming, she held out her hands to Benedict as he came striding across the lawn.

"Lilliana, where is your cloak? You'll catch your death!" he called, and began stripping his own cloak from his shoulders.

"I'm quite all right," she assured him, but he already had the cloak around her shoulders. He kissed her forehead in greeting and Lilliana immediately stepped back, out of his reach, to peer around him, blushing. "Did you just arrive?" *Where was Adrian?*

"This very moment. Come—I won't have you standing outside," he said, and wrapped an arm around her shoulder, forcing her into his side as he hurried her toward the house. Entering the terrace sitting room, Lilliana smiled brightly and glanced anxiously about, expecting to see her husband. *Where was he?*

"I could use a bit of brandy to warm my bones. It's frightfully cold out," Benedict remarked.

Lilliana pulled his cloak from her shoulders. "Max keeps the gold salon rather well stocked," she replied, inclining her head toward the door. Benedict took the cloak and followed her into the corridor. Adrian would appear at any moment, she thought, and give her that charming smile of his. He would act as if nothing had happened, just as he always did.

But Adrian did not appear as they walked the length of the corridor.

Benedict commented on one of her newly hung paintings—marvelous, he said, and she nodded, her eyes trained ahead, expecting him to step through a door at any moment. When they reached the gold salon, they found it empty, and Lilliana's heart sank.

Max entered behind them and quickly divested Benedict of the cloak, then walked to the sideboard, withdrawing two snifters. "May I pour you a brandy, my lady?" he asked. Lilliana shook her head, and Max put one snifter away. Now there was only one. Adrian had not come home, she realized, and was suddenly conscious of a dull ache in her chest.

Benedict accepted the snifter from Max and strolled casually to the hearth to warm his back. "I thought spring had come, but it is awfully cold out. I suppose winter is not quite done with us," he remarked sociably, and sipped his brandy. "Thank you, Max. That will be all."

Lilliana sank into a chintz-covered armchair, oblivious to the tight-lipped look Max gave her before he quit the room. "Did . . . did Adrian come with you?" she asked, wincing that her voice sounded so small.

Benedict hesitated. "I'm afraid not. He decided to stay a bit longer."

"Really?" she asked, trying very hard to sound casual. "How much longer?"

"I couldn't say, really." He suddenly turned his back to her, warming his front. "I cannot seem to shake the chill."

"Umm . . . did he say *why* he should remain there?" she asked, her voice even smaller.

Benedict responded with a shrug of his slender shoulders. "I rather imagine he will tell you it was business."

He would *tell* her it was business? Lilliana's hand fisted in her lap, and she dropped her gaze, commanding herself not to be so distrustful. When she lifted her head again, Benedict had turned and was watching her closely. Her cheeks flushed. "He must be quite busy with his work. It's been so long since he has been to London."

"Oh, I shouldn't fret—he didn't seem so very busy," Benedict offered, and smiled strangely; it seemed almost a sneer.

But Lilliana nodded dumbly, distraught that her husband had not returned. Might never return! Perhaps he found himself delightfully free of her and quite safe from another shameful episode in her suite. Her face flooded with the heat of shame as she recalled that night for the thousandth time, offering herself like a whore, shocked when he had angrily thrust into her, and then . . . then finding such *rapture* in it. She swallowed convulsively at the memory; how despicable . . . it would be a miracle if he ever found his way home again after what she had done.

"Dear God, I've upset you," Benedict said, and came away from the hearth.

"Of course you haven't!" she shakily attempted to assure him. "I've been a bit under the weather recently, and I rather think—"

"Lilliana, look at me." Benedict sank down on the ottoman in front of her and leaned forward so that she could see the concern etched around his eyes. "Lord help me, but I cannot bear to see you so distressed—"

"I am not distressed—"

"I cannot deceive you. I would do anything to avoid hurting you, but I cannot lie!"

The nausea of dread began to rise in her throat. "Lie?" she echoed, and with a limp flick of her wrist, attempted to laugh.

But Benedict caught her hand and held it tightly. "I tried to tell you what sort of man he was, but you would not hear me. . . . Jesus, this is so difficult," he said, grimacing.

"Please, Benedict, no more," Lilliana insisted weakly, but oh, God, she knew. She knew and the knowledge was knifing her through the heart. She yanked her hand free of his; he fumbled for it but let it slide through his fingers.

"My dearest Lillie, how very innocent you are," he said, sighing sadly. The sound of that name on Benedict's lips, the name *he* called her when he held her in his arms, made her nausea grow. "I know how painful this must be for you—poor Lillie, so very sweet and simple. Unfortunately, it is the way of some men and there is little one can do to change them. It is difficult to accept, I know, but you are strong—you *will* come to accept it, and I will help you with all that I have," he murmured.

She had no idea what to say to that! Stunned, she could only stare at him, wondering if she should thank him for being forthright or curse him for saying something so wretched.

He suddenly rose. "Let me fetch you a brandy. You'll feel better with a brandy." He returned a few moments later with a snifter, holding it between his hands to warm it before giving it to her. "I'll postpone my return to Kealing Park a day or two; I cannot leave you in such distress."

He handed her the brandy with such a look of pity that she wanted to pour it over his head. Simple and fragile—but look at her, for God's sake! A country bumpkin who threw iniquitous little tantrums in her bedroom! "There is really no need, Benedict," she said, but her hand, trembling as she took the brandy he offered, suggested otherwise. *Damn it!* How could she look at Adrian again, knowing he was keeping company with another woman in London? A woman who undoubtedly accepted his gentle caress without tears or dramatic displays!

"There is every need," he said in a distinctly patronizing tone. "Drink your brandy, love, and then perhaps you should lie down for a bit."

She didn't need to lie down. She needed to run out into the bitter cold so that her lungs would freeze and she would never have to take another tortured breath again.

Fortunately, Thunder liked the cold, and kept up a rapid pace for most of the trip to Longbridge. Adrian had made good time and was glad for it. The need to see Lilliana was eating at him like a virus, so much so that he had asked Arthur to bring the emerald jewelry he had commissioned because he simply could not wait another day. Naturally, he had been forced to endure a fair amount of ribald laughter for it, but Arthur had agreed.

Thunder trotted down the oak-lined drive, and Adrian anxiously glanced at his pocket watch again. Max had once mentioned she spent her afternoons painting; she would be in the orangery now. In the paddock he quickly tossed the reins to a groom and instructed him to have his bags delivered to Max, then headed for the orangery. As he round the corner of the stable, he could see the soft glow of candlelight illuminating the orangery windows, and amazingly, his heart beat a little faster.

He picked up the pace, jogging to the corner of the

orangery, then slowing to a walk as he headed for the door. As he approached one pane-glass window, he caught a glimpse of her inside, her brush raised to a canvas, her blond curls shimmering in the candlelight. He smiled warmly—but the smile began to fade as he neared. A man's arm came up near her head, pointing at something on the canvas. Max, perhaps? Or Benedict?

His eyes narrowed as he walked past the window. It was Benedict, all right, hanging over her shoulder. Reaching the door, Adrian rapped lightly and swung it open. Lilliana dropped her brush and came clumsily to her feet, hastily wiping the back of her hand across her forehead. "Adrian. You've come home."

Cool and to the point. Not exactly the reception he had hoped for, but not altogether unexpected. "A little later than I would have liked," he said blandly. He glanced around as Lilliana shrugged awkwardly from a smock that looked suspiciously like one of his shirts. There were paintings everywhere—covering the walls, propped like cards in one corner, and on three separate easels in various spots around the large, rectangular room. "You've been busy, I see," he said, and glanced to his right. "Ben, I am surprised to see you," he said, and walked forward, extending his hand. "Thought you had business elsewhere."

His brother's eyes darted nervously to Lilliana before he grasped Adrian's hand. "The weather," he mumbled. "Rather nasty the last few days."

It was cold, but hardly treacherous. Adrian shifted his gaze to Lilliana. "I hope you have been well," he said, and strolled toward her. Her eyes widened as he approached, the gray-green orbs exactly as he had imagined them these last few days, large and framed with thick golden lashes. "Are you?"

"Am I?"

"Well."

"Oh!" Her hand came up, and she nervously fingered the small gold cross at her neck. "Yes, quite well, thank you. And you?"

"Quite well," he mumbled, and leaned down to kiss her. She startled him by turning her head slightly, so that he just caught the corner of her mouth. He straightened slowly, silently cursing Benedict's presence. If only he could speak to her, in here, among her paintings. While she looked so terribly mussed and appealing. "I don't suppose I could entice you to join me in the gold salon? I should like to hear about Longbridge while I was away. I trust no boxing matches have occurred?" he asked, and smiled.

"Umm, no." She glanced at Benedict. A twinge of jealousy shot down Adrian's spine, and he followed her gaze over his shoulder. Benedict was standing with his feet braced apart, his hands clenched at his side. "Ah, actually, my lord," she said, "it is almost time for tea. If you please, I should dress first." She quickly pulled a tarp over the painting she had been working on and stepped around him, walking toward the door. Benedict was there in a trice, holding out her cloak. "Oh. Thank you," she mumbled, and fastened it around her neck. She turned halfway toward Adrian, her gaze riveting on his neckcloth. "Excuse me," she muttered. And with that she walked out of the orangery. There was no joy at his return, no need to see him as he needed to see her. Terribly conscious of Benedict, Adrian kept his expression neutral. He strolled toward the door, his eyes on his younger brother, who seemed oddly nervous. The weakling was hiding something. "Did I interrupt?" he asked mildly.

"Interrupt . . . ? God, no, Adrian. She's been a bit unsettled I think, what with you being gone."

"Has she? I would not have guessed," Adrian said dryly, and walked out the door, not caring if Benedict followed or not.

But he did, and Adrian was forced to make conversation with him while they waited a full hour for Lilliana to appear. Benedict chatted endlessly about nothing, and if pressed, Adrian could not have repeated a single thing he had said. His heart was full of foolish jealousy at her cool reception, impatience at her lack of gaiety. Had he been a fool to think he harbored some fondness for her? Had he been so disturbed by her performance that night in her bed that he had come up with some ridiculous notion of affection? Yes, and while he was convincing himself that he rather did care for her, she had been smiling at Benedict.

But when she walked into the salon wearing a pale gold gown of brocade and chiffon, the uncertainty rocketed to terrifying proportions. She moved as if she were gliding on air, the chiffon streaming out behind her like some sort of cloud. Her hair was swept back and bound up with little gold beads stuck carelessly about her coif. She was terribly alluring—had she always been so? Was it really possible he had been so blind to her charm?

She sat gingerly on the edge of a settee and accepted the cup of tea a footman handed her, but made no move to drink it. Her face was pale, and the faintest of shadows dusted the skin beneath her eyes. Benedict immediately engaged her in some useless conversation, and Lilliana smiled at him, and Adrian felt the gulf between them widen impossibly. This was hardly what he had hoped for or imagined. He had wanted to sweep her into his arms, make passionate love to her, and erase the memory of that awful night.

But Benedict's chatter continued well into supper. At the dining table, Adrian quietly endured the inane chatter and Lilliana's bright responses. Too bright. So bright that it seemed that tiny chinks in her armor were glowing with them. This was not the same Lilliana he had left a few days ago.

And if he needed any further proof of it, she did not touch her pudding.

By the time the dishes had been cleared and the port drunk, Adrian was sick to death of Benedict. He had to speak with his wife, alone, unguarded. He stood abruptly, his eyes riveting on Lilliana. "I would speak with you alone, Lilliana," he said curtly, and glancing to his left, said coolly, "Ben, you will excuse us, won't you?"

"Oh! Naturally! I should really be off to bed as I intend to get an early start tomorrow."

That Adrian would believe when he saw it. With a curt nod to his brother he walked to the door and opened it. "Lilliana?"

Her gaze fell to the table, and bracing her hands against it, she slowly pushed herself to her feet. Deliberately, she turned and walked toward him with her eyes on the carpet, as if she had been summoned to meet her maker. When she reached the door, Adrian grasped her elbow and propelled her swiftly into the east wing and to his private study.

Pushing the door open, he waited for her to precede him, then stepped across the threshold and leaned against the door with his hands shoved in his pockets. He watched her move to the far side of the room, nervously running her palms up and down over the chiffon overlay of her gown, until she at last clasped her hands at her waist and turned toward him.

"You seem out of sorts tonight, Lilliana."

She refused to meet his gaze. "I . . . I rather suppose I am," she murmured.

"Mind telling me why?"

She drew part of her bottom lip between her teeth for a moment. "I must ask you something I truly wish I did not have to ask," she muttered.

Adrian pushed away from the door and strolled into the center of the room. "How many times must I say it? Whatever pleases you, you may have."

Slowly she lifted her chin, and the green eyes pierced him. "That's splendid, because it would please me to live separately from you."

The softly spoken words carried as much power as a kick to his gut; Adrian unconsciously stepped backward. *Now* what insanity had invaded her head? "Are you ill? Mad, perhaps?" he asked, struggling to keep his voice even.

"I am not *mad*," she said indignantly. "But the circumstances being what they are, I believe it is the best course for us. For me, anyway."

Benedict. He knew that weakling had something to do with this as sure as he stood there. "Under the circumstance? *What* circumstance?" he asked, barely able to contain the anger beginning to churn just beneath the surface.

"Your indifference, Adrian. Your . . . your faithlessness. I cannot bear it, and I won't. I want to live in the west wing. Those rooms are never used, and it seems to me that we should be quite able to avoid one another."

She said it so smoothly, so clearly, he wondered how many times she had practiced it. Had Benedict helped her? "No," he said calmly. "Now perhaps you will explain this ridiculous notion you have that I am either indifferent or faithless."

"Ridiculous?" Her lovely eyes narrowed. "You have been indifferent to me since the day we married, and your faithlessness has made itself known in more ways than one."

When had dementia invaded this woman? "Do you have any concept of the *meaning* of the words you use, Lilliana? Do you even know what you are accusing me of?" he asked, folding his arms defensively across his chest. He saw the spark in her eye, the certain flare of anger that doused the sadness.

"And now you think me stupid—but I should hardly be surprised. Of *course* I know what I am saying! Do you think me so simple that I cannot plainly see what is before me?"

"What is *before* you? God, the idiocy that muddles your mind! Have you forgotten that I must constantly remind you that you may have whatever you would like? That I must constantly remind you that you are a bloody countess with all the privilege that entails? Where is the indifference, Lilliana? Where is the faithlessness?" he asked sharply.

Lilliana's knuckles were white now, and he realized she was gripping them tightly to her abdomen to keep them from shaking. But she held her ground and looked him square in the eye, her eyes flashing murderously. "You will give me every material thing at your disposal, but you will give me nothing of yourself! *That* is the indifference!" she snapped. "And as for the faithlessness, it is fairly obvious, isn't it? You keep your distance from me at Longbridge then escape to London and you do not return for *days*!"

Adrian opened his mouth to speak but, her eyes blazing, Lilliana rushed on. "Don't you dare tell me it was business," she said hoarsely, "because it is always business with you, Adrian! Or at least that is what you would have me believe! And do not attempt to give me some weak excuse, because I *know*!"

The urge to throttle the insane little minx rose swiftly. Adrian shoved his hands in his pocket and pivoted on his heel, stalking to the cold hearth. "I don't know whether to shake some sense into you or let you stew in your own folly, Lilliana. I have given you everything that is mine, yet it seems not enough! I go to London to see to my affairs so that I may *continue* to give you everything you want, yet it is not enough for you! What do you want of me? *Jesus,* just once, will you tell me what you want?" he roared. He realized he was shouting at her, and it seemed to take her aback almost as much as it did him.

"I don't want your *things,* Adrian," she said slowly. "I want the companionship you spoke of when you offered for me! I want to *soar* like you soar, to experience the sights and sounds and pleasures of this world just like you! I don't want to be kept hidden away here because you are ashamed of me!" She gasped softly at her own words, and instantly turned away from him.

Adrian immediately crossed the room and grasped her shoulders, pulling her back against his chest. "I am not ashamed of you," he said softly.

"But neither can you confess a particular interest in

me, can you?'' Before he could answer, before he could
say that he *was* interested in her, that he was bloody well
intrigued by her, she wrenched free and whirled around
to face him. ''Your attentions to me are for one thing
only, are they not? *That* is the companionship you spoke
of! My God, I was naive!'' she cried. ''But I am no
longer the country girl you married, Adrian—I understand clearly now, too clearly! You had best keep your
other companions,'' she cried, ''because I cannot live
this way! I will not live this way! You want me to tell
you what I want? I want separate quarters ! I want to be
away from *you*!''

He felt the painful slash of her rejection across his
chest. The wall was coming up, the wall he had battered
down the last several days in his earnest desire to tell
Lilliana that she mattered to him, that she made him
smile, that he felt an affection for her he had rarely felt
in his life. The wall was coming up, all right, brick by
impenetrable brick.

He smirked. ''Then by all means, be away from me,
madam,'' he said smoothly. ''Live in your little fantasy
for all I care—it makes not a whit of difference to me.
But you will not flaunt your disgust in full view of the
staff. You may not take separate quarters.''

''I already have,'' she said quietly.

He caught his breath to keep from exploding, remained rigid as she walked past him and quit the room.
And then he pressed his fingers to his eyes as another
raging headache threatened to split his skull open.

Fourteen

POLLY DID NOT care for her mistress's decision to move to the west wing, and frowned at the musty drapes and sagging bed. The room wasn't fit for a groom, much less a countess. But Lady Albright was just like the girls—headstrong and foolish. When the door burst open, Polly bestowed her disapproving frown on her ladyship. "It's dark as Hades in here," she snapped.

"Hades is lit with eternal fire," Lady Albright shot back, and moved quickly to the vanity, threw herself down onto the bench, and buried her face in her hands.

Polly snorted; bad humor was just what she deserved for being so petulant. A woman's place was with her husband. "Shouldn't be here, I'll say. It's not good for you."

"*Don't,* Polly! Please, I need to be alone."

Polly clucked her tongue disdainfully. "Just like the Albright girls," she muttered irritably as she marched from the room.

That was where Polly was wrong. There was nothing about her that remotely resembled an Albright in any shape or fashion, Lilliana thought angrily as she stood and struggled from her gown. And she did not want to *be* an Albright, either, not if it meant such cold, hard-hearted indifference! Oh God, oh God, how had she ever gotten herself into such a mess?

She would never forget the way he looked when he walked into the orangery, his thick sandy hair tousled by the wind, the impossible span of his chest, and that lop-sided grin that had made her knees shake and her hands tremble. And tonight, in his oh so precious study, the way he had leaned against the door, casually perusing her—

Bloody marvelous, her cheeks were flaming because of a bonafide, self-important *ass*! Who did he think he was, traipsing off to London and some woman, then waltzing back to Longbridge to protest that she seemed *out of sorts*? He must think her the consummate fool, an unsophisticated rustic with a brain the size of a pea! For all his faults, Benedict *never* treated her so poorly—a bit domineering, perhaps, but he was first and foremost a gentleman! She should have married Benedict. She should never have let a childish fantasy guide such an important decision.

Lilliana angrily fumbled with the fastenings of her gown, and in a moment of frustration yanked so hard that she succeeded in popping a button and launching it clear across the room. She should have married Bene-dict, settled at Kealing Park, and lived her life in famil-iar surroundings. What a fool to think she might have soared with Adrian! What a pathetic bumpkin to believe a man like him would want her companionship! Ah, but he was a scoundrel, a *liar* for letting her think it!

She jerked the gown from her body and threw herself on the bed, where she remained tossing and turning all night, hoping he would come to her and hoping just as fiercely that he would not.

The next morning, her anxiety was not eased in the least. A storm had passed in the night, coating the branches outside her window with ice and the ground with snow. It made her feel impossibly hopeless and impossibly *trapped*. This was hell. Somehow she had stumbled into an abyss from which there was no escape.

Adrian was thinking much the same thing as he sat in the breakfast room, staring across the table at Benedict. How long would he remain? One day, maybe two? He had already made some remark about being trapped here for God knew how long. Adrian could not bear another moment of Benedict's cheerful chatter about Kealing Park and all that he would do to it one day. Too disturbed to feign polite interest, he closeted himself in his study right after breakfast.

Just before *she* came down.

And there he remained for as long as he could, until he could stand the solitude no longer. When he at last ventured into the corridor, he could hear the sound of muted laughter coming from the music room. Against his better judgment, he walked in that direction. As he neared the door he could hear the tinkling of a pianoforte. A burst of laughter startled him, and he paused at the door, listening to Lilliana's voice rise above the other.

And then the silence.

The ignominious thought that they were kissing ignited a red-hot flame of fury in him. He flung open the door and strode inside, fully prepared to catch them in the act.

But they were not kissing. At least not at that moment.

Lilliana was scribbling something on a sheet of music while Benedict stood gazing out the window. "There," she said, and held the sheet up.

Benedict turned to see what she had and saw Adrian standing in the open door. "Adrian! Do come in! I will wager you didn't know your wife penned music." Bloody hell, of course he didn't know it! Startled, Lilliana jerked her head around to him, blatantly frowning at his intrusion. Hugo and Maude, lying at Benedict's feet, lifted their heads and thumped their tales, but neither moved to greet him.

Adrian glared at the traitorous curs. "Another hidden talent," he drawled, and forced himself to smile. Lilliana quickly turned away and set the sheet of music aside.

"Ah, her music is as lovely as her paintings. But I am sure you have noted that she is quite a talented artist."

"You would know better than I," Adrian said in a moment of irrational jealousy. What insanity! As if he *wanted* to sit at a pianoforte with the Princess! He hardly wanted to be in the same room with her, let alone listen to her conjure up some rudimentary country song. Nevertheless, the uncomfortable sensation of envy rifled through him. "I am sorry I disturbed you," he said stiffly, and turned to go, but not before catching the scathing look Lilliana bestowed on him.

"No bother," Benedict called after him as he left the room.

No bother my *ass*, he thought angrily as he strode down the corridor to the sanctity of his study. How long would he be forced to watch the two of them cozying up to one another? She had the audacity to accuse him of faithlessness? What a fool he had been. It was all he could do to keep from laughing at himself like a madman for having imagined he was somehow fond of that wench.

Through supper, and again the next morning, he was forced to endure the sound of that lilting laughter coming from somewhere in the house, feeling quite certain it was at his expense. At luncheon he had stalked to the dining room and had happened upon Max and Bertram standing in the alcove leading to the west wing, staring curiously at a painting. Judging by the way Max turned deathly pale, he had surprised them, and the two men immediately sidled past, each muttering something about duties and chores and a bucket that needed scrubbing. Confused by their reaction, Adrian glanced at the painting.

It was a portrait of him. A magnificent one, really, that portrayed him proudly astride a steed, his hair ruffled by a breeze, looking out over something in the distance. She really was quite talented, he realized, and inadvertently looked at the steed.

Which happened to be a mule.

And a fat one at that.

Adrian watched the snow from a window in his study until the last fragile flake fell midafternoon. Convinced it had stopped, he strode to the foyer in search of Max, where he found him polishing a brass wall ornament. *"Max!"* he barked, and startled the man so badly that he must have jumped two feet.

"Y-yes, my lord?" he stammered.

"Go to the stables and tell whoever is there that I want the road cleared."

Max gulped. "The road . . . ? But the snow, my lord—it must be a foot thick!"

Adrian folded his arms and leaned forward until he was only inches from Max's thin face. "I don't care if there are six feet of snow. *I want the road cleared.*"

Nodding furiously, Max gulped again and stuffed the cleaning rag in his trousers, then bolted for the massive mahogany doors, disappearing outside without even a cloak. Adrian smirked before starting for the music room, where he was certain he would find the mule lover with her beau.

The music room was empty.

Damn! He paused, hands on hips, as he tried to think of where two rustics might spend a snowy day. The terrace sitting room. He marched on.

The door of the terrace sitting room was open and Adrian sailed through, but it was also empty. Frustrated, he shoved a hand through his hair while he racked his brain for an idea of where they might be, forcing aside thoughts of where they had best *not* be. If he discovered the two of them had gone alone to the west wing—

A thud on the terrace window startled him from his thoughts. He glanced up just as another snowball went hurtling by. Good God, were they children? They were out there, all right, Lilliana's forest-green cloak a stark contrast to the snow. Benedict tossed a snowball at her, and with a shriek she jumped out of the way, slipping on the icy terrace. She went down so fast that Adrian started; Benedict, however, was immediately at her side, helping her up, then draping his arm around her shoulder as he peered into her face.

And then he kissed her on the cheek.

Something exploded in Adrian's head so hard and so violently that he did not see Lilliana forcefully shove Benedict away. He bolted for the doors like a madman and jerked them open, launching himself onto the terrace without really seeing anything, least of all the snowball she was hurling. It caught Adrian in the shoulder and he winced with surprise. Good *Lord,* she packed them hard!

"Oh my! I am terribly sorry!" she said, and rushed forward, sliding precariously on the terrace.

"I am quite all right," Adrian snapped, and angrily brushed the snow from his coat before slicing an icy glare across her. "Have you no care for your person? You could break your leg!"

Her cheeks, already rosy from the cold, flushed dark. "I . . ."

"You are foolish," he finished for her. "Come inside before you harm yourself," he snapped, and pivoted on his heel, angry that he had allowed any feeling for the twit at all.

The second snowball caught him completely unaware and squarely between the shoulders with a force that almost knocked the breath from him. Stunned, he turned slowly, disbelieving what he was certain had happened. And by God, as if to assure him, the Grange Princess actually laughed. Her eyes sparkled with little demon fires as she marched past him, a smirk on her lips. At least Benedict had the grace to look a bit sheepish.

For the first time in his life, Adrian actually contemplated murder.

When he stepped inside, she gave him a pert toss of her head, then flounced out of the room, leaving Benedict warming his hands in front of the fire. Adrian scowled at her retreating form, then turned his attention to his witless brother. "I didn't think you so careless, Benedict," he said curtly.

"Careless?"

"I saw her fall, no thanks to your silly games. What if she had broken a leg?"

Benedict shrugged. "She is not a child, Adrian; a little tumble is not going to hurt her. And she wanted to go outside—we've been cooped up in here forever."

"Yes, well, the road is being cleared as we speak. I rather imagine you should have no trouble getting through come morning, so there is no need to remain *cooped up* here any longer," he shot back.

Benedict slowly turned his head to consider Adrian. "I see," he said at last. "Then I shall take my leave of you in the morning." He turned back to the fire.

Bloody grand, Adrian thought, and left the sitting room without another word.

But he was feeling a bit churlish for having lost his composure when Benedict's coach was pulled around the next morning. Benedict was a weakling, not a man with courage enough to seduce his own sister-in-law. At least that's what Adrian tried to tell himself. Fortunately, the sun was out and already melting the dozens of icicles that hung from the eaves. Adrian made a lame jest about it as he walked with Benedict out onto the circular drive, but his brother did not laugh. Sighing, Adrian shoved a hand through his hair. "Look here, I apologize for being so terribly rude yesterday. I was worried about Lilliana." He winced inwardly at how pathetic his lie sounded.

Benedict glanced at him from the corner of his eye as he shoved his manicured hands into leather gloves. "I understand," he responded stiffly. "No offense taken.

And it is high time I returned to the Park. Papa is probably quite concerned by now.''

Oh, Archie was probably apoplectic by now—his golden child had been gone for almost a fortnight. Adrian nodded and stepped back so that Benedict could get in the coach. His brother paused to instruct his driver, and then opened the door, prepared to take his leave.

"Benedict!"

Both men turned as Lilliana dashed out the door without a cloak. The damn dogs that shadowed her every move scampered just ahead of her, barking excitedly. "Wait! I've something to give you!" she called, and holding her pale blue skirts high so they would not drag the snow, rushed forward. Adrian thought he would have to catch her before she barreled into the coach, but she stopped abruptly in front of Benedict and thrust a large sheet of music at him. "I finally finished it. If you be so kind as to—"

"Lilliana! It's such a wonderful gift, love," he gushed, and Adrian's chest tightened painfully.

She smiled shyly and waved an airy hand at him. "It's not a gift, really. But I promised—"

"Precious all the same," he said, and cupped her face with his hand, smiling down at her.

Indignation soared; Adrian clenched his jaw tightly shut and looked away, unable to look at the two lovers standing there, oblivious to the impropriety. Or were they? Perhaps the lovers enjoyed flaunting it! He yanked his gaze to them again, but Lilliana had stepped out of Benedict's reach, her traitorous face flaming. Adrian turned abruptly. "You must write," he called over his shoulder, and walked away from the coach, his pulse racing with mad jealousy. He had tried to give them the benefit of the doubt, berating himself every time he suspected them, and for that, they would flaunt it in his face! He paused in the foyer and looked back—Lilliana was speaking earnestly to Benedict and he was looking at her with such adoration that Adrian's gut twisted.

Hadn't he already lost everything to that weakling? Would he lose his wife to him too? The insult was more than Adrian could endure, and he whirled away from the touching little scene to glare at Bertram.

"Have Lady Albright come to my study the moment he is gone," he snapped, and strode to his study, where he paced for what seemed hours to him, alternating between anger and an acute sense of guilt. All right! He had stolen their happiness, goddammit—he understood that! But there was nothing that could change things now—she was married to *him* and he'd be damned if he would allow her to make a fool of him with his very own brother! Lord *God*, the quality of his mercy could not possibly get any worse than this!

It was a full quarter of an hour before Lilliana at last deigned to grace him with her presence, and he had worked himself into a frightening fury. He shooed the mongrels outside and shut the door loudly before turning a furious glare on her. Lilliana took an involuntary step backward, her eyes shimmering with surprise and a touch of fear. Adrian turned on his heel and walked to the far side of the room so he would not have to see those eyes, those eyes that made him insane. He began pacing again, trying desperately to collect his thoughts while Lilliana watched him intently, rooted to the floor.

After a few moments he managed to stop pacing like some stricken schoolboy, and very deliberately turned to face her, his hands clasped behind his back, his feet spread apart. "There is," he ground out, "no escaping our situation, madam. We are married, for better or worse, and there is nothing you can do to change that."

Lilliana faltered. Her lips moved as if she would speak, but there was no sound. Her gaze fell to the floor, hidden beneath the gold crescents of her lashes that fanned her cheeks.

"I know this marriage is not something either of us desires anymore," he continued, pausing only briefly to wonder where on earth that had come from, "but that is, unfortunately, too damn bad. We *are* married, and I would ask you do me the common courtesy of remembering that.''

Moments of tense silence passed before she slowly lifted her gaze, and Adrian's heart lurched at the fury he saw blazing in her eyes. "I beg your pardon?" she asked hoarsely. "You would ask that *I* remember that? Have you lost your bloody mind?"

With a derisive snort Adrian responded, "Quite the contrary, madam. I have *found* it. I had lost it when I thought to give you and my brother the benefit of the doubt, but I realize I have been an absolute fool to let your tender little attraction continue a moment longer than it already has.''

She gasped, clenched her hands into little fists at her sides; Adrian was quite certain she was restraining herself from striking him. "What in God's name are you implying?''

"I am not implying, Lilliana, I am *commanding* you to stop inviting his attentions. Despite what you may want your situation to be, you are married to *me*. As unfortunate as that is for both of us, you will not make a fool of me in my own house!''

Lilliana shrieked her outrage. "I cannot believe what I am hearing!" she cried, and whirled toward the hearth, covering her ears with her hands. "This is madness! My God, what ever made me think a marriage to you would be paradise? I beg your pardon, but it is not *you* who has lost your mind, it is *I*! I lost it irretrievably when I accepted your offer!''

"Your indignation is almost convincing," he sneered. "But do not take me for a fool. Don't you think I know—that I can *see* what the two of you feel for one another?''

That stunned her into speechlessness. She jerked around, her breast heaving with each furious breath. "I pity you, Adrian," she finally whispered. "You are so bereft of compassion that you cannot see and accept a friendship between your brother and your wife! Your twisted mind must interpret something lurid in it! And you would do so while you think *nothing* of your little escapade to London, or God knows where else—''

"Honestly! London again? What rubbish—''

"It is not rubbish! Do not try and deceive me! God, what do you want me to do? If you should happen to acknowledge that I exist, you treat me so indifferently that I cannot tell if I am your wife or another servant in your home! You cannot bring yourself to even *speak* to me for the most part, and when you do, it is with great condescension and obvious disinterest! You have no desire to be with me except to use me as a vessel for your seed, yet you would accuse me of taking a lover in your very own brother! At least he shows me the kindness you are apparently incapable of! Why *wouldn't* I prefer his company to yours, Adrian?" she shrieked hysterically. "*God*, I should have married Benedict!" The words were no sooner out of her mouth before her eyes flew wide with mortification and she quickly covered her mouth with her hand.

The stinging realization that he had been shunted aside in favor of Benedict again was like a knife in his gut. It was almost as if Archie were standing there, comparing him to his brother, enumerating the many different ways he was so very inadequate. The habit of suppressing the pain borne from years of Archie's abuse suddenly kicked in. "Yes, you should have," he muttered, and smiled wryly.

"I . . . I did not mean that," she said frantically. "It's not true!"

He shrugged indifferently. "Isn't it, Lilliana? I will admit it's true—why can't you?"

She sucked in a sharp, incredulous breath. "It's not *true*!" she insisted, almost pleadingly. "I may be confused about some things, but not *that*! He is kind to me, Adrian, that's all—there is nothing between us!"

Adrian laughed contemptuously. "Say what you will, *love*," he said, spitting Benedict's endearment, "but it is obvious." He lifted his hand before she could speak.

"Please God, do not argue with me. Do not invite his attentions, do you understand me?"

"I do not invite his attentions!"

"Really?" he drawled. "Oh, here's a gift, Benedict, you are too *kind,* Benedict," he mocked her.

"That music was not—" Lilliana strangled on a cry of outrage. "Why do I bother to try and explain? You are a beast!"

"Perhaps," he said with a slight shrug of his shoulders. "I am many things, I will grant you that. But a fool is not one of them. Avail yourself of my wealth, of my home, of my name, Lilliana, but *not* my horse and *not* my brother, do you understand me?"

She understood him. She understood him so plainly that she thought she might disintegrate into tiny pieces right where she stood. Her eyes were suddenly brimming, and she hastily turned away from him, swiping at the tears before he could see just how badly he hurt her. Hurt? Ah, but that was too mild a description for what he was doing to her. This was *hell*.

It was over for them—and there was no escape, no turning back. They were apparently doomed to a life of mutual distrust, and she had no one to blame but herself. Of all the imbecilic, foolish, childish things she had ever done, marrying *him* was the most fantastic. Her chest constricted around her heart until she was fairly certain it would burst, and she started unsteadily toward the door, her mind reeling with the knowledge that her marriage had ended before it had even begun. Hysterical laughter bubbled to her throat at the absurdity of it all. When she walked out of this room, her hope of living with the man of her dreams would be gone, crushed, completely obliterated.

She paused. But first, she would know why the *hell* he had ever offered for her in the first place! She glanced at him over her shoulder. He had moved to the mantel, and was leaning heavily against it as he stared into the flames, like some country gentleman quietly contemplating his supper. An overwhelming need to hurt him as he had hurt her took hold, choking the breath from her. "I *do* wish I had married Benedict," she said hoarsely.

Adrian shot her a furious frown and shook his head disgustedly.

"Tell me why!" she demanded. His frown deepened. "Tell me why you married me, Adrian!"

He suddenly pushed from the mantel, his eyes glowing maliciously. "You want to know why?" he asked nastily. "My father disowned me, Lilliana. He gave everything that was rightfully mine to your weak-willed lover. Kealing took *everything* from me, and Benedict never had the courage to stand by me when I needed him to! *That's* why!"

She flinched at the bitterness in his words, unable to believe him. "I know you and your father quarreled, but I do not see—"

"Don't you? Can't you see that I took the one thing Ben wanted?" He paused, watching the astonishment and hurt fill her. "You need not look at me with such horror. I have already commended myself to the devil for it," he said and casually shifted his weight onto one hip.

She could not move. Paralyzed with revulsion, she *could not* move. Revenge? He had married her for *revenge*? Somehow she managed to get a hand to her throat and gripped tightly against a swell of nausea. Unable to absorb it, she closed her eyes. *"It was a lie."* It was her voice, strange as it sounded.

"More or less." There was no remorse in his voice, nothing but the casual tone of observation.

It was more than she could bear; about to be violently sick, she whirled around, fumbling for the door. Grappling blindly with the brass knob, she pulled with all her might until the latch finally gave and the door swung open. An impulsive need to look at the monster before fleeing in horror compelled her to drag a blurry gaze to him—he was still standing there, expressionless, as if he had not just uttered the cruelest thing imaginable.

"You are your father's son," she muttered raggedly,

and raced from his study, running blindly down the corridor, her pups chasing behind her as she bolted up the stairs. The sobs were choking the life from her, the tears blinding her. Had it not been for Polly, she would have collapsed at the top of the staircase to die. But Polly put a strong arm around her and dragged her down the hall to the west wing, muttering under her breath that it was "just like the Albright girls all over again."

After a moment of confused terror at what he had done, Adrian stormed after Lilliana, watching in helpless frustration as Mrs. Dismuke gathered her up and dragged her away. Astounded by his own callousness, he pivoted around in the foyer, too appalled to witness her devastation, and caught sight of an ashen Bertram staring mutely at him. He was an animal! He strode angrily to his study, away from anyone who would remind him what sort of beast he was.

Once inside he marched to the sideboard and grabbed a decanter of whiskey, then seated himself at his desk with it. What had he done? What madness had caused him to do something so horribly vicious? What in the hell was *happening* to him? His world was turning upside down—he hardly knew himself anymore. Adrian drank, numb to the burn of the liquor in his throat as the demons from his past emerged and clashed with one another in his head, sending him into a tailspin. He had known disaster would happen. He had understood there would be a price to pay for Phillip's death. But he had never imagined it would destroy him.

If there was one person Max admired, it was Lord Albright. In the nine years he had been with him, he had never seen him falter. Completely unflappable, the man was a rock—calm, cool, and terribly sophisticated in the direst of circumstances, and Lord knew Max had seen his lord in dire circumstances.

But that was before he had married *her*. Oh, Max adored Lady Albright. He thought her very refreshing, and secretly laughed at her attempts to move the rock. But lately it seemed everything about her was trouble. Not *her* precisely, but . . . well, there was Lord Benedict, for example. That man acted as if he owned Longbridge, and his attentions to his sister-in-law were unnatural, in Max's humble opinion. And Mrs. Dismuke, good *Lord* but that woman was constantly prattling about disaster, and the Albright girls, and history repeating itself.

The worst was Lord Albright. Max had seen him in any number of dangerous situations, and he had never shown anything but that cool, silky demeanor. But he had changed; he seemed almost haunted, so completely unlike himself that it made Max even more nervous than usual. And now this . . . *this* was catastrophe. When Bertram had come running into the kitchens to tell him of the horrible argument between Lord and Lady Albright, Max had immediately gone off to see what could be done. But Lord Albright had locked himself in the study and would not allow anyone entrance.

The hearth had not been lit; it had to be freezing in there, so Max had hovered about, anxiously waiting to be called. When the noon hour came and went, he forced himself to go on with his daily tasks, reasoning that Lord Albright was a grown man and quite capable of caring for himself. No doubt he was studying his books. Bertram had probably exaggerated the whole thing.

But when Max returned an hour later, the study door was wide open and Lord Albright was gone. An empty bottle of whiskey lay on the floor. As Max walked through the foyer he stopped Roger, his lordship's valet. "Have you seen Lord Albright?" he asked.

Roger scowled. "Indeed I did, sir. He went that way, a bottle in one hand, his hat in the other," he said, and pointed toward the west wing.

The west wing? His lordship *never* went to the west wing, as he had once remarked he did not need to be reminded of a family past that was not his. Max hurried into the corridor, walking quickly from one door to the next. He was quite familiar with it, actually, as he made sure the rooms were swept and aired on a routine basis. As he came to the last door before the terrace and steps leading to the outbuildings, he paused to look inside.

The sound of the gun blast shook him from his boots. He caught his breath and brought a hand to his suddenly pounding heart. The blast had come from one of the outbuildings. Max suddenly thought of the game house, chock-full of the late Lord Albright's hunting trophies and old guns. He was running in that direction before he realized it, his heart pounding furiously with fear. He skidded across the terrace, stumbled down the steps, and careered to the door of the game house. With trembling hands, he fumbled about until he got the door open.

The acrid smell of gun smoke assaulted his senses, and he coughed as he fumbled for a kerchief in his pocket. Waving a hand in the air at the smoke, he anxiously looked around, and screamed with terror when he saw the earl's still form lying on the floor. He rushed to his lord's side and fell to his knees. The gun was lying a foot or so away, below an open window. The earl's hand, bent at an odd angle, was covered with black. Terrified, Max nudged him over onto his back, then released a keening cry that could be heard almost throughout the estate.

"Max! What in the blazes—" Bertram shouted as he rushed inside the game house.

"Dear God, he is *dead*!" Max cried.

Fifteen

Fortunately for the panicked residents of Longbridge, Max didn't know a thing about the human anatomy beyond what he was required to know, and he knew nothing about injury of any kind. When he had appeared on Dr. Mayton's doorstep wailing that the Earl of Albright was dead, the doctor had rushed to the estate, fearing the worst. He discovered that the earl was far from dead, although one would be hard pressed to convince his lordship of that. Apparently an old gun he had been handling had misfired, exploding in his face.

Thankfully, there were no broken bones or any apparent internal injuries, but in addition to a horribly deep gash at his temple, the earl had sustained a terrible injury to his eyes. Dr. Mayton would never forget the absolute horror when the earl regained consciousness or the shocked silence as he explained that when the bandages came off, he might very well be blind.

And the insufferable silence began. For several days Lord Albright lay in his massive bed, his bandaged eyes resembling an owl's. It was heartbreaking, even to a seasoned doctor like Mayton, that a young man as virile and commanding as the earl might be permanently blinded. Added to that was the scandal threatening to erupt—the entire estate was whispering of an attempted suicide.

But Lord Albright had grown quite agitated when Dr. Mayton had asked if he had intended to take his own life. "I am a fool, not a *coward*," he spat, and begrudgingly admitted having drunk himself into quite a state. Apparently, although he could not recall why, the earl had wandered into his grandfather's old game house and in a state of inebriation had toyed with one of many old guns. He recalled wanting to see if the gun worked, and had opened a window with the intent of firing at some target. Somewhere between opening the window and priming the ancient firearm, it had misfired in his face. The doctor felt a little better with that explanation— after all, his own foot had been the victim of an old gun.

But Lord Albright made the rumors worse by refusing to see anyone. The man was quietly but completely despairing of his destiny, often mumbling incoherently about something to do with mercy and idiocy.

How fortunate, the doctor thought as he flipped through the pages of his medical books again, that Lady Albright had proven to be such a rock of strength. Not that she hadn't been overcome with grief when she learned the unfortunate prognosis that night, but by the next morning her demeanor had become eerily calm and her eyes glinted with determination. As Lord Albright refused to admit her into his rooms, Lady Albright paced outside his door, walking slowly from one end of the long corridor to the other while her pups slept on a cushioned window seat. When anyone emerged from his room, she would demand to know how he fared, her pretty eyes narrowing with anger when she was told that he would not eat.

The entire estate endured two excruciating weeks of waiting for the bandages to be removed. When the morning came, the earl sat as rigid as a monument, unflinching as Dr. Mayton peeled the strips of cloth from his eyes. Beneath the bandages, his pus-filled eyes were scarred around the edges, which Dr. Mayton assured him would fade with time.

"Open them," the earl had stoically responded.

So he had, prying one open, then the other. His hand trembling slightly, he had lifted two fingers in front of the earl's face.

Nothing.

Dr. Mayton quickly bandaged them again as he awkwardly reassured the earl that his eyes were not quite healed, that they needed more time. Lord Albright had not uttered a word. Another week passed, and again the earl sat stiffly as the bandages were peeled away. Again, he could not see the two fingers the doctor lifted in front of his face.

There was nothing Dr. Mayton could do; there was no known cure for blindness. He tried to console the earl by suggesting it might only be a matter of time before his sight returned. But the earl had laughed darkly and shook his head. "Apparently, Dr. Mayton, you don't know the quality of mercy when you see it." With that he had turned away, refusing to say anything else.

Dejected, Dr. Mayton had met Lady Albright in her sitting room and explained that he had exhausted all resources available to him, that there was nothing more he could do for her husband. Her eyes glistening with tears, she had nodded solemnly and had asked, was it possible he might send for a surgeon? Of course, he had told her, but surgery on the head was almost unheard of and, moreover, there was no known procedure to restore sight. Lady Albright had turned away, walking slowly to the window that looked out over the gardens. She had looked terribly regal, dressed in a pale green gown—how sad, he had thought, that the earl would never gaze into her lovely countenance again. She stared out the window for an eternity it seemed, but at last she turned. Tell me what to do, she had asked.

Dr. Mayton had seized upon that—make him live, he had said, teach him how to live with his blindness. And by the time Lady Albright had shown him to the door of

Longbridge, he had no doubt that she would make her husband live again, whether he wanted to or not.

Make him live. Dr. Mayton's words reverberated in her mind. But exactly how did one do that? With a shawl wrapped around her shoulders Lilliana sat in a chair pulled up to the window in the suite adjoining Adrian's, staring at the stars. The room was bathed in darkness except for the weak moonlight that streamed in the window; even the fire had grown cold. She absently wondered how long she had been sitting in the chair, knowing only that the sun had just started to sink into the horizon when she had sagged into it, exhausted.

She had, of course, moved back to her rooms the same day of the accident, desperate to help him but unsure *how* to help him. Her efforts seemed awkward and contrived after the appalling words they had exchanged. But oh God, she was devastated by what had happened to him! Never had she felt such sorrow for anyone—the magnificence of him, the spirit of the strong and reckless adventurer—all of it cut down by blindness. Lilliana pulled the shawl tighter, shivering at the omnipotent forces that could do this to a man. She understood his terror—to rob him of his sight was to rob him of life. Regardless of what had gone between them, nothing that had been said could make her turn her back on him now, not when he was in such distress.

He *needed* her.

Not that he would ever admit it. He had sent her away a dozen times or more, refused to see her, and forbade the little maid who tended him from allowing her entry. He had even suggested through Max that she return to Blackfield Grange until such time his sight had returned.

Ridiculous. It was instinctive, she supposed, but she knew it was grief that caused him to act so petulantly. But she did not want to aggravate him, and tried to help in another way—by attempting to dispel the awful rumors circulating about the entire parish. Unfortunately she was not particularly successful, in part because the rumors were so fantastic they created a life of their own.

The "dangerous gentleman" was a danger to himself. The Earl of Albright had tried to kill himself, they said.

How those rumors angered her! Dr. Mayton had, of course, given her Adrian's explanation for what had happened, but it was hardly necessary. A man of Adrian's character would never attempt anything so cowardly. And if for some reason he had thought to end his own life, she was quite certain he would have succeeded. Whatever had happened that afternoon, he had not attempted to take his own life, and she had to think of a way to help him. She *would* think of a way.

Lilliana gathered her feet up under her dressing gown, propping her chin on her knees as she stared at the moon, thankful for the late-night silence so she could think. It was somewhere in the depth of that silence that she first heard the sound of a wounded animal. Straining to hear it, she lifted her head. There it was again—a low, aching moan, as if the animal were in pain. Immediately, she thought of her pups, relegated to a small pen Mr. Bottoms had built for her near the terrace. She came swiftly to her feet and went to the window, peering outside.

The sound came again, so faint as to almost be imagined, swelled a bit, then faded. Lilliana jerked her head around to the door that connected her rooms to the master suite.

Adrian.

Oh God, it was Adrian! She gasped softly as the low, keening sound came again, a sound unlike any she had ever heard a human make. It was coarse, sickening—and heart-wrenching. Adrian was in pain.

She moved quickly to her bedside and lit a candle, and without hesitation opened the connecting door, wincing as the moan grew louder. Carefully, she stepped into his room. He did not notice her; it took her a mo-

ment to remember he could not see the light. Lying on
his bed, he was curled into a ball on bedcovers that had
been thrashed into a furious heap. He moaned again,
and slowly, quietly, she moved across the room, lifting
the candle high. As she neared the bed his head suddenly
jerked up. Her gaze riveted on his hazel eyes—she had
no idea what she thought she would see, but she had not
imagined them to look the same. But dear God, they
were the same deep hazel eyes with the same gold flecks.
A little scarred around the edges, but the very same eyes
frantically roaming the room as he came up on his elbow.

"Who is it? Who is there?" he snapped.

She unconsciously took a step backward, and his eyes
flashed with unimaginable terror. Struck speechless by
the extraordinary display of emotion, Lilliana moved
cautiously to the bed table and set her candle down.

"For God's sake, who is it?" he demanded, the fear
evident in his voice.

"*Adrian*. It's me."

His hazel eyes widened, and he suddenly fell over on
his side. "Get out!" he groaned helplessly.

Her heart aching to the point of bursting, Lilliana
moved to the bed and laid her hand on his shoulder. "I
won't leave you," she whispered tearfully. "Not now,
not ever."

For a moment he did not move. But then his hand
abruptly shot out, flailing as he searched for her, grabbing at her shoulder, her breast, and finally her hand,
which he clutched so tightly, she feared the bones would
crack. He lifted himself up, pulling her into his embrace
at the same time. "Lillie, *Lillie*!" he whispered frantically. "Hold me. Dear God, please hold me—"

Choking on a frightened sob, Lilliana melted onto the
bed and gathered him in her arms.

"Hold me," he muttered helplessly, and clutched her
so fiercely that she could scarcely breathe. He pressed his
face to her breasts, taking tortured gulps of air.

"I won't leave you," she murmured, *"I will never leave you."*

Sleep came at last, after days of tossing and waking often in the hope that by some miracle his sight had returned. In the rare moments Adrian had actually slept, he had been tortured by recurring visions of Phillip's face in death, Benedict's eyes at his wedding, and the devastation on Lilliana's face when he had told her the true reason he had married her. This was hell, at long last come and richly deserved. An eternity of darkness to be endured with nothing but those hideous images forever playing in his mind's eye.

This was the quality of his mercy, and dear God, it was *terrifying*.

When he had finally determined he had gone completely mad, she had come and had touched him, had awakened something buried deeply within him that he hardly recognized. She had come and wrapped her arms around him, banishing the terror that engulfed him for a time, soothing his fear with her caress, the dulcet tone of her voice, and the soft scent of roses in her hair. And finally, he had slept.

For how long, he had no idea, but it had been a peaceful, dreamless slumber. When he awoke to the blackness again, it had taken him several moments to remember where he was, that he held her in his arms. She was sleeping—he could feel her steady breath on his neck. She smelled so sweet, he thought drowsily, and for the first time in days he felt safe, a comfort in her arms that soothed the ragged edges of his mind.

But then the powerful terror struck him anew. He was *blind*! God, dear *God,* how could this have happened? What sin had he committed that the Lord would strike him blind? The punishment seemed so cruel—too cruel to allow her to bear it with him. Was his hell to be hers too? What sort of life was this, bound to a blind man who had married her for revenge? *Cast me to hell, but not her, dear God, not her.* No! He would not commend her to hell with him—she had to go. As soon as possible, without looking back. She had to go!

He suddenly shoved her away, ignoring the small, sleepy cry of alarm. "Go on, Lilliana. Go to your room," he growled.

She stirred; the mattress dipped next to him and he understood she had come up on her elbow. "Adrian, are you all right?" she murmured. "Can I get you something?"

"Please God, don't treat me like an invalid," he said nastily, and rolled away from her. "Go. Go back to your rooms."

Her hand touched his bare shoulder, and he jerked away from her lest he succumb to the comfort of her arms again. "Adrian, I meant what I said. I won't leave you."

"I don't *want* you here, Lilliana! Go!" he said more forcefully.

"I will not allow you to push me away," she said stubbornly. "You need me, and I—"

"Jesus, did you hear me? Get *out*!" he bellowed. Silence. What was she doing? He at once felt very self-conscious and unsure of himself . . . he was not in control.

"No," she said quietly.

Now she was alarming him. All right, all right, in a moment of weakness he had turned to her. But the Princess of the Grange would *not* talk herself into some foolish sense of responsibility. He rolled again, groping for the edge of the bed. Swinging his legs over the side, he gripped the mattress on either side of his knees, afraid to stand, afraid of the awkward steps into blackness. "Go back to your rustic little Grange and leave me be!" he growled.

"I'm not going anywhere. Have you forgotten? I am *married* to you," she said firmly.

His alarm gave way to panic—sheer, unarguable panic. Was she insane? Was she so dense she could not comprehend what he had become, how it would ruin her life? "Not for long," he said bluntly. "I intend to divorce you." He heard her swallow convulsively. *Good.* Someday she would thank him for his cruelty.

"I will fight you," she muttered softly.

Good *God,* she was stubborn! He made a sound of great disgust and shook his head. "You are unabashedly stupid, aren't you?" he sneered. "A plain little idiot. What must I say to get through that thick head of yours? I am *through* with you, Lilliana. I don't want you here. I am releasing you so you can spread your thighs for Benedict. Go!" he snapped, and winced, nauseated by his own reprehensible words.

"Don't be an idiot, Adrian," she shot back. "I married you for better or worse, and I am not going anywhere. So just stop this!"

He shoved to his feet, wildly praying he did not stumble headlong into a chair. With his hands he groped in front of him. The wall. *Thank God.* He turned so that his back was pressed against something familiar. "By all that is holy, I cannot speak any plainer, madam. I want you gone from Longbridge. I don't give a bloody damn about your misguided sense of duty. I want you out of my sight—"

His breath stuck in his lungs. She was out of his sight, all right, but he could feel her eyes on him, imagined them full of pity, and his anger soared. "It would not matter if I could see you now. I wanted to be rid of you long before this happened. It was a mistake to have married you, a *colossal* mistake. Heed me, madam, I do not want a parish princess for a wife. I want you gone!"

She said nothing for a moment, but then he heard the bed creak, the rustling of the linens as she climbed out of bed. "All right," she said softly, and he heard her move away, then the door open and close. Adrian waited for a moment, his fingers spreading against the wall at his back to make sure it did not go anywhere. She was gone. Oh God, hopefully one day she would understand. He sagged against the wall as another blinding headache forced his chin to his chest.

"I'll go, but only for the moment. I *will not* leave you."

Her voice cracked the air; Adrian lurched upright, straining uselessly to see her, his pulse racing at having been so shamelessly fooled. He heard the door open and the sound of her dressing gown as she whisked through it, then the loud, resounding slam of it when she shoved it closed.

This time, he had no doubt she was gone.

It had been four weeks to the day, Lilliana thought as she marched down the long corridor of the east wing. Hugo and Maude followed closely behind, the bells she had fastened around their necks jangling loudly. The door to the breakfast room was open, and she could hear Adrian's loud groan before she reached it. A smile slowly spread her lips; she marched across the threshold, and punched her fists to her hips as she surveyed the room. Adrian was sitting at the table, his face buried in his hands. Max stood at the sideboard behind him, shaking his head fiercely in warning, grimacing and pointing wildly at Adrian.

Lilliana blithely ignored him. "Still in high dudgeon, I see," she quipped, and glided into the room with her dogs close behind.

"High dudgeon!" Adrian snapped, and straightened slowly, his eyes staring blankly in front of him. "I assure you I am hardly afflicted with such a feminine weakness, but I *am* sick to death of those curs!"

Max shook his head so hard that fine wisps of hair stood straight out as he anxiously pointed at the dogs. Lilliana merely smiled; the staff was intimidated by Adrian's fierceness, but not her. She had made the discovery that he was capable of feeling after all, and on some level she delighted in provoking those feelings. And since his accident, she rarely had to try. He reserved the most bitter of his emotions for her.

"My pups adore you, Adrian," she announced sweetly, and settled herself directly across from him. His sightless eyes unabashedly fascinated her; she marveled at their ability to convey the emotions he so easily masked when he could see. Judging by the glint in them now, he was greatly displeased.

"I don't give a damn—I hope to heaven you take them with you when you return to Blackfield Grange," he snarled, and shoved his hands through his hair, making it look as if it hadn't been combed in weeks.

Lilliana chuckled. "What, the Grange *again*, Adrian? You have apparently forgotten—for at least the hundredth time, I am quite certain—that I am not going to the Grange."

Adrian's face darkened. "Do you want my opinion?" he drawled nastily.

"I don't know," she said thoughtfully. "Why don't you give it to me first, and then I shall decide?"

Max's mouth dropped open in amazement before he threw back his head and closed his eyes in mortification. Adrian punched his elbows to the table and leaned forward, glaring at a point over her shoulder. "Very well, then, Princess, brace yourself," he drawled nastily. "It is my opinion that you are an immature, selfish, and woefully ignorant country bumpkin who is not fit to shine my shoes!"

"Is that all?" Lilliana laughed, and winked at the butler. "You must congratulate me, Max. I have apparently improved over yesterday. As you are in such fine spirits, my lord, perhaps you would agree to walk in the gardens with a woefully ignorant country bumpkin?"

"Don't be ridiculous," he snapped. "If you won't leave Longbridge, then at least have the decency to leave me be," he said, and motioned angrily for Max, who rushed forward, grasping Adrian's arm and the chair at the same time. Adrian rose cautiously, his hands gripping the table until he was confident on Max's arm. "To

my rooms,'' he muttered irritably, "and kick the stuffing
from those beasts if they dare step in our path.''

Lilliana rose too. Hugo and Maude immediately
sprang to their feet like chubby little sentinels, paying
rapt attention to her every movement.

At the door, Adrian paused at the sound of their
bells. "Do not follow me!" he all but shouted.

"I am not following you," she replied calmly. "I am
going to *my* rooms. Come, pups.''

"What are you waiting for?" he snarled at Max. "Be
quick about it!" With a nervous hitch, Max gingerly
placed one hand on Adrian's waist, then wrapped the
other around Adrian's upper arm, and began to lead him
with great care down the corridor. Frowning at the pair,
Lilliana followed slowly behind with her hands clasped
behind her back. Adrian walked as if he were one hundred and fifty years old, one arm stretched far in front of
him, his steps measured and shuffled. Exasperated, she
sighed loudly.

"You may remedy your impatience by leaving Longbridge," he irritably reminded her.

"Why? I am hardly bothering you."

"I beg to differ. You have bothered me since the day
we were wed."

Again, Max shook his head—this time, at his feet.

"You needn't remind me of that," Lilliana replied in
a singsong voice. "You've been quite plain about it, actually. Oh, Hugo! Give that to me!" The puppy obediently relinquished the linen napkin he had helped
himself to in the breakfast room, and waddled over to
see what Maude was so frantically sniffing. Bells tinkled
softly as the two dogs sniffed around the leg of the furniture.

"This house is not a barn, and I want those mongrels
out of here!" Adrian growled. "Those bells are enough
to drive a man out of his mind."

"It is still too cold outdoors—"

"They are *dogs,* for God's sake—"

"And the bells let you know where they are at all times."

"I don't want to know where they are! Good God! Will you not *leave*?" he roared.

Max was positively cringing now; he cast pleading glances at her over his shoulder as he carefully eased Adrian up onto the first step of the great spiraling staircase, and the next.

Like an invalid.

Lilliana's frown deepened. "Max, don't you think he could climb the stairs by himself? There is a perfectly good railing he could hold—"

"Get *out*!" Adrian suddenly exploded, and clutched desperately at Max to keep from toppling over. "I will not abide this constant harassment! If you are not gone by morning, I shall send for the constable, do you hear me? Do us all an enormous favor and get *out*!"

Lilliana stilled. As accustomed as she was to his frequent railing, the rabid way in which he spoke stung her. Lord, how he hated her! Because she was the one person on this godforsaken estate who insisted that he at least *try* to live. Even as determined as she was in that, she was weary of the endless stream of scorn. Anger shuddered through her, and she moved quietly up the stairs, pausing on the step where he stood. "If you want me gone, Adrian, you will have to remove me yourself," she said calmly. "That is, if you are man enough."

The world seemed to stop for one bizarre moment. Adrian's hazel eyes clouded with fury and, wrenching free of Max, he suddenly lunged for her. Lilliana easily sidestepped him, and he landed on Maude. The pup's frightened yelp infuriated him, and he lunged again, crashing headlong into the wall. That caused him to explode in the vilest curse imaginable—she didn't know the meaning of half the words he used, and cringed as Max quickly grabbed him.

"My lord, please!" the butler cried. "Have a care!" A footman came running to the foot of the stairs; two maids rushed into the foyer, clinging to each other as they watched Adrian thrash about until Max had righted him. He cast an imploring look at Lilliana as Adrian took deep, ragged gulps of air. "Please, my lady," he begged her, "*please*! Give him some peace!"

Somewhere below her, she could hear one of the maids moaning softly. Shaking her head with disgust, Lilliana continued up the stairs to where Polly was waiting, having witnessed the whole exchange and Adrian's near topple. "Ah, my lady, his lordship . . . he needs your support now," Polly pleaded.

Lilliana glared at her as she marched past. "You are right, Polly. He needs my support. He needs me to help him *live*, because the rest of you would allow him to waste away like some old fool!"

"Oh this house, this house," Polly moaned as she hurried after her mistress. "Will it never see an end to the tragedy?"

"Honestly, Polly!" Lilliana snapped. "He is *blind*, not dead! I will not allow him or anyone else to think otherwise! It is truly beyond my comprehension how the lot of you can watch a man as magnificent as Adrian Spence shrivel up and die! Well, I won't, and I don't give a fig what any of you think about it!" she ranted, and stepped into her rooms, quickly ushering her dogs in before turning an enraged glare at Polly. "He is *drowning* in self-pity, can you not see that? I will not allow it!" she shouted.

Polly blinked down at her big hands, clasped tightly together. "Heaven help us, this family is cursed! First the girls, now *this*!" she wailed, and turning, rushed away from Lilliana.

Just grand. Now she had succeeded in alienating even Polly. Frustrated and weary from the emotional battering she was enduring, Lilliana slammed the door and restlessly began pacing. Why could they not see what he was doing? Why did they cater to his frailty? Or was it possible that she really *was* being destructive? Marvelous. Now she was second-guessing herself at every turn. But Dr. Mayton had said to make him live—he *had* to live! Indeed it was tragic that his sight was gone—but did that make him any less a man? Only if he allowed it, and it made her exceedingly angry that Adrian would not stand up to this adversity. Just where was the fearlessness, the reckless living?

Well, *she* would stand up to it. He could utterly despise her if he so chose, but she'd be damned if she would watch him sink and drown in his own terror. He would face it or she would die trying to make him!

Escape. Oh God, to escape, if only for a time, for the space of a few hours. Lilliana abruptly left her rooms, marching past his door and down the stairs, ignoring the disapproving looks from the servants who had witnessed her challenge to him. *Damn* them! Yanking a cloak around her shoulders in the foyer, she marched outside after Hugo and Maude, heading for the stables at a near sprint.

When she reached the paddock, she was startled to see two strangers, one holding Thunder and the other speaking with Mr. Lewis. What on earth? Did Mr. Lewis think to allow these men to *ride* Thunder? Lilliana hurried across the paddock to him; Mr. Lewis paused the moment he saw her and quickly bowed. "Good afternoon, Lady Albright."

"Mr. Lewis? What is going on here?" she asked curtly, glancing warily at the man to whom the steward was speaking.

"He's come for the stallion, my lady. His lordship has sold him."

Lilliana almost choked. Oh no. No, no, no. He *wouldn't*! He could not give up so easily! "What do you mean?" she demanded.

Mr. Lewis glanced sheepishly at the stranger. "Lord Albright has sold—"

"No!" she shrieked, and whirled around, grabbing the reins from the man who held Thunder and startling him badly. "That is impossible, Mr. Lewis! I forbid it!"

Mr. Lewis's eyes grew wide, and he took a careful

step forward. "But my lady," he whispered loudly, "his lordship has an agreement—"

"No! No agreement, Mr. Lewis! He will not sell Thunder!" she cried, and yanked at the reins, pulling Thunder around. Mr. Lewis moved to take them from her, but Lilliana quickly pulled Thunder back farther, jerking the bridle hard when he pulled in protest. The three men exchanged glances and, as one, began to move toward her. Hysteria bubbled in Lilliana. Her heart beat wildly with fear, but she would die before she would allow them to take Thunder. Adrian held the horse dearer than everything else, and without him, he would truly wither away, she was *certain* of it. So certain, she was prepared to fight. Except that her heart had climbed to her throat in sheer terror, threatening to choke her senseless.

"Lady Albright!" Mr. Lewis warned, as if talking to a child.

"No! You cannot sell this horse!" she shrieked hysterically. "And if you think to take him from me, you will have to kill me to do it!"

That stunned the three men into silence. A moment passed; the taller of the two gentlemen shifted his gaze to Mr. Lewis. "Perhaps there has been a misunderstanding," he said gently.

"No!" Mr. Lewis said hastily. "You must forgive her ladyship, sir. She is . . . well naturally, she is distraught at what has happened, but Lord Albright was quite clear—"

"No!" Lilliana screamed.

The two men started backing away. "I suggest that you verify Lord Albright's intentions, sir," one muttered, and the two turned on their heels, walking quickly from the paddock and slapping at the noses of the dogs as they attempted to greet them.

Lilliana gulped as Mr. Lewis turned slowly to look at her. "What have you done, my lady?" he muttered hopelessly.

With that, her fear gave way to fury. Was the entire

world as blind as Adrian? Her brows snapped into a frown; she thrust the reins at a groom who was gaping at her. "Have him saddled," she said icily. "Thunder and I are going for a ride." She glanced at Mr. Lewis, her eyes narrowing dangerously as her gaze sliced across him. "Please listen carefully, sir. I will not—under *any* circumstance—allow that horse to be sold. My husband will ride again. Do you quite understand me? He will ride that horse again!"

It was quite clear he did not understand, and disgusted, Lilliana marched into the stables. She didn't give a damn if Mr. Lewis understood her or not. Adrian would sell Thunder over her dead body.

Sixteen

ADRIAN KNEW SOMETHING was wrong. He could hear the frantic conversation down the corridor, could tell by the muffled tone of Max's voice that he was distressed. The sound of doors banging and bells tinkling further testified to some little bickering, but as long as they left him alone, he could not have cared less. Sitting in front of the fire in what he thought was the gold salon, he did not need or want their attentions.

Was it really a gold salon? Honestly, he couldn't recall anything but vague details about the room. The chair he was sitting in, for example, he knew to be embroidered. But with what design, he couldn't say. He knew his grandfather's ornate clock stood on the mantel, but he had no idea if it kept time. There were so many things, so many *little* things he had never really noticed. Little things that he would give his life to see again.

Resting his head against the chair, he closed his eyes. As loath as he was to admit it, he would give his life to see *her* again.

The bickering filtered into his consciousness again; he sighed wearily when the door of the salon opened. "What *now*, Max?"

"Not Max. Me!"

Adrian groaned and rolled his head from one side to the other on the back of the chair. Marvelous. And the little demon was not alone, apparently, judging by the sound of those intolerable bells and the distinct panting of dogs. "Get those beasts out of here!" he warned her, angrily swiping his arm into black space, hoping to punch at least one of them in the nose.

"Here, pups, go find Max so that I might have a word alone with your papa."

Adrian scowled at that. The Princess of the Grange apparently had come to torment him again, starting with her annoying habit of speaking to those beasts as if they were human. God in heaven, when would she take her opportunity and *leave* him? He listened to her usher the two beasts out the door, and when it closed, he warily cocked his head to one side, confused as to whether he was alone or not.

But the rustling of her skirt and the whiff of her perfume as she sailed past assured him he was not alone. "Now what?" he asked testily.

"Would you like a brandy? Or perhaps a whiskey? I confess in the time we've been married, I have never known your preference," she said from somewhere near the sideboard.

"I don't want anything but for you to go," he growled, ignoring the little voice in him that disagreed.

"You don't want anything but to waste away like some old man! *Damn* you, Adrian!"

That surprised him. For the last weeks, she had been unerringly cheerful in her responses to his innumerable attempts to make her leave. He could sense her anger, could sense her pacing in front of the hearth. "What concern is it of yours if I do?" he responded evenly. "I know you are too thick to grasp this simple concept, but I don't want you here."

"*Hush,*" she said, her voice threatening. "I am sick unto death of your pathetic attempts to make me leave you."

"If that is so, madam, then you can ease yourself quite readily by leaving."

"I don't care how vile you are, I won't leave you," she said, and he imagined a pert toss of her head. "Nor will I allow you to dispose of the few things you hold dear in a fit of self-pity."

Self-pity? Adrian snorted contemptuously. Did she think blindness was something a man could easily take in stride? "You know nothing."

"I refused to let Lewis sell Thunder."

Instantly, a shot of anger rifled through him and Adrian sat up. "You did *what*?"

"I sent those men away, and then I rode Thunder until he was laboring to breathe," she blithely announced.

Fury rapidly uncoiled in Adrian's chest—the little demon was treading on dangerous ground. "*Jesus,* Lilliana!" he bellowed. "You have no right to countermand me! Regardless of how feeble or infirm you may think me, *I* am the lord of this estate, and you will not contradict me!"

"If you are lord of this estate, then act like it," she responded calmly.

Livid, Adrian gripped the arms of his chair. If he could see her, if he could get his hands on her . . .

"Thunder has not been ridden in weeks and he was desperate to be given his head. Before you launch yourself from that chair, let me assure you he is quite content at the moment. As for those men, well, I could not let you send away the only thing you love because of some silly notion—"

"Look at me, Lilliana!" he roared. "*Look* at me! I am *blind*! I cannot ride that stallion any longer—surely even *you* can comprehend that!"

The rustling of her skirts and the sound of her falling to her knees in front of him startled him. He flinched when she put her hands on his knees and instantly pushed back into the chair in a futile effort to get away from her touch.

"Oh Adrian," she moaned sorrowfully. "You can't ride him the way you did, but you can still *ride*! Don't you see what you are doing? You are giving up, surrendering to this tragedy and allowing it to drain you of all will to live! I can't sit idly by while you allow this sorrow to swallow you whole," she said, gasping on a sob in her throat. "I don't *care* that you despise me! I will fight you until you realize you are no less a man for your infirmity! You can *live*, Adrian, as you did before, and there is nothing to stop you but your fear!" She made a soulful sound that gripped his heart. "Perhaps you can't see the sun, but you can still *feel* it fall down around you and know it is there. It's still there, don't you know? The sun is still there!" Another sob escaped her throat, and she buried her face on his knees.

Stunned, Adrian sat perfectly still as her tears seeped through his trousers, awed by how her weeping seemed to fill the black space around him. What sort of woman was this? What sort of woman would remain with a shell of a man when he had granted her freedom? What sort of woman would place his sorry life so far above her own?

It moved him—jolted him, really—and he lifted his hand, slowly extending it until he found her head. Gently, he laid his palm on her head and caressed her hair; desperately wishing he could see that mass of curls again and the dozen shades of gold that caught the sun and refracted its brightness around her.

But he would never see it again.

"Lilliana, please listen to me." He spoke earnestly; the Princess had to understand how hopeless it all was. "I appreciate what you think you are doing, I swear it. But you must understand that I will never be the same again. I cannot provide for you now. I cannot guarantee your safety or protect you from harm. I have ruined your life in more ways than one, and I am asking . . . no, I am *begging* you to please release us both from this nightmare and go home. I can never make you happy—go home to the Grange, to Benedict. Go home, Lillie, and leave me to my hell.''

A long moment of silence passed before her head lifted beneath his hand, and he had the unearthly sensation that her gray-green eyes pierced his heart. ''How can you say you are less a man?'' she murmured tearfully.

''Because it is plainly true,'' he said patiently.

All of a sudden she moved and surprised him by placing her hands on his shoulders, effectively pinning him to the chair. ''What are you doing?'' he exclaimed.

She answered by pressing her lips to his, by crawling onto his lap when he tried to wrench free. With her hands she caught his face, holding it with remarkable strength as she kissed him, her lips sliding across his, her tongue darting delicately along the seam of his lips. A fire lit his belly, and fearful of it, Adrian tried to push her off his lap. But she was amazingly strong and continued to kiss him, fighting him every step of the way.

Liquid fire ran through him like a sieve. Her lips, her scent, the press of her breasts against him as he tried to dislodge her—all of his animal instincts and raging desires were suddenly alive and gathering in his groin. He fought her—or at least he thought he did, but his arms were somehow around her now, crushing her lithe body to him, eagerly devouring her lips. He sucked at them, tasted the saltiness of her tears on them, and greedily filled her mouth with his tongue. She responded by pressing her body tightly to him, wriggling against his rigid arousal, caressing his shoulders, his arms. His hand found her breast, and he cupped it, reveling in its weight against his palm. He wanted more, and searched for an entrance to her warm flesh through the fabric of her gown.

But suddenly, it was over. She abruptly lifted her head and left him panting. ''Can you still honestly say you are less a man?'' She slid off his lap. ''If you want me, come here,'' she murmured hoarsely.

Adrian unsteadily wiped the back of his hand across

his mouth. He wanted her back in his lap, her soft, plump lips on his again, but felt helpless to find her and draw her near. Even if he did manage to go to her, it was pointless. "It won't change anything," he said bitterly. "I am still blind. I am still unable to ride Thunder, or see to my business, or to travel freely in this world. I am still sentenced to a life of darkness and this estate. *You*, on the other hand, can have everything I cannot, the freedom to do all the things I cannot. Do not be a fool, Lilliana. *Take* it!"

That was met with complete silence. He turned his head in the direction of the sideboard, then the opposite wall, trying to catch a movement, any sound at all. And then he heard her walking away, away from *him*, and strangled on the urge to call her back. "I will leave," he heard her mutter, "when the moon turns to cheese!" With that, he heard her yank the door open and shut it resoundingly behind her.

A fierce headache began to press behind his eyes. The tantalizing feel of her lingered in his arms and that incredible kiss still burned with a heat so strong that it alarmed him. He thought of her tears on his knee and tried to imagine how her eyes had looked. Damn it, why couldn't he see her eyes? Why hadn't he looked at her, *really* looked at her, even once, so he could remember? And he vowed, then and there, if he ever saw again, he would not squander the chance to look into her eyes. Not a single chance.

Lilliana spent the next morning with Hugo and Maude removing the thick velvet cords from dozens of drapes hanging in the west wing. The servants watched her covertly, exchanging curious glances as she went from one room to the next with a bundle of cords in her arms. They soon gathered in the kitchens to speculate as to what her ladyship was doing *now*. A footman hypothesized that she was systematically destroying the house in retaliation for Lord Albright's cruel treatment of her. A

maid shook her head to that, insisting that Lady Albright had lost her mind to grief—which prompted a
spirited debate over which Albright was actually the
more demented one. After all, the cook loudly insisted,
his lordship had tried to take his own life.

Max listened quietly to their talk, then slipped out of
the kitchen, unnoticed.

He smiled when he entered the front corridor. His
lady was a clever one, he would give her that, he thought
appreciatively. In the east wing, she had strung the cords
along the wall from one end of the corridor to the other,
just where the wainscoting met the wallpaper. The
string of cords disappeared around the corner and up the
great staircase. She was working at the very end of the
corridor, bent at the waist as she tried to fasten the cord
to the wall.

Max walked briskly down the length of the corridor.
"Lady Albright?"

Her head snapped up, and she straightened quickly,
the better to glare at him. "Don't you dare," she said in
low tones, "don't you *dare* tell me to leave him be."

She had a bright, almost wild look in her eye, and
Max quickly flung his hands up, palms outward. "No,
milady."

Her suspicious gaze raked over him before she turned
back to her chore. She was exhausted, Max realized. Her
hair was a mess, curls springing out in every direction.
Her gown was covered with vertical lines of dust from
where she had held the old drapery cords against her.
Her slender fingers were rubbed almost raw from laboring to tack the cords to the wall.

He reached for the cord, holding a hand up in peace
when she whirled around, prepared to do battle. "I
should very much like to help you," he said calmly, and
pried the cord from her fingers. Her shoulders sagged—
with relief and exhaustion, he thought—as he went to
work on the cord, smiling to himself.

When Max finally returned to the kitchens—having
seen to it that all the cords were hung to her satisfac-

tion—he informed the witless staff that she had strung the cords as guides so that his lordship could walk freely. That earned him several looks of surprise—and a few tenuous grins of approval.

Lilliana wasn't done yet. Later that afternoon she waited patiently in Adrian's study, her brows knitted together in a devilish vee. She had sent Mr. Lewis for him, ignoring the steward's fearful pleas to leave him to his rest. "He has rested on his laurels quite long enough, Mr. Lewis," she had cheerfully responded.

She heard Adrian before she saw him; his displeasure flowed freely as he walked down the corridor. He appeared with his hand clamped firmly on Mr. Lewis's shoulder, his face dark. "Good afternoon, my lord!" she said brightly.

"What havoc do you wreak now?" he drawled, shrugging Mr. Lewis off once he had found a chair and had eased himself into it.

"I am reviewing the books," she said pleasantly. "Mr. Lewis thought to invest in a new roof for the Baineses' cottage, and when he mentioned it, I thought I should have a look at the expenses first." Mr. Lewis grew white as a sheet at that bald-faced lie, and began shaking his head, drawing his hand across his throat, mimicking a cutthroat. Lilliana glared impatiently at him. "Thank you, Mr. Lewis. Lord Albright shall be quite safe for a time, I promise."

"You have no business prowling through the books," Adrian said tightly. Mr. Lewis cast her another pleading look, and with her hand Lilliana shooed him away. He backed up slowly, his teeth nervously nibbling his lip.

"Well, as you won't, I thought someone should do it," she responded amicably. Mr. Lewis rolled his eyes in mortification and quickly disappeared through the door.

Adrian sighed wearily. "Now I know you are mad. Exactly how would you expect me to *look* at the books?"

"Obviously, with help," she said, unable to hide the

twinge of exasperation in her voice. "But as you haven't shown the slightest interest in your affairs, I feel duty-bound to make sure everything is in order."

"Get up from there and send for Mr. Lewis," he said sharply.

Lilliana defiantly opened the ledger. "Aha. I see here that you expended fifteen pounds for paraffin oil and beeswax. My, that is awfully expensive, isn't it? Do we need beeswax? Ooh, and here is another five pounds for tallow . . . I can plainly see I shall have to cut that expenditure in half. I'll just draw a line through this figure—"

"Lilliana!" Adrian exclaimed, and miracle of miracles, he came out of his seat, standing unsteadily in the middle of the room. "Please put it down. You don't know what you are doing," he said anxiously, and shoved his arms out in front of him as he took a step forward.

"Oats? What need of oats do we have? I shall draw a line through this too."

"If you want Thunder to eat, you will not touch that entry," he breathed. "Please put the ledger away—" He knocked into a low ornamental table and cursed under his breath, but caught himself with his hands and straightened slowly, inching carefully around the obstacle.

"The footman's liveries are a bit worn, I think. I shall order some bolts of fine English wool cloth. Ten bolts, I should think, and two competent seamstresses. Honestly, I've no idea of the cost! I suppose I could enter a guess for now—"

"Lilliana!" Adrian cried, and lunged forward, taking several steps until he had found the desk. He gripped the edge of it tightly and leaned forward. *"Put the ledger down,"* he said, carefully enunciating each word.

Lilliana couldn't help it; she smiled happily at the muscle jumping in his clenched jaw. Thunder had not worked. Her kiss had not worked, but at last she had found the one thing that could bring him to his feet. Why hadn't she thought of his affairs before? "Why?" she asked flippantly. "*You* can't see it," she said, and eased back, waiting for the explosion she was sure would come.

Adrian dropped his head between his shoulders in an apparent attempt to contain his anger. When he at last lifted his head, his hazel eyes looked tired. "Did you write anything? Did you make any mark at all?"

"No. But if you will tell me what to do, I will be your eyes."

He groaned and squeezed his eyes shut as he pushed himself from the desk. "You are going to send me to an early grave, you know that, don't you?" he muttered.

"Better there than this state of helplessness you insist upon," she said, her smile deepening. He shook his head, and with his hand felt for the edge of the desk. Carefully, he came around it to where she sat.

"Fetch a chair, or would you have me attempt that, too?" he asked dryly.

Her heart soared. Lilliana sprang to her feet, pulling the chair out so he could get into it and eagerly rushing to pull another around beside him. With his hand he felt for the ledger; his fingers traced lightly down columns he could no longer see. "What have you got?" he asked.

"Several invoices, it would appear—"

"Read one to me."

"To the sale of one hundred pounds of raw oats, five pounds, six pence."

Nodding, Adrian pointed to the ledger. "There is a page labeled 'stable.' When you find it, you will notice there are four columns. . . ."

And for the remainder of the afternoon he talked her through the books, guiding her to enter the expenditures, review the revenues, and balance the accounts. It was the most blissful afternoon Lilliana had spent in her life. At long last she felt needed, as if she was really contributing something of value. Adrian sat calmly beside her, smiling faintly when she picked up the accounting techniques he explained to her. Not once did he raise his voice. Not once did he show her any disdain. He was pleasant, almost relaxed, and she felt keenly the sense of companionship she had longed for.

She watched him closely, free to marvel at his handsome face and the square cut of his jaw, the thick hair that brushed well below his collar. He was truly magnificent, she thought dreamily, a veritable god—something she had lost sight of several weeks ago and something that made her tingle to observe so unabashedly. When Adrian asked her to send for Max and tea, she happily obliged, hoping the magical moment between them would go on forever.

But nothing lasts forever.

Max arrived before she could ring the bellpull, announcing guests. Adrian stiffened instantly in his chair. "Who?" he asked bluntly.

"Lord Kealing, my lord. And . . . and Lord Benedict," Max said reluctantly.

His expression melted to bland, and Adrian motioned to the chair next to him. "Move this. Have tea brought after you show them in." As the door closed behind Max, Adrian asked quietly, "Lilliana? How does he know?"

She cringed. Of course she had not written his family, not without his permission. And she had only lightly suggested Dr. Mayton do it. "I . . . I don't . . . Perhaps Dr. Mayton?"

Whatever he might have thought of that died on his tongue, because Archibald Spence, Lord Kealing, stalked into the room at that very moment, Benedict trailing behind. Lilliana had not seen Lord Kealing in many years; his angry countenance surprised her. Benedict smiled nervously at her, but his attention was quickly on Adrian, who rose slowly, his knuckles white as he gripped the desk, the only outward sign of uncertainty that showed. "Father, you will forgive me if I do not come to greet you," he said blandly.

"Bloody hell," Lord Kealing whispered. "It *is* true."

"Unfortunately so," Adrian responded with a smirk.

"I don't believe you have had the pleasure of making the acquaintance of my wife. Lady Lilliana Albright," he said.

To Lilliana's great surprise, Lord Kealing did not even look at her. His face reddened as he glared at Adrian. "I was given to understand that you blinded yourself by attempting to blow your fool head off!"

Lilliana gaped at him in shock, but Adrian merely chuckled. "Rather sorry I missed, are you, Father?"

"You won't stop until you ruin everything around you!" Lord Kealing spat contemptuously. "I knew your recklessness would ruin you in the end, and I was right! Look at you now! Useless to your wife, to your *title*! Is this how you would honor your grandfather? Is this what you would do to me in the end? Heaven help me, the expense I will incur in taking your foolishness to the Court of Faculties and Dispensations—"

"Lord Kealing!" Lilliana interjected, horrified by his ignominious words and posture. But Lord Kealing did not seem to hear her. Benedict responded with a weakly imploring look that made her stomach knot in revulsion.

"The burden now falls to me," he went on. "What more would you do to me?" he bellowed.

"Father, please," Benedict tried lamely.

Across the room, Adrian laughed softly. Lilliana jerked her gaze to him; he was standing with his arms folded across his chest, glaring in the direction of Lord Kealing so sharply that for a moment she thought he could see his father. "Father, only you could take a tragedy such as this and make it seem willful on my part. I did not ask you to come here. I do not ask *anything* of you. Whatever scheme you may have concocted is pointless."

"Pointless, is it?" Lord Kealing bellowed. "I will not allow my name to be scandalized, and as much as I wish it were untrue, *your* name is tied to *mine*. How many lives will you ruin before it is all said and done? One would have thought Phillip's murder was enough—"

"Father!" Benedict cried. "Please! Be civil! Come,

sit near the fire. Lilliana, is there perhaps a bit of whis-key about?'' he asked nervously, and grabbing his fa-ther's coat sleeve, forced him to turn around and walk to the fire.

Lord Kealing went, but he was not done. ''I don't want any whiskey, Ben,'' he muttered. ''I don't intend to stay a moment longer in this house than I must.''

''You already have,'' Adrian said indifferently.

''Unfortunately, Albright, I have a duty to assess the damage to Longbridge. You may deserve to rot, but he was Benedict's grandfather, too, and I will not allow you to ruin his legacy!''

''He has not ruined Longbridge!'' Lilliana gasped with outrage. ''He has done nothing but improve it! It was in horrible disrepair when we came, but he has—''

''Lilliana,'' Adrian gently interrupted, ''save your breath.''

''Lady Albright,'' Lord Kealing said icily, turning his little black eyes to her, ''do me the enormous courtesy of allowing me a private conversation with my son.''

Astounded, Lilliana gaped at him, unable to conceive of someone behaving in such a rude manner. And in her own house! Indignant, she deliberately planted her hands on her waist. ''I beg your pardon?'' she asked slowly.

''Benedict!'' Adrian said sharply. ''Please . . .'' he said, motioning in the general direction of Lilliana.

Benedict seemed to know exactly what he wanted, and quickly strode across the room to grab Lilliana's elbow. ''I would that you show me your recent paint-ings.'' He did not allow her to respond, but forced her to the door as Lord Kealing began his contemptible drivel again.

''Benedict, stop! I must—''

''You must let Adrian and Father talk,'' he muttered, and pushed her out the door, almost colliding with Max and his tray of tea. ''Take my advice and keep the tea for yourself, Max, unless you relish cleaning up the car-nage later,'' he said and proceeded to march her down the corridor toward the terrace, then practically dragged her down the flagstone steps and into the garden.

When Lilliana tried to pry his fingers from her elbow, Benedict urged her forward. "Let him be! There is much that must be said between them just now, and it is not appropriate for you to hear," he admonished her, and propelled her to the orangery as Lilliana struggled alongside, imagining Adrian walking unsteadily to a seat near his father, too proud to ask for help. She had met Lord Kealing on very few occasions, but she had never taken such an instant dislike to anyone in all her life. How dare he come and assail his son! Could he not *feel* Adrian's devastation?

Benedict threw open the door to the orangery and shoved her in ahead of him, closing the door securely behind him before allowing his gaze to sweep over her. He frowned at what he saw. "Ah, love, don't be so vexed. Their differences are long-standing."

"That hardly gives your father the right to treat him so ill!"

Benedict shrugged and strolled into the room. "It may seem so to you, but Adrian has treated him just as ill on more than one occasion."

That gave her pause. Suspicious, she asked, "What do you mean by that?"

"Just that Adrian has been as cruel to Father," he said matter-of-factly, and glanced toward the wall, where several of her paintings were hung. "There were times when Father desperately needed him, and Adrian merely laughed. He despises Father, you know." Benedict glanced at her over his shoulder. "I am quite fond of Adrian, you understand. But surely you know by now he is not the man he would have you believe. He has a dark side that is just as contemptible, if not more so, than you think my father has."

"He would never treat anyone so harshly," Lilliana said defensively, inwardly wincing at how false she knew that to be. The things he had said to her sounded just as vulgar as Lord Kealing's utterances. She uncon-

sciously shook her head, unwilling to engage in another
internal debate about Adrian. "What is the Court of
Faculties and Dispensations?" she asked, quickly changing the subject.

Benedict smiled patiently. "A court where special
circumstances are heard, love. Nothing you should fret
about, I assure you. You finished the painting of the old
chapel, I see. It's marvelous! You should really consider
selling some of your work," Benedict said, and began
strolling about her many canvases.

Lilliana kept her mouth shut. Something was terribly
wrong, and whatever it was, Benedict knew it. She
watched him wander about her little studio for an hour
or so, chattering easily, never really giving her an opportunity to question him further. There was something uncomfortably jovial in his manner, inappropriate after
what they had heard. She grew increasingly fretful, and
Benedict finally gave in to it, escorting her back to the
house. As they walked down the corridor to the study
where they had left the men, Lilliana could not help
fearing that the silence meant father and son had killed
each other.

But when Max hurried down the hall to meet them
with Benedict's hat in his hands and an unusually vivid
look of worry about him, Benedict grabbed her hand
and squeezed it. "You see there? It is already over."

She jerked her hand free as Max shoved the hat between him and Lilliana. "Lord Kealing is waiting for
you in the chaise, my lord. He would that you come at
once."

"And Lord Albright? Where is he?" Lilliana asked.

"Upstairs, madam," he said, and glanced anxiously
at Benedict. "His lordship was quite insistent." He
turned to hurry off in the direction he had come.

Benedict's gaze fell on her lips. "I'll come again
soon. Everything will be all right, you'll see." With a
reassuring smile he started down the corridor—his steps,
Lilliana noticed, every bit as anxious as Max's.

Seventeen

INCOMPETENT HIS FATHER had called him. Too infirm to manage his affairs. A blight on the fine tradition of his title. And then the bastard was off to find a barrister he could convince to prepare a case and present it to the Court of Faculties and Dispensations. Adrian had no doubt Archie would have a decent chance in gaining Longbridge in trust—all of his holdings, for that matter—until an heir came of age.

Assuming Archie didn't find some way to keep him from that too. Not that Adrian was terribly anxious to bring into this world a child he could not even see, let alone provide for. Bloody hell, he could hardly disagree with anything Archie had said. He was a reckless fool—the moment he had killed Phillip, he had started a downward slide into hell, and had taken an innocent parish princess along with him. Even if she wanted to be free of him, she could not marry Benedict. There was no custom or law in the land that would allow her to find true happiness, not after what he had done.

Ah, but that Princess had shown him a strength of spirit he honestly envied. Her unfathomable dedication to him was exasperating, yes, but extraordinarily admirable in light of everything. This monstrous thing he had done—ruining her life irrevocably—was just the beginning. Should Archie be successful in his suit, the scandal would be devastating. His recklessness and need for revenge had ruined her, and the irony of it all was that Archie would win after all.

When he heard the door to the master suite creak open, he waved her in, actually grateful for the intrusion for once. He was sick of himself.

"Adrian?" Her voice was small. "When you didn't come down for supper, I wondered if . . . I thought perhaps . . ."

"I have not expired, nor lain on the counterpane and wept myself to sleep," he said dryly.

"Oh. Well. Then I shall leave you—"

"What is this sudden reticence, Lilliana? You have so enjoyed demanding my attention," he said, and rose carefully, turning in the direction of her voice.

"I don't wish to disturb you if you are . . . you know. . . ."

"Please, come sit with me. I am rather eager for company tonight." In an unusual gesture he stretched his hand in her direction, smiling at her soft intake of breath. A moment passed, then another, and at last he heard her moving across the room. When she slipped her slender hand into his, he brought it to his lips in an almost unconscious act of penitence. Another little gasp. When he released her hand, it slipped from his and he heard the soft whisper of her skirts as she sat down. He groped in the darkness for his chair, falling into it without aplomb. "You are undoubtedly wondering what transpired," he said impassively.

"I, umm . . . yes. Yes, I am."

"Well, Lillie, I hate to be the one to inform you, but the moon has, apparently, turned to cheese." She made no response to his quip; he could sense her holding her breath. Sighing wearily, he shoved a hand through his hair. There was no sense in prolonging the inevitable. "Archie intends to take Longbridge from me. I hope that you will at last see reason and return to the Grange before I can cause you any more harm.''

"B-but that's impossible!''

"Not impossible . . . not easy, perhaps, but not impossible. He will engage the finest barrister he can afford to present his case.''

She made a small sound of disbelief. "His *case*? What case?''

"A case of incompetency, an inability to care for my holdings properly. A case that argues on behalf of future heirs. He will argue that as I blinded myself in a botched attempt to take my own life, I cannot possibly be of a mind to see to my own affairs. Therefore, my assets should be held in trust for my son. And naturally he will put forth that he should be the executor of any such trust.'' Adrian paused; how strange that he could sense her deep blush.

"You . . . you don't have an heir,'' she said quietly.

He smiled. "That is putting a rather fine point on it. I suppose in theory I am capable, and that is all that matters. He'll stop at nothing to gain Longbridge from me.'' Funny, but he heard himself speak as if he were talking of another person, someone only remotely familiar to him. He felt no emotion at all, nothing but the numb, vague sense of emptiness he always felt when it came to Archie. In that, at least, nothing had changed.

"But why would he do such a thing? Why should he feel so . . . so . . .''

"Why should he hate me so?'' Adrian chuckled derisively. How could he possibly explain? "It's a rather long story, and one that is hardly suitable for a lady.''

"Oh, honestly,'' she snapped, surprising him with her sudden impatience. "I know you think me a simpleton, but you needn't resort to treating me like a child.''

She was glaring at him, he knew it very well, and he smiled. "I don't think you a simpleton, Lilliana,'' he said laughingly. "Far from it, actually.'' He might have thought so once, but not any longer. "I think you are a Princess, a woman of great valor,'' he said solemnly, "but I have hurt you enough." He *did* regret it, more than anything else he had ever done—and that was saying quite a lot for a rogue.

Lilliana's skirts rustled as she shifted uncomfortably in her chair. A moment of silence passed, and he could almost see her staring into the fire, her green eyes clouded with pained confusion. "There is little you can say that will hurt me anymore," she finally said, and cleared her throat as if gathering her courage. "Whatever it is, I am quite prepared to hear it. I don't know how to speak any plainer, Adrian. I *want* to help you and I will do whatever is in my power. What has passed between us cannot be taken back, but . . ." She faltered; he almost reached for her, but there was no point in it. Any comfort he would try and give her now would seem so . . . *late*. "There is nothing you can say that will change the way I feel," she murmured softly.

Why? Dear God, *why*? What had he done to deserve this? What impossible logic of hers could perpetuate such a sentiment? All right, then, there was nothing to be done for it but to tell her everything. Every ugly aspect. She had to go for her own sake, and he knew no other way to make her see reason than to lay it all out for her, plain as day, and hope she would at last comprehend. "You leave me no choice," he said hoarsely.

"Then you might as well say it."

He spoke—haltingly at first—finding it difficult to voice aloud the fact that his father had despised him since birth and had thought his mother a whore. But he forced himself to speak, admitting things about his childhood that he had never told another living soul. In the background he heard the small sounds of distress she made as she listened, but he continued undaunted, his voice growing stronger. Words flowed out of him, words he had kept locked away in some remote part of his soul all his life spilled out, tumbling over one another in their haste to be set free.

He spoke of the abuse, of Archie's doting on Benedict. Of how Benedict had gone from an eager, devoted lad to a sullen, weak young man who hid behind Archie's promise of Kealing Park. Strangely embarrassed, he admitted to taking Archie's challenges and turning them into gold, all the while pushing him, pushing him, with everything he could think of. Nor did he shy away from telling her of the whoring, the gambling, and the reckless reputation the Rogues had eagerly earned, of the friends that meant more to him than his own kin.

At one point as he gathered his thoughts and his breath, he heard her move from her chair, caught the scent of her as she brushed past him. For one terrified moment he thought she had left in disgust, but she returned, wrapping his fingers around a snifter of brandy. Adrian gratefully took the snifter and let the fire stream down his gullet. Then hoarse from the brandy, he told her how he had finally given Archie the reason he needed to disinherit him.

Everything tumbled off his tongue, every minute of the appalling weekend when he had killed Phillip, every thought, every moment of horror on that field. The shock at seeing a gun pointed directly at his chest. The terror upon realizing he had killed one of his very best friends. The guilt that would not leave him. He told her how Archie had disinherited him, and how he had sought her out in an almost mad state of revenge. How he regretted what he had done to her, for telling her the truth in such an abhorrent manner. And how that regret had led him to drink himself into such a state of oblivion, he could not even tell her what had happened with the gun.

When he at last finished, the pounding in his head was relentless, the pain almost nauseating.

An eternity seemed to pass before she spoke. "I understand everything but this. Why would he despise his son from birth?"

Ah, yes, the one thing he could not quite put a voice to. But it was all there, his whole life, lying like bits of debris scattered on the floor between them—except the one thing that had shattered it all in the beginning. "Because my birth was conceived outside the bounds of lawful matrimony.'' And he laughed bitterly, almost choking on it.

''How do you know that?'' she asked quietly.

''Because nothing else can explain it. The names he called her, his disdain for me, his absolute adoration of Ben. I am my mother's bastard son, Lilliana, and Archie hates me for it.'' He laughed again, desperately this time, suddenly wishing he could retrieve every word he had uttered and stomp the truth that damned him and gave everything to Benedict. ''He cannot bring himself to admit he was cuckolded. He would prefer to ruin me, as I am the single reminder of her infidelity. And, I fear, he may finally succeed.'' Adrian sucked the thin air around him. ''That is why you must go, Princess. This is my fate, not yours, and I cannot bear to see you harmed. It is my dirty secret, and you should not have to pay the consequence.''

The silence that filled the room unnerved him; his breath came harshly as his secret hammered in his ears and his head. Adrian gulped for air, silently crying to God to let him see her one more time, to see her *now* and if the light was still in her eyes . . . or the revulsion that he feared.

He didn't realize she had moved until he felt her hand in his, then her lips brush his fingers. ''I won't let him hurt you,'' she murmured.

He groaned; there was so much she could not possibly comprehend. What a father and son could do to one another—her tender soul should never know what darkness men were capable of. ''On my *life*, I won't let him hurt you ever again,'' she said, and pulled lightly on his hand. ''No one will hurt you.'' She tugged again, pulling him to his feet.

''Lilliana—''

''Shhh.'' She pressed a finger to his lips, then drew him slowly away from his chair. Adrian followed her mindlessly, moving carelessly across the carpet, not really conscious of anything but his desperate need to see her. Surprised when his leg bumped up against the bed, there was no time to react before she pushed him down. He fell onto his side; Lilliana fell on top of him.

"I love you Adrian," she whispered, and quickly covered his mouth with hers.

Impossible! his mind screamed, and he struggled to push her off, afraid unto death of what those words meant, that they should come *now,* after everything he had told her. But the touch of her lips detonated something inside him, and his pushing suddenly turned to a fierce embrace. He raked his hands through her curls, cupped her face, felt her neck and eyes and ears with his hands. Lilliana straddled him; there was nothing but a gossamer layer of undergarments between them.

Adrian's hands and body operated feverishly, stroking every curve, seeking her warm flesh. He buried his face in her neck and ran his tongue inside her ear as he inhaled her scent. Lilliana worked just as feverishly, ripping the neckcloth from him, then sending her fingers flying down the buttons of his waistcoat. He felt his shirt being pulled from his trousers, then somehow, she managed to claw it off of him. Her delicate hands were everywhere, caressing him, gliding over his chest, stroking the soft down of hair trailing to his groin.

Adrian caught a breath in his throat when her tongue flicked across his nipple as her hands fumbled with his trousers to free his arousal. It was an assault, a blind assault on all his senses, and he was mad for her. Frantic, he sought the fastenings of her gown, releasing her breasts from the confines of fabric. He groped for the softly pliant flesh, moaning with pleasure when they began to swell in his hands. He suddenly sat up, holding her tightly on his lap to take one succulent breast in his mouth, sucking the hardened peak into his tongue.

Her hand surrounded his rigid erection, making him ache with desire. With her other hand, she shoved him backward again, then covered his face with kisses, pressed her lips to his blind eyes, his nose, his lips, and trailed a river of simmering kisses to his chest. And then, *Lord God,* down the length of his torso, pausing to flick her tongue into the crevice of his navel. Adrian held his breath; every fiber was burning with a fire that licked at the deepest recesses of his soul. He felt her body as he had never felt a woman, aware of every place they touched, of the scent of their lovemaking, of the sound of their eagerness.

When her lips touched the velvet head, Adrian lurched violently. "Shhh," she whispered, and with her tongue traced the length of him. Gasping, he tried not to writhe beneath her like an animal. But it was no use; she was destroying his control, pushing him to the brink of yearning that made him shudder with anticipation. Her lips left him long enough to glide across the slippery skin of his testicles, and Adrian shot upward in the dark, bracing himself on his elbows. But his mind went blank when her lips slid slowly down the length of him and back, tantalizing him to the point of madness.

The seduction was overwhelming; dangerously close to losing his control, he groped for her, yanking her up to him like a rag doll and encircling her tightly in his arms. Her lips landed softly on his, and she continued the wild seduction of his soul with the thrust of her tongue into his mouth.

Adrian fought her skirts until they were hiked above her hips, then slipped his hand between her legs. Lilliana gasped against his lips; he breathed a silent moan into her body upon discovering she was slick with desire. His fingers slipped inside her heat; his thumb stroked her mindlessly until she made a little cry and shifted suddenly, lifting herself above the hardened length of his passion.

Adrian impaled her. Fiercely, completely, he thrust into her, again and again, burying his face in the valley of her breasts, struggling to take them as fully into his mouth as her body took him. Over and over again he thrust into her, rashly seeking to touch her very soul. With every stroke he came closer, and when he felt her tighten around him, he was unable to contain the power-

ful need to release his life's blood into the very core of
her.

It was Lilliana who cried out first. Her fingers dug
into his shoulders as she shuddered, contracting around
him and drawing a powerful climax. With a strangled
sob of ecstasy, Adrian released himself into her with a
potent thrust. And another. And one more, until he was
spent, drained, and in absolute awe of what had just
happened. He somberly gathered her in his arms and
pressed his face to her neck, rocking gently as the heat
ebbed from their bodies. Lilliana held him just as tightly,
her arms wrapped around his head, her breath ragged in
his hair, the dangerously erratic beating of her heart
keeping time with his own.

Slowly he leaned back, taking her with him until he
was prone on the bed, and leaving himself buried
somewhere near the warmth of her womb. "My darling
Princess," he whispered reverently. "My demon Lillie,
what have you done to me?"

A sob lodged in her throat; she buried her face in his
neck. He felt the hot path of her tears and he finally,
finally understood them. He had been almost moved to
tears himself.

They lay entwined in each other's arms for what
seemed hours, until he could tell from her breathing that
Lilliana was sleeping. Still, he did not let go of her,
afraid of losing the magic they had just shared. He felt
alive, and Lord save him, he had never made love so
intensely or experienced such heartfelt emotions, such
wondrous joy at giving her the fulfillment he so desperately wanted and received for himself.

And as he held her tightly to him, he was, strangely,
reminded of what the vicar had said at Phillip's funeral.
*Know ye the quality of love, the quality of life, and the
quality of mercy.*

What a mockery those words had seemed then. How
extraordinary they seemed now. He must be incredibly
unperceptive, but now he understood with vivid clarity.
This Princess of the Grange, the woman he had married

in an act of revenge, had shown him the quality of mercy. *Had* been showing him, many times over, forgiving him everything he thought had damned him, even though he had begged God for mercy, had deemed himself cursed and unworthy of it. And all along, unrecognized and unappreciated, his unremarkable country wife had been trying to show him the true quality of mercy. But he had been too damned blind to see it.

God forgive him! He had been blind *long* before the accident—blind to her many qualities, to her unique and forgiving spirit, to the life she could give him, whether he deserved it or not. She had not turned away, not once, not even when he had been so brutally honest. She had heard the whole ugly truth and had responded by showing him what it meant to make love, guiding him through one of the most extraordinary experiences of his life—if not the most terrifying!

He had no idea what it meant to feel like this, no notion of what would come, if the feelings would be as intense on the morrow, or if they would only grow stronger.

If only he could see her! He would give his life to look into those wide, gray-green eyes once more, to see the dimple of a cheerful little smile that seemed glorious in his mind's eye. *Dammit!* Why hadn't he looked at her more often? Why hadn't he memorized her features, her luscious body, her silky hair?

Adrian suddenly came up on his knees.

Lilliana thought she was dreaming; the soothing caress felt like a whisper of a breeze on her skin. She drowsily opened her eyes to find him bent over her, on his knees, his face burrowed in a frown of concentration that looked quite fierce in the dim light of the waning fire. With his hands, he was touching every inch of her. But not just touching her—*examining* her. She stirred.

"Be still, love," he murmured, *"be still."* Her heart fluttered wildly; she watched in fascination as he continued his examination, leaving no patch of skin untouched in a trail of tingling warmth. Slowly, methodically, he traced her body with his hands, moving from her toes, to her knees, drifting over the apex of her thighs, then her torso. Reverently, he stroked the skin of her arms, her breasts, and then her neck.

"W-What are you doing?" she whispered as his fingers curved around her ears.

"Seeing you," he muttered, and traced a line over her lips before moving to her eyes, then her hair. When he reached the top of her head and ran his fingers through the curls there, he sighed longingly and lowered himself to her, kissing her tenderly as his hand slipped down to her breast again.

He made love to her with great deliberation, taking his own sweet time to touch every part of her with his hands and mouth, stroking and tasting her skin and the heat of her desire between her legs. His tongue was everywhere, in every crevice, in all the places that she was certain would condemn her directly to hell—but she didn't care. This glimpse of heaven was worth every moment of eternal damnation. The warmth began to build in her belly as he laved the tender flesh between her legs. She squirmed as his tongue flicked in and out of her, then over the most intimate part of her. Adrian grasped her hips in his hands as she began to thrash beneath him, holding her firmly as he buried his face in the valley between her legs, torturing her with his teeth and tongue.

Intense pressure was reverberating through her, but Adrian did not allow it, not yet. He rose up, and slowly he entered her while he feathered her face and neck with kisses. Smoothly and gently, he provoked her with a tantalizing rhythm, pausing when she was on the brink of losing herself, then starting the whole extraordinary experience again, all the while touching her, feeling her. *Seeing* her. When she at last begged him for mercy, he took her to yet another pinnacle of ethereal fulfillment, whispering her name again and again . . . groaning it one last time as he found his own release. And Lilliana felt as if she was floating far above herself as he wrapped

her tightly into his arms and rolled to his side. It wasn't
until she heard the deep breath of his sleep that she finally floated back to earth, secure in his arms.

When Lilliana finally roused herself from a deliciously
deep sleep, Adrian had gone. Her first thought was that
he had left her again, just as he always did. No, *no*, she
thought frantically, not after last night! She climbed out
of bed, wrapped a sheet around her and rushed to her
own rooms, where she washed and dressed quickly while
fighting a growing sense of urgency and fearfulness.
What had occurred between them last night was a
dream—and she couldn't be entirely certain it *wasn't* a
dream. Had she imagined an outpouring of emotion?
The desperate way he clung to her? Had she somehow
seen emotions he truly did not have? It certainly
wouldn't be the first time she had done so. But last
night—last night had been different than all the times
before. He could not be so unfeeling!

She rushed downstairs to the foyer, where the footman Bertram was at his post. "Good morning, milady,"
he said, peering curiously at her hair.

Lilliana quickly raked her fingers through the unruly
curls, self-consciously stuffing as many of them as she
could behind her ears. "Good morning, Bertram. Have
you . . . ah, have you seen Lord Albright?" she asked
nervously.

Bertram suddenly grinned. "Aye, milady. He's gone
to his study."

His study. To lock himself away from her? Lilliana
nodded, walked calmly in that direction until Bertram
could no longer see her, then flew anxiously down the
corridor. The door of his study was closed, naturally,
and she reached for the brass knob, but quickly withdrew her hand. What if it *had* been a dream? How
would she bear it if he were indifferent to her this morning? Or worse yet, what if he began his insistence that
she leave all over again? She would never be able to

leave him! *Never.* It would be impossible to live without his touch—her body was still warm from his caress!

She reached for the brass knob again, and just as quickly withdrew her hand with a confused shake of her head. No, no, *no!* It would be impossible to stay if he had not felt the same as she did last night! But she had seen him—she had *felt* him—give in to her passion, and oh God, what passion he had shown her in return!

Yes, but he had been passionate before. All right, he had, but not with the same . . . *intensity.* Nonetheless . . . he might insist that she leave Longbridge for her own good. *The moon has, apparently, turned to cheese,* he had said, throwing her oh so elegant refusal to leave back in her face. What if he *did* tell her to go? Oh, but that was simple, she thought, rolling her eyes. She would die. Straightaway and without ado.

This was ridiculous! Lilliana took a deep breath, reached for the brass knob, and pushed the door open. Nerves attacked her with surprising force; she had to make herself poke her head into the gap between the door and its frame and glance toward his desk.

Her husband was there, all right, looking impossibly handsome. Max sat across from him, reading a weekly paper. Aloud. Mesmerized, Lilliana slipped inside the room, self-consciously remaining at the door as she listened to Max.

"The two percents have ex-hibed a tenderly—"

"Exhibited a tendency," Adrian muttered patiently.

Max glanced at him, then squinted at the paper. "Ah." He cleared his throat loudly. "Exhibited a tendency to . . . to rubbish goat—"

"I think you mean rapid growth," Adrian said, a hint of a smile on his lips.

Max frowned and squirmed in his seat as he squinted at the paper. "Rapid growth and sharp designs," he muttered quickly.

"Declines," Adrian said, his smile growing broader.

"Blast it all, my lord, but I can hardly *see* the words on this page!" he blustered in frustration.

Adrian laughed. "That's a bit better than I can do!" He laughed again, unaware that the blood was rapidly draining from his butler's face. "Perhaps Lady Albright will relieve you," he said, and cocked his head toward the door.

Lilliana's mouth dropped open. How in God's name did he *do* that? As if reading her thoughts, Adrian chuckled. "I cannot see, but I can certainly hear well enough. Please, Lilliana, do come in and relieve Max. He is pathetically farsighted."

"*Please,* milady," Max implored her, and leapt to his feet, waving the paper at her. Lilliana walked forward uncertainly, taking the paper he thrust at her. "If you will excuse me, my lord, I should really be about . . . something else," Max muttered, and bobbing a quick, birdlike bow to her, bolted for the door.

Adrian chuckled warmly as the door closed behind him. "He has a fine head for house management, but the man is hopeless with the written word. Perhaps you would be so kind as to finish the business news?"

"Of course," she murmured and, sitting on the edge of the chair Max had vacated, began to read, her mind whirling as she mouthed words about securities, a shipping company gone under, and the latest news from Paris. She stole surreptitious glimpses of him, looking for something, *anything* to suggest he had not felt as deeply as she had last night, that it was just another coupling to him. But he gave her no indication—his eyes were fixed straight ahead as though he were casually studying one of her paintings.

When she began to read the news of the coal industry, he muttered softly, "You smell heavenly."

"W-what?"

"The scent of roses. You put the scent of roses in your hair." His eyes still fixed on the painting, he smiled faintly. "What is the weather today?" he asked.

A deep smile curved Lilliana's lips and she lowered the paper to her lap. "The sun is shining."

"Ah. I had heard it is still there. I suppose if I were to

indulge in a turn about the gardens, I might feel it fall down around me?''

Her heart surged with renewed hope. "Every ray, I should think," she answered, smiling.

Adrian flashed a charming, boyish grin. "Then might I ask the enormous favor of your company? I couldn't possibly absorb all that sunshine alone.''

She wanted to cry. Good heavens, the urge to weep with joy was overwhelming. He *had* felt the depth of their lovemaking! He had given in *finally,* he had given in to some feeling for her! Lilliana leapt to her feet, oblivious of the paper's slide to the floor. "I would like nothing better. But wait!" she said brightly, and rushed to the door. "I have something for you.''

He responded, but Lilliana did not hear him. She was already flying down the hall to the foyer, where she came to an abrupt halt in front of Bertram. "The walking stick, Bertram. Do you recall? I gave it to you a few weeks ago.''

The footman grinned widely. "Yes, the walking stick. Fine day for a turn about, indeed, milady.''

Lilliana shifted anxiously from one foot to the other. "Indeed—the walking stick, Bertram?''

"It is just here," he said reassuringly, and fished about in an umbrella stand, producing a cane of fine mahogany wood with a brass top shaped like the head of an eagle. Having discovered it in the first days she had roamed Longbridge, Lilliana had retrieved it after Adrian's accident, hoping he would learn to use it to walk freely about. With a smile she snatched it from Bertram's hands and hastily started back to the study, but halted in midstride.

Adrian was walking down the corridor unaided, as easily as if he could see, using the cords she had strung as a guide. Lilliana bit her lip against a sudden surge of grateful tears.

Adrian would live again.

Eighteen

THE TRANSFORMATION IN Adrian was miraculous.

With a fervor that left the inhabitants of Longbridge breathless, he began to tackle the enormity of adjusting everything he had ever known to a dark world. No one could keep up with him—except for Lilliana.

Her fervor was just as intent because she had at last found her freedom. It did not occur as she might have expected, but came to her in the days she spent exploring a new world with the man she loved. She became Adrian's eyes, and as such, was suddenly seeing familiar things as she had never seen them before. Objects she had taken for granted she now viewed through new eyes. This new vision of inanimate objects made them almost animate—and her paintings took on that quality, a depth she humbly recognized as art. *This* was soaring; this was experiencing life, deep in her heart where it counted most.

And oh, how Adrian had changed! It was preposterous, she knew, but it seemed to Lilliana that in blindness, her husband was more the reckless adventurer than he possibly could have been before. He knew no bounds—his desire to get on with his life was earnest and contagious. To think that he was the same person who had hobbled about like an old man in the first weeks of his blindness was almost laughable. Now, with the walking stick she had given him and the cords that were strung all over Longbridge, Adrian strode down the corridors and grounds as purposefully as he ever had—a stranger had to look very closely to know he was blind.

He insisted on "seeing" the estate. They walked at first—miles and miles they walked, Adrian's stick striking the path determinedly ahead of them. Lilliana strolled beside him, happily smiling like a half-wit at everything around her, lost in the magic of just being with him. Her admiration for him grew in leaps and bounds on those walks—the more time they spent together, the more freely Adrian spoke of himself and his life. Amusing anecdotes from his youth, scandalous acts committed with the infamous Rogues, dangerous adventures abroad. Instead of being shocked by the things he told her, as any proper lady would be, she was enthralled by them. She could almost imagine herself there when he reminisced, could almost feel the heady sense of recklessness.

On rare occasions in those moments of reflection, Adrian would speak of his birth. He bore clearly painful memories, particularly of his mother. She was a broken, desolate woman, he said, living a quiet lie. "Imagine, no siblings or friends to speak of, and only two small boys to rely upon. It is a wonder she endured as long as she did." Lilliana's heart went out to him—that so-called *quiet lie* had defined his life. She had not been raised so far removed from society that she didn't understand how that secret would ruin his life if it were to be made public. Nonetheless . . . something nagged the back of her mind, a vague sense that not everything about the secret fell neatly into place.

The one topic Adrian refused to discuss with her was Phillip Rothembow. It was poignantly clear how dis-

tressing it was for him, and while he seemed to have
come to some sort of peace with himself, he would not
mention Phillip's name nor allow it to be mentioned in
his presence.

Actually, much to Lilliana's sheer mortification,
Adrian preferred she talk of her simple life. Embarrassed to the core by her own undistinguished and uneventful upbringing, she hesitantly gave him the dull
details and waited for the smirk or the signs of tedium.
So it was nothing short of miraculous that Adrian never
seemed bored with her life. He laughed when she sheepishly admitted the most contemptible thing she had done
was to put pepper in Mr. Willard's snuffbox. He arched
a brow when she reluctantly admitted her habit of racing Jason behind her mother's back, but smiled broadly
when she informed him she won nine times out of ten.
He nodded sympathetically when she wistfully spoke of
her mother and the constant struggle to be good as was
expected, of never quite measuring up to those expectations. And when she admitted her lifelong fear of per-
ishing at Blackfield Grange without so much as seeing
London, he pulled her into his embrace. "I know how
heartbreaking it is," he mumbled, "to want something
so desperately and believe you can never have it."

She didn't know what he meant by that, but Lilliana
did not pine away for the world as she once had at the
Grange. She was experiencing her dream now, with him,
and much more richly than she had thought possible.

As Adrian became more confident with his affliction,
he resumed more of his life. He took to riding again,
holding on to her waist as she pushed Thunder to the
stallion's limits. He reviewed the books with her every
morning, taught her how to balance them, and eventually entrusted the task to her.

As the precious days with him piled on, it was impossible for Lilliana to remember the man who had once
been so callously indifferent to her. It was as if he were a
different man from the one she had married—he even
seemed to delight in catering to her silly whims. One

night she had coaxed Polly into playing the pianoforte—if one could call it playing—and had asked Adrian to dance with her. He had been a bit taken aback, but when she pulled him from his chair, he had swept her into a waltz, and she had been embarrassed to learn that *she* was the one with two left feet. He moved so elegantly and seductively that in a mad moment, she had peered intently into his eyes, quite convinced he could actually see. Her unspoken question had been answered by a crash into the sideboard a few moments later. Adrian had laughed uproariously at his blunder before gathering her in his arms and abruptly kissing her—in full view of Polly, Max, and a young footman who turned as red as a tomato.

He became a fixture in the orangery, agreeing to sit for a portrait after extracting her solemn promise that she would remove the painting of him on a mule. Those sittings were at first unnerving, but Lilliana quickly grew accustomed to his seemingly pointed looks as she painted. So accustomed, that she stopped bothering with any modicum of modesty. If it was warm, she unbuttoned her blouse. She hiked her skirts far above her knees so she could better attack the canvas. Her mind on some forgotten tune, she twirled aimlessly about the orangery, not caring if she appeared addled. In there, with him, she was free to do what she wanted, to be *who* she wanted.

And so was Adrian free, seemingly at peace with himself and his life. Never had Lilliana understood that as clearly as she did one morning when she caught him with her dogs. As she passed the open door of his study, she saw him sitting with Hugo stretched out asleep, his head propped on Adrian's foot. But even more extraordinary, Maude's head was on his knee and he was stroking her ears. Seeing him with "the beasts" had touched her so deeply that she had pressed a hand to her mouth and smothered a spontaneous cry of joy. If anything marked the transformation in him, if any one thing demonstrated his capacity to feel, it was his attention to her dogs. It was absurd—insane, really—but Lilliana firmly believed that when Adrian lost his sight, he also lost some invisible shackles that had kept his feelings bound deeply inside.

The truth of that was driven home to her each night. Lord *God,* the things he did to her! She became a shameless wanton in his arms, a Jezebel exalting in the purported sins of the flesh. Incredibly, she was not ashamed of what they did. For reasons lost to her, Adrian's inability to see her unabashedly covet every masculine inch of him freed her to pleasure him shamelessly. She was not afraid of anything, least of all exploring new and terribly immodest ways to love him. Why God did not strike her with a bolt of lightning for all her indecency astounded her. But until that happened, she would strive to learn the many ways to please him, constantly in awe at how easily he pleased her. The man was a master with his tongue, an absolute artist with his hands. It seemed as if all he had to do was touch her and she was panting for release, begging him to give himself to her, harder, faster, longer. Their lovemaking was so utterly without bounds that she was quite certain the entire household heard her cries of ecstasy when she lost herself in him.

And he called her darling; the word curled around her heart every time he uttered it. His darling demon, he whispered, his beautiful Princess Lillie. As he thrust into her, he murmured how beautiful she was, praised her wicked response to him. And when she was frantic for the eruption of searing heat inside her, he would murmur her name. *My darling Princess Lillie, come with me, come with me now.*

In those magical moments they were one heart, one spirit, one body. In those moments her life with Adrian was better than she had ever dared to hope. Her soul was completely liberated in her love of him—she knew no restrictions but was free to be who she was, abandoning herself to the magic he had created for them. She was at long last soaring—in her heart, higher than she would have dreamed possible, far above the earth and everything she had ever known.

Until Benedict would appear.

Which was too often to suit her. Privately, she resented his calls—she wanted Adrian all to herself. But even in her newfound freedom, she was still her mother's daughter, and she greeted him with all the respect due a brother-in-law. What else could she do?

Adrian certainly did not seem to mind his calling—he was unfailingly polite to his brother. Certainly Benedict did nothing to earn her resentment, but she couldn't help feeling uncomfortable around him. For one thing, it seemed to her that he was forever making veiled insinuations about Adrian. Nothing terribly blatant, of course, but enough to give rise to a feeling of protectiveness for her husband. One day, Benedict coaxed her into a stroll about the gardens and spoke plaintively of the rift between his father and brother. "Father has struggled to accept him, but Adrian has not made it very easy," he said on a weary sigh. "He has always been so wild, you know—but I rather suppose that is to be expected, isn't it?" He had left that question dangling in front of her, almost daring her to snatch it up and ask him what he meant by it.

Lilliana would not rise to the bait. "It seems awfully cruel to disinherit him then seek custody of his holdings," she had replied with some bitterness.

"Yes, well, I am endeavoring to make sure that doesn't happen," he responded. "Trust me, Lillie. I will not allow Father's actions to harm you." With that, he had squeezed her hand and bestowed a tender smile on her.

That was the other thing she did not care for. He was *always* touching her, or looking at her in such a way that made her feel uncomfortably exposed. He would kiss her cheek and allow his lips to linger, or brush a curl from her temple with undue familiarity. And just when she thought she might explode and say something awful, he would smile and say, "I am so grateful you are happy

with him, Lilliana. If only Father could see how happy
you are, he would drop his suit.''

It was all very confusing—at times she trusted Benedict, times she forced herself to trust him. If there was
even the slightest chance he could influence Lord Kealing, she had to endure his attentions for the sake of
Adrian.

Adrian endured his visits for the sake of mercy.

As much as Benedict's presence irritated him, he was
as deserving of mercy as Adrian was. And mercy had
been granted to him; his sole regret was that it had taken
him too long to see it. How long might he have drowned
in his self-pity before he understood that the one person
who could grant him the treasure of mercy stood before
him?

Dammit, there was so much to Lilliana that he never
saw before the accident, so much *beauty* that he had
been too blind to see. The woman was very caring of
others, and he had thought that a weakness. She was
selfless to a fault, and he had thought *that* the character-
istic of a country bumpkin. She was compassionate, and
he had found that bothersome. God help him, he
couldn't see outward any longer, but he could certainly
see inward, and he did not like what he saw. Not even
remotely. He had been heartless, indifferent, absorbed
with obsessions and blind to everything around him.

Heart blind.

Well, he now appreciated her qualities enormously
and credited her with saving him from the edge of hell.
The night she had come to his room and had quietly
listened to all the reasons she should utterly despise him
had left an indelible mark on his very soul. Not once did
she raise a word against him, or cry out in revulsion, or
voice a fear of the scandal in which she would undoubtedly be mired. His Princess had taken it in very calmly,
had borne his trouble as her own, and then, astonishingly, had vowed no one would hurt him. *He* should
have made that promise to *her*. And then she had hum-

bled him completely by showing him just how deep was her capacity to forgive.

That night, God had shown him the quality of mercy and given him a reason to live.

But he had never really *looked* at her, and now all he had was the fading memory of her face. He was left to imagine her painting in one of his best shirts, splattering little drops of color on it. Or throwing a stick into the lake for Hugo to fetch. Or laughing with the cook as they perfected the puddings she devoured, and frowning at Max with those sparkling demon eyes when he complained of Mrs. Dismuke's high-handed ways.

He could even imagine the face of determination when she strung those cords about the house, or the devilish glint in her eye when she tied the bells around the necks of her dogs. In his mind's eye, he could see her twirl about the orangery as she hummed an old Gaelic tune and the way her eyes sparkled when he had danced with her. She was alive, he realized, more alive than he had ever been in all of his thirty-two years, and the life in her was contagious.

Just the sound of her musical laughter sent a shiver down his spine. Her chatter, which he had once feared, was now a source of great comfort to him. He suddenly found himself well versed in every aspect of Caroline's adoration of Horace Feather; the exact day, down to the likely minute, her family would return from Bath; the dozen things that separated her two mongrels from all the other dogs in the world; and the hour Mr. Bottoms's recent fever had broken. She brightened everything around them, and the sound of her breathless voice as she eagerly described things she saw to him went straight into his heart. Incredible though it was to him, he realized he actually *could* feel the sun fall down around him when she was near.

His parish princess was terribly bright, too, had quickly understood the accounting principles he used, rapidly learning everything he could teach her about the books. Honestly, he could leave the management of

Longbridge in her capable hands, something he never would have even contemplated before now.

Longbridge . . . now there was another great error on his part. His mindless drive to build an estate to rival the grandest of Europe had been an act of jealousy. Nothing he might do to Longbridge would ever restore Kealing Park to him. But amazingly, he was coming to understand that he did not *need* Kealing Park—whatever solace he had once thought he could find there had faded long ago. His solace was at Longbridge now. With Lilliana.

Yet her face haunted him as he struggled to remember it. It seemed the only place he was free of that struggle was in his bed. He did not have to see her there; he could *feel* her. Her passion reverberated around them; her sensuality searing him every place they touched. Her hands, her lips, her hair, all enveloped him in a surreal seductive dance that catapulted him to the heavens on wave after wave of sheer pleasure. In his bed he breathed her in, from the rosewater in her hair, to the scent of the dampness between her legs. He felt her, every beautiful, lissome inch of her, with his hands. He tasted her, from the hollow behind her ear to the tender skin behind her knee.

And his heart came near to bursting when she whispered her love.

Even he, the master of suppressing all emotion, could see what was happening to him. As guarded as he was, as hard as he strove to bury his emotions, he had come to care deeply for the unremarkable little Grange Princess he had married—so deeply, he was afraid to even attempt to put a name to it. All he knew was that she had, miraculously, lightened his soul. For the first time in his life, he felt at peace.

How odd that it should come now, with the loss of his sight.

It had been two months since his accident; the weather had turned warmer and the sun was beginning to stretch longer into each day. On the terrace one morning, Adrian relished the feel of the sun on his face, the cool, crisp sensation of rebirth evident in each breeze as he sat listening to the tinkle of dog bells and Lilliana's laughter. Smiling warmly, he shifted in his seat so that his face was directly to the sun. How strange, he though idly, that he could almost *see* the light.

His heart suddenly lurched in his chest.

Impossible! He *was* seeing light! Adrian quickly shook his head at that mad thought, blinking rapidly—imagining things again, he thought bitterly, imagining that he saw light, as he sometimes imagined he saw Lilliana's eyes. In a moment the darkness would return, just as it always did.

He waited, fidgeting impatiently with his neckcloth. The light, though an obvious figment of his imagination, was oddly disconcerting. When would the darkness return, the state of being he knew so very well now? He blinked again, but if anything the light seemed to grow brighter. Adrian's hand began to shake, and he suddenly lifted it, waving it in front of his face. No, he could not see his hand; of *course* he could not see his hand! Then how could he see light?

He turned his head away from the sun's rays; the light dimmed, but it did not go away. Oh Lord, there was light, a tiny shard of it knifing through the darkness and into his consciousness, playing havoc with his emotions. It was so baffling, he did not hear Lilliana come onto the terrace.

"Adrian? Are you all right?"

He jerked around to the sound of her voice. "Yes. Yes, of course!"

"Would you like to walk in the gardens?" As he lifted his face to the sound of her voice, the light brightened. *What was happening?*

"Adrian! What is it?" she exclaimed.

He suddenly grasped her hand resting on his shoul-

der. "A bit of a headache, Princess—it's nothing. I
believe Lewis is due any time now," he said, and stood
slowly, fixated on the light. "I've some correspondence
to review with him."

Lilliana slipped her hand into his. "You look as if
you have seen an apparition," she said, the concern
evident in her voice.

He *was* seeing an apparition. But he forced himself to
smile as he felt his way up her arm and to her neck, then
pulled her forward. "No apparitions," he said, and
leaned down to kiss her. As he slanted his lips over hers,
the light faded completely. Just a cruel trick his mind
was playing, his blasted imagination, a part of his brain
that refused to accept his blindness. This had happened
before—fleeting images that sometimes flickered across
his mind's eye, so real that he thought he had seen them.
But those images were gone as quickly as they came—
they never lasted as long as the tiny beam of light.

But when he lifted his head, the light reappeared and
his entire body seized with fear. "I shall join you for
tea," he forced himself to say, and began to sweep the
path in front of him with his walking stick.

Once inside the terrace sitting room, he brought his
hands to his eyes, probing roughly. There was no light.
Stunned that he was almost grateful the light had left
him, a tremor of fear swept over him—what in the
bloody hell was the matter with him? What if he *was*
seeing light? That thought caused an odd wave of nausea to rumble in his belly. There was no plausible explanation—his mind was playing ugly tricks on him. How
very rich—he was to lose his mind as well as his sight!
But it was *not* light, he thought miserably, and started
for his study, his stick banging on furniture and doors as
he went.

The next day, however, he had no doubt he was seeing
light. Lilliana had asked him to walk with her down to
the lake. The light had come to him the moment they

had stepped outdoors, and grew brighter with each step. Faint as it was, his eyes stung and his head felt close to exploding. He made some excuse to turn back, and Lilliana had obliged him, unaware that each step sent a jarring jolt of pain behind his eyes.

The rest of the afternoon he spent in his study, blinking over and over again in a desperate attempt to bring back the light, but to no avail. By the time the supper hour came, he had once again convinced himself that he was imagining things.

Lilliana was already in the dining salon when he entered; he could hear her bustling around the table. "At last!" she cried happily.

"Hungry, are you?" he asked dryly.

"Famished! I climbed all the way to the top of the hill on the other side of the lake. Do you know the one I mean? It doesn't look so very tall when one is standing in the garden, but it is *quite* tall! I thought I might very well perish before I reached the top."

"You shouldn't go off alone, Lilliana."

"Perhaps I should have told Max, but he was engaged in a ridiculous argument with Polly—"

"Again?"

Lilliana laughed, a rich sound that curled around him. Gently, she took his hand and led him to the table. "A bucket, it seems, belonging to Polly was used . . . ah, well . . . *inappropriately* . . . by one of the footmen. Polly was quite beside herself, and Max felt compelled to defend the poor man." She patted his arm, signaling him to sit. "You know how practical Max can be. He suggested to Polly that she clean the bucket with lye, but Polly took great exception, insisting she would *never* use that bucket again, and demanded that Max purchase a new one for her."

Adrian turned his head in the direction of her voice, and in doing so, almost came out of his chair. Three pinpoints of light had formed in front of him. They were watery and faint, almost without form, but he could see

the light and the hint of silver beneath it! It was, he was
quite certain, the candelabrum.

"Max, however, thought that quite an extravagance.
He insisted the bucket was quite serviceable, and that
Polly was making much too much of it."

Adrian barely heard her. He could not tear his eyes
away from the hazy image of a candelabrum. Dear God,
could it be possible? He could see nothing else, just the
three points of light and the glint of the silver candelabrum. The smell of duck soup drifted by his nose; a
footman placed a bowl in front of him.

"I finished your portrait," Lilliana continued.
Adrian nodded, groping for a spoon, his eyes fixated on
the wavering object in front of him. "I had Bertram
hang it on the ground floor of the west wing with all the
family portraits. He commented that it was the exact
likeness of you."

"You are very talented," he muttered.

"Don't you adore duck soup?" she asked. He had
the sensation of everyone pausing, looking at him. His
gaze, faint as it was, dropped to where the soup should
have been.

He could see nothing.

With his hand, he found the bowl, and very gingerly
slipped the spoon into the liquid, straining to see something, *anything*. The clink of Lilliana's spoon on her
bowl sounded as loud as a church bell, and a bit of perspiration dripped down his side.

"—Bertram thought so too." *What was she saying?*
He forced himself to lift the spoon and take a mouthful
of soup. "In fact, he pointed it out to me."

"I beg your pardon?" he muttered, trying desperately to keep his voice even as he lifted his gaze to the
pinpoints of light again.

"The portrait of the two girls. One of them bears a
strong resemblance to you. And then I remembered what
has been bothering me. That painting reminded me of a
portrait at Kealing Park. I used to study the portraits in
the gallery for hours, it seems, when I was a child. Do

you recall the portrait of a man with his leg propped on a chair and the riding crop across his thigh? You bear a strong resemblance to him, too." She paused, sipping very daintily. Adrian placed the spoon on the table and shifted his eyes to the left.

The blood drained from his face.

Dear God, this was impossible, bloody well *impossible*! He could see the dark, fuzzy shadow of a human! Anxiously he rubbed sweaty palms on his thighs, afraid to look to his right, to Lilliana. *Was* it possible? Would God grant him such an enormous reprieve? An irrational and strong fear swept through him at the prospect, and he realized he was perspiring terribly. What lunacy! If he were to regain his sight, he would fall to his knees in thanks!

"—And of course, she did."

Adrian jerked toward her voice and thought he might faint for the first time in his life. He could see her! Not really *see* her, but the vague shape of her head. "She?" he echoed hoarsely.

"Polly. Of course, she knows *everyone* who has ever carried the name of Albright, but what with her ankle so swollen, she really couldn't come to the west wing with me. Nonetheless, she was quite adamant that it was your mother."

Adrian stared in her direction, straining to see more than the strange shape of what he was fairly certain was her head. What would she say if she knew he could almost see her? They had been so happy, so terribly happy . . . was he addled? What sort of idiot would be reluctant to gain his sight? No, no, of course he wanted his sight back! But he couldn't say anything, not yet, not until he had time to think it through. Not until he was *sure*.

"Why are you looking at me so strangely? Oh! Polly's ankle!" Lilliana sighed with exasperation. "Well, she *did* surprise us all, and had I known she was going to barge in like that, I would have moved the ottoman.

Honestly, Adrian, why are you looking at me so strangely?"

"I am not looking at you, Lilliana. I cannot see you," he said bluntly.

A moment of silence passed. "Of course not," she murmured.

Of course not, he thought numbly, and groped for his spoon again. He spent the remainder of the meal trying to converse with his wife while staring at what he thought was a candelabrum, or trying to catch a glimpse of the footman's form, or the shadow of Lilliana's head. It was preposterous that he should be so rattled. If he weren't completely mad, he'd be leaping from his chair to rejoice in his blessing. Yes, well, he wasn't *certain* of it. At the moment there was nothing but varying shades of darkness, undefined shapes, and the barest hint of light. He could hardly suggest he was regaining his sight!

Then how would he possibly know that she stole his pudding?

He smelled it—he *knew* it had been placed at his side. He had thought the footman had stopped serving him pudding long ago, but he saw it, just as plainly as he saw the shadow reaching for it. Stunned, he swallowed a gasp of surprise. He could not *possibly* have seen . . . first of all, Lilliana would not *steal* his pudding. Secondly, he could not see something as defined as an arm. The madness was mocking him! Oh, he was losing his mind, all right . . . or was he?

He swallowed. "Enjoy your pudding?" he asked casually, desperate to know if he was right.

Lilliana did not answer right away, and once again he had the eerie feeling that the whole room had paused to look at him. "I'm sorry," she murmured. "But you *never* eat it." Adrian's heart seized at her admission. He *had* seen it! "It's . . . it's bread pudding. I adore bread pudding," she muttered, clearly embarrassed.

Stunned, Adrian shook his head. "You may have the pudding, Princess," he absently assured her. They finished their meal in silence; Lilliana too appalled at having been caught, and Adrian, too confused by what was happening to him.

And when they retired, he grew more confused than ever. Once they left the dining room, he was unable to make out any other shape. Nothing—just blackness. He made love to Lilliana with deliberation, burying his face in the skin of her belly and her thighs. He entered her slowly, holding them both back from a climax, lingering in the place he had found such solace in the last two months. It was *here* that he had found his mercy and his peace. And dammit, he was fearful of losing that in the naked light of day.

Sight began to come back to him in bits and pieces. Nothing really consistent or constant, but vague shapes and strange shadows that drove him to distraction while giving him a surreal sense of what was happening around him. Still, he refused to believe it until the shapes began to take a sharper form and the weak light began to sting his eyes so deeply that he could no longer deny it.

Lilliana, in particular, was beginning to take shape for him, and he was almost sick with dread. He had discovered in his blindness that there was so much more to her than he had ever realized, but now he feared—perhaps irrationally—that he had just convinced himself of that. Was it possible that he had been so terrified of the darkness that he had imagined the happiness he had found with her, clinging to her in desperation? What would he think when he actually saw her again? What would *she* think? Had she stayed with him because she truly loved him, or had she confused pity with love? Had it all been a false sense of peace?

He was duly astounded when he began to see the watery image of her face. Not that he could actually *see* it, but in certain conditions, such as the noonday sun, he had a sense of a beauty there, one that was natural and honest, born of a vibrant spirit more than cosmetics. It astounded him that he had ever thought her plain. Lilliana was . . . *brilliant*. He believed he could see the sparkle in the dark circles that were her eyes when she laughed, the gleam of her gorgeous smile, and the long, shapely shadow that was her figure. As he began to see her more clearly, he understood quite plainly what a consummate fool he had been. She was lovely, but he had been too engrossed in his own troubles to notice.

Oddly enough, the more he could make out her face, the more afraid he became of telling her about his sight. At first he was afraid that his feelings would somehow change when he saw her. God knew that they did—impossible though it seemed, he cared for her more. No, he *loved* her, he finally realized, but cringed with alarm at the very idea. Years of conditioning, years of experience, told him that to love her was to lose her. He felt trapped, stuck between a world of darkness that had been his peace, and the world of shimmering light in which Lilliana lived, freely and joyously. And the feelings that invaded him were foreign and certainly damning.

As Lilliana's shape began to gradually develop edges, Adrian discovered just *how* freely his wife lived. In the orangery, for example, she made little pirouettes that seemed to come from somewhere inside her; careless little pirouettes that made him smile. She chased her pups on the bowling lawn. *Pups*, she called them, but Hugo and Maude were now the size of small cattle. At night, in the gold salon, she would read to him, and he discovered that she had little patience for his indifference to popular literature, something he would never have known without seeing her shadowy image. "That novel is positively asinine," he remarked about a Jane Austen tome one night, to which Lilliana wordlessly shook her head—the light of her curls distinguishable from the darkness around her. She continued reading, and in the middle of the next chapter, he exclaimed, "What absurdity! She writes like a child!" That prompted her to toss her head back against the settee and roll it from side to side in a show of great frustration before answering sweetly, "It is not meant to be a treatise, my lord. It is meant to entertain." He had refrained from making any more comments after that, fearful that he would burst into laughter.

The worst was when he had come to her rooms and had been shown to her bath. Sitting in that tub with soapy water sloshing carelessly over the sides, he could make out her succulent breasts riding the water like two porpoises, disappearing beneath the suds only to emerge again in a triumphant arc. It had taken a great deal of will to pretend to listen to the latest spat between Max and Polly. As she related the controversy having something to do with drapery, he was certain he saw her swirl the water around her breasts, running her hands over them and fingering her nipples. It was terribly erotic, and it had taken every ounce of his self-control not to fling himself into the bathwater with her. But his sight was still blurred, and he could not help wondering if he saw what perhaps he *wanted* to see.

And then there was the small matter of having fallen in love with her. Of course, he could not actually say something like that, because he could not be entirely certain he had not put the word *love* to a deep sense of gratitude. And even if he did convince himself it was love—there were times he was quite certain he loved her—it did not erase a lifetime of losing those he cared about. He could not risk that. Not yet. Not like this.

So he plodded along each day, realizing that as his sight steadily improved, withholding the truth from his wife grew more monstrous. But then Benedict returned to Longbridge, and something happened to convince Adrian his sight had indeed been restored.

Over tea with his wife and brother, Adrian was quite certain he saw their hazy forms come closely together, followed by muffled laughter that Lilliana claimed was for her dogs. A seed of suspicion took root, and as the day wore on he gained himself a terrible headache as he strained to see them, convinced they often moved as one, and castigating himself for even thinking such a thing.

He understood, of course, that he was spying, watery images or no.

He also understood that now he was convinced he could see, he must tell her. And he had every intention of doing just that, the moment his sight was pure.

But not a moment before—because he had to know the truth about them first.

Nineteen

THERE WAS NO denying it. A week after Benedict's last visit, Adrian could no longer deny that his sight was fully restored. If he had any doubt, he needed only to look at the glorious color of her hair.

He had to tell her. But uncertain about what was going on between his wife and his brother, and uncertain how to explain a week of sight, he waited for the right moment. In the meantime, Lilliana had coaxed him into picnicking at the lake with a large basket of food and wine. From his perch atop a flat rock, Adrian watched her beneath heavy lids as she tossed the stick into the water for the dogs, her laugher sounding like chimes. It was a miracle that he noticed the snake at all, its silvery head just barely visible above the grass and poised to strike at her ankles.

Adrian reacted without thinking. "*Lilliana!* Don't move!" he barked, and came swiftly to his feet. She turned; surprise and confusion scudded across her face as he began walking toward her, his eyes fixed on the snake. He caught the almost indiscernible movement of the reptile and suddenly lunged for her, jerking her off her feet and around.

The snake struck air, then fell to the ground. The dogs began barking wildly and chased after the snake as it slithered quickly through the grass and into the water, their tails high and erect as they trotted back and forth along the water's edge in case the snake thought to return.

And then Adrian remembered. Cautiously, he turned his head. She was peering up at him, her bright eyes awash in confusion. So much for his plans to tell her at the right moment, he thought uneasily, and smiled sheepishly, like a child who had been caught pilfering sweets.

Lilliana sluggishly pushed his arms from her and stepped back as the look of confusion turned to utter disbelief. "You can *see!*"

"Yes," he said simply.

Without warning, she suddenly flung herself into his arms, knocking him off balance as she hugged him tightly to her. "Oh Lord, I am so grateful!" she cried. "Thank God! It's a miracle, isn't it? I have been so afraid to hope. . . . Oh Adrian, this is *wonderful!*"

The rare heat of shame crept under his collar as Adrian held her in a tight embrace.

And then she abruptly jerked backward to gaze up at him with eyes filled with wonder. "*When?* Did you just discover it, just now? You . . . you just opened your eyes, and it had returned?" she asked breathlessly.

Oh God, he wanted to tell her that was *exactly* how it had happened. "Not precisely," he muttered. "Actually . . . it's been several days now."

Her eyes widened; that luscious mouth of hers fell open as her hands slowly slid from his neck and fell heavily to her sides. "Several days?" He nodded. She continued to stare at him, apparently unable to fathom the fact that he could see. But then her breast began to rise and fall, and she deliberately stepped back, slipping out of his arms. She could fathom it, all right.

"I can explain—" he said hastily.

"You *lied* to me!"

Adrian winced; he looked to the lake, to where the dogs were still sniffing about. "I didn't *lie* to you. I just wasn't certain."

"You weren't certain?" she asked, her voice full of disbelief.

I wasn't certain the peace would not end. "I . . . I wasn't certain it was *real*. It came back in pieces, really, and I wasn't . . . I had to be certain it was real," he said, cringing at how ludicrous that sounded.

"B-but . . . can you see? I mean, can you see everything?" she asked, clearly confused.

"I can."

"Your sight is fully restored? You have no question of it?"

"None."

"And you've been able to see for several days?" she asked, her voice falling to a whisper.

He hesitated. "Yes."

A range of emotions flicked across her eyes before she abruptly pivoted on her foot, marching for the blanket she had spread. Adrian quickly followed, feeling awkward and guilty. "You weren't certain it was *real*?" she shrieked, and bent, grabbing a corner of the blanket and jerking it upward. Bread and cheese went flying into the grass along with two crystal goblets and a wine vessel. "What were you unsure about, Adrian? Was the grass not green enough? The sky not blue? You see the entire world around you, and you are not certain it is *real*? I cannot *believe* you would hide this from me!"

Adrian grabbed her wrist as she tried to fold the blanket. "You think that is so ridiculous?" he breathed. "Do you know what it is like to lose your sight, Lilliana? Have you *any* idea what it means to be thrust into total darkness, to be forced to learn how to live again? My sight came to me gradually, in pieces—and as ridiculous as you may think it is, I could not be completely certain that my mind wasn't playing some cruel trick on me! I had to be certain!"

Lilliana jerked her wrist from his grasp and wound

the blanket up into a big ball, which she promptly tossed aside. "I can understand how shocking it must have been to regain your sight!" she said, fighting mightily to contain her composure. "But what I cannot understand is how you could keep that from me! And for so long, Adrian—days? Pardon, but it feels like *you* are playing a cruel trick on *me*!"

"No, Lilliana," he said evenly, and reached for her hand.

She lurched backward, out of his reach. "How many days? How many days have you watched me, pretending to be blind, knowing that I would give you my eyes if I could? How long have you known?" she demanded hysterically.

Dumbstruck, Adrian blinked. He had no good answer for that, no way to explain how his lie had spiraled out of control, how he had looked for the perfect moment to tell her, knowing every hour that passed was damning. "I have known it was real for at least four days now," he admitted. "Maybe five."

Lilliana gasped. Raw confusion blanketed her eyes as they wildly roamed his chest. "Five *days*?" she squeaked. "Oh no. Oh no . . . do not tell me you could see . . . the other night, when I was bathing. . . ." She looked up and peered helplessly at him, her green eyes wide with mortification. Adrian had never despised himself more than he did at that moment. He did not dare to answer. He did not *need* to answer. Her cheeks blushed furiously as she dropped her gaze. "And in the orangery, I suppose," she muttered weakly. When he declined to answer, one fat tear slipped from her eye and trailed to her mouth. "Did you enjoy yourself?" she asked hoarsely.

"Oh *God,* please let me explain," he moaned.

"You already have," she said bitterly, and stooped to pick up the basket. "You have explained quite clearly, actually." She dropped the basket and pierced him with a scathing look. "You didn't trust me enough to tell me the truth. And you *spied* on me, Adrian! How could you? How *dare* you?"

"Take a deep breath, Princess," he said frantically, "try to be calm."

"Don't you *dare* tell me to be calm!" she shouted, and whirled away from him. Picking up her skirts, she began running for the house, oblivious to the dogs nipping playfully at her hem.

Lilliana ran, blinded by frustration and shock. Turbulent emotions roared through her heart—the joyous relief upon realizing he had regained his sight warred with a cruel sense of betrayal. How could he have kept this from her? After everything they had become in the last two months, how could he have so ruthlessly *spied* on her? Those moments she had thought she was private, when she believed she soared—he had been *watching* her!

She ran until she reached the manor grounds, stopping just below the gardens to press her hand to a stitch in her side as she tried to catch her breath.

"Lilliana? Are you all right?"

Oh God, not now, not today. Lilliana turned reluctantly toward the sound of the voice. "Benedict," she gasped. "We weren't expecting you."

He came forward, his hand falling on the small of her back as he leaned over to peer in her face. "What have you done, run from the lake?" he asked. "What on earth is the matter?"

Perhaps it was the concern in his voice, or maybe just the need to hear the truth spoken out loud. "It's . . . it's Adrian! He can see!" she said, and instantly pressed her hand against the stabbing pain in her side. "Everything! Every blasted thing around us, he can *see*!" She caught a sob in her throat and swallowed hard against the emotion boiling within her.

Benedict did not immediately respond. His hand slipped around her waist, and he attempted to pull her into an embrace, but she resisted. He settled for stroking her arm. "There now, Lillie," he said softly. "This is wonderful news. I should think you would be happy for him.''

''I *am* happy for him! I am ecstatically happy! God knows how I have prayed for such a miracle!'' she cried.

''Then what has you so upset?''

''He didn't tell me! He has known for days, and he didn't *tell* me!''

''Do you mean to say . . .'' He paused. ''Dear God, he didn't *tell* you? I thought surely . . . But never mind. The important thing is that he *has* regained his sight.''

He thought surely . . . *what*? Lilliana snapped her head up to look at him; Benedict's brown eyes flicked to her lips. ''You thought surely what?'' she demanded.

He shrugged; a queer smile snaked his mouth. ''This is wonderful news, of course—''

''You thought *what*?'' she demanded again, and slapped his hand from her arm, stumbling backward.

''I thought surely he would tell you before now,'' he said slowly.

Impossible! Adrian had told *Benedict*? He had confided in his brother when he had last called, but not his wife? Painful fury shot through her. ''Would you have me believe you knew?'' she asked, her voice breaking.

''Ah, Lillie, I hate to see you so distraught.''

''Did you know?'' she shrieked.

Benedict shrugged helplessly. ''I am his brother.''

That was it? That was his explanation for Adrian's lie to her—that he was his brother? By God, what was *she*? Some country bumpkin who happened to live at Longbridge? What a colossal fool she was! All those nights she had lain in his arms convinced that he loved her as much as she loved him! She *knew* better than to believe a leopard could change his spots!

Infuriated, she began marching toward the house.

''Lilliana! Wait!'' Benedict called. ''Believe me, I have tried to tell you!''

That brought her up short. She jerked around and raked a scathing glare across him. ''You have tried to tell me *what*?'' she snapped. ''That my husband could actually see me when I thought I was private?''

''I tried to tell you that he could not be trusted,'' he said gruffly. Unwilling and unable to hear his insinuations now, Lilliana rolled her eyes and continued toward the house. Benedict caught up to her. ''I tried to tell you, but you would not listen! Lilliana, I have known him all my life! Adrian thinks of no one but himself—he cannot be trusted, he has alienated everyone who ever loved him, and he will lie to you without thought or reason!''

''What in God's name are you doing?'' she exclaimed, and halted midstride to face him. ''Why do you seek to denigrate him?''

''*Denigrate* him?'' Are you truly so naive? I am trying to keep you from hurt! My only hope is that you will understand him as I do so you will not allow yourself to be hurt by him! Lilliana, *think* about it! He has never been truthful! Do you know why he married you? Do you *truly* know why?''

She faltered, ashamed to admit that she did.

''It was sick revenge,'' Benedict continued hastily. ''A strike against me because Father had disowned him. Oh, I am sure he has told you that Father is overbearing, distrustful, and God knows what else! Believe me, I have heard it many times! But on my honor, my father raised him like his very own son! He gave him every opportunity, every chance to be his heir, and Adrian squandered every one! It was *he* who caused the rift between them, *not* Father! It was *he* who had a quarrel with Rothembow, not the other way around! He will twist everything to suit his own ends, including something as tragic as his blindness! Why do you think he didn't tell you?''

''I . . . I don't know,'' Lilliana stammered helplessly.

Benedict grabbed her shoulders and shook her. ''For chrissakes, Lilliana, open your eyes! Why didn't he tell you? To keep you exactly where he wanted you, don't you see that? He *needed* you! If you left him, Father's chances in the courts would be much improved, for what wife would leave her husband? It is unheard of, and it would prove he cannot provide as he should!''

No! This was too fantastic, complete madness—she shook her head, but Benedict stubbornly dug his fingers into her shoulders. ''Appearances mean much to the peerage, Lilliana. He needed you by his side for the sake of appearances. Nothing more!''

Everyone around her was mad, she thought frantically, and something . . . *something* did not make sense. ''If you care so much for me, why didn't *you* tell me?'' she demanded.

Benedict immediately let go, frowning at her. ''Because he told me in the strictest of confidence, and I am a man of my word. Besides, you are *his* wife, not mine,'' he ground out. ''It was not my place.''

There was something in the way he said it, a twinge of bitterness that did not ring true. ''Excuse me.'' She stepped around him and hurried on to the house, suddenly sick to death of the Spence family and their mysteries.

Their mysteries kept her pacing in her rooms for the better part of the afternoon. Twice she turned Adrian away, too confused and hurt to speak to him. Frantic, she tried to find a plausible reason why he would keep his sight from her, trying gamely not to think about other secrets he might have kept from her. And then there was Benedict—as detestable as his words were, could he be telling the truth? *The truth is that my father raised him as his very own son.* Could Adrian lie so easily? *Adrian is not to be trusted.* She could not help herself; she questioned everything he had ever told her. The sad tales about his mother, about Phillip Rothembow. Was any of it true?

One of the Spence brothers was lying to her.

All right, all right, she had to *think*. One of them was lying. Certainly Adrian was—his so-called blindness was a testament to his lies. No, *she* was the one who had been blind to everything around her. *She* was the one who had stupidly married for freedom and the chance to soar. But marriage was not about freedom, it was about honesty. And loyalty and commitment—concepts that had never crossed her mind until now. These concepts struck at her with a vengeance now because she understood she had signed over her fate to the notion of *amusement*!

Well, there you had it. Everything that soars must eventually come down. She had come down, all right, like the little sparrow that had plummeted to earth in her mother's garden. Adrian had lied to her while garnering her deepest sympathies. And in the course of it, he had blithely enchanted her, had made her fall hopelessly in love with him.

Oh, and there was Benedict, too, always charming, always *present*, doing nothing that would suggest he would be lying. But something about him rang false. Could it be Benedict's own need for revenge had caused him to try and poison the well of her feelings for Adrian?

And swirling in the middle of it all was the question of Adrian's birth. His birth was the very root of dissension between the two brothers, the very reason Adrian had married her to avenge the loss of his inheritance. Yet even here—there was something about the supposition that Adrian was illegitimate that did not seem quite right. It was nothing more than a vague intuition that had been bothering her, but—

Polly.

It was Polly! Lilliana suddenly realized. Adrian had said his mother was an only child. Polly often spoke of the *girls*. Lilliana suddenly pitched for the door of her rooms and went in search of her lady's maid.

She found her sewing contentedly in her rooms with her mending ankle propped on a tiny little stool. "Good afternoon, milady," she said cheerfully after bidding Lilliana to enter. "It's early yet, isn't it? I shall be down to tend you at five o'clock, just as I always do," she said, glancing at a clock.

"Polly, do you recall the painting in the gallery I mentioned to you?"

"Of Ladies Evelyn and Allison? Fine painting it is too."

Lilliana hastily moved to her vanity, grabbed the bench there, and dragged it to where Polly sat. "Who *are* Evelyn and Allison?" she asked.

Polly grinned. "Why Lord Albright's girls, of course! Darling little girls, they were."

"Were they cousins?"

The woman snorted. "They were *sisters*, Lady Albright!" she exclaimed, and shook her head at what she obviously considered a ridiculous question.

"Lord Albright believes his mother was an only child," she stated, and watched Polly's gray brows arch high, almost into her receding hairline.

"Beggin' your pardon, mum, but that's silliness. Of course Lady Kealing had a sister! The two were thick as thieves!"

At that bit of information Lilliana eagerly leaned forward. "What happened to them?"

"Why, what happens to all young girls, naturally. Lady Evelyn, she went off and married Lord Kealing, and Lady Allison, she went off to London. I don't know after that. The girls never came back to Longbridge, and Lord Albright, well, he wasn't the talkative sort. I corresponded with Lady Kealing for a time, but she rarely spoke of her sister, not after . . ." Polly suddenly shifted. "Lady Allison always talked of living in Italy. Perhaps she did."

"But don't you know where she is?"

"No, milady. It's been more than thirty years now." A slight frown creased Polly's brow for a moment before she resumed her sewing. "Ah, but they were the loveliest girls in the parish. Lady Evelyn was the youngest, and she was married first. Lady Allison left about the same time."

"But I don't understand! Why wouldn't Adrian know of his aunt?" Lillian insisted to the wall.

Polly's frown deepened. "You'll have to ask him."

Ask him indeed.

Lilliana left Polly's rooms, lost in thought as she slowly made her way to her own rooms. It was as if pieces of a puzzle were scattered across her mind—the portrait of two girls at Longbridge, the portrait at Kealing Park of a man who so closely resembled Adrian. The paintings somehow fit together, she was certain, but for the life of her she could not see how.

The afternoon was proving unbearable for Adrian. Having followed Lilliana to the house after retrieving their things, the first thing he had to do was face the dozens of servants and accept their congratulations for the miraculous recovery of his sight. He felt almost sinister, as if he had perpetrated some fantastic scheme on all of them. More than one looked at him a bit suspiciously, and who could blame them? What blind man went out for a picnic and came back with his sight fully restored? Still others marveled at the glory of God, insisting that he had been blessed. That was almost cruel—he wasn't blessed, he was doomed.

The second thing he had to do was face Benedict, who had appeared unannounced, as he was increasingly fond of doing, without invitation, and strutting about the place as if he owned it. Oh, but Benedict was in fine form. After proclaiming himself to be ecstatically happy about Adrian's restored sight—and naturally, the end to Archie's ridiculous suit, Benedict chatted easily about his attempts to soothe Lilliana, not caring who heard, and describing in great detail her pretty, tear-filled eyes. But he assured Adrian he had done his best to comfort her. Adrian could just imagine that he had. Now that he could actually *see* Benedict again, he did not trust him for a moment. Yet that ignoble thought made him cringe with self-loathing. Where was the mercy he was so intent on showing Benedict? Where was the benefit of the doubt?

His insides felt as if they had rotted, but as the afternoon wore on he grew more distrustful of everyone around him. Damn it, he *had* seen the shadows of his wife and his brother together when they had thought he was blind. And as much as he would love to dispel that suspicion, Lilliana had locked the damned door to her rooms and refused to speak to him. And just what had he done that was so horrible? Could she not understand how awesome the gift of sight could be to a blind man? Could she at least attempt to comprehend how he might have felt at that moment?

Or was there another reason she was so angry?

When she came down to supper—wearing a rich blue brocade gown that hugged her curves and succeeded in lighting a torch in him—she walked past him with just a flick of her eyes. She glided to a seat across from Benedict, who immediately engaged her in some pointless chatter until Adrian thought he might explode. How he endured the meal, he hardly knew. It was impossible to take his eyes from her. God, oh God, how could he have missed her natural elegance? In the warm light of the candelabrum, her porcelain skin and rosy blush made her look ravishing. Her hair had grown well past her shoulders, and she swept it back and up in a very simple but graceful style. The Princess was gorgeous, he realized with a jolt.

Benedict saw it too.

Hell, he not only saw it, he *catered* to it. When they retired to the green drawing room after supper, his brother proceeded to practically make love to his wife right before his very eyes! He spoke softly to her, constantly touching her hand, her shoulder, her knee. He laughed at the things she said, hung on every word that fell from those full lips. Lilliana responded politely, Adrian noticed, but was never coy. Was her restraint for his benefit? Just what *had* gone on while he had been blind? As hard as he fought it, he was growing furiously jealous of Lilliana's dimpled smile, particularly when that smile shone upon the weakling Benedict, no matter how briefly.

When at last it came time to retire, Adrian made his way to his rooms after Lilliana had gone up, an irrational anger mounting in him with every step. His crime was not so great to warrant such cool haughtiness from her. Granted, he should have told her about his sight, but he could hardly see how that should condemn him. Perhaps he had misjudged her—perhaps she was much shallower than he had recently come to believe. Or was she perhaps more conniving than he had thought, even angry that they could no longer carry on their little affair right under his nose? He was uncertain about everything. Except that he was furious. And that his head was killing him.

Fury pushed him to crash through the door of his rooms, shove out of his coat and drop it on the floor. He did the same with his neckcloth, practically clawing it from his neck, and then his waistcoat, which he also carelessly discarded onto the floor. All of this he did as he walked to the door to her rooms. God help her if he found it locked, he thought, and shoved hard against it. The door swung open, bouncing against the wall.

At her dressing table, Lilliana shrieked and whirled around, bringing a hand to her throat. "You startled me!"

Adrian clenched his jaw and surveyed the room as he made a half-assed attempt to get hold of himself. Honestly, he did not *want* to get hold of himself! He had been blinded for two months and had regained his sight, and *he* was not the villain here! And he had thought her so passionate, so extraordinarily forgiving. "You owe me a bloody apology," he said through clenched teeth.

Her eyes widened with shock, then narrowed dangerously. "I owe *you* an apology?"

He walked farther into the room, facing her with arms akimbo and legs braced apart. "First and foremost for locking your door to me. Don't *ever* lock your door to me," he growled. "This is *my* house and you are *my* wife. I will enter here when I bloody well please."

Lilliana slowly rose, her hand gripping a hairbrush so tightly he could see the white of her knuckles. "The inventory of your chattel is duly noted. Is there anything else?"

"Oh yes, madam, there certainly is," he snarled. "You further owe me apology for having behaved so childishly today."

She gasped with outrage. *"I beg your pardon?"*

"You heard me. Funny, isn't it, that I should think my wife would be grateful my sight had returned? Yet I find myself wondering why she is incensed that I can see her!"

"You must be out of your mind!" she snapped, and slapped the brush down hard on the vanity. "Of *course* I am grateful, but you are forgetting one important fact, Adrian. You *lied* to me! You didn't tell me your sight was restored, and I can only presume it was because you were too preoccupied with spying on me and everyone else on this estate!"

"I walked around this estate seeing *nothing*, hardly trusting what I was seeing! Do you have any idea how many images I saw in my mind while I was blind? *Hundreds* of them! Images so real that I questioned my own sanity! When my sight began to come back, I could not be sure it wasn't my mind conjuring up those very same images!"

"I am quite certain," she said raggedly, "that it was traumatic. I could never have endured what you did, or as bravely as you did! But the fact remains that you did not trust me enough to tell me! Nothing has changed, Adrian, and I honestly thought it had!" she cried. "This . . . this is not about your sight, it's about *us*. About you and me, and your ability to trust me, to be *honest* with me! You were *spying* on me!" she cried, and swiped angrily at a tear that spilled from one eye.

"God in heaven, I was not spying on you!" he roared to the ceiling. "I have tried to explain to the best of my ability why I didn't tell you! Oh, but you have made it exceedingly clear that you don't like the reason, Lilliana. And I cannot help but wonder why you are so god-dammed intent on *not* believing me! Perhaps *you* are the one who is hiding something!''

"Me?" Lilliana's eyes clouded with confusion. Or guilt. With a trembling hand she wiped another tear from her cheek. ''What could I possibly be hiding?'' she asked, her voice ragged.

''Oh, I don't know,'' he said snidely. ''Perhaps we should ask Benedict.''

Like a bolt of lightning Lilliana's hand shot out to strike him, but Adrian caught her wrist and flung her arm away. ''How *dare* you imply such a thing? My God, you are *obsessed* with him! Everything comes back to Benedict, doesn't it? Everything about you is about him! Well, hear this, Adrian! At this very moment I can truthfully say I find him *far* more desirable than you!'' she shouted hysterically.

His head burst into a thousand tiny shards. Without thinking, he grabbed her arms, hauling her into his chest. A thousand retorts, a thousand threats rifled through his brain. But as he glared down into her gray-green eyes, he saw his own fear and anger reflected in them. The fact that he, of all people, could be driven to such a jealous rage disgusted him.

The whole, emotionally sickening scene instantly reminded him of Archie. It was almost as if he was holding *Archie* in his arms. But it wasn't Archie. It was Lilliana rejecting him, Lilliana despising him, Lilliana loving Benedict.

He hated her.

He hated her for turning against him after he had opened his rusty heart to her. What a pathetic fool he had become, a weak, pathetic fool who had let a silly parish princess affect him! And he had convinced himself that he *loved* this little cretin? Appalled, he shoved her away. Lilliana stumbled into her vanity, catching herself on the edge. With an indolent smile Adrian shrugged at her pretty little pout of fear. "Madam, you may believe what you will," he said indifferently, and casually strolled out of her room as if nothing had happened.

Twenty

JULIAN DID NOT want to go, but Arthur made him. They argued the entire way to Longbridge, Julian protesting that their vow to meddle in one another's affairs was to be on the anniversary of Phillip's death, and not willy-nilly in between. Arthur countered that they had vowed not to allow another of them to fall, arguing effectively that when a man lost his sight—and under questionable circumstance, no less—then *that* certainly constituted despair. And if that wasn't enough to suit Julian, they had promised to deliver the emerald and diamond jewelry Albright had commissioned for his bride.

As there was no adequate retort for that, Julian turned his complaints to the road conditions, the weather, and the very irritable notion that Albright's *despair* stemmed from his turning into one of those soft-bellied country earls. As they turned onto the mile-long drive leading to the Longbridge estate, Arthur spat, "The Lord as my witness, I shall *never* so much as cross the *Thames* with you again!"

"Please God, don't make me idle promises," Julian sighed. "As I have been coerced into accompanying you on more than one useless excursion, I should be forever thankful if—Bloody hell, that's Thunder!'' he exclaimed.

''Pardon?'' Arthur muttered, and glanced to his left, instantly recognizing Adrian's prized stallion galloping toward them. Both men cringed when it looked as if the rider would hit them broadside, but the stallion was reined to a halt just short of that.

''Mary and Joseph,'' Julian muttered under his breath. Arthur peered closely at the rider—just as he had suspected, it was a woman riding astride in a pair of buckskin trousers! Which, he could not help noticing, hugged two very shapely thighs. She also wore a man's hat beneath which blond curls peeked, and a lawn shirt that skimmed two very delectable breasts. Arthur glanced at her face—large gray-green eyes, thick blond lashes . . .

''Who are you?'' she demanded.

Julian, looking quite surprised, responded, ''I am Julian Dane, the Earl of Kettering, and my companion—''

''Lord Arthur, I presume,'' she finished for him. ''I know all about the two of you. I suppose Adrian is expecting you?''

Arthur exchanged a startled glance with Julian. ''I, uh . . . well . . . no,'' he stammered, and the woman swung those eyes to him, piercing him to the very core. ''We, ah . . . it was a spur-of-the-moment thing,'' he muttered lamely, completely cowed by the pair of pretty eyes.

The woman shrugged indifferently. ''Follow me,'' she said, and with a tug of the reins turned Adrian's prized stallion around.

''I beg your pardon, madam,'' Julian said quickly, ''but might I inquire as to your name?''

The woman turned her head slowly, slicing a gaze across Julian that made even Arthur cringe. ''Lilliana Spence,'' she answered tightly, ''the mistress of this godforsaken place.'' With that, she spurred Thunder forward.

Arthur and Julian looked at one another in disbelief. "*That* was Lady Albright?" Julian gasped. "The sweetness and light for whom Adrian had that dainty little bracelet made?"

"Not exactly what one would expect," Arthur muttered, and the two of them spurred their mounts after her.

But she was too fast for them; by the time they reached the large circular drive, Lilliana Spence, the mistress of This Godforsaken Place, was nowhere to be seen. Max, however, was standing on the steps, anxiously directing two young grooms to take their reins as Julian and Arthur alighted. "Welcome to Longbridge, my lords," he intoned with a bow.

Julian paused to slap the dust of the road from his trousers. "Thank you, Max. I hope we haven't called at an inopportune time?" he said, casting Arthur a narrow I-told-you-so look.

"Indeed not, my lord. Lord Albright is away presently, but he should return before nightfall. He would insist you avail yourselves of Longbridge."

And how exactly was it that a blind man could be away? Arthur wondered.

"His lordship is with his steward," Max continued, and gestured nervously toward the foyer. Aha, Arthur, thought, not *away* precisely, but accompanied somewhere. What a tragedy for a man like Albright.

"Apparently they haven't nailed the coffin completely shut," Julian muttered sarcastically as he brushed past Arthur and followed Max. Frowning, Arthur followed.

Max ushered them to a large salon, done up in soft golds and greens and sporting a dozen or more paintings. An avid fan of quality art, Arthur wandered about the room, admiring the paintings. They were really quite fine: appealing landscapes, an amusing scene from a country dance, a portrait of Albright—Arthur did a double take—a portrait of Albright on a *mule*.

"*Kettering!*" he hissed. Julian turned from his own

examination of a painting. Arthur stabbed his finger at
the portrait of Adrian. Strolling casually to Arthur's side,
Julian withdrew a pair of wire-rimmed spectacles from
his coat pocket, placed them on his nose, and put his
head to one side in thoughtful consideration. "The nose
is all wrong," he mused.

"Ah! You are admiring our paintings, I see!" Simultaneously, Arthur and Julian whipped around toward
the sound of Lord Benedict Spence's voice. "We are
quite pleased with them. Rather good, don't you think?"
He strutted across the room like a cock, his hand extended, beaming at the two of them.

We are quite pleased? All right, Arthur did not know
much about what had happened between Adrian and his
father, but he had heard Adrian make enough comments
through the years, and of course, he knew what had
transpired between the brothers recently. All of that,
coupled with the fact that Benedict was far too cheerful,
made him instantly suspicious. Benedict was the last
man he would have expected to see here, save Lord
Kealing himself.

He glanced sidelong at Julian, who bowed slightly.
"Lord Benedict. What a pleasure," he said smoothly.

"Oh no, my lord, the pleasure is ours! How fortuitous
that you should come! Adrian will be quite pleased, I
should think. But do have a look around. We are all very
admiring of Lilliana's paintings," he said, and nodded
toward the portrait in question with a strange smile.
Correction—a *smirk*.

"Lady Albright?" Julian asked, sounding a little
choked.

"Oh my, yes. All of these are her paintings! She is
enormously talented, wouldn't you agree?"

"Yes indeed," Arthur muttered.

Benedict slapped Julian on the shoulder too eagerly,
causing him to lurch forward. "Julian Dane, my old
tutor! Still lecturing at the university?"

"On occasion," Julian responded tightly.

"And those sisters of yours, are they well?"

"Thank you, they are indeed quite well."

"Marvelous," Benedict drawled. "Well, Christian, I suppose the duke is still in Italy?"

"Ah . . . yes," Arthur said.

A footman entered carrying a tray. "Yes, yes, just put it there," Benedict instructed, and hurried toward the man. Once the tray was set to his satisfaction, he glanced over his shoulder at Julian and Arthur. "Might I offer you a brandy?" he asked cheerfully.

Arthur nodded; Julian mumbled something. With a flick of his wrist Benedict instructed the footman to pour three brandies. How very odd, Arthur thought as he strolled into the middle of the room, that Benedict should act as if he owned the place. Perhaps there had been a reconciliation—stranger things had happened.

He took the brandy Benedict handed him and seated himself. Julian selected a chair directly across from him, arching a curious brow as Benedict bustled in between them as if they were old friends. "I sent a groom after Adrian—he'll undoubtedly ride very hard when he learns you have come," Benedict blithely offered.

"Ride?" Arthur asked.

"Hmmm? Yes, of course," Benedict said, and plopped onto a settee, crossed his legs, and casually stretched one arm along the camelback.

"But . . . how?" Julian asked carefully.

"How?" Benedict's brows shot up. "Why as anyone—oh dear, you haven't heard, have you?" he asked, and suddenly laughed.

"We learned of the accident . . ." Arthur started.

"But not the miraculous recovery." Benedict laughed again at the twin looks of bafflement. "I am terribly happy to tell you that Adrian has regained his sight. The doctor claims he was never really quite certain, and insisted Adrian's chances of regaining it were as good as losing—"

"He can *see*?" Julian interrupted, incredulous.

"As well as you or I," Benedict noted cheerfully.

"B-but *when*?" Arthur demanded.

"Now *that* is a matter of some controversy," Benedict said, smiling. "Sort of the miraculous aspect of it all. Apparently, he regained it well before he let on. Caused a bit of strife between him and Lady Albright," he said, and chuckled lightly. "But then again, it seems as if there is always a bit of strife between them. I am given to understand from my dear sister-in-law that my brother has a very nasty habit of hiding things from her. But that hardly surprises me, I confess. He's never been very forthright, has he? And I have often said Adrian is not the marrying type."

What in the hell was Benedict talking about, hiding things and marrying types? And the extraordinary news that Adrian could see! Arthur frowned into his brandy. *That* news had most definitely not reached London as of yet. "I beg your pardon. Hiding things?" he asked, unable to suppress a twinge of impatience in his voice.

"I merely refer to the *usual* sorts of things a man might hide," Benedict responded with a salacious grin. "Need I remind you of the little visit the three of you paid to Madam Farantino's when we were last in London?" He chuckled, then casually sipped his brandy.

"How would you know of that?" Arthur asked quietly.

"I heard it at White's. Lord Dalhurst was complaining that his favorite lady had been unavailable, as the Rogues had come and claimed the best for themselves." He chuckled again, and raised his snifter in a mock toast to Arthur.

Arthur glanced at Julian; he could see the ire in Kettering's black eyes, and quickly deduced Benedict was too dense to see it—he had never thought Benedict overly bright. "But Adrian was not with us that night," he said pointedly.

Benedict's snifter wavered just slightly at his lips, but he shrugged indifferently. "Well, perhaps not *that* night—"

"Not any night," Julian said calmly, fixing an icy glare on Benedict.

The young man turned red, and he slowly lowered the brandy from his mouth. "I assure you, I am not in the habit of keeping tabs on my brother's whereabouts. But before you defend him too ardently, you should know that he has not been completely truthful with his wife, and *that* is the cause of the friction."

Extraordinary, Arthur thought. The little bastard was spilling the family's dirty linen onto the floor for them to examine. Benedict was up to no good. But he artfully changed the subject, and chattered endlessly about some venture he had brewing in Cambridge. None of it made any sense to Arthur, nor did he particularly care. He never had much countenance for Benedict to begin with; the sniveling boy had turned into a sniveling man as far as he was concerned. And he was thinking of offering to fetch Lord Albright himself just to escape Benedict's boring chatter when Adrian strode into the salon with an urbane expression.

"Kettering and Christian, as I live and breathe," he drawled. "I consider myself right fortunate that you have called." He shifted a cool gaze to his brother. "Thank you, Ben, for entertaining them until I could return."

With a smile Benedict inclined his head and sipped his brandy. A long moment passed before he realized that Adrian was still looking at him, as were Arthur and Julian. A flush crept into his cheeks as he slowly came to his feet. "Yes, well, if you will please excuse me," he muttered, and walked out of the room.

When the door had closed behind him, Adrian motioned for them to sit. "So glad you have come," he said unconvincingly.

"Thank God, Adrian. You have your sight!" Arthur exclaimed.

Adrian smiled thinly. "A rather extraordinary little journey." He settled himself in the spot Benedict had vacated and glanced out the window.

"Lady Albright must be terribly grateful."

"Indeed she is," Adrian responded with a curt nod.

Shifting uncomfortably in his seat, Arthur remarked, "We met her on the drive."

A faint tick appeared in Adrian's cheek and he slid his gaze to Arthur. "Did you? Astride Thunder, I suppose?" It could very well be his imagination, but Arthur had the distinct impression that Adrian was on the verge of erupting. "She has taken quite a shine to him," Adrian added insouciantly.

"As a matter of fact . . . she seems an excellent horsewoman," Julian offered.

"Yes, doesn't she?" Adrian drawled.

"Speaking of your lady wife, I brought the jewelry," Arthur added cautiously.

Adrian stiffened noticeably. "I am in your debt." He suddenly sprang to his feet.

"Let's have a look around, shall we? I confess, I never fully realized how grand Longbridge could be"— he started quickly toward the door—"but not nearly as grand as it shall be when I am done with it." With that he abruptly ended their conversation about Lady Albright.

It was just before the supper hour when Arthur rapped on the door to Julian's room, who opened it in a state of half dress. "Ah. I was hoping for a good valet," he drawled.

Arthur strode past him into the room, ignoring the gibe. "Explain it to me, will you? What in the hell is going on in this house?"

Julian strolled to the mirror and began to loop the loose ends of his neckcloth around his neck. "It appears to me that Adrian is doing what he always does—seizing upon something and turning it into gold."

"Not *Longbridge*," Arthur huffed in exasperation, although he had to agree that Adrian had indeed turned Longbridge into gold.

"Then what?"

"*What?* Shall we start with Benedict, strutting

around like a gamecock? Or his lovely wife for chrissakes, astride Thunder! I should like to have that
woman on the back of my ponies at Ascot," he muttered
irritably.

"If I were you, I'd be willing to try just about anything at Ascot. What did you lose last time, five hundred
pounds?" Julian quipped.

Arthur snorted. "Come now, you see what I mean,"
he insisted again.

"I don't know that I do," Julian answered calmly as
he tied a knot in his neckcloth. "Perhaps he and Benedict have reconciled. Perhaps his wife is an avid
horsewoman."

Folding his arms across his chest, Arthur released an
impatient sigh. "Don't you think it just a *bit* odd that
Albright seemed so smitten with her when he was in
London, and now one can barely mention her name in
his presence?"

"I would suggest that perhaps the bloom has fallen
from the rose," Julian muttered, and peered closely at
his neckcloth as he arranged the folds just so. "It happens to all men, Arthur. Juvenile affection quickly passes
and the cold reality of matrimony sets in."

"I *know* that," Arthur exclaimed, annoyed that Julian did not see things exactly as he did. "But there are
plenty of marriages where the happy couple is quite civil
to one another. Didn't you notice how he seems to avoid
the subject of her? And *she* was hardly in a civil mood!"

"I don't know that he avoids the subject of her at all.
Really, you know Albright as well as I—if the lady is not
worth mentioning, he will not. He should have taken a
mistress, if you ask me. Unfortunately, he chose to listen
to your sentimental drivel."

"Honesty with one's wife is not necessarily *drivel*,
Kettering," Arthur responded sharply.

Julian flashed a charming smile over his shoulder.
"You worry too much, Christian."

"And you don't worry enough, my lord," he shot

back. And if Kettering was too . . . *stupid* to see it, he wasn't. Something was quite wrong in this house.

Adrian felt like a caged animal, forced to make small talk with his closest friends, cringing inwardly every time he heard Benedict's overly boisterous laughter, and wondering if the Princess of the Grange would deign to make an appearance tonight. As he could hardly bear to look at her, part of him hoped she would not. But another part of him wondered what his guests would think. That he had been emasculated by her desire for his brother and therefore could not stand to be in the same room with her?

"I noticed you are erecting something near the gardens—a gazebo?" Arthur asked, interrupting his train of thought.

"Yes," he muttered, and glanced out the window toward the stables.

"I rather think he hopes to build one to rival Kealing Park," Benedict remarked, then laughed, paling a bit when three pairs of eyes riveted on him.

"I am so hoping it will be completed in time for summer."

Everyone started at the sound of her voice. Seeing her standing at the threshold, Adrian could not help the pang of desire that struck his chest as he gazed at her golden hair, her spectacular celery-green gown, her vivid eyes. How had he ever thought her plain? When Benedict stood, he quickly came to his feet, unwilling to let his brother near her, and forced himself to walk across the room for her.

Her eyes flicked to his for a suspended moment as he neared, assessing him warily, then quickly shifted away.

"Come and meet some good friends of mine," he muttered.

"We met this afternoon," she said politely, and placed her hand—hardly touching him at all, really—on his proffered arm.

Adrian led her to where the men stood among a cozy grouping of furniture near the hearth. "Lord Arthur Christian of the Sutherlands, and the Earl of Kettering, Julian Dane. My lords, may I present my wife, Lady Albright."

"A pleasure to meet you again," she said demurely.

"The pleasure is most assuredly mine," Arthur said gallantly, and bowed.

"And mine," echoed Julian, and smiled admiringly. "Please allow me to comment that you ride exceedingly well, Lady Albright."

Lilliana smiled shyly. "Actually, I cling to Thunder's back quite well," she said. Arthur and Julian chuckled as Adrian sat her in a chair as far away from Benedict as he could get.

"Oh, come now, you are much too modest, Lillie," Benedict said. "You are an excellent horsewoman. Shall I fetch you some sherry?"

A shot of anger rifled through Adrian. It was a seemingly innocent compliment, an innocent gesture. But as with all of Benedict's actions of late, it felt like a blatant slap to his face.

Lilliana barely glanced at Benedict as she murmured her decline, and turned a charming smile to Arthur. "My lord, I have heard such wonderful things said about your sister-in-law, the Duchess of Sutherland. Her work with orphans is quite admirable."

"Ah, indeed," Arthur said with a genuine smile. "Rarely have I known such charity."

"Lilliana is rather charitable in her own right," Benedict offered proudly. "The tenants adore her, and I daresay their welfare comes before her own."

Did Benedict have to hold everything she did up to the standard of sainthood? "She is indeed a fine mistress, Ben, but I hardly think it the same as the work the duchess performs," Adrian remarked impassively. That earned him a scowl from Benedict and a look of surprise from Arthur and Julian. Lilliana did not so much as move.

"Well," Julian hastily interjected, "charity is commendable in all its forms."

Adrian shrugged indifferently. "I suppose that is true."

Arthur looked appalled, and Adrian thought to clarify his statement, but was saved from it by the appearance of Max, announcing supper. He quickly moved to help Lilliana to her feet before Benedict could do it, and escorted her from the room, rolling his eyes when he heard Benedict stop Arthur and Julian to show them yet another painting done by the very talented Lady Albright.

"Must you be so open with your disdain?" Lilliana whispered as they walked down the corridor to the dining salon ahead of the others.

Must *she*? Adrian slanted a smoldering look at her. "I am not displaying my disdain, Lilliana, believe me," he muttered through clenched teeth.

She choked on a bitter laugh. "I beg to differ! You display it at every opportunity, but I hoped that you would at least have the decency to refrain from belittling me in front of your guests."

"*Belittle* you?" he scoffed. "That's rich. You belittle me in my own house. I had hoped that you would have the decency not to display your affection for my brother," he said nastily, and paused to let her precede him into the dining salon.

Lillian stopped to glare at him over her shoulder. "My apologies, Adrian," she said, and inclined her head graciously. "I foolishly thought you had regained your sight, but now I understand that you are as blind as ever."

Adrian opened his mouth to retort he was no longer blind to *anything* about her, but Julian and Arthur walked up behind him, and Lilliana turned and glided away. The muscles in his jaw working frenetically, Adrian stepped aside and allowed his guests to enter before him, then seated himself at the head of the table, hoping like hell Bertram had the good sense to bring the wine *now*.

The first course passed uneventfully. Except that Adrian drank enough wine for two meals, smiling thinly if someone directed a comment to him and silently drowning in a pathetic sense of longing for the woman at the far end of the table. Why in God's name would he still desire her? Why couldn't he push her down to the bottomless pit of his black soul as he did everything else? Had he been cast to hell *again*?

It was when the beef almondine was served that he took new notice of Benedict. Arthur and Julian were politely listening to his brother's long-winded dissertation on life, but he was aware of the frequent exchange of glances. Motioning for the footman to fill his wineglass, he glanced at his brother—with one elbow on the table, he leaned forward, droning on about Kealing Park to Arthur and Julian as if he was an old, old friend.

Kealing Park. The words suddenly burst into his consciousness, pricking him. If Benedict wasn't flaunting his adoration of Lilliana in his face, he was flaunting Kealing Park.

"I told Father that I could hardly sanction another mill. We produce far more than we can use as it is. But he is quite determined to profit from it, and I daresay he can," Benedict said, laughing. "I shall have quite an enterprise on my hands one day. *Another* one."

When neither Arthur nor Julian responded to that, Benedict turned abruptly to Adrian. "Tell me what you think of this, will you? I've been toying with the idea of putting a track on the lower portion of the west side of the estate. Not terribly arable, but it is accessible from several roads. The summer months would be perfect for a little weekend wagering, don't you think?"

Adrian slowly lowered his wineglass.

"You know Kealing Park well enough, don't you? I mean, you know the portion I am speaking of?" Benedict flashed a derisive little smile.

Adrian's eyes narrowed slightly as he calmly considered his brother. He reminded himself he was a master at affecting indifference. Benedict could no more openly goad him than *she* could.

"Benedict," Lilliana interjected softly. "This hardly seems the time—"

"I think a track is a marvelous idea," Adrian quietly responded. "You and Archie could race your nags around it."

A stunned hush fell over the dining table; Julian took a sudden interest in his beef; Arthur seemed intent on the carrots.

Benedict chuckled and lifted his wineglass in a mock toast. "That's very amusing. On our nags indeed!" He chuckled again and, shaking his head, turned to look at Lilliana. "You recall the sitting room at the Park you were so fond of?" he asked her. "The one you had hoped to make your own?"

A chill seized Adrian; Lilliana paled.

"It could use a new coat of paint, particularly the ceiling moldings," Benedict blithely continued. "What color would you recommend?"

Slowly, Lilliana lowered her fork and placed it carefully aside. "I have no idea," she muttered.

"Oh come now, don't you? You *adore* that room, and you've such an eye for color."

A rage was building in Adrian that he feared he would not be able to contain. "Perhaps she would like to visit before she states an opinion. Wouldn't you rather like to see it again, my dear?" he asked, and stared pointedly at Lilliana down the length of the long table. A small groan escaped Julian as he closed his eyes and pressed the bridge of his nose between his finger and thumb.

Lilliana placed both hands on the table, pushed her chair back before the footman could reach her, and stood. "My lord, if you will please excuse me. I find I have a rather sick headache," she said, and began walking toward the door.

Julian, Arthur, and Benedict all scrambled to their

feet as she passed. Adrian did not stand, but sipped his wine as he watched her gliding toward him, her eyes fixed on a point beyond him. "Sweet dreams," he muttered as she walked past.

When the door closed softly behind her, Benedict fell heavily into his seat. Julian and Arthur slowly resumed their seats as well, but not their meal. Adrian lifted the wineglass to his lips again, wincing at the sudden stab of pain behind his eyes.

Julian could not wait to leave Longbridge. He said as much to Arthur when they retired after that awful supper and earned a smirk for it. "You see?" Arthur had crowed. "These people are quite mad."

Julian had politely informed Arthur he saw nothing of the sort, but meant merely that he was anxious to get to Whitten where a historical manuscript was waiting for him.

Arthur rolled his eyes. "God, Kettering, you are so bloody obtuse."

"I'd rather be obtuse than a meddlesome old woman," he had replied, and ducked artfully before Arthur could cuff him on the shoulder. "I'll see you in London, my friend," he had said, and with a chuckle left Arthur grumbling that it was apparently his sorry lot in life to look after everyone.

But Julian was far from obtuse. He privately agreed with Arthur—something was very wrong here. But Julian—despite his immense guilt over Phillip's death— did not feel comfortable interfering in another man's affairs. Not with his track record. He had tried in his own way to help Phillip, and look where that had ended. But Adrian was not Phillip. Adrian was not despairing—he was paying for a particularly hasty and bad decision. He was locked in the hell of matrimony.

Julian could scarcely *wait* to leave Longbridge.

He was so eager, he reached the breakfast room just after sunup, a time of day he very rarely saw. It surprised him to find Adrian already there, nursing a cup of tea. Unnoticed, Julian paused at the door. What was happening here was none of his affair, none at all. But he had spent a rather restless night, bothered that he had become somewhat angered for Adrian's sake. Having observed the residents of Longbridge, the situation was crystal clear to him: Adrian was allowing his brother to wreak havoc here, whether he realized it or not. He might have erred in his decision to marry, but that did not mean he must allow Benedict to take such blatant advantage.

Strangely enough, as he stood there gazing at Adrian rest his forehead in the palm of his hand, Julian was struck with the memory of their vow after Phillip's funeral: to *make sure that nothing goes unsaid between us. To make sure that not another of us slips away* . . . Well bloody hell, then. He had vowed it over Phillip's grave, and here he was, looking at one of his oldest and dearest friends slip away into a man's private hell. Benedict, the little weasel, was doing his damnedest to make sure of it. Julian knew then that he had to say something—he owed it to Phillip if nothing else. Wouldn't Christian be proud of him now, he thought, and abruptly shoved away from the door and walked into the room. "It would appear that our good friend Arthur has led you to the evil of drink, has he?" he quipped.

Adrian grimaced when Julian called a cheerful good morning; he had a monstrous head from too much wine last evening. "Rather hysterical coming from you," he muttered miserably. "Must be the one night you have gone to bed quite sober, isn't it?"

"Please, you offend me," Julian said, smiling. "It is at *least* the second. But then again, I didn't have a lovely woman waiting for me."

Adrian closed his eyes. "Neither did I." There was no smart retort to that, and he opened his eyes. Julian's smile had faded; he removed his wire-rimmed spectacles from his breast pocket and put them on, regarding Adrian thoughtfully. Bloody fantastic. Now *Julian Dane* was staring at him as if he were mad. Adrian groaned and shoved the tea away from him.

"Look here," Julian started awkwardly. Adrian cocked his head to one side, expressionless. It was so very unlike Julian to meddle. Arthur, yes—Julian, never. Since his sister Valerie had died a few years ago, the man had been too busy drifting through his own life to remark on others.

Julian awkwardly cleared his throat. "Ah, I know this is none of my affair, but I am your friend, Albright, and we . . . well . . . we did make a vow to one another."

"A vow?"

"You know," he said, clearly uncomfortable. "We vowed never to let another of us slip away again."

Indignation rose swiftly in Adrian. He had had his fair share of hard times recently, but to suggest he was as cowardly as Phillip . . . "What exactly are you suggesting?" he snapped.

Julian winced lightly and cast his gaze to the table. "I am suggesting that you are perhaps . . . in need of some sound advice."

"Advice," Adrian growled.

Julian impatiently waved a hand at him. "I am not speaking of . . . look, think what you will, but I must say this. Your brother is causing more harm than I think you realize. He is far too attentive of your wife, he purposely attempts to goad you, and I have no earthly idea why, but I would trust that you might find your peace with her if he weren't here. There, I've said it."

Surprised, Adrian blinked. "Perhaps she is attentive of *him,*" he said slowly.

Julian immediately shook his head. "He makes her rather uncomfortable, obviously. Hell, I only know that he intentionally seeks to drive a wedge between you and your wife. I can't possibly fathom why, but his intentions are malevolent, I am quite certain. Take my advice, Albright, and send him home. At once."

That rendered Adrian speechless, and he stared at his

friend as his mind began to click. Julian stood abruptly. "I beg your pardon," he said sheepishly. "It is none of my affair. Look here, I'm off to Whitten to see after an old manuscript that may be of some importance to my studies. I had best get an early start." He turned on his heel and walked quickly to the door. Adrian had yet to speak, his mind still reeling from the few words Julian had uttered. "I'll see you in London soon, I hope?" he asked over his shoulder. When Adrian nodded, Julian lifted a hand and disappeared into the corridor.

Adrian stared after him, still stunned. He didn't need Julian to tell him Benedict was a problem. He did, apparently, need Julian to tell him that Benedict was intentionally driving a wedge between him and his wife. It suddenly all made sense, and he marveled that he had not seen it before. Of *course* that was what he was doing! He was seeking his own revenge and using Lilliana to do it. Adrian had certainly been pricked by Benedict's talk of Kealing Park, but had thought it nothing more than Benedict's childish attempt to needle him. He had not seen what Benedict was really doing, not until Julian had said it aloud.

The little bastard was *intentionally* pushing him from Lilliana. And she, perhaps unwittingly, was playing along with him.

It was high time he had a talk with his brother.

Twenty-one

LILLIANA FELT THE faint nausea begin to rise again as Polly fastened her blond curls to the back of her head. The sickness had not really left her since that horrible night when she had stood just where Polly was standing now and had told Adrian she preferred Benedict to him. She closed her eyes—what made her say such things? Nothing could be further from the truth; the mere thought made her belly lurch again. But she had been angry with him, and the words had tumbled out of their own accord. If only she had caught them, held them back . . . but she hadn't, and Adrian's mask of indifference had slid into place. Now he avoided her like death.

Fine, she thought as the nausea passed, and opened her eyes. She couldn't take those words back, and she was still furious with him for lying to her. They were hopelessly arrested in a strange and silent standoff, the gulf between them growing wider and wider with each passing day. The strain was taking its toll on her; she felt constantly ill. Desperate to air their differences, she was absolutely sick of Benedict's constant presence! Adrian simply acted as if his brother didn't exist—just as he pretended his wife didn't exist. In the meantime, Benedict grew increasingly obnoxious. He treated the staff as if he paid their wages, was relentless in his unwanted and unwelcome attention to her, and belittled Adrian with veiled remarks about his father and Kealing Park.

As if things couldn't get any worse, those two *Rogues* had appeared unannounced, and undoubtedly suggesting all manner of things they might do now that Adrian's sight was restored. The irony was not lost on her that there was a time she would have given anything to know the Rogues and experience their reckless ways. But that seemed like years ago—now, all she wanted was the blind Adrian back. Not a *blind* Adrian, but the Adrian he had been then—loving, gentle, and completely open with her. The Adrian who had made her sob with wonder when he took her, who would hold her tightly to him in sleep, who would reach for her at dawn's first light. The Adrian who had allowed her to look into his soul. She wanted *that* Adrian, not the indifferent, coolly civil, pompous . . . incredibly distant Adrian.

She did not know how to get him back.

"My stars, but don't you look lovely," Polly said, beaming behind her.

Lilliana glanced at herself in the mirror, unnoticing of the little wisps of blond curls that blanketed her neck and temple, or the stylish lavender gown she wore. She saw the dark circles, the bottom lip swollen from her chewing on it, the almost translucent skin. "Thank you, Polly," she muttered sadly.

Polly clucked her tongue. "Here now, milady, you've been moping about since his lordship got his sight back. You're happy for him, aren't you?"

"Of course!" Lilliana said, and forced a smile.

"Well, you don't seem yourself a'tall, if you don't mind me saying. I don't suppose you're carrying?"

Lilliana's heart skipped, and she caught Polly's amused gaze in the mirror. "I beg your pardon?"

"I *said,* you must be carrying," Polly repeated matter-of-factly, and bustled to the bed to pick up a silk wrapper and drape it carefully along the foot. "Has it not occurred to you? Well, I am your lady's maid, and if you don't know, I *do*," she said with supreme self-assurance.

Lilliana's eyes rounded as she quickly calculated the days since her last cycle. Oh God. Oh *God!* It *couldn't* be! Oh God, but it could . . . what else would explain the sickness, the turbulent up-and-down of her emotions, the constant threat of tears?

Unconsciously, her hand slipped to her abdomen as she stared at herself in the mirror. She was carrying his child. It should have made her ecstatically happy. But the sickness came over her again, and folding her arms across the vanity, she dropped her forehead onto them.

Polly patted her back. "There now, it's nothing to be afraid of. His lordship will be very pleased," she said soothingly, and walked to the door. "The sickness will pass soon enough, I warrant. I'll leave you to your thoughts, milady," she said blithely, and quit the room.

Polly was wrong about one thing—the sickness would never pass, it was too firmly rooted in her soul. A million thoughts bombarded Lilliana as she tried to fathom the incredible knowledge that she was carrying a child. Everything that had gone between her and Adrian the last few days seemed foolish to her now. Moreover, with the life budding inside her, it seemed terribly sad. She would bring a child into the world who would know nothing but disdain from his father, just as Adrian had been raised. . . .

She abruptly lifted her head and stared at herself in the mirror. Maybe she couldn't bridge the gulf between them, but she at least could put the question of his birth to rest once and for all. The painting at Kealing Park had haunted her for days . . . she had admired it enough times to remember now that Adrian was the spitting image of his grandfather, and therefore could not be anyone's son but his father's. And if that were true, then why did his father despise him? Surely *he* had noticed the resemblance between his father and his son?

There had to be another reason for his disdain, and suddenly, knowing the reason was paramount to everything else. If Adrian was truly Lord Kealing's son, she had to know it, for the sake of the child she carried if nothing else. And she knew one person who might be able to help her.

Mr. Pearle, the solicitor in Kealing who knew everything about everyone.

But how on earth could she possibly go and speak with him? She couldn't tell Adrian of her suspicions. He would not listen to her, and even if he did, he would not believe it. No, she had to go, and she had to think of a way to do it without letting him know.

After seeing an unusually somber Arthur off to London, Adrian sent for Benedict. He was seated behind the massive desk in his study when Benedict strolled in, his face a wreath of smiles. "Ah, Adrian, you look more confident each time I see you. Glorious day out, you know. You might enjoy a stroll about the gardens. Lilliana and I certainly did."

Adrian unconsciously gripped the arm of his chair. "Have a seat, will you?" he suggested.

Benedict did as he asked, casually stretching his legs in front of him, one hand shoved into the waist of his trousers. "I should very much like to show Lilliana the gardens at the Park. They are so much grander than here, and I think she would thoroughly enjoy them again—"

"Ben, I think it is time we were honest with each other," Adrian interrupted.

That startled Benedict, but he quickly recovered. "Of course! What is on your mind?"

"I think it high time you returned to Kealing Park—"

"Oh yes, I do too. Now that I am assured you are wholly recovered—"

"And not come back again."

Benedict's eyes rounded; he pushed himself up and peered closely at Adrian. "I beg your pardon?"

"I should have asked you to leave long before now," Adrian said wearily, "but I confess I did not fully understand what you were attempting to do. I am truly sorry for what has happened, although I rather doubt you will ever believe that," Adrian continued, noticing that the color was rapidly draining from Benedict's face. "Marrying her for the reasons I did was a stupid thing to have done. But Lilliana is my wife, Ben, and there is nothing you can do to change it," he said evenly.

Benedict's lips began to move, but no words came out. He shook his head as if to clear it, then gaped at Adrian again. "I am quite certain I do not know what you mean. I think surely you have misconstrued—you can't honestly be thinking clearly if you think I should want to change anything. I am happy for Lilliana. She is a sweet girl, and I am glad that she has married well."

Adrian nodded thoughtfully. "Then you would have me believe that you never really cared for her? That you don't, even now?" he asked quietly.

The hint of a flush began to fill Benedict's cheeks and he chuckled nervously. "Lord, I *told* you!" he blustered, then laughed as if it was the most absurd suggestion in the world. "I *never* cared for Lilliana, not like you seem to think! And certainly now all I feel for her is a brotherly concern!"

"A brotherly concern," Adrian echoed. "I rather think it more than that."

Benedict blinked—then suddenly surged to his feet and strode to the desk. "If you are jealous, you should speak with your wife!" he spat. "If there is an unnatural affection between us, it is most decidedly *hers* and not mine!"

The fury that Adrian had been fighting to contain all morning began to leak out of him. Very deliberately he stood, towering over Ben by several inches. "I am quite certain you did not mean to imply that my wife harbors some *unnatural* affection for you."

"You can hardly hold me responsible if she now wishes she had married me!" he blustered angrily.

He would throttle him! Adrian moved from the desk; Benedict matched it by taking several steps backward. "Be honest, Ben," he urged. "Admit what you are doing here." Benedict responded by pressing his lips firmly together into a thin line. "Let me help you," he said, and took another step toward him. "You have attempted to drive a wedge between us. You have tried to make me think that there is something between the two of you, and you have done your best to poison her against me in the course of seeking your revenge." He stopped there and shoved his hands into his pockets, waiting for Benedict to deny it.

But Benedict surprised him. His brown eyes blazing, he scowled hatefully at Adrian. "You *betrayed* me! God, when I think of how I admired you!" he spat, his face contorting in pain. "I have *always* admired you, more than anyone I know. But when you took her from me . . ." His voice trailed off, and he squeezed his eyes shut, fighting for composure. "When you took her from me, I hated you," he muttered. "I hated you more than I thought was possible to hate another living soul. You are right, Adrian. I came here hoping to find you broken as well as blind. I hoped to find you miserably contemplating the rest of your life in darkness, *alone,* without comfort. As I can *never* have her, I would that you live your life in misery," he said, his voice trembling with emotion. "She hates you, too, you know," he continued, and sneered. "She regrets this marriage far more than I think you are capable of even comprehending."

Adrian's heart constricted painfully; but he shrugged and blandly regarded the brother who had everything that should have belonged to him. He kept his hands in his pockets as he looked at a man who loved Lilliana so much, he would seek to destroy her for the sake of his jealousy. In no small measure he actually pitied Benedict. "I would that you go now, Ben. You are no longer welcome at Longbridge," he said quietly.

Benedict pivoted sharply on his heel and stalked to the door, where he paused to cast a final, scathing look at Adrian. "You are an unfeeling *bastard*," he angrily declared. "I hope that you will one day feel the same pain I felt when you stole her from me! But I fear it is a futile wish of mine—you are incapable of hurt. You are incapable of *love*. I pity Lilliana for that, but God, how I pity *you*," he ground out, and followed his words with a slam of the study door.

Adrian stood staring blindly at the door, Benedict's harsh words ringing in his ears. There was a time when he might have agreed with him, but he knew now that he was not incapable of hurt or love. At the moment, he felt them both rather acutely—he just didn't know how to express them. He damned sure didn't know what to do with them. He didn't know how to do anything but push it all down to the farthest recesses of his soul.

And for that, he pitied himself.

Lilliana devised a plan, which unfortunately entailed lying to Polly Dismuke. Banking on Polly's sentimentality, she told her that she had a surprise for Adrian that she must fetch from Kealing, but that Adrian would suspect what it was if he knew where she was going. She could not divulge the surprise, she coyly explained, not yet. And just as she had suspected, Polly had eagerly accepted her plan, proclaiming a surprise was just the thing his lordship needed to bolster his spirits.

Now all Lilliana had to do was convince Adrian she needed to go and welcome her family home from Bath, and hope he would not remember they weren't due until next week. She was actually grateful that the Rogues were at Longbridge—Adrian would not question her in their company.

As she went in search of the men she realized she was rather nervous. There really wasn't a dishonest bone in her body, and she hardly relished the thought of lying to Adrian, regardless of how strained things were between them. But she had no choice, no other alternative that she could see. If there had never been a question of his birthright, if she had never *seen* the portrait of his grandfather, she would not be doing this. But that question was a fundamental part of who he was, at the core of his very being, and she could not let it lie, especially now that she carried his child. She could not live with herself if she did not at least attempt to uncover the truth.

Walking into the gold salon, her nervousness increased tenfold when she discovered Adrian was alone. Seated in front of the hearth, he was quietly reading a newspaper. "You've come down," he remarked, and folded the paper neatly before looking at her.

"Where are your guests?" she asked timidly.

"They departed early this morning."

They had *left*? Hadn't Lord Arthur said something about seeing the irrigation efforts today? "So soon?" she asked dumbly.

Adrian rose from his chair and turned to face her. His eyes leisurely swept her body before settling on her face. "I think they were rather uncomfortable," he said bluntly.

Lilliana felt herself color and moved uneasily into the room. "And Benedict?"

A smirk slowly spread across his mouth. "A rather surprising inquiry from your lips, madam. Surely Benedict told you he was leaving?" he drawled, arching a brow.

No, she had quite convinced herself that Benedict would reside at Longbridge forever, and swallowed her surprise. She had spent the morning locked in the orangery, avoiding Benedict and devising her plan. "He did not mention—he has gone to Kealing Park?" she asked, for wont of anything better to say.

Adrian's smirk deepened. "Yes, he has. No doubt he is eager to paint your sitting room."

She frowned at that; she had no earthly idea what Benedict had meant last night—she had never said much about that particular sitting room that she could recall, other than she recalled it as being very cozy.

"Don't look so chagrined, Lilliana. It is not as if he has left the continent." Adrian chuckled, then looked at her strangely, almost as if he was seeing her for the first time. He motioned to a cluster of chairs. "Won't you join me?"

Her nerves grew worse as she walked slowly across the plush Aubusson carpet. The two of them had not been alone since the night she had said— She would not think of that now! She settled on the edge of a chair and clasped her hands tightly on her lap. Adrian lackadaisically resumed his seat. She could feel him watching her, and kept her gaze on her lap.

"It looks as if it's just you and me now," he said quietly. Lilliana glanced up at that; Adrian was staring at her, his gaze piercing hers. "I gather from your expression you find that rather unappealing," he said flatly.

She didn't know how she found it, other than rather unnerving. Everything was so different now, so wholly different from when he had been blind. Her mind was suddenly flooded with the memory of climbing onto his lap and kissing him one night when he had sat in that very chair, proving to him and to herself that he was still a man. Other memories, little moments of happiness they had shared in this room, came back, moments sitting in quiet companionship while she read to him, or watching the firelight flicker in his blank eyes. Had he actually been watching her then? She scarcely knew anymore! It seemed as if an eternity had passed since then, an eternity in which the gulf had widened so impossibly that neither of them knew how to cross it.

Her stomach roiled, and she clutched her hands to her abdomen.

"Unappealing and nauseating, too, apparently," he said roughly.

"I am not well," she said softly.

"Does the thought of being with me make you so ill?"

He was annoying her now, pushing her, challenging her to say he sickened her. "It has nothing to do with you," she said sharply. "I am simply unwell."

He shrugged. "Perhaps you should take to your bed," he said indifferently.

His apathy disgusted her! "Perhaps I should," she bit out.

Adrian flicked a piece of lint from his trouser leg. "Please, don't let me keep you. I have grown quite accustomed to your frequent absences. If you prefer to be alone, then by all means . . ."

Her anger surged. The man was a *goat*—unfeeling, uncaring, and devouring everything in his path! "I hardly prefer it, but as I have not grown accustomed to your apathy, I find I prefer solitude."

Adrian quirked a brow, smiling thinly. "Apathy? I beg your pardon, but I thought we had established our course. You may do whatever you like, Lilliana, whatever makes you happy. You may even covet my very own brother if you so desire. How more accommodating can I be?"

Something inside her exploded into raw heat. She leapt to her feet, glaring down at him in absolute fury. "*Stop* it! I do not *covet* your brother! I don't particularly care for your brother and I am rather pleased he is gone!"

Adrian lifted the other brow to meet the first. "Is that so?" he drawled. "And I thought your sudden illness was the pang of regret."

Lilliana rolled her eyes to the ceiling, fighting the sudden urge to cry. Stubborn. Stubborn and hateful and maddening. She whirled away from him, stalking to the hearth. "It is impossible for me to understand you," she muttered. "It goes against my very nature to be so . . . *callous* to everything as you are! I thought you had changed, Adrian! I *know* you are different now!" She glanced at him over her shoulder. "But you won't allow it, will you? You won't allow yourself to feel. You will feel *nothing,* not caring who you hurt, just as long as you don't have to *feel* anything! I truly pity you!" she cried.

Adrian's mouth tightened into a thin line and he rose from his seat. "What would you have me feel, Lilliana?" he asked slowly. "The dishonor of my birth? The guilt at having killed my very own cousin?" he breathed. "Or perhaps you would prefer that I *feel* the pain of having married you under false pretense, the agony of being despised by my own father, or your *rejection* in favor of my spineless brother? Is that what you want? Because I will feel it all if it will make you happy," he said hoarsely.

His words stunned her into silence. He regarded her through cold hazel eyes, boldly sweeping her face and daring her to argue with him. Unconsciously she stepped backward, bumping into the hearth implements and rattling them loudly.

"What is it, my love? Does it go against your very nature to make a man feel all that?" he mocked her.

Yes, dammit, it did! She had to get out of there—and was suddenly marching for the door. She had to get away from him and this heartless indifference. Away from the man she had thought so magnificent, the man who harbored more pain than a body had a right to know and would not allow love into that black soul. She could not help him. The fight was too much for her, too deep.

Lilliana reached the door before she remembered what she had come to tell him. Closing her eyes, she drew a deep, steadying breath, then whirled around, intent on getting it over and done with as quickly as possible.

And she saw it.

She saw the ravaging effects of pain in the set of his mouth, the hard glint of his eye. He was watching her walk out, and it had hurt him. He quickly looked away. Lilliana bit her lip, fighting the urge to go to him. And what if she did? He wouldn't let his guard down.

All at once she felt very ill. "My . . . my family returns from Bath on the morrow, and I thought to welcome them home," she said, weakly. "I shall be gone a few days, I expect. Polly is coming with me. And Bertram."

He nodded and picked up his paper. "Whatever you would like," he said, and resumed his seat to read. The wall had come up again, but now she knew there was a crack in it. Lilliana's heart cried out to her once again, urging her to go to him. But she turned and walked out the door, too confused, too afraid to try again. And besides, she *had* to know the truth. For his sake.

Adrian listened to the sound of the door being quietly closed, and brought a hand to his forehead. The pain was knifing through him, piercing the back of his eyes and shooting like fire down his spine. He dropped the paper and pressed the heels of his palms into his eyes. He was a monster! Too proud to admit she had hurt him, too goddammed proud to get on his knees and beg her to love him again! No wonder she preferred Benedict to him—for all that man's weaknesses, he was not a monster. At least Benedict could give her the affection she needed. He could not—bloody hell, he could not even bring himself to tell her he thought her beautiful, or utter the words *thank you* aloud for having seen him through the darkest of days! No matter how he tried, he could see nothing but the disgust in her eyes, feel her complete disdain, and he could not find the words to change it. They just weren't in him. *He was a monster.*

Adrian came clumsily to his feet and staggered toward the sideboard to pour a double whiskey. Anything to dull the pain.

Twenty-two

M<small>R</small>. P<small>EARLE WAS</small> up to his elbows in pastries, methodically testing the quality of the product—a task he considered his most important as proprietor of the bakery. As he fastidiously dabbed the evidence of the "testing" from his lips with a linen napkin, he spied Lady Albright walking briskly down the street toward his establishment. Good heavens, she was coming to *his* shop! Ah, what a banner day!

He was at the door to swing it open just as she reached for the knob.

Nervously touching the folds of his neckcloth, he bowed and said, "Lady Albright! What a pleasure you should call! Is there something I might do for you?"

Lady Albright smiled graciously. "Good morning, Mr. Pearle. Lovely day, isn't it?" she asked as she swept past him and into the bakery. She glanced quickly around the small room, then turned a very charming, dimpled smile to him.

"An absolutely glorious day, madam. I had not heard you were in Kealing. Shall I take it that you have come for some buns? I've a delicious assortment—"

"Actually, Mr. Pearle, I've come on a matter of some delicacy."

"Ooh, I *see*," he said, and leaned forward, his mind suddenly rifling through the possibilities. "I am certain I can be of assistance. I am quite renowned for my . . . *tact*." He beamed at her and adjusted his neckcloth once more. "Shall we talk in my office?" She nodded, and he showed her up some rickety steps to a little alcove, made sure she was seated in the most comfortable chair, then gingerly lowered himself onto a wooden chair that groaned in protest beneath his weight.

Lady Albright smiled again; Mr. Pearle noticed she was twisting her gloves in her hand. "I confess, sir, I hardly know where to begin."

"Might I suggest—being accustomed to this sort of thing, you understand," he hastily reminded her, "that you begin at the beginning. Always a fine place to start, in my opinion." Eagerly, he shifted forward, oblivious to the ominous creaking of the chair.

"An excellent suggestion. Well. You will recall that I married a few months ago, and that my husband and I took up residence at Longbridge."

"Yes, yes, of course. After the unfortunate falling out . . . well, that is none of *my* concern, mind you, but I was aware that the earl was in need of a . . . *residence* he might call his own," Mr. Pearle informed her, pleased to tactfully demonstrate that he was aware of her circumstance.

She blushed a bit. "Yes, well, we reside at Longbridge, the seat of the Albright—"

"Inherited from his maternal grandfather in 1829," Mr. Pearle eagerly recited.

Lady Albright blinked. "I believe that is correct," she responded cautiously. "It is the seat of the Albrights, but my husband had visited there only a handful of times since his grandfather passed away, and—"

"Unfortunate, that," he said, and fingering his neckcloth, smiled sympathetically.

"Umm, yes . . . Well, sir, as you may have surmised, Lord Albright and his grandfather were not very close—''

''I would say *estranged*. Of course, it wasn't the *earl's* fault, you know, because his grandfather was estranged from his daughter, your husband's mother,'' he quickly interjected. Naturally, the details were as firmly etched in his mind as they were in Journal 6 of his *Pearles of Wisdom*.

Lady Albright, however, was apparently not aware of that small fact, judging by the rounding of her lovely eyes. ''Yes. Well,'' she murmured. ''Ah, the ah, items left by the late earl—personal items, you understand—are not looked upon with great . . . *sentiment* by my husband,'' she said.

''Naturally they would not be!'' Mr. Pearle nodded his vigorous agreement. ''Particularly the guns, I hear. How terribly trying that incident must have been for you.''

Lady Albright studied him warily for a moment. ''Umm . . . there are many articles, and I thought to seek your advice on what to do with them. I should think . . .'' She paused, and Mr. Pearle leaned forward a bit more, balancing himself by clasping his hands on his knees. ''I should think that there is *someone*—a family member, perhaps—that would cherish the articles.''

Ah, but she was a clever young woman! ''How very astute of you, Lady Albright. And how very kind.''

Lady Albright startled him by suddenly leaning forward, so that her face was just inches from his. ''Might you help me, Mr. Pearle? I haven't the foggiest notion of how I might find such a family member, what with the *unfortunate* circumstances my husband and his father find themselves in today,'' she said earnestly.

Mr. Pearle could not help his sad sigh. The Spence family was as tragic as any he had ever known. ''They are *indeed* most unfortunate,'' he moaned, and shook his head.

''But I know . . . well, I have *heard* that there was

another daughter. If that is true, then I should be honor-bound to make every effort to find her, shouldn't I?''

Goodness, but Lady Albright had always been a little firestorm of energy, hadn't she?

He was hardly surprised that she should come all this way to inquire after a distant relative. Caroline was the beauty of the Dashell family, but what this one lacked in comely appearance she made up for in spirit. And *he*, of course, would be more than happy to help the young countess bestow sentimental property on the descendants. Which was, naturally, why she had come to him in the first place—he could *always* be counted on to help. He abruptly slapped his knees and shoved to his feet. ''Well! I am quite certain I have kept *some* record of the family.'' He walked to a bookcase, and legs braced wide apart, he tapped one finger against a thick lip as he scanned the dozen or more leatherbound volumes there. At last he picked one from the middle and, holding it reverently, brought it back to the little chair, sitting heavily on the rickety thing, mindless of the groan of the wood.

Mr. Pearle wet one finger and began flipping through the pages. ''Let me see, let me see,'' he murmured to himself. ''That would have been around 1800, I should think.'' He paused, scanning the dozens of entries on each page until he found what he was looking for. ''Aha!'' he exclaimed, and lifted a beaming grin to Lady Albright as he tapped rapidly on a page. ''I was right—1802, it was?'' 1802? Had it been *that* long ago? Goodness, time had escaped him! He quickly resumed his study of the book.

''It was 1802?'' Lady Albright echoed, confused.

''That was the year, 1802,'' he muttered, his attention on the book. But there it was, plain as day on the page. ''Oh my, it *is* as I recalled.'' With that, he shut the book with a resounding *thud* and looked at Lady Albright.

''Is . . . is there something . . . I mean, might you

possibly know where I could find her?'' she asked delicately.

"Such a sad story,'' Mr. Pearle sighed, and indeed it was. "Lady Evelyn Kealing was so terribly young at the time—a mere sixteen, I believe, and her sister Allison, perhaps eighteen, not more.''

Lady Albright's fine brows sank into a confused frown. "A *sad* story, Mr. Pearle?'' she asked anxiously.

"Well,'' he said with a dismissive flip of his hand, "the estrangement and all. But of course, what would one expect? You have a sister, Lady Albright. I am sure you can well imagine how terribly divisive it might have been had *your* sister abruptly married *your* intended.''

Lady Albright's mouth fell open. She shut it. Then she opened it again, and said slowly, "I . . . I don't understand.''

Young dear, of course she didn't! Sordid events such as those that plagued the Spence family did not happen in *good* families. "Let me endeavor to explain, if I may,'' he said charitably. "The betrothal had not been formally announced—that was all set for the spring assembly, you see, when it was customary for the families to announce them. Lord Kealing had been courting Lady Allison for a year, if I recall correctly.'' He leaned forward, peering intently at the countess, and lowered his voice. "*Everyone* was expecting the announcement. Can you imagine the astonishment when he announced for Lady Evelyn and *not* Lady Allison?'' He leaned back, shaking his head. "My goodness, what *calamity* that caused between the sisters! And old Lord Albright, he was positively beside himself, he was. He sent one daughter to Kealing Park, the other to London, and then worked very diligently to sweep the entire thing under the rug.''

A rush of air escaped Lady Albright. With wide eyes she glanced at the bookcase with the dozen identical volumes, then at Mr. Pearle again. "But . . . but Lady Allison? What happened to her?''

"Off to London, I'm afraid. Lord Albright packed her off so as not to invite gossip after the wedding was

concluded. A wedding that occurred in a *fortnight*," he
added, and frowned disapprovingly. Although the reasons were not actually recorded in his *Pearles of Wisdom*—he had his standards, after all—it was quite
apparent why there had been such a rush. But far be it
from him to spread vicious gossip. No, indeed. He smiled
reassuringly. "The entire affair is completely forgotten
now. Which is why my notes are so terribly valuable,
you see. I was just explaining to Mrs. Rasworthy not two
days ago that it is my notes that separate me from Mr.
Farnsworth of Newhall. *My* clients know they can count
on me to keep a precise record of events—"

"Is she in London now?" Lady Albright interrupted.
Startled from his little speech, Mr. Pearle slowly shook
his head. "Poor girl never cared for London, I am told. I
suppose that's why she came back, in spite of her sister's
perfidy."

The young dear's eyes widened even more. "She is
here?" she asked in astonishment.

Mr. Pearle nodded. "Near Fairlington, not more than
three miles from here," he added matter-of-factly, and
once again mentally patted himself on the back for keeping such succinct and meticulous notes.

Much to his great surprise and annoyance, Julian found
himself in Kealing. That crofter must have been nipping
his ale a bit early today, because Julian was quite certain
he had taken the road the man had directed him to. But
Kealing? Hell, he couldn't be any farther from his destination if he tried! Trotting down the main thoroughfare,
he pondered how it was possible he could have gotten so
far off track. A dry goods establishment caught his attention; he swung down and pushed the hat from his forehead. Two hours from London! He could not make it
before evening fell, and he hardly relished the thought of
being on the turnpike when darkness came—who knew
what sort of ruffians waited for lone riders?

There was always Longbridge. Julian sighed and

dusted the grime of the road from his cloak. He hardly relished the thought of *that* place any more than the turnpike, but at least it would be safer. And it would be a quick ride into London if he left very early on the morrow. Of course, he could retain a room here, but Lord knew who he might bump into in Kealing—the least odious being Lord Benedict, which immediately set him against the idea—and besides, there was not a blasted thing to do in this little village.

Longbridge, then.

That decided, he walked purposefully toward the little shop, intent on purchasing some sugar for his damned horse, and reminding himself for the hundredth time to thank his sister Eugenie the next time he saw her for ruining his roan. He was reaching for the handle of the shop when his eye caught a movement inside, and he started.

Bloody hell, it was Lady Albright. He could see her plainly through the window, speaking with a man he assumed was the proprietor. Julian stepped back and quickly looked up and down the thoroughfare for any sign of Adrian's coach. Seeing none, he shifted his gaze to her again, fumbling for his spectacles just to make doubly sure. As she came to the door, he stepped aside, out of sight. Not entirely certain why he would avoid her, he nonetheless stood in the shadows of a nearby doorway and watched her walk in the opposite direction with her reticule bouncing pertly on her arm until she reached the Kealing Inn and disappeared inside.

Impossible, he thought, that Adrian would have sent her here without escort. A smile slowly curved his lips. If Adrian was at the inn, that meant Longbridge was deserted. He could get a good night's sleep there after all, pen a short note to Adrian bemoaning the fact that he had missed him, and avail himself of the very fine whiskey his friend kept. *Perfect*. Whistling, Julian entered the dry goods store to charm the proprietor's wife out of a pound of sugar.

———

Exhausted and emotionally spent, Lilliana disregarded
Polly's admonition to eat and retired to the rooms she
had rented at Kealing Inn. Wearily, she sat down at the
small writing table and stared at the paper in front of
her. The last two days had been an incredible journey
into Adrian's past, a journey that still had her reeling.
The pieces of the puzzle had fallen into place, but there
was one last piece of information she needed before she
returned to Longbridge. She picked up the pen and
dipped it in the inkwell, then quickly dashed off a note.

When the ink had dried, she folded the paper carefully and wrote on the outside, *The Lord Benedict
Spence, Kealing Park*.

She stood then, and pressing her hands to the small of
her back, sighed deeply. What Adrian had endured as a
child, she could not begin to fathom. The lies, the abuse
. . . it was little wonder he was as guarded and con-
trolled as he was. Her insight had been well honed in the
last few days—and the ache for him, so recently dulled
by her own hurt, was sharply focused and wearing her
down. Lilliana thought of her own mother and the many
times they had collided. There had been times in her life
that she had wished for a different mother, one who
would view life exactly as she did, and would not put so
much store in the notion of propriety.

She glanced at the ceiling, blinking back the glimmer
of tears. Now, knowing what she did about Adrian's
family, she could not thank God enough for her mother's
love. For her kind, *gentle* father, and for Caroline and
Tom, the two people in the world she knew would never
hurt her. How empty her life might have been without
her family, devoid of love and affection—gifts she had
taken so terribly for granted.

She dearly wanted Adrian to know what it was to be
cherished.

But she had one last task.

Lilliana was waiting for Benedict in the common room
of the inn when he arrived, practically bounding into the
dark interior. She immediately sent Polly to their rooms,
frowning at that woman's snort of disapproval as she
marched away. Benedict's eyes shone when he found
her, and he strode eagerly to the little table at which she
was seated. "I came the moment I received your note,"
he said breathlessly, and reached for the hand she had
not offered, drawing it quickly to his lips.

"Thank you for coming," she said quietly, and withdrawing her hand from his, motioned to a chair across
from her.

Benedict sat, his eyes searching her expression. "Are
you all right? Has something happened? Honestly, Lillie,
but you look so terribly pale. Can I get you something to
drink, a wine perhaps?"

"I am quite well, Benedict," she said on a weary
sigh.

"Is Adrian here?" he whispered.

She shook her head.

His brown eyes were suddenly gleaming—oddly
enough, his expression was almost one of triumph. He
glanced surreptitiously around them, then leaned across
the table. "There is an irreparable rift between you, isn't
there? Don't be surprised—it has been so very obvious.
My dearest, there must be something I can do to help
you," he murmured. "How you managed to stay as long
as you did . . . just tell me what you would have me
do."

Lilliana looked at the man sitting across from her, the
man she would have married, in all probability, if
Adrian hadn't appeared from out of the blue. She had
been so sheltered, so inexperienced, she had never really
seen him. She had never noticed the strange glint in his
eye, the way he held his mouth so prim and taut. There
was nothing he did, nothing he *ever* did, that outwardly
suggested what he was doing, but Lilliana knew in her

gut he had seen the break between them and had pried the pieces apart. He *wanted* to push them asunder and destroy any chance for happiness she and Adrian might have had. How naive she had been not to see that Benedict wanted his revenge for her marriage to Adrian.

She suddenly felt as if a huge weight was crushing down on her, bending her shoulders and back. It was little wonder her mother had fretted about her so—her naiveté was staggering.

"Lillie? Dear me, you look quite ill—please let me get you some wine, will you?"

"No," she muttered, shaking her head.

"Tell me how I can help you!" he insisted, and reached across the table, covering her hand with his own. Lilliana looked down at his hand and felt revulsion rumble through her. "You know I would do anything for you, including harboring you from my very own brother, if that is what you need," he whispered.

He would certainly relish that, wouldn't he? She withdrew her hand from his. "There is one thing you can do for me, Benedict." He nodded quickly. "I want to go to Kealing Park—"

"Yes, yes of course. Where are your things? It will be much safer there for you—"

"There is a portrait there I must see."

That clearly startled him. He glanced covertly to his right, where the innkeeper was busy cleaning a table. "A *portrait*?"

"It is in the family gallery—a portrait I often admired when I was a child."

Benedict laughed tautly. "Lilliana! You are thinking of a portrait from your childhood at a time like this? You are so sweet, my dear, so very sweet," he murmured, and reached for her hand again, but Lilliana moved it before he could touch her.

"It is important that I see it, Benedict. It means something, I am quite certain."

"Means something? Means *what*?" he asked sharply, then quickly checked himself as he shot another anxious glance at the innkeeper. "Forgive me, but it hardly seems the thing to do just now, what with your marriage in a shambles. . . ."

He certainly presumed to know a lot, but she refrained from saying so. "Please, I must see it. What harm is there in it?"

Regarding her suspiciously, he slowly leaned back and drummed his fingers on the table. She could almost see his mind clicking through the myriad reasons he did not want her to go to the Park merely to see a portrait. "Very well," he snapped at last. "If you think you must see this portrait, I shall take you. But I think you should plan to stay at the Park. If Adrian comes for you, I shouldn't want him to find you here alone, not like this."

Like *this*. Did he mean heartbroken? Confused as to how people born of the same flesh and blood could be so cruel to one another? Or revolted by his eagerness to see an end to her marriage? "He won't come for me, I can assure you," she replied in all honesty. "Nonetheless, I must see that portrait."

Benedict frowned, leaning forward again. "Whatever you think you may find, Lillie, it won't be enough. I tried to warn you about him. He can't be trusted, and he will only hurt you in the end. You should accept the fact that it is over," he whispered gravely.

"The portrait, Benedict," she muttered in response.

Throughout the drive to the Park, Benedict did his damnedest to convince her that she had lost Adrian, continuing his attempts all the way into the long hall that served as the family portrait gallery. But Lilliana ignored him. She was too engrossed in her search of the portraits and feared—not finding it right away—that she might have been wrong. But she hadn't imagined it! Frantic, she walked up and down the long gallery, halting abruptly when she found it.

It was much smaller than she remembered. The oils had darkened with time, so the image of the man was

not as vivid as she recalled. But it was him. Standing
with one foot propped on a wrought-iron bench, one arm
draped carelessly across that leg, holding a riding crop.
Bold and proud, his sandy-brown hair was swept back
and tied at the nape, and his hazel eyes seemed to pierce
through her.

The very image of Adrian: his face, his shoulders, his
hands. Adrian was the embodiment of his grandfather—
his *paternal* grandfather.

Everything fell into place now; everything she had
suspected and verified the last two days was painted on
a canvas before her. She gazed up at the portrait, wondering why Adrian had never noticed the resemblance.
But he had been young when his mother died, sent away
so soon after that. And certainly no one here had pointed
it out to him. She tried to imagine him walking up and
down this hall, studying the paintings, but she realized
he must have kept hidden away as a boy, fearing abuse,
and then as he grew older—

"What in the hell is going on here?"

Lilliana turned calmly toward the sound of Lord
Kealing's voice. Amazingly, she was actually looking
forward to this moment. "Good afternoon, Lord Kealing," she said impassively.

"What are you doing here?" he demanded, his eyes
slicing across Benedict, who seemed to shrink beside her.

"I asked Lord Benedict to bring me here," she said
matter-of-factly. "There was a portrait I very much
wanted to see."

Lord Kealing's eyes narrowed dangerously. "Apparently, then, you've seen it. Benedict, take her back to
wherever you found her," he snapped, and turned on his
heel, prepared to march out the door.

"I noticed the resemblance of your father to one of
your sons," she called after him.

Lord Kealing stopped dead in his tracks and slowly
turned to face her, his gaze searing her with rancor.
"Benedict," he snapped, "leave us."

"But Father—"

"*Leave* us!" he bellowed.

Like a puppet on a string, Benedict jumped; he glanced nervously at Lilliana. "I shall wait for you in the drawing room," he murmured, and quickly walked away.

Lilliana lifted her chin as he fled the hall and returned Lord Kealing's steady gaze. Funny, but he did not frighten her. Instinctively, she suspected he was as much a coward as Benedict was. "As I was saying, my lord, your son Adrian bears a strong resemblance to your very own father, wouldn't you agree?"

Not deigning to look at the portrait to which she pointed, he folded his arms across his chest. "What do you want?" he growled.

Without hesitation, she replied, "I want you to tell your son the truth."

Lord Kealing smirked, his gaze raking across her as if she was so much garbage. "You are a ridiculously pathetic creature," he sneered. "That portrait was painted posthumously. Of course it looks like him—who do you think the artist used as a model?"

Lilliana faltered and glanced at the portrait. Lord Kealing chuckled ominously. "You must think yourself particularly bright. Tell me, did *he* send you here? Does he send his hapless little wife to beg for him now?" he scoffed. "Get out before you make an even bigger fool of yourself." With that, he turned, walking away from her.

Lilliana grabbed her reticule and hastily snatched a folded parchment from it. "You might be interested in this, my lord!" she called after him, and held the parchment up. But Lord Kealing continued walking, shaking his head and muttering under his breath. Lilliana fumbled to open it. " 'My dearest Allison . . .' "

Lord Kealing stopped; he turned, glancing over his shoulder with such a look of hatred that she could not help but shudder. "You are a *fool*," he breathed.

———

It was well past nightfall by the time Julian reached Longbridge, having stayed a little too long to share a pint or two with the cheerful wife of the shopkeeper in Kealing. The mansion was completely dark save a dim light at the far end of the west wing, but Julian stubbornly knocked a third time, refusing to believe that he might have to sleep under the blasted stars. No one answered. How very splendid, he thought wearily, and walked down the front steps, wondering just what he would do now.

The door suddenly opened behind him. Julian jerked around; in the thin light of a single candle stood Max. "Lord Kettering?" he exclaimed, clearly surprised.

"Max! Thank God!" Grinning with relief, Julian bounded up the steps. "I have surmised Albright is away, but I am hoping you might see your way into allowing me a place for the night," he said, and clapping the butler on the shoulder, pushed past him into the foyer.

Max quickly shut the door. "He is not away, my lord," he anxiously whispered as his eyes darted to the corridor on his right. "But I daresay he was not expecting callers. Of *any* kind."

"Unfortunately, I was given some rather faulty directions from a simpleton in Whitten, and as I found myself in the middle of nowhere, I thought to beg for mercy from my old friend. He is here, then? Has he retired?"

"No, my lord," Max said, looking very uneasy. "He is where he has been for almost two days. In the gold salon," he muttered, and motioned frenetically toward the east wing.

In the gold salon for two days? That didn't sound like Adrian, but then again, nothing much about Adrian seemed familiar anymore. A vague, dull sense of panic seized Julian—an image of Phillip popped into his head, an image of a dear friend whose spirit had been lost to this world while his body continued to function. He tried to shove it aside, tried to tell himself he was being ridiculously sentimental, but started quickly after Max all the same.

As he stepped across the threshold of the gold salon, Julian's eyes needed a moment to adjust to the weak light of a single candle. Adrian sat in a chair near the cold hearth, a glass of whiskey in one hand, his chin cupped in the other. Max looked at Julian helplessly before stepping out of the room. Frightened by the dismal scene, Julian strode toward his friend. "What in blazes is the matter with you?" he asked, his voice booming in the silence.

"God, Kettering, do you *ever* send a note ahead?" Adrian asked apathetically. Julian snorted his response to that and began fishing around for a light. He found a three-pronged candelabrum and strode to Adrian's side, using his single candle to light it.

When he was satisfied there was sufficient light, he glared down at Adrian with his hands on his hips. "Are you ill? I certainly hope that you are, because I cannot imagine what could be ailing you if it is not some horrid malady."

"I would that I was so fortunate," Adrian muttered, and lifting the whiskey to his mouth, took a long drink. With a disgusted roll of his eyes, Julian stalked to the sideboard and helped himself to a whiskey. "Bring the bottle, will you?" Adrian mumbled.

Julian pretended not to hear that, and returned to the hearth, falling heavily into a chair next to Adrian. He peered at his friend, his frown growing deeper. "What in God's name has come over you?" he demanded.

Adrian shrugged.

Julian bristled with fear and indignation all at once. "Look here, man, I thought things bad enough a few days ago, but this is ridiculous. *Look* at you! How much whiskey have you drunk?"

Adrian slid a cool gaze to him. "I beg your pardon. I didn't recall you were delivering a sermon here this evening."

The look in his eyes struck a chord of fear in Julian—

it reminded him of Phillip! The last few evenings of his life Phillip had had the same desperate glint in his eyes, the look of a man who was drowning. A deep-seated panic he had never before felt propelled Julian forward. Fumbling for his spectacles, he shoved them onto his nose and peered at Adrian. "What is it, Albright?" he asked earnestly. "This is so unlike you—"

"Oh, for God's sake!" Adrian groaned, closing his eyes. "Please don't attempt to mother me, Kettering. It doesn't suit you in the least!" He stood abruptly, moving unevenly toward the sideboard, and filled his glass to the brim.

Just like Phillip used to do.

The dull panic took a painful hold—Julian frantically tried to assure himself that Adrian wasn't the same man as Phillip had been, but he could not dismiss the guilt of having seen the signs of self-destruction and not doing enough about it. As hard as he tried to force the bitter memory down, he could not. The fact of the matter was that he had seen Phillip's despair, but did not do all that he could—for a lot of reasons, true—but not all that he could do, and look what had happened. Perhaps he was reading more into Adrian's demeanor than was there, but if there was any chance, the *slimmest* of chances, Julian could not allow the same thing to happen to Adrian. Lord God, *never* to Adrian.

"What are you doing to yourself? It is *her*? Is she doing this to you?" he suddenly demanded, surprised by the anger in his voice.

Adrian laughed bitterly. "You would like that, wouldn't you? The Earl of Albright, done in by a woman in the end. Christ, how terribly amusing." He chuckled darkly before tossing back half of the whiskey he held.

"Adrian!" Julian implored him. "I don't know what has gone on here, but it can't be worth *this*," he said, sweeping his arm mindlessly to the side. "Would you destroy yourself over a woman?"

Adrian chuckled, "I should warn you, you are beginning to sound like Arthur."

That stung. Julian hesitated, hiding behind a gulp of the whiskey he had poured. Whatever had happened between Lord and Lady Albright was none of his affair. He had said what he could but he could not force Adrian to listen. Yet he had made a vow. All right, but Adrian was not Phillip; he was not going to come up with some ludicrous way to kill himself. Phillip had been plagued by debt—a woman plagued Adrian. The two were hardly the same! Yet Julian could not suppress the sense of uneasiness. He had never seen Adrian look so gaunt, so haunted . . . this man was their leader, the one among them who was never intimidated. *Nothing* bothered this man.

Oh, but he was bothered. He was absolutely possessed.

Woman or no, Julian shuddered and closed his eyes for a moment. What in the hell could he say to convince him? "Don't squander it," he blurted helplessly, and opened his eyes. The glass froze halfway to Adrian's mouth as he slowly turned toward him with a look of confusion in his eyes. "Don't squander your life!" Julian said again.

"What in the hell are you talking about?" Adrian scoffed. "I've had a bit too much drink, that's all! Certainly *you* should know the signs, Kettering. God knows you have fallen into your cups a time or two."

True, but he was not Earl Albright, the original Rogue of Regent Street. "Remember Phillip," he muttered helplessly.

Adrian's wince was painful, and he quickly looked away. "Have a care, Kettering," he growled through clenched teeth.

It was too late for that—he had already opened his mouth. Julian suddenly leaned forward. "Don't you see? Phillip *let* it destroy him—don't let it destroy you, Adrian. You can survive this, whatever it is. Just go to Kealing and fetch her."

Adrian's head jerked up; his gaze riveted on Julian. "Kealing?"

Julian anxiously waved a hand in the direction of the door. "A quick trip to the inn—throw her on the back of your horse if you must, but just go and fetch her."

Adrian sagged deep into the leather. "*Kealing,*" he muttered under his breath.

Julian left early the next morning. Embarrassed at having been found so incredibly intoxicated, Adrian could hardly look his friend in the eye as he mumbled a faint apology. Seemingly just as embarrassed, Julian nodded curtly, lifted his hand, and departed without another word. Adrian watched him until he could no longer see horse and rider, then began walking to no particular destination. Just moving.

If he kept moving, maybe he wouldn't have to think.

Unfortunately, he could not help but think. *Kealing.* She had gone to Kealing when she had said she was off to the Grange. He suddenly remembered that the Dashells weren't due until next week. She had lied to him, and he could think of only one reason why she would lie to him.

Benedict.

She had gone to Benedict, whether to consult him or feel his arms around her, he did not know or care. It mattered only that she had gone, had abandoned *him* for that sniveling bastard.

A sharp pain suddenly stabbed at the back of his eyes, and Adrian stumbled into the gardens. He had lost everything to Benedict, all that he was. Kealing Park, Archie . . . What was he thinking? Those things didn't matter anymore. *Nothing* mattered but Lilliana. He had lost the most precious part of his life. Wincing at another stab of pain, Adrian squeezed the bridge of his nose between his finger and thumb. It always ended the same— no matter what he did or achieved, Benedict always won in the end.

Adrian paused, blinking rapidly at the pain. He glanced upward, saw the cords strung along the walkways, cords she had strung for him so that he could walk freely despite his blindness. So that he might live again.

The pain suddenly blinded him, and Adrian went down on his knees. The wetness on his skin scared him, and he frantically lifted his hands to his face. What in the hell was this? His tongue darted across his lips, tasting the saltiness. God in heaven, these were *tears*! He had not produced tears since the day his mother had died, not once in all those twenty years, not even when he had been blinded. But these were tears, leaking from his heart and through his blind, blind eyes.

"*Lilliana*," he gasped, and squeezing his eyes shut, he wrapped his arms around his middle, fearing that he might also be sick. *Lilliana, Lilliana, don't leave me, never leave me*. Holding himself tightly, Adrian rocked back and forth, the irrefutable proof that he had a heart slipping from his eyes and sliding down his cheeks. His gut churned with nausea, every breath contracted painfully around his chest. All these years he had thought it was Kealing Park he wanted. But it wasn't Kealing Park; it was *her*, the Princess of the Grange, the little demon who made him laugh, the vibrant angel capable of such incredible compassion and worldly pleasures. He wanted her. He *loved* her. Finally he understood what had been eating at him, destroying him bit by bit—he had lost the one thing on God's green earth that mattered. Not Kealing Park, not his father. Lilliana.

Adrian threw his head back and looked heavenward, blinking rapidly to clear his eyes. "'Show me mercy, Lord,'' he groaned. "Show me mercy once more, and I swear on Phillip's grave I shall never squander it again.''

He waited, almost breathlessly. But the heavens did not open up and strike him with a bolt of kindness and mercy.

And Adrian doubled over with grief.

Twenty-three

LILLIANA HAD NEVER felt so exhausted in all her life. Or sick—her pregnancy seemed to keep her constantly nauseated. She trudged up the stairs of the Kealing Inn, using the railing to pull herself up to each step. When she reached the first floor, she walked slowly down the narrow hallway, believing that her heavy heart actually dragged on the floor. She desperately hoped Polly had gone to the public rooms as she had no desire to speak of the events at Kealing Park.

When she reached the door of her room, Lilliana took a deep breath and prepared to endure Polly's disapproving questions. She walked inside, tossed her gloves and reticule on a chair, and lifted her arms to remove her bonnet. As she was quite certain Polly would come barreling out of the adjoining rooms at any moment, she was hardly surprised when she heard the woman's heavy footfall behind her. Lilliana lifted the bonnet from her head and smoothed her hair into place before turning around.

He caught her completely by surprise, but she was too tired, too emotionally spent, too ill, for Adrian's presence to do anything but register mild alarm. Leaning against the doorframe with one leg crossed negligibly over the other, his arms folded tightly across his chest, he looked impossibly handsome and proud . . . and angry. Lilliana wearily tossed her bonnet onto the chair and attempted a halfhearted smile. He did not even blink, but locked his glittering gaze with hers. She waited for him to speak; when he showed no inclination of doing so, she asked simply, "How did you find me?"

"Kettering," he answered without hesitation. "Passed through Kealing yesterday and saw you. I was fortunate enough to find Bertram wandering about, peering in shop windows. Seems he is rather bored," he said idly.

Lilliana nodded.

Adrian pushed away from the door and moved into the middle of the room, his arms still folded defensively across his chest, his eyes blazing with a curious glint of anger and trepidation. "Mrs. Dismuke has packed your things. I hope you have taken your tender leave of Benedict, because I am sending you home to collect your belongings."

Lilliana's heart wrenched; his voice carried no rancor, but the glint in his eye turned hard. She supposed she should be incensed that he would assume she was carrying on some illicit affair with his very own brother, but she was too nauseated to dredge up much more than a deep sorrow for the man she loved with all her heart. How he must have suffered all these years! "I know you are angry, but there is something I must tell you—"

"Don't, Lilliana," he said quietly, and lifted one hand. "Just . . . don't. I am sick to death of the lies."

Sick of the lies! And he didn't know how many of them there had been, she thought miserably. *God,* she was tired. She pressed her hand to her forehead. "I did lie to you," she admitted, and noticed the painful grimace that scudded across his features before the mask slid into place. "But I did not deceive you with Benedict or anyone else. There was something I had to know—"

"I don't want to hear it. Gather your things. The

coach is waiting to take you to Longbridge," Adrian said, and clenched his jaw so tightly that his cheeks bulged with the exertion. He was angry, so angry he could hardly contain himself, she realized. She clasped her hands in front of her and bowed her head slightly as another wave of nausea bubbled up. She wasn't going anywhere until she told him what she knew. "I came to Kealing because I suspected there was more to your birth than you realize—"

"What?" he fairly exploded, and stared at her as if she had lost her mind. "Don't you understand? I have caught you in a dreadful deception, madam. I have every right and every reason to send you away from me—I even have grounds to divorce you. I don't know what the two of you have planned, but don't compound it by creating some ridiculous tale—"

"It's not a ridiculous tale—"

"Have you seen Benedict, Lilliana? Just answer that question, would you? Have you seen him?"

She opened her mouth to speak, but he quickly shook his head and raised a hand to stop her. "Before you attempt to lie to me again, consider this: You turned against me when my sight was restored. You even said . . . bloody hell, there is no point in repeating it. You *know* what you said, then you lied when you said you were going to meet your family. But you came to *Kealing,* didn't you, the one place on this earth to which you knew I would object! It all seems so . . . ." He closed his eyes for a moment as he obviously sought the right words. When he opened them again, he cast her a look full of suspicion. "For all your protestations to the contrary, I can't help wondering what really occurred while I was blinded. Take care in answering, because when I began to regain my sight, I saw the two of you! Answer me honestly, Lilliana. Have you seen Benedict?"

The accusation stung and angered her. She could hardly speak, much less respond to such rubbish. Adrian groaned and whirled away from her. Running a hand through his hair, he stalked to the window. The nausea swelled; beads of perspiration erupted on her scalp, and Lilliana sank into a chair. "For the last time, Adrian, you saw *nothing*!" she insisted. "Yet what difference does it make what I say? You will believe what you want to believe, and why shouldn't you? I, too, find myself wondering what really occurred when I thought you blind! How often did you sit and observe me? Lord *God*, you have your nerve!" she snapped, and forced herself to take a deep breath. Only moments ago, she had been ready to forgive him everything, but now she felt the seeds of distrust sprouting in her all over again. "Perhaps because you are prone to deception, you believe it of everyone else. Need I remind you of London?"

"That's enough!" Adrian roared, and jerked around to face her. Confronted with her own treachery, she acted as if this was nothing more than having sewn his neckcloths together! Adrian feared he might explode at any moment. "I have never so much as looked at another woman since the moment I offered for you, Lilliana. Not once. Do not attempt to use that as a shield. Now gather your things. I want you out of my house by the end of the week." *And out of my heart* . . . "You are not welcome at Longbridge any longer."

She shook her head, dislodging a silken strand of hair that draped her cheek. "This is ridiculous! I didn't come here because of Benedict! If you could put aside your foolish suspicions for just a moment, I am trying to tell you that I know about your past, Adrian. I know someone who can explain it all. If you will just listen to me— better yet, *come* with me—"

"*Lilliana!*" he snapped. Amazingly, she appeared to have no concept of what she had done! "You are obviously not hearing me clearly," he said evenly, trying desperately to keep calm, "Under the circumstances, you have no grounds to ask me to do a bloody thing. You are going to Longbridge *now*."

She blinked up at him as she pushed the strand of hair from her cheek. "You don't understand—I am trying to help you."

"By lying to me? Deceiving me?" he asked, incredulous.

A noticeable change came over her green eyes—they hardened somehow, the light in them dimming. "No more than you have deceived me, husband," she muttered low.

That pierced him; he cut a scathing glance across her. "Gather your things." She made no attempt to move. Adrian stared at his wife, noticing for the first time the dark circles under her eyes, the weary way in which she held herself. A flicker of sympathy struck him from nowhere, but he quickly smothered it. She had betrayed him in the most egregious way imaginable. "If you don't do as I ask, I'll send Bertram up to do it for you," he said stiffly, and walked to the door.

He heard her catch a sob in her throat. "All right. You win, Adrian. I can't fight you anymore," she muttered. "I just don't have the strength to fight you anymore!"

Her voice, suddenly small and weary, shot right to the middle of his soul. His hand stilled on the brass knob as his wounded heart warred with what was left of his senses.

"Then don't," he said, and walked out the door.

He decided to go to London so he wouldn't have to see her again. But then again, he couldn't bear not knowing if she had left Longbridge. Did Benedict know? Was he waiting for her? In a state of rare emotional confusion, Adrian skulked around Kealing for two days. When he at last could take it no more, he had the hostler saddle Thunder, determined to let the wind decide where to take him. And as he was waiting in the courtyard for his mount, he heard a familiar, odious voice.

"Lord Albright! Good day, my lord!" Mr. Pearle shouted. Adrian winced and glanced over his shoulder to see the rotund solicitor waddling as fast as his stout little legs would carry him. Groaning, he looked anxiously to the stables. What was taking them so long?

"My lord! Oh my!" Mr. Pearle exclaimed as he came to a halt, and panting, took several deep breaths before he could speak. "It's rather warm," he explained between gulps of air.

"Good day, Mr. Pearle," Adrian muttered.

"Pardon, my lord, but I simply had to thank you for allowing Lady Albright to come to Kealing on her charitable mission. I naturally had the enormous pleasure of meeting her. What a delightful ray of sunshine! But then again, I am quite certain I said as much when you inquired—"

"Mr. Pearle, is there something I might help you with?" Adrian snapped. Charitable mission indeed!

Mr. Pearle nervously fingered his neckcloth. "Well, actually . . . I wondered if Lady Albright enjoyed meeting your lady aunt. It's been a rather long time since anyone actually *saw* Lady Allison, and I would inquire after her health, you see. Charming woman."

His lady aunt? What nonsense! Adrian turned his head just slightly and peered down at the little man as he sopped up the perspiration on his brow with a frilly handkerchief. "I beg your pardon, sir?"

"Lady Allison, that is. Ah, but your lovely wife is such a dear, kindhearted soul to think to pass along the family keepsakes to your aunt. How terribly *thoughtful*! But she's always been known in these parts for being so thoughtful." Mr. Pearle beamed at Adrian.

What aunt? *I know someone who can explain it all.* . . . A pinprick of pain settled behind his eyes, and as the hostler brought Thunder into the courtyard, Adrian repeated dumbly, "Lady Allison?"

Mr. Pearle adjusted his neckcloth. "Why, yes! No doubt it's been a fair number of years since you've seen her, but she still resides on the abbey road just north of Fairlington," he said, and squinted up at Adrian. "You *do* know where she lives, my lord?" he asked, cocking his head thoughtfully to one side.

If you'll just listen to me—better yet, come with me.
. . . His mind was suddenly reeling and his heart was
banging against the wall of his chest. Somehow Adrian
managed to make his legs move toward Thunder. "Of
course," he said over his shoulder. "I am on my way to
pay her a call now." He swung up on Thunder's back
and glanced down at the beaming Mr. Pearle. "Good
day, sir," he muttered, and didn't hear Mr. Pearle call
after him to give his warmest regards to Lady Allison.

He stood in front of the spacious thatch-roofed cottage,
simply staring at it, trying to make sense of it, until a
man appeared dressed in rugged knee-high boots and a
sturdy cotton shirt stained with perspiration. How on
earth a woodsman had entered this bizarre story, Adrian
could not begin to fathom. The woodsman tipped his
hat.

"Pardon, sir, but I am looking for Lady Allison."

The woodsman's cheerful countenance rapidly fell;
he peered closely at Adrian. "It's Mrs. Fletcher you
want," he said, and at that moment, a woman appeared
in the door of the cottage that made Adrian's heart
plummet to his boots. *His mother had awakened from
the dead.* Several strong shudders racked his frame; his
heart began to pound so fast that he was certain he was
having a seizure. God help him, it was his *mother*! Except that her face was broader, and her hair, though
flecked with gray, was almost the color of his own. His
mother's hair had been blond.

As he was trying to make sense of the apparition in
front of him, the woman walked slowly forward, her
eyes full of wonder. "Oh my," she whispered, *"Adrian?"*

He took an involuntary step backward, unable to
speak. Confusion seized his brain; his mind raged with
the improbability, trying to understand how his mother
had risen from the dead.

"You don't remember me, do you?" she said as she
stepped out of the little yard, nearing him.

Fearful that his voice would betray him, Adrian clamped his jaw shut.

"We met only once, and it was many years ago," she said, and smiled sweetly—*exactly* as he remembered his mother's smile. "In Cambridge. You were only six or seven years old, I think."

Cambridge. He had been to Cambridge when he was eight, with his mother and Benedict. He had met his grandfather there; he could recall very clearly the imposing figure of the man.

She reached out and touched his arm. "Look at you," she murmured. "Evelyn would be so proud. I am your mother's sister, Adrian. My name is Allison."

His mind could not absorb those words. His mother had been an only child, the only issue of the cold Lord Albright. Had she a sister, he surely would have known it! Was this woman deceiving him? But the resemblance! He could not help gaping at her in disbelief, madly wondering how he could not have known! The woman smiled again, and for a moment she looked so much like his mother that he feared he might fall into her arms.

"Why don't you come inside? William has a good batch of ale—you look as if you could use a pint."

Adrian nodded and found a rough voice. "You will forgive me, but I rather think I could use several pints."

"I've some work to do in the clearing. I'll leave you to your talk," the man said, and with a look at Adrian, picked up his tools and started off. Smiling at her husband's retreating back, Allison motioned him into the cottage. It was tasteful and cozy; a dozen or more handcrafted works of needle art graced the rough-hewn walls. A worn settee, two upholstered chairs, and a small table were the only furniture in the front room. Adrian sat heavily on the chair to which his aunt gestured.

"I told your lovely wife that you certainly knew of my existence, but I can see now that you truly did not," his aunt remarked as she handed him a pint.

Adrian took a long drink, wiped his mouth with the back of his hand, and nodded solemnly. "You have me at a great disadvantage, madam. I was quite unaware of your existence.''

She smiled warmly as she settled across from him. ''Please call me Allison. You look so like her, you know. Her eyes, her mouth.''

That unnerved him. ''Until I saw you a moment ago, I scarcely remembered what she looked like,'' he said raggedly.

Allison leaned forward and placed her hand on his knee. ''She would have been so very proud of you, Adrian. She always was, but to see you grown, such a fine figure of a man—I know her heart would have burst with pride.''

His breath felt thick in his lungs, and he downed the ale. She rose to replenish his tankard while Adrian tried to regain a modicum of composure.

When she had reclaimed her seat, he set the tankard aside. ''Why have I never been told?'' he asked bluntly. ''Why are you not known to me—if you are indeed my lady aunt, why are you *here,* in a woodsman's cottage?''

That earned him a distinct look of disapproval. ''William Fletcher loved me when no one else would, my lord. He is a fine man, and he is my husband.''

Ashamed, Adrian swallowed and looked at his hands. ''I beg your apology. It's just that—''

''You are astounded,'' she said charitably. ''Oh Adrian, it was so long ago, and I haven't thought of it in many years.'' She glanced away, her eyes gleaming with a view of the distant past. ''But your darling wife told me of your troubles and implored me to explain all for your sake.'' Allison glanced at him from the corner of her eye. ''She loves you very much.''

Yes, he was beginning to believe that, and nothing could make him feel worse at the moment. Lilliana had been telling the truth! When he thought of what he had said to her . . . never mind that now. ''Tell me, please,'' he insisted.

She sighed. ''Evelyn and I were quite close. Living at Longbridge with no other children about, we were the

best of friends.'' Nervously clearing her throat, Allison
reached for a small, heart-shaped pillow and clutched it
apprehensively in one hand. ''I was two years older than
Evelyn—eighteen when your father came courting. Oh,
but he was terribly handsome and so very charming.''

Archie charming? It was unfathomable.

Allison's cheeks flushed pink, and she picked at the
lace trim of the little pillow she held. ''I was quite taken
with him. I thought him the most dashing young man I
had ever known, and as our acquaintance grew I was
rather excited when he hinted at something more enduring between us.''

Adrian frowned. ''But he married my mother,'' he
unnecessarily reminded her.

A shadow of misery blanketed her eyes, and Allison
quickly dropped her gaze again. ''So he did. You must
understand, he was really the only young man Evelyn or
I had ever known. There were others, but my father did
not consider them suitable for an earl's daughter. That
was just the way things were in those days.''

That was just the way things were today—he could
understand how Archie might have insinuated himself
into their lives, but how had his mother come to marry
him? Allison shifted uncomfortably in her chair and
clutched the little pillow tighter. ''I tell you this so you
may understand how we thought, how things came to
pass. You see, your father was also the most charming
man Evelyn had ever known. She adored him. But Archibald held *me* in great esteem—so great, that he spoke
to my father of marriage. We planned to announce our
engagement at the spring assembly.'' With a sad smile
she brushed the lap of her gown. ''I rather thought I
might expire before then, as it was a full four months
away. But Archibald thought it best—it was the custom
of young men to announce their betrothals at the spring
assembly each year.''

She glanced again at Adrian, but he was dumbfounded, staring mutely at the sheen of tears in her eyes.
''Unfortunately, I had no idea how much Evelyn adored

Julia London

Archibald. Very much, you see, because she . . .
she . . .''

Adrian swallowed as Allison groped for the right
words. He did not want to hear this, he was quite certain
he did not. Yet he could not find his voice to tell her to
stop, and gripped the arms of the chair to steady himself.

Allison took a deep breath; her clutch on the little
pillow was very close to squeezing the stuffing out of it.
''She truly adored him once, I think.'' Color flooded her
face; her lower lip began to tremble, and Allison bit hard
on it for a moment to keep tears from falling. ''And she
must have felt as if she was losing him to me, because
she . . . seduced him.''

Adrian's mouth fell open in shock. This woman was
lying! She *had* to be lying, because his mother had
despised his father, and she *never* would have done
something so lewd, he was quite certain.

''And . . . and he got her with child,'' she added in
a whisper.

He bolted from his chair and stalked unsteadily
toward the hearth, unwilling to believe such atrocious
lies. ''Forgive me, madam, but I cannot begin to imagine
why you would wish to defame my mother in such a
contemptible way—''

''You'd best sit down and hear it all before you pass
judgment,'' she said calmly. Stunned, he glanced over
his shoulder. She returned his gaze with one of sadness
and pity. How much she looked like his mother! She
smiled weakly and motioned toward the chair. ''There is
so much more that you should know.''

Before he even understood what was happening, he
had resumed his seat. Allison drew another, tortured
breath and continued. ''You cannot imagine the scandal that might have erupted. But my father and Lord
Kealing, your grandfather, were eager to hide the ugly
truth. Evelyn and Archibald were quickly married, and
I was sent to London. But naturally everyone surmised
what must have happened, and the fact that you were

born seven months after their marriage proved the suspicions.''

He was the product of that seduction? His conception had occurred in some haystack? Adrian was suddenly having trouble breathing, because even more startling—if what she said was true—was that his birth was legitimate. Conceived out of wedlock, perhaps, but he was Archie's natural son. ''Then . . . then his disdain . . .'' he mumbled, trying to make sense of it all.

''Oh, Adrian! He believed he was forced into marrying her, and he could never quite forgive her for it,'' she said sadly.

Furious, Adrian jerked his head up. ''His disdain for *me*!'' he all but shouted. ''I am his *son*!''

Allison blinked with surprise. ''Of course you are his son. How could you think differently?''

''What in the bloody hell was I *supposed* to think?'' he roared. ''My father despised me from the moment I was born!''

''Oh no,'' she said softly. ''Oh *no*, Adrian! You are his son!'' she insisted.

''Then tell me *why*.''

Her gaze slipped away from his. ''I can't explain why, precisely. But he never forgave Evelyn, and he never stopped caring for me. I suppose all of it, wrapped up together—''

''That's not good enough,'' he said angrily. ''He got another son on her, a son he loves dearly—''

''No,'' she quietly interjected.

No? Speechless, Adrian gaped at her as myriad doubts about everything that he had ever known rifled through his brain. ''Wh-what do you mean by that?'' he stammered.

''Please, allow me to say it all, because I fear I shall never be able to speak of it again. I was sent to London, but I complained to my father. I thought it horribly unfair that I was the one to be punished for Evelyn's . . . indiscretion. So Father sent me to Venice as the companion of two young girls, where I was quite miserable.

A few years passed, and I finally came home of my own volition, sick to death of being hidden away. My father was furious—he was frightened to death of scandal and did not want me anywhere near this parish. But I still loved Archibald. And I was terribly angry with Evelyn. I felt betrayed . . . robbed of a happiness that should have been mine. I defied my father and took a small house near Kealing Park and changed my name.

"It wasn't long before Archibald learned of my presence and came to me. It was obvious that the esteem we held for each other was still quite strong. Oh God, how ashamed I am to tell you these things!" she suddenly cried. Reluctantly, she looked him squarely in the eye. "It wasn't long thereafter that I discovered I was carrying your father's child."

Adrian was incapable of speaking. He was incapable of *breathing*. He had another sibling; another child of Archie's lived somewhere.

"Archibald was enthralled, but I was terribly frightened. An illicit affair was one thing—I *wanted* to hurt my sister as much as I wanted to love the man who should have been my husband! But a *child* . . . a child was such an enormous responsibility—and to be born out of wedlock! But Archibald was ecstatically happy—he called the baby his love child and doted on him from the moment he could hold him in his arms."

Adrian gripped the arms of his chair so tightly that his hands were hurting. "Where is he now?" he asked, his voice barely above a whisper.

Allison closed her eyes. "He is Benedict," she whispered.

The room began to spin; Adrian lurched forward and buried his face in his hands. An eddy of deep-seated pain churned ruthlessly in him, and he unconsciously released a moan. He heard Allison's choked cry, felt her hand on his head.

"Oh my dear, I would not hurt you for all the world, you must believe me! But it is high time you knew these things, and if what your wife tells me is true—"

"What more?" he blurted angrily, lifting his head. "What more is there?"

She withdrew her hand. "Archibald wanted his son to have the best of everything, to be raised in the bosom of his family home. I fought him as best I could, but I was powerless against him. He stole my son from me. That is when he began to treat Evelyn with such terrible hatred. It happened that I knew one of the maids at the Park—my resemblance to Evelyn was apparently unnoticed—and she spoke freely of the goings-on there. She told me everything—the horrible things he said to her, the way he treated you. When I tried to speak with Archibald about it, he became very angry. It was his belief that she deserved all that he could give her for having ruined his life. I never knew he could be so cruel! I began to despise him for it. The more I understood how shallow and cruel he was, the stronger his tendency toward abuse turned on me."

Allison labored to rise from her chair and walked to the small window in the room. "After a time, he stopped coming. I wrote him, begging him to bring Benedict to me, but he would not let me see my son. I suppose Evelyn must have found the letters, because it was she who arranged to meet Father in Cambridge, and begged him to bring me along. I remember every moment of that day. It was the first time I had seen my son in two years, and it was the first time I knew that Evelyn loved him as her own.

"After that, just a few years passed before Evelyn died. I received a letter from her shortly before she died, in which she explained everything. My sister died of a broken heart for having betrayed me—something Archibald would not let her forget a single moment of her young life. When she died, Benedict was lost to me forever too. I was terribly despondent. Father settled a small stipend on me with the understanding that I would remain here, under an assumed identity. I had no one . . . I don't know how I survived the years that passed before I found William. He knows everything, of course, and loves me just the same. And I swear to you, I never would have told another living soul if Lady Albright had not convinced me it was necessary for your happiness and, ultimately, the child she carries."

Those words kicked him squarely in the gut. Astounded, Adrian felt something snap inside, and his heart surged to his throat, choking him. *The child she carries* . . . In shock, he stared at Allison's back. A child. *A child?* Never in his wildest imagination could he have conjured up something so fantastic. A sharp pain jabbed at the back of his eyes, and he squeezed them shut as he tried to fathom it all. The startling revelation of his birth, of Benedict's birth. *Of the child she carries!* And then the inevitable image in his mind's eye he could not suppress, the image of the ogre who had done this to all of them.

Archie.

He declined the offer of tea, anxious to get away from the little cottage that had turned him inside out. He thanked her for her honesty, promised to call again soon, and strode out the door.

He rode dangerously, taking the crow's path to Kealing Park. He pushed Thunder as his mind unraveled all that he had ever been, revealing the brittle foundation, brick by crumbling brick. The well of hate that sprang in him now shook him to the core. Archie had stolen everything from him—his mother, his heritage, his sense of who he was. And he had given it all to Benedict, his bastard son. His bloody *love child*. And how frighteningly close he and Benedict had come to repeating his mother's doomed history made Adrian queasy. He couldn't think of that, not yet. He first had to attend to some unfinished business.

The windows were ablaze with light at Kealing Park, and as Adrian stood in the drive he was somewhat amazed that the desire to have this home no longer burned in him. No, at this moment he rather preferred

Longbridge, where at least there was a measure of peace. But not here. This house had never known a peaceful day in its life.

He walked up to the door and lifted the brass knocker, rapping loudly. A few moments later the door was opened by Peters, the butler who had served his family since Adrian could remember. He frowned when Peters's face fell, and before the butler could react he pushed past him. "Where is my father?" he demanded curtly.

Peters looked terribly pained and glanced sheepishly toward the front hall. "I beg your pardon, my lord, but I am under strict instructions—"

Adrian did not wait for him to finish but abruptly headed down the long corridor to the main drawing room. He rather suspected Archie and Ben were having a glass of port and a friendly chat about all the magnificent things they could do to Kealing Park, *his* rightful inheritance. When he reached the double oak doors, he flung them open and strode across the threshold.

Archie was alone and shoved to his feet, spilling the book on his lap onto the floor. "What are you doing here?" he demanded.

Adrian smiled dangerously as he clasped his hands behind his back. "I think you know very well, Father. It appears there have been some details of my past that have been . . . *lacking*."

The blood drained from Archie's face. "She has told you then. That wife of yours is a high-and-mighty miss—the two of you deserve each other. All right, so you know. Whatever you may do, do it to me. But I beg of you, do not ruin Benedict."

Adrian's pulse soared to dangerous heights. "Do not ruin *Benedict*?" he shouted. "After what you have done to me, you would ask that I *protect* him?"

Archie fell into his chair. "Benedict is my true son, no matter what you will say to me. I love him. I cannot bear to see him dishonored," he mumbled helplessly.

He might as well have pierced Adrian's heart with a

bloody arrow—his words squeezed the very life from
him, made him fight for breath as he gaped at the father
who had allowed a son to believe he was a bastard. "*I*
am your son! I am your rightful heir!" he roared.

Archie shook his head, still unable to look at him.
"You are *her* son." In disbelief, Adrian stalked to
where his father sat. "All these years you allowed me to
believe I was a bastard. How in the *hell* could you be so
cruel?" he demanded.

"You have no idea the suffering I have endured because of you! I loved Allison; I would have married her!
But Evelyn—that girl seduced me and forced me into
marriage because of *you*! She ruined my life!" he cried.
"*You* ruined my life!"

Dumbfounded, Adrian was absolutely incapable of
speech. Lord knew he despised his father, but he had
never thought him so . . . pathetic. "She was sixteen,"
he heard himself say. "You were what, two and twenty?
Would you have me believe a sixteen-year-old innocent
overpowered you and *forced* you to fornicate?" he demanded harshly.

Archie colored. He suddenly sprang from his chair
and moved unsteadily to the hearth. "She was a wanton, taunting me with her body and her eyes," he spat.

Fighting the urge to strangle the foul breath from
Archie's lungs, Adrian snapped, "You have done me a
grave disservice, my lord. I have all the necessary proof
I need that you have attempted to ruin me without
cause. I could drag you through the courts—you are
aware of that, I presume?"

Archie's eyes widened with fear. "What do you
want? Tell me what you want, and I will give it to
you," he pleaded.

What he wanted, had wanted all his life, was no
longer relevant. The monumental struggle to be accepted, the many ways he had desperately sought this
man's approval, now seemed like some macabre joke to
him. It was almost a relief—at the very least his indis-
cretions and mistakes over the years, including Phillip's

death, had never amounted to the cowardice and irre-
sponsibility embodied in the man standing before him
now. It seemed to Adrian, in this clarifying moment,
that what he had really ever wanted was Archie's attention. But no more. He never wanted even to *look* at him
again.

Unnerved by his silence, Archie took a step forward.
"Just tell me what you want and it is yours, but I am
begging you, do not dishonor your brother," he pleaded.

"You mean my bastard brother, don't you?" Adrian
asked, then smirked when Archie's face turned almost
gray. "I'll tell you what I want," he said, almost amicably. "I want my rightful inheritance restored to me. I
want you to rescind the papers that have labeled me a
scoundrel in so many words. And naturally I want you
to drop your ridiculous suit to hold Longbridge in trust.
In exchange for that, I will keep your dirty little secret."

Archie nodded quickly. "Anything," he said. "I will
have the papers drawn up and sent to Longbridge without delay."

Disgusted, Adrian turned on his heel and strode
across the room, anxious to be gone before his blood
turned sour. But . . . there was one last thing. He
turned sharply to face his father for the last time.
"There is one more thing," he said quietly. "You must
tell Benedict."

"Tell me what?"

Both men jerked around; Benedict had stepped into
the room unnoticed, was standing just at the door, looking like a frightened boy. "Tell me what?" he asked
again, his voice quivering.

Adrian shifted his gaze to Archie, whose pallor suggested he would be ill at any moment. "Tell him about
his mother," he said, and without another word walked
out of that room, leaving Benedict regarding Archie
with grave curiosity.

Twenty-four

Hᴇ ᴘʀᴀʏᴇᴅ ꜰᴏʀ a full moon and rode through the night to Longbridge, unconcerned with the inherent dangers. He refused to allow himself to dwell on the question of whether he was too late, which left him to struggle with his enormous burden of guilt. He was drowning in a sea of confusion; he had accused of every perfidy the one person who could toss him the lifeline he so desperately needed, and then had banished her from his life. Just as Archie had once banished him.

He had sunk to a new, unfathomable low—he had no idea how to climb out of the abyss he had fallen into. But, oh God, he loved her—and it was almost beyond his ability to comprehend why that was so bloody difficult for him.

It occurred to him on that wild moonlit ride that he wanted nothing more than to be like the Princess of the Grange. With all his heart he wanted to illuminate the world around him as she did, to trust as she did, to *believe* as she did. But he couldn't do it alone; the only thing he knew with certainty was that he was frightened unto death with the prospect of losing her. For a man who had never needed anyone, he needed that parish princess with all the desperation of a dying man. The irony was not lost on him—all his life he had been careful not to form attachments of any kind, convinced he would lose in the end. Well, he was losing. Badly and completely.

Frankly, he had been losing all his life. It was crystal clear to him now—how terribly prophetic he had been, crediting the painful losses in his life to his uncanny knack for destroying those he cared about. Now he could plainly see that the destruction had come not because he cared too much—but because he didn't care enough.

His mother, well, he had lost her before he ever understood what caring meant. His father had never been his to lose. But there was Phillip—he hadn't cared enough to look past the deterioration of that man's spirit, had allowed himself to believe that Phillip was a grown man and capable of taking care of himself. Phillip had no one, really, to whom he could turn, no one who truly cared. And he had let Phillip slip, numb to the signs of despair.

And what of Benedict? His brother had done unspeakable harm to his marriage by lying to them both and forcing the wedge of suspicion between them. As much as it troubled him to think of his traitorous brother, he could not help wondering what course their lives might have taken if he had just shown Benedict how much he cared for him. And he *had* cared once, somewhere deep down where the affection had festered like a disease until it had eaten through his heart and destroyed whatever relationship they might have had. For all his weaknesses, Benedict was what Archie had made him. In fairness, Adrian could not hold that against him. If only he had taken a greater interest in his brother, if only he had tried to love him. *That* was what Benedict had needed from him.

Which was precisely what he would write to Ben, along with the promise of an annuity and a hope that things might one day be reconciled between them. And

he would send another letter to the little cottage near
Fairlington, thanking his lady aunt for her honesty and
requesting that she and Mr. Fletcher join them soon at
Longbridge. He had lost his mother, but he would not
lose his aunt, not now, not when he needed her to help
him through the quagmire that was suddenly his life.

Which left him with the most gaping wound—the
seemingly impassable gulf that spread between him and
Lilliana, hopeless to span. It was his fault. Regardless of
what Benedict had done, it was *he* who had at first ignored her, then looked for something to distrust. She
had saved his sorry life, and for that he had accused her
of loving Benedict.

Ah, yes, he was indeed a desperate man. As hard as
it was for him, he was willing to flay himself open to her
inspection, show her the ugly madness that had caused
him to accuse her, the deep shadows and cobwebs that
surrounded his heart. He would do anything for that
woman, he grimly realized; he would lay down his life
for Princess Lillie of the Grange if that would bridge the
gulf. Because without her, he was hopeless—a veritable
dead man.

He needed her to save him.

The sun was beginning to show itself on the horizon,
and Lilliana spread her hands across her abdomen as
she gazed out her window over the gardens for the last
time. For once her belly was calm, but the illness in her
heart and mind churned with confusion. How could she
possibly leave this way? What should she do, leave a
note behind to tell him she was carrying his child? Since
that awful encounter in Kealing she had been torn between the responsibility of carrying his child and the
deep hurt that urged her to leave.

Her dilemma was simple: If Adrian Spence needed
anything, it was his own child to hold, his own flesh and
blood to draw the love from that wretched heart of his.

But neither could she live without the life she carried in her womb. And she couldn't live with Adrian.

Lilliana sank onto the cushioned window seat and pressed her forehead against the cool panes of glass. She had long forgotten her anger; the fury had been replaced with a deep despair. After all she had been through, the thought of losing him forever was far more painful than the shallow reasons for his lying to her. He had been distrustful of her, but what could she expect? After the life he had led, it was a wonder he had not tossed her out altogether with his suspicions. Unfortunately, she had no hope that he would ever change.

He was such a sad figure of a man, really, and not the dashing young earl with whom she had been so enamored. How empty his lonely life must have been— devoid of true human companionship, of love. His father had laid the foundation upon which Adrian had built an impenetrable wall around him, and that single inability to allow someone into his heart was what had created the deep chasm between them. She felt helpless standing on this side of the chasm, desperate to reach him in some way but hopeless to bridge the gap. He might as well be standing on the other side of the world.

Lord, she was tired.

There was nothing to be done for it. She had tried, she really had tried, but it was over. She had another life to think about now, and as soon as the coach was ready she would leave Longbridge forever.

Exhausted, Adrian entered the long circular drive at Longbridge and cringed at the sight of the traveling chaise packed high with trunks. His heart sank; she was actually going to leave him. *Please God, please show me Your mercy once more, just once more, and I swear it, I will not squander it!* he hopelessly prayed.

It was even worse than he imagined. As he reined Thunder to a halt on the drive, at least a half-dozen pairs of eyes were on him, including Max's and a crying

Mrs. Dismuke's, Lewis's, Dr. Mayton's, and those of a few of the servants. And in the middle of them stood Lilliana with a fat mongrel on either side of her.

There was no time to think; Adrian slid off Thunder and handed the reins to a young groom who actually frowned at him. Having ridden all night, he was covered with grime and hardly prepared to face her out here, in front of her army. But he had no choice—he would not waste this chance. He swept the hat off his head and raked his fingers through his hair. For a man who had lived life on the edge and had seen his fair share of danger and adventure, there was nothing—*nothing*—that frightened him more than what he must do at this moment. In front of all these *people*. Awkwardly, he moved forward, almost afraid to look at her. A silence fell over the little group as he lifted his head and gazed at Lilliana. *"Don't go,"* he rasped.

The color left her face; she glanced sheepishly at those gathered around her. Mrs. Dismuke, with her beefy arms folded tightly across her barrel chest, glared hatefully at him. Bertram, the footman, pretended to be looking at the coach, but glowered at Adrian from the corner of his eye. Even Max, loyal Max, pressed his lips tightly together and riveted his gaze on the tip of his boots. Only Dr. Mayton looked even remotely sympathetic. There were no secrets here today, that much was obvious.

Lilliana nervously cleared her throat. "I . . . I beg your pardon, my lord, but I promised I would meet my family when they returned from Bath, don't you recall?"

Adrian ignored her attempt to cover the ugly truth. "I am asking you, please, don't go."

Her eyes welled. "I have to," she said simply.

"No. You don't." He took several shaky steps forward. "Grant me a word, Lilliana. Just a word." God, did he sound as desperate as he felt?

Lilliana looked down, silently debating his request for what seemed like an eternity. Adrian shifted uncomfortably, tried not to notice the eyes staring at him, but had the distinct feeling that he might as well be standing on the gallows. He felt the butterflies of shame in the pit of his stomach, the heat of it under his collar. And just when he thought he would expire, she nodded. "A word," she murmured. Several looked disapproving of that decision, particularly Mrs. Dismuke. But Lilliana walked out of their protective circle to where Adrian stood.

He grasped her elbow and anxiously pulled her a few feet away from the others. "Don't go, Lilliana—"

She stubbornly shook her head. "I can't live like this anymore, Adrian."

"Don't say that! Oh God—*Listen* to me. I was so wrong, Lillie, so *wrong*! I know why you went to Kealing! I know everything now, and in addition to being extremely grateful to you, I realize now how deeply Benedict poisoned us! No, no—that's no excuse for my enormous stupidity! I should have trusted you. Lord, there are so *many* things I should have done! If you will but give me a chance, I will prove to you how sorry I am," he whispered frantically.

Lilliana lifted her pale green eyes to him, eyes that had once sparkled with life. But all he could see was pain. Those eyes pierced his soul, flooded him with her doubts, which were so clearly evident. And as tears began to fill her eyes, she slowly shook her head. "You may trust me at the moment, Adrian. But I think your wounds are too deep. I . . . I don't know when you'll close yourself off again, or find something else to distrust! I simply can't live like this. I can't . . . I can't *breathe* like this!"

No! his mind screamed. Frantic, he pulled her even farther from the crowd. "All right . . . you wanted to soar, remember? You told me you want to experience life! I swear it, I'll experience it with you, whatever you want to do! If you want to climb mountains, we'll climb them! If you want to sail to the ends of the earth, we shall sail! You and me, Lilliana . . . and our child," he pleaded desperately, and placed his hand over her abdomen.

With a sharp intake of breath, Lilliana flinched at his touch. A single tear drifted from the corner of one eye, and she squeezed them tightly shut. "God help us both, Adrian, but I fear it's too *late*," she gasped. "We can never go back, don't you understand? This was a foolish marriage from the start, and the damage has been done. I can't stay here! I can't live with you!"

And as if he had burned her, she suddenly pivoted away from him.

Wild with despair, Adrian blurted, "What about the child you carry?"

Her hand unconsciously went to her belly, and reluctantly she turned her head slightly, glancing at him from the corner of her eye. The regret shimmering in her tears wrenched his heart. "I honestly don't know," she whispered hoarsely, and started forward.

Speechless, Adrian racked his brain for something, *anything* to stop her. He had no idea how to plead for his life—it was as foreign to him as everything else she had taught him. As Lilliana neared the little crowd Mrs. Dismuke opened her arms to her and Adrian saw his moment slipping away. Something deep inside him suddenly reared, and he shouted, "You promised you would never leave me!"

Lilliana halted dead in her tracks. Several of the onlookers gasped; Adrian caught his breath and held it. *Turn around, turn around, turn around,* he silently begged her, and merciful God, she slowly turned to face him.

"That was different," she muttered weakly.

Adrian violently shook his head. "No! You swore you would never leave me, and you can't deny it! You promised me, Lilliana. You *promised*!"

A stream of emotion paced wet paths down her fair cheeks; she looked so helpless and forlorn that Adrian took several steps toward her, his hands itching to hold her. But Lilliana shook her head and stumbled backward. "You can't hold me to that vow, Adrian! Everything is different now!"

"Oh, yes, my darling," he said in a low tone, and took another small step forward. "Everything is different. *I* am different—and so are you. That is why you can't just walk out of here, isn't it? Everything is different! There is so much unsaid, so much hurt between us, so much we have feared! We owe it to our child, Lilliana, we owe our child at least the chance to heal the wounds! Given what you know about my family, can you disagree? You can't go, Lilliana, not like this!"

His plea was met with a softly strangled cry, and Lilliana buried her face in her hands. Her resolve was slowly crumbling. Clinging desperately to a tiny thread of hope, Adrian anxiously watched her. After a few agonizing moments, he began to realize that Mrs. Dismuke was gaping at him, slowly shaking her head . . . and astonishingly, sniffling through a few tears of her own. Behind her, Dr. Mayton was beaming over the heads of the others and patting Mrs. Dismuke on the arm. And Max! Max looked curiously at him, then at Lilliana, and after several long moments, he bent over to pick up her small portmanteau. Adrian's heart seized—but Max startled him by wordlessly turning on his heel and carrying her bag into the house.

And then Lilliana lifted her wounded gaze to him. "One more day. That's all I can give you."

He nodded solemnly, belying the crest of renewed hope in his heart, and ignoring the grin Dr. Mayton and Bertram exchanged.

Another blasted tear slipped silently from her eye, and Lilliana bit her lip to keep the flood from coming. In the hours since Adrian had returned, she had been closeted in her rooms trying to make sense of her confusion, trying to decide what she should do. Though it was almost dusk, she was still no closer to an answer than she had been two days ago.

The truth was that she loved Adrian as much or more than she ever did. She realized now, after hours of reflection, that it wasn't Benedict who had ruined everything by lying to them—in spite of his many attempts to harm them. In the end, it was the distrust that destroyed everything. Oh, she believed Adrian was sorry for it, just as she was. And he might be grateful to her now for uncovering the truth of his birth—but what would he feel a year from now? Or tomorrow? Would he ever allow himself to feel without a struggle? And how long would it be before he lost the struggle? He had never once said he loved her—did he? Would he ever? She was deathly afraid of the heartache, afraid it would find a way to worm itself back into her life and destroy her.

The tinkle of bells distracted her; she turned to see Hugo wandering in through the door she was quite certain she had shut, wearing the bright red ribbon with a little bell on it she had made when Adrian was blind. Wagging his tail, Hugo eagerly lifted his snout to her face. "Hugo, where did you find your ribbon?" she mumbled, and reached down to scratch his ears. Running her hands through the fur on his neck, she felt something hard and bent down to examine it. A gasp of surprise escaped her—a diamond and emerald bracelet dangled next to his little bell. She quickly extracted the exquisite piece, and as she examined the bracelet Maude came bounding in and crowded in next to Hugo, lifting her snout over his for Lilliana's attention. Maude, Lilliana quickly noticed, had a little pouch attached to her ribbon. She untied it, then turned it upside down over her lap. A folded square of vellum fell onto her lap next to a necklace made of emeralds and diamonds.

"Oh God," she whispered, and snatched up the vellum, fumbling to open it. *I implore you, please come to the gazebo. Please.*

That was it—nothing more, no signature—nothing. But it was enough.

———

Adrian anxiously paced the length of the massive gazebo, around the expensive champagne chilling in a bucket of the river's icy-cold waters, past the little table set up with a variety of puddings, and almost colliding with the massive bouquet of orchids and lilies. Irritably, he stepped around the bouquet to continue his pacing. With Max's considerable help, he had scrambled like a madman for this moment, knew it his last and best chance. And he was sick with fear that she would not come.

He grit his teeth—she *would* come. And when she did, he had the perfect speech planned, one that would explain the forces of the universe in such a way that she could not possibly misconstrue what he was telling her. It was a very fine speech of contrition; he had thought about nothing else since that horrifying ordeal on the drive. His initial victory was fragile, that was plainly obvious, but this speech—he had examined it for flaws, and she could not possibly find anything lacking in his logic.

He pivoted sharply on his heel, preparing to pace again, and gasped with surprise. Lilliana stood at the entrance to the gazebo. Adrian's heart flipped in his chest as he gazed at her—good *God,* had she always been so beautiful? In the golden light of sunset, dressed in a gown the color of her eyes and sporting a plunging décolletage above which his peace offering glittered, the woman he had married looked every inch the Princess. For the hundredth time he was sharply reminded of how very blind he had been—to the beauty that glowed from within her, to the brilliant smile that could bring a man to his knees. To the curvaceous shape, the glorious hair, and the sparkling eyes—the depth of his stupidity astounded him.

She clasped her hands demurely behind her back, and he was, he realized, staring at her like a simpleton. Drawing a deep, steadying breath, he said, "I have been so wrong, I can't imagine that you would want to listen to a word I have to say.''

Lilliana smiled sadly, her gaze flicking to the orchids. ''We were both wrong.''

''Yes, well, I have been quite . . . obtuse, really. *Thick* is another word that comes to mind,'' he muttered, more to himself. ''All in all I was spectacularly wrong about you.''

Her brows dipped slightly into a puzzled frown.

''That is to say . . . I *wronged* you. I should have trusted you. I should have done so many things—'' His speech. Where was his speech? Where were the grand comparisons of their troubles to life in general? The promises he intended to make? Out of his mind, because gazing at her, he felt a surge of warmth in his chest, the unmistakable, irrefutable proof—

''I love you,'' he blurted. ''Hopelessly so, I'm afraid.''

Her eyes widened, and she drew her bottom lip between her teeth.

''The fact of the matter is that I can't live without you and I am in mortal fear that you will truly leave me,'' he announced, and had the sensation of his heart winging far ahead of his brain. And he couldn't stop it. Clutching her hands tightly together, Lilliana lifted them to her mouth, and peered at him with such a strange look that he couldn't say if she was appalled or merely fearful. He braced his hands against his hips, looked wildly about the room as he tried to think of the right words, but it was no use—his heart plunged ahead. ''Lillie . . . please *God,* don't leave me. I *need* you! If you will just let me try and show you how very sorry I am for everything, that I love you . . . that I love you so much I *ache* with it—''

Adrian would never really be certain how it happened—he was quite sure he never even saw her move. But she was suddenly in his arms, kissing him madly. He grabbed her waist to keep from falling, but his knees were buckling from the gravity of his emotion, and the next thing he knew they were lying prone on the cushioned benches that circled the interior of the gazebo.

"I love you," he muttered again, astonished at how the words lifted the invisible weight from his heart. Her hands were fumbling with his neckcloth, then the buttons of his waistcoat. "I never knew what love was until you—and I don't deserve it," he continued with breathless determination as she pushed his coat from his arms. "I don't deserve *anything* as precious or as good or as beautiful as you. And . . . and I had you, but I didn't recognize what you were doing to me until it was too late and I had no just cause to distrust you so, and now, God help me, I haven't the faintest idea what to do," he babbled as she forced him onto his back and started on his shirt. "But beg you. Yes, beg you, down on my knees, I beg you Lillie, *please* love me—"

She silenced him with a deep kiss. Her tongue darted between his lips, and Adrian groaned, all thoughts suddenly vanquished from his head. Her fingers scraped at his shoulders, down his chest and across his hardened nipples, then lower, drifting over the desire straining against his clothing.

Adrian grabbed her head, pulling the pins from her hair and raking his fingers through the silken tresses. He inhaled her into his soul, and then somehow she was beneath him, the fastening of her gown loosened enough that her magnificent breasts had spilled out. He devoured them while his hand fought her skirts, shoving them upward until he could feel the creamy skin of her thighs. "I love you," he muttered.

"Then show me," she responded hoarsely in his ear, and Adrian thought it the most erotic thing ever uttered in the history of the world. Lilliana squirmed beneath him and nipped his bottom lip with her teeth. "Show me *now*," she insisted. He did not need to be asked again; he freed himself from his trousers and entered her greedily, reveling in the sheer seduction of her body wrapping tightly around his. Lilliana grasped his shoul-

ders and raised herself to him. "I love you, Adrian.
More than my very own life I love you."

And he thought he might very well explode. He
thrust hard into her, watching her eyes shimmer with
desire and her lips purse with her rapid breath. She
rocked against him, meeting each thrust with her own,
squeezing him tightly with her legs. Their lovemaking
was almost barbaric in its intensity yet equally magnificent in its splendor, and as the desire in him began to
uncoil toward a frightening climax, Lilliana's head
dropped backward. She whimpered as she convulsed
around him, each spasm of heat branding him. And
Adrian lost himself deep inside her, near the womb that
held their child and the promise of their future.

They lay spent, each gasping for breath. To think
that he might never have held her again made him suddenly shudder, but Lilliana's fingers twined through his
hair, soothing him with feathery little strokes. "Tell me
again," she whispered. "Tell me so that I may soar."

Adrian lifted his head and looked into the gray-green
eyes of his wife. Humbled and grateful that God had
shown him the quality of mercy a second time, he
smiled tenderly. In that moment he silently vowed never
to squander another moment with her again. "I love
you, Princess, more than the very air that I breathe."

And Lilliana closed her eyes and laughed, exactly as
she might if she were soaring high above the earth.

Twenty-five

Adrian frowned as a groom led Thunder onto the front drive. Standing with her hands pressed against the small of her back, Lilliana shook her head firmly and frowned right back. "You are making a goose of yourself, my lord husband," she announced.

Max could not suppress a chuckle at that, and Adrian's frown deepened.

"Nothing is going to happen," she said blithely. "I am only seven months, and if anything *should* happen—which it *won't*—Max has already promised at least one hundred times to send for you at once. Mother and Caroline are here with me, so stop worrying and go," she said, making a shooing motion with her hand.

"It is precisely because you *are* seven months along that I am worried," he snapped irritably, and bestowed a look that suggested he might strangle Max if he grinned one more time. "What if the child should come early?" he doggedly continued.

"This child is not going to come early, darling, Dr. Mayton told you so himself. Please, would you go? The Rogues are going to think you are dead on the turnpike."

"I don't give a bloody—"

"*Adrian,*" she softly admonished him.

It was useless, he realized, and sighed heavily. Giving Max another scathing look for good measure, he wrapped his arm around his very pregnant wife—the part of her he could reach—and kissed her fully on the lips. When he lifted his head, his eyes narrowed. "I have your word, Princess. You will send for me the moment there is even a hint of trouble," he muttered.

Lilliana's dimpled smile drew a soft moan from him. "I promise!" She kissed him on the corner of his mouth before giving him a healthy shove away from her. "Take care!" she said cheerfully.

Muttering under his breath, Adrian strode toward Thunder and swung himself up. Taking the reins from the groom, he uttered the thousandth curse against the damn Rogues and their silly, stupid, inane vows. "I love you, my darling," he said, and smirked at the look of shock on Max's face before he sent Thunder galloping down the drive.

Leaning against the pillar of Arthur's Mount Street mansion, Julian watched the promenade of a dozen young ladies on the street through half-hooded eyes. Next to him, Arthur was just as engrossed in the sashay of petticoats as the ladies glided away, giggling uncontrollably behind gloved hands. And the two of them might have stood on the front steps enjoying the scenery all day had the Earl of Albright not suddenly appeared from nowhere and blocked their view.

He leapt down from his mount and strode quickly forward, an irrepressible grin on his face. Julian knew, of course, that his bubbling wife was carrying his child. Judging by Albright's idiotic expression, the earl was rather pleased with himself on that score. He jogged up the steps, and with arms akimbo, surveyed each of them before speaking. "Well? Either of you feel you are on the verge of ruination?" he quipped. "Be quick about it if you are. My beautiful wife is carrying my child, and as much as I enjoy your stellar company, I much prefer hers. Come on then, who's first?''

A smile slowly spread across Julian's lips as Arthur chuckled.

''You, Kettering,'' Adrian said, and motioned with his hand for Julian to divulge all.

Laughing, Julian pushed away from the pillar. ''You'll need wild horses or a good bottle of whiskey to drag it out of me, and let me state for the record that I prefer the latter,'' he said, and winked at a grinning Arthur.

Adrian walked across the stoop, shaking his head. ''No time for that, I'm afraid. Come on, then, we made our blasted vow, but I am quite certain no one determined how long must be spent on your little troubles.''

Arthur laughed and clapped Adrian on the shoulder. ''Good to see the old Albright alive and well, even if he is a horse's ass!'' Laughing, the two Rogues disappeared inside. Julian watched them cross the threshold. It was amazing, he thought, that when Phillip had died a year ago, he was quite certain Adrian would never be himself again. Honestly, after what had happened at Longbridge, he had feared Adrian was as lost to them as Phillip ever was. Despondent, full of self-pity, and suffering from more trials than Job, their leader had slipped from their grasp.

Well, miraculously their leader had recovered.

And the most amazing thing of all was that the antidote had been a woman. No one distinctive, just a simple lass from a grange. But that lass had opened Albright's heart and mind to a way of life that looked almost enticing.

Almost. If there was one thing of which Julian was quite certain, it was that he did not need a woman mucking up his life. Inexplicably, the very comely image of Lady Claudia Whitney popped into his mind, but he quickly and violently shook his head. He especially didn't need *her* mucking up his life. No thank you, he had sisters, and that was enough to turn a man from the ridiculous notion of matrimony for a lifetime. Albright . . . well, he was to be excused. The poor fool never really had a family to speak of, much less a woman about, and one could hardly fault him for falling prey to one.

Ah, but never the Earl of Kettering, he thought smugly. He knew *exactly* what women were about, and he would do just as well with a handful of demimondes and a supply of fine whiskey.

"Kettering! Come on, man—I am quite certain you will take the most of our time, so please do hurry along," Adrian shouted, and that was followed by a loud guffaw from Arthur. Chuckling, Julian sauntered inside to join his fellow Rogues and assure himself that not another one of them would fall.

About the Author